MIDNIGHT
IN THE
GRAVEYARD

"One of the decade's finest feasts of fiction."—Matt Hayward, Bram Stoker Award-nominated author of *What Do Monsters Fear?*

"*Midnight in the Graveyard* is a collection of ghostly stories that will keep you awake at night long after you finish the last story. From vengeful spirits to sympathetic haunts, every one of these modern tales is a classic in its own right."—JG Faherty, author of *Hellrider*, *The Cure*, and *Carnival of Fear*

"*Midnight in The Graveyard* is a tome packed with the best of the macabre, with a table of contents that will surely lure in horror fans of all tastes, with both heavy hitters and rising stars of the genre displaying some of the most original ghost stories penned. With tales of wandering spirits, those trapped here by the madness of their former deeds, and those doomed to walk the earth in limbo for atrocities they had no part in. Reading it is like a walk through a cemetery by the light of the moon, you can feel the souls reaching out to you from each grave, desperate to tell their stories, some will whisper to you of their sorrows while others scream for your blood and suffering. A wonderfully spooky read!"—Michelle Garza, co-author of *Mayan Blue*, *Those Who Follow*, *Tapetum Lucidum*, and *Isolation*

"Seriously creepy and deliciously disturbed, you can practically smell the moldering earth on your fingertips as you turn the page... or swipe the screen."—Craig Spector, bestselling author of *Underground* and *The Light At The End*

"*Midnight in the Graveyard* gathers a collection of some of the most talented authors in the genre today, both well-known names and up-and-comers. The stories are spooky, creepy, emotional, and gripping. If you want a sampling of great horror, this anthology is for you."—Mark Allan Gunnells, author of *Daylight Will Not Save You* and *Book Haven and Other Curiosities*

"Featuring work from a bevy of talented newcomers plus legends such as Beth Massie and Robert McCammon, *Midnight in the Graveyard* is the ghoulish grimoire of ghost stories you need to conjure scares this Halloween."—Mark Steensland, co-author of *In the Scrape*, *The Special*, and *Jimmy the Freak*

"With stories ranging from macabre to melancholy to the downright frightening, this incredible mix of veterans and up-and-comers will surely give even the most jaded of horror fans something fresh and unique to discover. I absolutely adore this collection, and I think you will too. And keep this in mind: This is only their first anthology. With a book this good, the future is looking awfully bright for Silver Shamrock Publishing."—Wesley Southard, author of *One For The Road* and *Resisting Madness*

"Silver Shamrock's debut anthology features an all-star line-up of today's best horror authors. These are not your father's ghost stories." —Tom Deady, Bram Stoker Award winning author of *Haven*

"Reading *Midnight In The Graveyard* is a haunting experience that will have you flipping on the lights and jumping at shadows. The book is full of ghosts, both real and imagined. Some are restless spirits from beyond the grave, others are failures and regrets that torment our mind. While each story offers a fresh look at a familiar theme, they combine to make you feel like something hungry is hovering right behind you, reading over your shoulder. I dare you to read this book alone at night. Just remember, when you hear whispers coming from the other room, run."—Brian Kirk, author of *We Are Monsters* and *Will Haunt You*

"I can't tell you the last time I read an anthology where every story grabbed my attention and wouldn't let go. Not only does *Midnight In The Graveyard* start out strong, oh man, the stories just kept getting better and better. Silver Shamrock comes flying out of the gate with this collection of superlative ghost stories."—Tony Tremblay, Bram Stoker Award nominated author of *The Moore House*.

" *Midnight In The Graveyard* gathers an outstanding mix of ghost stories running the gamut of the creepy subgenre. From legendary authors, to talented newcomers, this anthology will leave you unsettled and questioning that cold draft in the hallway in the middle of the night."—Glen Krisch, author of *Where Darkness Dwells* and *Little Whispers*

MIDNIGHT
IN THE
GRAVEYARD

Edited by Kenneth W. Cain

www.silvershamrockpublishing.com

Table of Contents

Legends, Ghosts, and Predictions

An Introduction to *Midnight in the Graveyard*
by Jonathan Janz

I don't have a crystal ball, I can't read tea leaves, and I never catch flashes of future events a la Stephen King's Johnny Smith in *The Dead Zone*. So if you're looking for an accurate prediction, you best cruise on by.

I can, however, make educated guesses. One of those has to do with Silver Shamrock Publishing, and another involves the book you are now holding.

Speaking of Silver Shamrock, I'm guessing they'll be around for a while. Horror publishers shut their doors every day because it's a heck of a tough business. Some close up shop due to circumstances beyond their control; others simply aren't in it for the right reasons.

The folks behind Silver Shamrock are unquestionably in this for the right reasons. What's more, they love horror (which is one of the best "right reasons" I can list). I've interacted with Ken McKinley for years and can state with certainty that he loves the genre. Loving horror isn't a guarantee of success, but it's a damn good start.

That love for the genre shows in the writers he has included in this, Silver Shamrock's first anthology. And that leads me to another prediction:

You're gonna love these stories.

On what do I base this prediction?

Silver Shamrock has gathered for you a rogue's gallery of legends and rising stars, an absolute embarrassment of fabulous writers. I'd like to talk about all of them, but to whet your appetite and prevent this introduction from overstaying its welcome, I'll just mention a handful.

Robert McCammon is one of the best writers to pick up a pen or a keyboard in this or any other genre. He's one of my primary influences and one of the few writers who deserves to be mentioned in the same breath with Stephen King, Richard Matheson, Shirley

Jackson, and Edgar Allan Poe. Any anthology that includes a McCammon tale is an anthology you should have on your shelf. For a new publisher to score a story by McCammon is an absolute coup. And a McCammon *ghost* story? That's worth the price of the book by itself.

Tom Monteleone is an award-winning author and editor who knows a thing or two about spinning an eerie yarn. A legendary editor and author, Tom has forgotten more about storytelling than most of us ever learn. The tale he has penned here is guaranteed to give you the shivers.

And then there's Elizabeth Massie, the wickedly talented creator of the novel *Sineater* and the short story "Abed," which is arguably the most disturbing zombie tale ever written. Elizabeth has brought her macabre sensibility and remarkable precision to this collection via a story that'll linger with you long after you've finished it.

Kealan Patrick Burke is one of the best in the business, and saying he brought his A-game to this anthology is misleading because I'm not sure he possesses anything other than an A-game. His story is sure to electrify. I don't recommend reading it before you attempt sleep.

Ronald Kelly's voice is totally his own, and this story is vintage Kelly. Like all his work, it contains heart as well as goosebumps, and it's all served up in his unmistakable voice, which is equal parts southern-fried fun and certified fright.

And I might as well say it now: I could talk at length about every one of these tales and every one of these outstanding writers. I have dear friends (and killer writers) in this book like Kelli Owen and Hunter Shea; there are rising stars on display like Somer Canon and Tim Meyer. As if that weren't enough, Silver Shamrock has brought on board ace editor/author Kenneth W. Cain to give these stories the attention they deserve and to maximize their impact on you, the reader. Heck, even the cover is a stunner, a whispered promise of the hauntings to come.

I've kept this introduction brief so you could get to the good stuff. I told you in the beginning I stink at making predictions, and I stand by that. I have no idea if the Cubs will win another World Series, whether or not Glenn Close will win an Oscar, or what the odds are on that George Strait/Metallica collaboration for which I've always yearned.

What I do know is this: Silver Shamrock is doing this thing right. They've assembled a ferocious roster of talent for *Midnight in the Graveyard* and created an anthology certain to give you hours of pleasure and more than a few nightmares.

It's time for you to go now, to venture into the cemetery on the cover with your lantern held aloft and your body stiff with fear. What's waiting for you amongst these gravestones and moon-kissed oaks is getting impatient. And though you're not wearing a wristwatch, the timepiece in your coat pocket reads one minute to midnight.

Enter, friend. I wish you well, but I've got to warn you.

These ghosts are hungry.

Devil's Dip

by Shannon Felton

Allison would freak out if she caught me smoking in the garage. Yet there I was, lighting one after another, the place heavy with the smell of sweat and ash. One right after another, until a pile of butts spilled out of an overflowing ashtray onto the workbench and floor.

Knowing her, she'd come in screaming about my health, the baby's health, about what a fire hazard I had created. And she wouldn't be wrong. With all the wood chips and shavings scattered across the floor, it was a wonder the place hadn't already gone up like a tinderbox.

But then again, *she* was the one who was screwing her boss, so fuck her, right?

Which was probably why she was staying upstairs in the guest room; she was giving me space. How considerate. I guess it was the least she could do after nuking our marriage.

Fifteen years. Right down the drain.

I grabbed another smoke from the pack, lit up, and started digging through some old boxes. Talk about a trip. And by 'trip' I mean 'heartbreaking'. I popped an old cassette tape into the stereo and wondered where the fuck I had gone wrong in my life. What had happened to that kid who sneered at the suburban sheeple, who laughed at the old losers who mowed their lawns on Saturday so that they could grill on Sunday? Who had I become?

You know what the funny thing was, though? I'd actually grown up and wanted all that shit. I'd gotten out of that craphole town, conquered my demons, and had done everything right. I worked hard. I didn't mess around. And the truth was, I really loved her. Somehow, it still hadn't been enough.

It made me feel like a goddamn fool; that was the worst part. No, that was a lie. The worst part was that she had finally gotten pregnant and now I wondered if the baby was even mine.

To think, we'd just gone halfway across the country so our families could meet Evelynn and there was a chance I wasn't even her father. It was embarrassing how proud and stupid I'd been, driving through my hometown for the first time in a decade, looking down on it all like I was king of the world. I'd been relieved, believing my childhood in Stewartville was nothing more than a dream, a toothless nightmare made of the sort of stuff and nonsense that gave you a good laugh in the morning. And all the while, my wife sat in the seat beside me, sexting with Alan Fuckhead, potential sperm donor of my baby girl.

I hadn't even bothered to visit Mike, that's how good I was feeling. Who needed him anymore, I thought. Certainly not me, not Mr. Bigshot with his gorgeous wife and beautiful baby.

Could you blame me, though? It's not like I hadn't tried my best to stay in contact with him. Even after I moved, even after twenty years had passed, I still called him, still checked in, still tried to hang on to some of that friendship we had back in the good old days.

He'd stayed in Stewartville, married some girl I'd never met (she was older than us, a waitress at the one good Italian place in town), and worked for a living at his dad's auto body shop.

He hardly ever answered when I called, and when he did, he'd let me go within minutes, promising to keep in touch, talking down to me like I was some needy loser. Almost had me believing it, too, though most times I convinced myself he was just jealous and bitter. To be honest, he'd always been kind of a dick, even back in high school, even to me. Now he was a full-blown asshole. But he was the best friend I ever had. One of the only friends.

I wished I could call him, what with all that was going on with Allison and that old cassette tape bringing back a bunch of memories. Maybe I'd give him a ring in the morning just to check in. Remember a bit of who I was before Allison had destroyed me.

So imagine my surprise—sitting there in the garage with my head in my hands—when my phone chimed and Mike's picture popped up on the screen.

I took a drag from the cigarette held tight between my lips, squinted against the streaming smoke, and read the message.

"Awake?" he'd texted. It was 11:00 p.m.

I picked up the phone and leaned back in my chair, flicking ash onto the floor, down onto all that wood.

"Yeah, man," I typed. "What's up?"

I watched the text bubbles stream across the screen, thinking how it was kind of nice he was reaching out to *me* for a change. And maybe he hadn't been so wrong after all, maybe I had been needy. Hadn't Allison said the same thing every night for the last five years I'd asked her for sex, said it every time she'd beg off or give me a half-hearted hand job that I wound up having to finish off for myself anyway?

"Joanne's dead," he wrote.

Joanne was his wife. I'd heard the news on Facebook, so this wasn't some big shocker. I probably should have written, should have said something and stepped in when he'd started babbling incoherently in his status updates. But after twenty odd years, you eventually take the hint that you aren't wanted.

Thing was, I couldn't even remember how it had come to that anymore, but it was a damn shame considering how close we'd been. He'd been there for me when my dad died. I was the only one who understood his home life and why everything had to be a joke.

Ash fell from the end of my cigarette as I took a drag. I wrote back: "I was sorry to hear the news. How you holding up? Anything I can do for you?"

"Thanks. I'm good. Staying up at my dad's place."

Mike's dad lived up on Poplar Hill in an old ranch home. It had a cactus garden out front, which had become a hulking mass of tumbleweeds and litter over the years.

I'd been inside exactly once. His mom was sick, her brain was unhealthy, and try as he might, Mike's dad just couldn't care for her the way she needed. She'd woken up that day and had decided to smear her shit on the walls. Mike and I had walked right in on it, the smell hitting us as soon as we stepped through the door. But it wasn't just that. Sometimes she'd get a hankering to cut her face up with a razor blade. One time, she had tried to pour a bottle of bleach down her throat. Mike grabbed it from her just in time and had thrown the bottle across the room. The bleach sprayed out and splashed right into his younger brother's eyes, who'd been watching the whole thing in frozen horror. That was the end. Protective Services showed up then, had taken control where Mike's dad couldn't.

And shit, *my* dad, who I thought was just a boring old accountant, hadn't been so boring after all. He'd walked out of work, went to the IGA across the street, and blew his brains out in the cereal aisle.

It had always creeped me out how a person could just go nuts like that. I didn't know what was worse: The idea that someone could go through so much shit that their mind began to degrade, or the idea that it was just a random roll of the dice and you were stuck with a bummer brain for no reason at all.

"Well, you know I'm here if you need anything," I wrote back.

The message was received but there were no streaming bubbles to indicate a reply. I figured that was it, he'd said what he needed to say and I wouldn't hear from him again. I put the phone back down, wondering why people found it so easy to use me and cast me aside, then the phone chimed again.

My hands stilled and I looked down at his message.

"I can't do this anymore, man."

I took a drag, unsure of what to say. Finally, I typed: "I hear ya. Life's a bitch, then you marry one." As soon as I hit send, I slapped my forehead. What a dope I was.

"You remember Devil's Dip?" he texted.

Now that was something I could answer. "Shit yeah," I wrote. "Of course I remember it."

Devil's Dip was this road in Stewartville that went straight down and straight back up, giving you that roller coaster feeling in your gut. They called it Devil's Dip for two reasons: one, when you came up on it, the dip was so immediate and deep that your headlights glanced right off the top, giving the impression of a bottomless black pit that stood between you and the other side of the road. And two: because of all the jackasses who took it way too fast or way too drunk. The roadside was littered with those little white crosses you see whenever someone dies in an accident.

"Ha!" I texted back. "The creepiest place in the world, how could I forget?"

"You remember that night we bought an ounce of skunk weed with Joey and went driving around?"

I was grinning now, the first time since seeing Allison's phone sitting unlocked on the bathroom counter, the messages between her and Alan socking me in the gut. "Lol. Yeah, I remember. That was a lot of nights though, man."

It was true. We'd been your average teenage shitheads, spending our time getting drunk or smoking weed out in Bumfuck Egypt, swimming the river when it got hot, talking about the rumor of Anne Lynn's hairy tits while we flipped through *Hustler*. What dumbass kids we were. Nowadays, I wouldn't have cared if Allison had dog nipples so long as she gave me some affection and acted like she loved me a little.

"This one there wasn't any moon," he wrote. "And Devil's Dip showed up out of nowhere cause we hadn't realized where we were going. Remember?"

Now that he mentioned it, I *did* remember. In fact, Devil's Dip had always made me nervous because I could never seem to remember where it was. When I did come across it, it always felt more like it had found me instead of the other way around.

I did know you had to take a left off Ninth onto the road with that old Gothic mansion on the corner. I also knew that on the left side of the road there was a cow field and, on the right, a bunch of old houses. But once you took a right into the neighborhood, Devil's Dip could be anywhere. The road where you thought you found it last time would be normal the next. Eventually, you'd give up looking, take a few turns to leave, and then there it would be, on a road you swore you'd just driven down. And the weirdest thing? Once you were on Devil's Dip, it felt like you were out in the middle of nowhere instead of smack dab in Stewartville.

It also seemed like the trees were always bare on Devil's Dip, or maybe I was just always remembering that particular night, right before Halloween, when the autumn winds had stripped all the leaves away. Whatever the case, ashy grey trunks with brittle branches had reached out and scraped against the car windows, like the nails of the dead, and I remembered being in the backseat—

Ding.

"I saw him at the market a few days ago."

"Who? Joey? How'd he look?" Thinking to myself: *Hey, we're finally reminiscing and catching up. Perfect.*

"Bill, it was like seeing what true evil can do to a person."

That gave me pause. As I mentioned earlier, Mike had been saying some weird shit online lately. Not that he didn't have a right to a breakdown. I mean, his wife had just died and all. But this wasn't the Mike I knew.

"Listen, Mike, I know you've had a hard time of it lately. I'm worried about you."

"Don't be worried. God has forgiven me and shown me the way. I'm protected now."

I read his messages a few times over, getting the heebie-jeebies as his words sunk in. He was totally off his rocker. But he was also my friend. "Protect you from what?" I texted.

"From what we picked up that night at Devil's Dip."

The ceiling creaked above me, probably Allison awake with the baby, and then it occurred to me she might be up there talking to that prick.

Picking at my nicotine-dried lips, I fought back the urge to run upstairs and catch her in the act. Who knew what I'd do then? What I needed to do was stay calm. I put my cigarette out and lit another.

"All right," I texted back, my thumbs moving over the screen. "I'll bite. What did we pick up at Devil's Dip?"

"You're the one who saw her."

The words popped up on the screen like a bad omen, making the hairs on my arms stand up like someone was right behind me blowing on the back of my neck. An old familiar darkness descended upon me. One I'd ran from so many years ago.

"Saw who?"

"The White Lady."

Maybe because it came over the screen so impersonal, so detached and hollow, or maybe because as soon as the message appeared my stereo started eating my cassette tape, causing the lyrics and music to distort and warp into some weird, scratchy chanting. Whatever the case, I got that itchy, antsy feeling like I wasn't the only one in the garage anymore.

I pulled the shredded tape out of the player and then texted him back. "I don't know what you're talking about, man."

"Holy shit? You really don't remember?"

Did I? I thought back on that night, remembered being in the back seat of Mike's crappy car, passing the joint up front to Joey. Remembered the headlights coming up on that black hole in the road...

Mike had to be fucking with me. That was the only reasonable explanation. He wasn't crazy, he was just being his usual self. He'd always liked pushing my buttons, freaking me out. A classic prankster.

So I wrote back, "You're just fucking with me now, aren't you?"

I waited awhile for his reply, waited to see those streaming bubbles, but none came. There was another creak upstairs, which got me thinking about what I'd read in the text messages, like how Allison and Alan used the guest bedroom when I was gone because she felt weird using ours. *That's* what made her feel weird. Not actually cheating on me, mind you.

I put in a new tape and turned the volume up.

Ding.

"You're not fucking with ME are you?"

I sat back and rested the phone on my gut as I typed. "Seriously, Mike. I have no idea what you're talking about."

"Fuck me. You gotta remember, man."

I didn't answer and the phone stayed quiet a minute more. Then:

Ding.

"You don't remember stopping at the bottom of the dip, and you crying in the backseat?"

Did I remember? I saw a vision of myself, like in a dream, sitting in the backseat like he said, with tears streaming down my face. And hadn't there been someone else there? A fourth person, one sitting right next to me?

I sighed and rubbed my forehead. "Look, Mike," I wrote. "Why don't you just quit playing games and tell me what it is you think I should remember."

"That thing we promised we'd never talk about. Remember now?"

His words rang a bell and I thought back on senior year, remembering how we'd sit together at lunch holding our tongues, not wanting to look at one another, until finally we stopped hanging out altogether and spent our time instead with other crowds in other—safer—conversations.

"If we promised, then why are you talking about it now?" I bent forward, shoulders hunched, and watched the phone.

"You're the one who keeps calling me. It has me thinking you WANT to remember."

"Yeah! I call to catch up. Reminisce." I sent the message, started furiously typing another. "I don't call to be a dick and play games."

"Reminisce about what?" he asked.

My head jerked back from the screen. What the fuck did he mean *about what*? I was so confused I barely noticed the music had shut off.

"About life," I wrote back in the quiet garage. "Hanging out. Smoking weed and getting drunk. The laughs we had."

"You want to do that every year? On October 13th? Think about it, man. "

I made a face but looked at the clock. It was 11:59. October the twelfth. "I don't call you every year on October 13th," I answered. But I had a weird, dizzying feeling in my gut as I recalled that I had, in fact, planned to call him in the morning.

"Sure man. Whatever you say."

That was it. I was done for the night. "Hey, it was nice talking with you, but I gotta head to bed."

Bubbles floated on the screen and I watched them as I smoked, listening to Allison moving around upstairs again. Wasn't until my cigarette was nearly gone that he finally texted back.

Ding.

"K. Be careful."

Yeah, right.

It took a minute to clean up the cigarette butts, dump the ashtray, and sweep up the shavings. Mostly because I was thinking about what Mike had said, thinking of his words, *The White Lady*. Upstairs Allison kept thudding around. What the fuck was she doing up there?

She must have heard me come in. The house was quiet and the stairwell dark. I turned down the hall, flipped on my bedroom light, and powered on the TV. I couldn't go to bed in silence, my mind would race too much. The noise would occupy my thoughts, distract my brain from the idea of the two of them together.

Shirt off, I took a minute to sniff my pits, hating the stench of myself. Maybe she cheated because I'm disgusting, I thought, hating myself even more. When I glanced back up, something was in the mirror behind me. I spun around to an empty room.

Fucking Mike. He knew that BS would get to me. I turned off the lamp, crawled between the sheets, and closed my eyes.

Ding.

I rolled over onto my side and reached for the phone on the nightstand.

"She was sitting right next to you in the backseat and you started crying like a baby."

The image of something flashed through my mind, and, with it, the air grew heavy. So heavy, in fact, I was pretty sure if I looked over my shoulder at the other side of the bed, there'd be—

Don't think of the eyes—

My thumbs jabbed at the phone. "I don't know what the fuck you're talking about, asshole."

Ding.

"Yeah, keep telling yourself that, buddy."

Ding.

"She's been with me every second since that damned night and nothing I do has gotten rid of her."

Ding.

"Except this. It's your turn now."

My thumbs flew over the keyboard. "Dude. Are you fucking high?"

Nothing. I laid my head back on the pillow and watched the ceiling flicker with blue light. There was a knot in my stomach, and I wasn't sure if it was there because Mike had gone crazy, or because of the things he made me think about as I drifted off to sleep.

Like the thought of his car pulling up slowly to the dip that night my dad had died and Joey saying, *Hey, you know how there's all these accidents here? My brother's friend Ricky says it's because of a ghost at the bottom of the dip. The White Lady...*

Mike wanted to check the story out. So he crept the car down the hill and stopped it right at the bottom of the dip.

"See anything?" he asked us after a minute.

Joey and I had looked around at the dried weeds in the circle of headlights, at the inclines both in front and behind, and shook our heads.

"That's a fucking bummer," Mike said.

And just like that the radio fritzed, bleeping out static one minute and then a hundred different channels the next, a cacophony of voices and instruments that filled the car. Mike lurched forward in his seat and snapped the radio off, and then we stared at one another in the silence of the night.

"What the fuck," Joey breathed, and then we heard it: the low hum of an engine.

Lights shone overhead, glancing over the dip and hitting the top of the incline. The engine raced closer, it's hum now a roar.

"Fucking *go!*" I yelled. "They're gonna hit us, *go!*"

Mike put the car in drive, hit the gas, and the fucking thing stalled out. So Joey and I kept yelling at him to go, even though we knew he was trying, and then he finally got it in gear, finally got it to jerk forward, only for it to shimmy and sputter as he slammed down the gas.

It was too late. We were flooded with light. The car was right on us and it wasn't slowing down. Its engine growled, a hungry beast that we couldn't outrun.

Eyes closed, hands over my face, I braced for the impact. Brakes squealed, metal screeched against metal, and glass shattered. Then there were screams that turned to wailing that turned to silence.

But I hadn't felt anything. I opened my eyes.

We were the only car on an empty road.

"*Hol-ee fuck,*" Joey said.

Mike sat back in his seat, hands gripping the wheel. "What the fuck was that?"

I didn't answer. I couldn't answer.

She sat next to me, her head hanging back over her right shoulder, her sliced neck gaping at me, looking like cherry pie-filling. Her eyes rolled around in their sockets until they caught sight of me and they latched onto mine with the desperate stare of a woman drowning at sea, an animal caught in a trap.

I couldn't look away, even as my body heaved out a sob that made Mike and Joey swivel around in their seats.

"What?" Mike asked.

I was blubbering now, staring right into the horror of that girl with her head almost lopped off, her mouth gasping for air that wouldn't fill her lungs but came out instead as bubbling blood down the front of her white dress. I couldn't speak, couldn't think, but somehow, I managed to raise a finger and point.

"Do you see something?" Joey asked. He looked out the side window, his head and shoulders bobbing as he tried to make something out in the moonlight.

"S-s-she's right there," I said, finding words between sobs, tasting the saltiness of my own snot across my lips.

"Outside?" Mike asked. He craned his neck and his voice had cracked so I knew he was afraid, knew he believed me.

"In—in the seat," I gasped, fighting the urge to vomit.

Joey and Mike turned to look. I could tell when the stillness fell over the car that one of them had seen her, could tell by the way her terrified eyes finally broke away from mine and rolled in her sockets to the front seat.

I squeezed my eyes shut as soon as she looked away from me, thinking I'd never be able to open them again.

"Jesus Christ," Joey said in the black void of my head. *"Jesus Christ, make her stop looking at me!"*

I cringed against the window at his screams, still bawling like a baby at what I knew sat beside me.

"What?" Mike asked, "Where is it?" His voice was frantic, shrill.

"She's right there," Joey whispered. Mike gasped and I knew he'd seen her, knew by the way Joey now sobbed quietly instead of like a madman. And I also knew, somehow, that if she was busy looking at someone else, she wouldn't be looking at me.

Mike finally spoke, sounding as if he were choking on his tongue "Bill, get her to stop. God damn it, look at her, Bill."

I covered my ears. *"Don't talk to me about it,"* I screamed, knowing that if he did, my mind would turn her way, drawn involuntarily to the horror of it, a primal urge to make sure it was real. *"Don't talk about it,"* I screamed again.

The phone rang. I rubbed my eyes and picked it up off the nightstand, feeling groggy and disoriented. Mike's name flashed on the screen. Jesus fuck. I didn't want to talk to his crazy ass, but for some reason I answered and held the phone up to my ear anyway.

"Hello?"

"Hey man," Mike said. His words were slurred. He was drunk. It fucking figured. "How you doing?"

"Go to hell, Mike. Your crazy ass bullshit gave me some fucked up dreams last night."

"Oh yeah? Well, I slept like a baby for the first time in *years*."

Something made a noise outside the door. I pulled the phone away from my ear and swung my legs over the bed. Mike's voice squawked at me. "I really hated to do this to you, man. But I just can't take it anymore."

From the light coming under the door I could see a pair of feet standing out in the hall. For a minute I thought Allison had heard the phone ring. That her guilty conscience had forced her to eavesdrop, to come see if I was taking a secret call with a secret lover.

I figured that had to be it as I turned the knob. Mike's voice continued to crackle over the line. "I had to make her stop looking at me, man," he said, his voice distant and small. "I had to."

I'd stopped listening. The White Lady stood with her back to me, her head dangling over her shoulder, her face pointing up at the ceiling. As I stood there, frozen, I barely made out Mike's apology as the phone tumbled from my fingers to the ground. In paralyzed horror, I watched as the girl pivoted slowly in my direction and then it was too late. She found me with her eyes.

I screamed so loud it woke the baby up and hearing her cry was the only thing that kept me from going totally crazy. I couldn't let the baby see her, that was the most important thing. The idea of that little angel being haunted by this vision of death sent me stumbling back, fumbling to lock the door before Allison could open hers.

The White Lady stood beside me in the bedroom.

Within seconds Allison was there, banging on the other side of the door. "Bill? Bill? Are you okay, Bill?" She must have had the baby in her arms, I could tell by the wails that came through the door.

"Leave me alone!" I shouted to my wife. "Just leave me the fuck alone."

"Bill, is this about Alan? Please don't do anything crazy."

I crawled into bed on my hands and knees as the baby continued screaming and Allison shouted and pounded on the door. I wept as I pulled the blanket over my face, knowing that The White Lady stood at the edge of my bed, her eyes staring down at me, her head swiveling to keep me in sight no matter where I turned.

"Bill, please!"

"Just get the fuck out of here, Allison. Take Evelynn with you!"

"Just talk to me, Bill. I'm worried about you."

I pulled the blanket down.

The White Lady was contorted over the bed, her face only inches from mine.

"Oh god, Allison," I groaned, my voice catching on a sob. "God help me, Allison." The White Lady's hair fluttered against my breath.

"What is going on?!"

"Get out now!" I shouted, crazy and mad and desperate. "*Get out, get out, get out.*"

I had scared her. Her footsteps were hurried, and Evelynn's cries quickly faded into the guest room. I curled into the fetal position, squeezed my eyes shut, and wept.

Ten minutes later, Allison left, yelling down the hall at me that I was fucking nuts. I thank God every day she never came back.

Because The White Lady stayed.

When I shower, she's there. When I work, she's there. In the car, at the store—when I piss, shit, and eat, she's there. She never blinks. She just stares at me, her eyes always on the verge of death, begging for something I can't give her. Eyes so full of fear and panic I can't help but feel it, too.

Sometimes I'll wake up and she's gone. Hours will go by and I'll start thinking maybe I can visit Evelynn, get my life together, and then I'll hear a creak in the house, footsteps, and she'll be there when I turn the corner or shut the fridge, her gash of a neck grinning at me like a twisted fucking clown.

Mike calls me every once in a while now, ever since he got word of my breakdown. He's forgotten everything, even our talk that night, as if it were all just a nightmare made of the type of stuff and nonsense that could be laughed at and forgotten in the morning. At least he's happy again. Joking again.

He wants to talk about the good old days, rekindle our friendship. But how can I? How can I talk to him with a scream on my lips and terror in my heart? How can I talk to him, knowing that if I lead him down memory lane, he'll see something he can't look away from?

Oh, but the temptation is there. How close I've come to saying the words, *Remember that time at Devil's Dip*, so that he'll ask and begin to see her again. But I can't do to him what he's done to me. Not after he bore the burden of it for twenty years, lied about things instead of telling the truth, hurried off the phone when the lure of escape became too much. All to save me from the agony of it.

The least I can do is return the favor.

But I want to do more than that. The White Lady and I are together in the garage now, October 13th. I'm smoking one cigarette after another while she stares at me, choking on her own blood. Shavings are everywhere and the smoke from the cigarette burns my eyes.

I pull it away from my mouth and let it fall to the floor. A minute later and my nostrils are full with the smell of burning pine.

She'll have to find someone new on Devil's Dip.

Tug O' War

by Chad Lutzke

The three of us pulled together and camped out in Jonathan's living room while he lay in bed upstairs, dying. After a week in the hospital, the doctors had sent him home with little hope for recovery, his body lacking the strength to fight the infection. A fever persisted, peaking at dangerous levels, never dropping below 100. His wife called us all, asked if we'd come see him. She thought familiar faces would boost his spirits, perhaps up his chance of recovery. It was a desperate attempt, full of pessimism.

When we'd first arrived, we all donned surgical masks and stood only at the threshold of Jonathan's room. This distance kept was at the insistence of the visiting doctor—an older gentleman who still made house calls. While the doctor couldn't be sure of any possible contagion, he wanted to be safe. I think we all did, just in case. Jonathan would have it no other way himself could he express so, but the few minutes he was awake each day were spent sipping water and calling out to the Lord for help, for either healing or a merciful death.

On one occasion, the three of us attempted small talk with our friend from the safety of the hallway. And while he seemed happy to see us, his eyes couldn't stay open long enough to clarify exactly who was who. It was hard to watch. His face was glazed alabaster with deep-set eyes. A sunken husk. Barely a trace of the man he used to be. To each of us, it was clear that without divine intervention, Jonathan would pass before the weekend was up.

The house smelled of antiseptic and sickness, a warning sign for the healthy to steer clear. And it felt as though Death itself camped out in that living room with us, waiting its turn to visit Jonathan, when the smell would change to loosened bowels and cooling flesh.

We spent the weekend fueled by alcohol and entertained by poker, dealing cards into the wee hours like we did in our younger years, when Jonathan would occupy a seat with us each Saturday night.

Jonathan's wife insisted on feeding us, slaving over more than one meal. But the rest of her time was spent in her room, grieving the inevitable loss of her husband. And while our drunken behavior on the first floor seemed inappropriate under the circumstances, she insisted we carry on, stating it sounded like happier days and was helping her cope.

It was our last night there, and we were deep into a bottle of single-malt scotch. As the alcohol loosened lips and weaved us in and out of intermittent episodes of sorrow, then drunken joy—as harsh drink tends to do—the conversation turned dark.

"When I go, I want the birds to eat me," Bill said. "A Tibetan thing, I think. Saw it on TV."

"Mausoleum for me. My own little apartment after death," I said.

"Better start saving now," Tom said. "They don't just hand those out, you know."

"A man can dream."

"My buddy at work died. His wife had him cremated, uses his ashes to make paintings. Makes her feel like he's watching over her. She finds it comforting," Bill said.

Tom furrowed his brow. "That's some grim shit."

I disagreed. "Not really. Bereavement is a sonofabitch. I can't imagine losing Carol. If I could paint, I'd probably do the same thing…if I found that it helped."

Tom shuffled the cards, dealt out another hand. "My mother-in-law held a séance so she could talk to her husband after he'd gone. She made us join her."

"Seriously?" I asked. "What happened?"

"Typical movie shit. We joined hands, focused on him while she spoke."

"Lights flickering, cold chills, and all that?" Bill asked.

"My mother-in-law claimed she saw him sitting next to her, smiling. She said she could smell him, taste him even. But I didn't see anything."

"Is she nuts, or do you think she really saw something?" I asked.

"I don't know, but she sure as hell thought she did."

Then came the sound of glass against wood, and our eyes were drawn to the stairs as Jonathan's drunken wife descended them, a drink in her hand that threatened to spill. Her robe was open, her breasts exposed, and her face a black mess, muddy with mascara.

"Deal me in, boys." Her voice cracked, struggling for composure.

Two things went through each of our minds, I'm sure. The first was a sense of guilt at the sudden arousal of seeing our friend's wife naked. Whether our loins stirred from the alcohol or from merely being a man, I don't know. But the feelings were there and, under the circumstances, were disgusting. The second was the utmost sympathy we had for the woman as she fell apart before us—eyes swollen with grief.

It was Bill who stood up first. But it was me who ran to her, cradled her, closed her robe. She sat with us and struck up conversation while we put the game on hold.

"What were you guys talking about? Death and ghosts?"

We looked at one another, stumbling over our tongues. Never finding the words.

"Do you think my Jonathan will haunt this house once he's gone?"

"Wherever he's going, Beth, he'll be at peace, I'm sure." Tom offered.

"But what if he's not? What if he's trapped between here and there, with unfinished business?"

"I don't think that's how it works," I said.

"Who's to say? None of us know." Her tone was carried by desperation and the comfort of booze. "I heard you talking about séances. I want to know I can count on you guys...to do for me what Tom did for his wife's family."

"Jonathan's not even dead yet." Bill said.

"He will be! He smells like it already. You haven't been up there tonight." She lowered her head into her hands and spoke the rest through a wet, grimacing face. "I can smell him rotting."

The three of us said nothing and laid consoling hands on her while she wept. We remained like that for several minutes. Then Beth collected herself and went up to be with her husband. Glasses were filled and the poker game continued, along with memories voiced aloud regarding Jonathan and the type of man he was—a loyal man filled with integrity. It was no wonder he'd landed a wife before any of us. And kept her. Right to the end.

Well after 2:00 a.m., we could hear the panicked voice of Beth speaking frantically into the phone upstairs. Our thoughts turned bleak, and we found ourselves gazing at the floor, tossing our cards into a pile, never to pick them up for the remainder of our stay. After the phone call, Beth came downstairs, dressed in pajamas, her face the same swollen mess.

We stood in anticipation of bad news.

"I think it's happening," she whimpered. "He's dying... *right now*!"

We scrambled to her and repeated the laying on of comforting hands. Like unbalanced calves drunk from recent birth, we stood awkwardly around Beth, out of our element and struggling to stand under the weight of a soon-to-be widow's grief and a bottle of scotch.

"I've called Dr. Hammond. He's on his way. If you want to see him while you can, you should head up."

We each took turns hugging Beth, and Bill stayed behind to console her. Tom and I put hand to bannister and climbed the stairs. Two steps from the top, the smell hit us. Beth was right. He already reeked of death. Perhaps Death *had* been waiting downstairs, patiently, listening in on our discussions, watching me bluff my way through every hand I'd won, knowing things we didn't. Eyeing each of us with an expiration date in mind and knowing that tonight was the night our friend would leave us.

Jonathan's door hung open. His hands were kept rested at his sides, his eyes open, their gaze fixed on nothing. There was no shine to them. They were drying.

Like the day before, Tom and I remained right outside the room. We stared at Jonathan's gaping mouth, the all-too-short breaths he took, ending in quiet wheezes. October leaves in a Hallow's Eve gust.

I looked at Tom. Like myself, he had cupped his mouth, his vision blocked by tears that didn't want to jump but would soon enough. We each said a few heartfelt words, then headed back downstairs to Beth and Bill, and to the bottle.

The doctor had arrived—mask over face—and was offering his coat to Beth, who'd handed the man a cup of coffee. He gulped it down as though it were cool water. We welcomed him and listened as Beth gave her report of Jonathan's decline. Dr. Hammond headed upstairs with a case that resembled luggage more than something you'd expect a doctor to be carrying, like the small black leather bags just big enough to hold a stethoscope, thermometer, some iodine, and a pint of whiskey.

While the doctor was upstairs, the rest of us sat at the dining room table, drank and listened to Beth as she spoke of funeral arrangements and finances and how they never had the child they'd always wanted and how, oh God, she wished they had. To have a small part of him still here, something that carried his smile, maybe his dimpled chin, his appreciation for art, his eye for photography, and his quick wit. Maybe then she would feel like life was still worth living.

Finally, Bill excused himself to go and visit Jonathan while Tom and I stayed with Beth. And as I listened to her talk, I wondered if Jonathan truly knew the blessing he had in the woman. Never before had I witnessed such sadness, such disdain for life without their better half to share it. Her stuttered speech and quivering chin scarred me to this day.

Our attention was then drawn to Bill, who stood at the bottom of the stairs. His face was long, as though holding a mouthful of rocks. Or bad news.

"No!" Beth whimpered. "No, no, no."

"I'm so sorry, Beth." Bill could barely get the words out.

"Are you sure?" I asked.

"He quit breathing."

Bill didn't mention the long, quiet moan that preceded the halt in the rising of Jonathan's chest, or the smell of feces as it spilled onto the sheets, and especially not the fly that had landed on Jonathan's open eye and stayed there longer than it should have.

"Oh, God!" Beth threw herself into me, sobbing uncontrollably.

Tom had an empty stare that seemed to see through walls and down the street and just kept going, anywhere but here. Bill sat, eyes fixed on the wooden table. Beth shook in my embrace, her sobs muffled by my shirt, where it was being branded by what was left of Beth's mascara.

"I can't...I can't go up there... Not now." Beth managed.

"We'll take care of everything," I said, looking at the others. "We'll do everything we can to help."

"We're here for you, Beth."

"Anything you need..."

Abruptly, Beth quit crying and pulled herself together. She cleared her throat and began to speak, alluding to our earlier discussion regarding séances. She drilled Tom with questions concerning the ceremony, specifically about materials. When he noted only a dimly lit room, a table, and candles were needed, she ran for the kitchen and gathered a book of matches and five candles, then set them all on the table.

Seeing the bewildered look on our faces, Beth cried: "I need this, you guys."

"Beth. I think...," Tom started.

"I have to do this, Tom...I want him to know...I want him to know I love him and that...that I'm going to be okay. Will you guys help me? Please!"

Again, be it the alcohol or the weakness of a man against a grieving woman's eyes, we all agreed, with the hope it would provide closure for Beth.

Beth lit the candles and grabbed my hand, grabbed Bill's hand.

"Join hands," she said. "Tom, will you please take us through?"

"Okay, but you should know, I don't really know what I'm doing." Tom took my hand and Bill's and rested them on the table.

And with no further hesitation, Tom began.

"Everyone close your eyes and think about Jonathan. Think about him being alive." He paused, then: "Think about him being here with us...and...invite him into your hearts...into your minds."

Beth squeezed my hand, tight. I could feel her wedding ring press hard against my knuckle and wondered how long after Jonathan was gone would she continue to wear it and knew if she had to answer that now, she'd say forever, that there'd never be a day it would leave her finger.

"Jonathan, if you can hear me, we invite you here to be with us. We are friends and family...your wife is here."

Beth broke down, the table shook under her sobs.

"Jonathan. Beth wants to speak with you...and if you could...if you could maybe speak to her somehow, she would love that."

Tom's voice was full of insecurity, but Beth seemed to overlook it.

"Honey, can you hear me? It's me. Beth. I'm here, honey. Please speak to me."

We sat in silence for a full minute before Beth said: "It's not working, Tom. I can't hear him. I can't feel him."

"Everyone invite Jonathan to be with us. Right here, right now." Tom said.

For ten minutes there was a cacophony of voices as we spoke simultaneously with invitations and pleading, all the while Beth squeezed my hand with voracious determination.

"Please, honey. Come to me. We invite you here. Please come to me, Jonathan. I need to feel you... I need you to hear me. Even if just for a moment."

What we were doing felt unnatural, uncomfortable. And there came a point I wanted nothing more to do with the ceremony. Something I never believed in in the first place. But I wanted peace for my friend's wife, and if the desperate act could somehow help, then I was willing to stick it out despite my true feelings toward it.

Then came a strong breeze that chilled me to the bone. I opened my eyes and found Beth smiling, her hair blown about, hands in the air.

"Oh, honey. I'm here. I can feel you... I can feel you, baby. I love you so much. I'm gonna be okay... I'll miss you like crazy, but I'm gonna be okay."

Beth's cries of grief turned to those of exhausting relief. As for myself, I saw my own face reflected in my friend's as they watched slack-jawed and wide-eyed. The cooling breeze rushed through us once more, then left. We waited for a moment, but it seemed to be over. That's when Dr. Hammond called out from the other room.

As though ashamed by the act, Beth blew out the candles and turned on the light. "In here, Dr. Hammond."

The doctor entered the room, his bag with him, his face downcast. "I'm sorry, Mrs. Davis, your husband has passed."

"I know. Thank you, Doctor. Bill told us."

"Bill told you?"

"Yes, about fifteen, twenty minutes ago."

"Excuse me, Mrs. Davis, but your husband just passed only moments ago."

We looked at Bill who spoke up. "I was up there. I saw him. He wasn't breathing. I saw him take his last breath. He...he messed the bed. I was there at the doorway."

"Sir, it's true that he did..." The doctor glanced at Beth with apologetic eyes, ashamed such details were being given. "...mess the bed. And temporarily he did cease breathing, but that was all the result of a small seizure, which ultimately broke his fever. After the episode, he was actually improving, if I'm to be honest."

"Improving?" Beth asked, her hand to her mouth.

"Yes. When the seizure subsided, he was cognizant of his surroundings, of me, of his situation. For a moment, I was slightly optimistic for his recovery."

"I don't understand. My Jonathan was awake and alert, and now he's gone?"

"Yes, ma'am. He took a very sudden turn for the worse. He struggled to stay with us, to stay with you, Mrs. Davis. He really did. I could tell. He tried so hard. Your husband was a very strong man. But I'm afraid the pull to the other side was stronger."

The weight in the room was a black cloud that bruised every one of us as we dropped our eyes to the floor, searching for answers in a hardwood ocean of regret, the only sound the whoosh of life blood that rushed through our ears as it mocked our being alive and healthy. And of being responsible.

Finally, a whimper killed the silence as Beth Davis broke—a fine crack that would spread and never heal. We all cracked. And none of us would ever make another attempt at speaking with the dead again.

Or the not quite dead.

Euphemia Christie

by Catherine Cavendish

It began with a gravestone. Or, more accurately, a whole cemetery of them.

My best friend, Fran, and I loved wandering through graveyards, trying to find the oldest stone there, reading some of the more colorful memorials. This sunny Saturday in early spring was no exception. I drove us to St. Christopher's Church a few miles out of town and we ambled through the grounds, picking our way carefully through overgrown grassy paths, avoiding stinging nettles and thistles.

"Here's one, Marie." Fran read out the inscription. "'Here lies Ebenezer Fernsby. Born 10th September 1798. Departed this life 29th December 1887. A more sober, honest and pious soul could ne'er be found. Also Maude, wife of the above, a woman much beloved and pure in heart with never an evil thought, word or deed'. Bloody hell, I'll bet she was a barrel of laughs. Not."

I laughed and then a feeling of sadness swept over me as I stared down at a poorly carved, bleak stone. "At least someone cared enough to write something about her."

Fran wandered over and peered down. "Oh. That's sad. I can barely make it out." She crouched in order to get level with it. "It's just a name. Grace Farmer. No dates, no mention of relatives. Nothing."

I shivered. "Makes you think they just wanted rid of her. Nothing to say. Stick her in the ground and forget about her. The stone's practically obliterated by the bindweed."

"Maybe she had no family to pay for anything much."

"Perhaps."

Fran moved on, but I lingered for a few moments. Who was Grace Farmer? Mysteries had always intrigued me. I blamed it on an early diet of Agatha Christie, John Grisham, and Patricia Cornwell.

Fran had moved on a little distance and was dragging weeds away from an inscription. Her giggles rang out across the peaceful graveyard.

Bidding a silent farewell to the unknown Grace Farmer, I wandered along the path until my attention was diverted by a tall gravestone on the opposite side. The wording was a little difficult to make out, marred as it was by lichen. I bent closer and peered at it. 'Euphemia Christie of Barton Longhope. Born 8th April 1861, Died 2nd July 1903, wife of Raymond Christie and mother of Caroline, Lucinda, and Judith, who all perished 25th June 1903. She died as she lived.'

I touched the stone, my fingers traveling over its gnarled, cold surface. The sun disappeared behind a fluffy white cloud and, for the second time in a few minutes, I shivered in the sudden chill. I felt someone move up behind me and turned, expecting to see Fran. Instead, a middle-aged man dressed in worn and frayed brown corduroy trousers secured with a black leather belt and sporting a collarless shirt looked as if he had stepped out of a Thomas Hardy novel.

He met my eye, blinking behind unfashionable tortoiseshell spectacles, and nodded toward the gravestone. "You don't want to trouble yourself with the likes of her."

I tore my eyes away from him to glance back down at Euphemia Christie's memorial. "Why would you say that?" I asked, switching my attention back again. But there was no sign of him.

Fran was a few yards away, smiling at yet another amusing find. I called to her. "Hey, Fran."

"Yeah?"

"Come here a minute. I want to show you something."

She hurried back to join me, and I pointed at the stone, which she leaned in closer to read.

"Did you see a strangely dressed man here a minute ago?" I asked.

She shook her head. "No, why?"

"He looked like a Victorian workman, laborer or something. He spoke to me and then he…well…vanished." It sounded as crazy to me as it must to her.

Fran cocked her head on one side and gave a little laugh. "Well he's not here now. Maybe he's one of the sextons."

"Do they still have sextons?"

Fran shrugged. "Euphemia. I used to have an Aunt Euphemia. We called her Auntie Effie."

"You would never have called this one Effie."

"How do you know that?"

The thought had sprung into my mind as if someone had whispered it to me. "I haven't the faintest idea." Something bothered me about the inscription. "The last bit is in a different font as if it was added later by another stonemason. What do you think it means by 'She died as she lived'? Is that good or bad?"

"Who knows? Poor woman, though, losing her husband and three children all on one day. Some accident perhaps?"

"She was dead herself within a week so it could well have been. Or maybe some contagious disease."

The sun emerged from behind its blanket but did nothing to warm me. I hugged myself.

"You okay?"

"Yes, I'm fine," I lied. How could I explain that, at that moment, I felt anything but fine? I stared back down at the inscription, removed my phone from my jacket pocket and took a couple of close up shots. Then I backed up in order to photograph the stone in the context of its surroundings. That way I could find it again when—or if—I returned. Why I would want to come back to this particular place, I had no idea. But I knew I needed to find out more about Euphemia Christie.

"Marie, aren't you becoming a little obsessed about this?" I could hear Fran's concern over the phone.

"Not particularly. It's fascinating. I love doing research. You know that. But she's a tough one to track down. She only seems to come up as an adjunct to her husband. Raymond Christie owned a substantial part of Barton Longhope and was the squire of the village. You were right about the accident. He and their three daughters all perished in a devastating fire, which pretty much destroyed the house. I can't find any mention of Euphemia after that date, other than a brief note in the local paper reporting the combined funeral of her husband and children. She's described as the grieving widow and mother. It says she was, 'dressed in deepest black and heavily veiled'. I think I've exhausted the Internet, so I'm going to Barton Longhope tomorrow. It's not far. Want to come with me?"

"I think I'll pass, if you don't mind. And you should too. We've got to get our essays in by Wednesday or there'll be hell to pay from Crabby Crabtree. You told me you hadn't started yours yet."

"Yeah, yeah. I'll get it done." Although, how was a different matter. I hadn't typed a word yet. My notes sat in an untidy heap next to my laptop, but all they had been good for so far was to act as a coaster for my coffee mug, as a number of brown ring stains would attest to. "I just need to follow through on this first."

"Euphemia Christie and her secrets will still be there next week, or at the end of term. That's only a couple of weeks away for Heaven's sake."

She was right, of course. I couldn't explain the overpowering need I had to trace this long-dead woman and, besides, at the back of my mind lay the unsolved mystery of the man who had been there one minute and gone the next.

"I'll see you on Monday, Fran." I didn't need to see her face to know she was mad at me. We had known each other since primary school and had never kept any secrets from one another. Boyfriends had come and gone, but we were always there for each other. We were even reading the same subject at university and were postgraduate students in English. Now, for the first time I could remember, I felt a distance had sprung up. And all because of Euphemia Christie. Who was this woman, and why did I care so much?

Barton Longhope was one of those typical English villages, set in the heart of rural England with gentle, sloping hills as a backdrop. None of the cluster of houses looked less than three hundred years old. All were stone-built in similar style; their honey-toned walls and mullioned windows showing the effects of centuries of weathering. I parked in a bay outside the village stores. If anyone knew about a former inhabitant, the local shopkeeper was a good place to start.

Crossing over the threshold felt like stepping back to the 1950s. The jangling bell, long, polished wood counter, even the till which, although electronic, owed more to the 1970s than the present day. Behind the counter, a man I gauged to be in his fifties was stacking shelves while a woman of similar age smiled and greeted me.

"What can I do for you?" she asked, her voice friendly and pleasant, with a hint of the local accent.

I spotted a chocolate bar I was partial to. "A couple of those, please." I could hardly ask for information and not buy anything.

"Just passing through?" the woman asked.

"Yes. Actually, I wonder if you can help me?"

"I will if I can," the woman replied.

"I wonder if you have ever heard of a woman named Euphemia Christie."

A sheet of ice seemed to crash down between us. The woman's smile froze with it, and the man almost growled as he spoke. "What do you want to know about her for?"

"I'm doing a bit of research..." Their hostility gave me no encouragement to continue.

The ensuing awkward silence was broken by the woman. "Euphemia Christie and her family lived in the Old Manse but it burned down."

"Could you tell me where the ruins are?"

"Go out of here and continue towards Favershill. It's about half a mile. You'll see the skeleton of the building from the road."

"Thank you." I couldn't get out of the shop fast enough. Anyone would think the events that had them both so riled had only taken place weeks ago.

All the while I picked my way through the wilderness that had grown among the ruins of the Old Manse, I couldn't escape the strong impression of being watched.

A slight breeze rustled leaves, and grasses flickered. An early butterfly—a Red Admiral—fluttered past, trying out its new wings before alighting on a bluebell. I stared up at the sad and ruined walls, almost obliterated by ivy, bindweed and convolvulus, and stepped gingerly over broken slates while hidden ones cracked under my feet. The whole impression was one of loss. What remained of the Old Manse stood in perpetual mourning. Trees encroached on what had surely once been formal gardens, leaves twitching and rustling as the breeze tickled them. I smelled wild garlic, mingled with earthy aromas, but another smell took hold. Charcoal. Smoke. Fire.

I looked around. No sign of anything burning. The closer I came to the building, the stronger it became, making my eyes water, and my nose sting. My skin felt hot, and, when I pulled up my sleeves, my arms hurt as if they were red raw, yet they looked perfectly normal.

Nevertheless, I persevered and crossed over into the house itself, now open to the elements, the upper floors and windows gone, only some blackened timbers peeping through the lush green vegetation. The stench of burning was almost overpowering, and the sound of roaring flames filled my head. Could I really be imagining all this? Fear overtook me, and I scrambled back outside.

"I wouldn't go back in there if I were you."

Maybe I heard those words. Perhaps someone really did utter them. The voice I heard—or thought I heard—was the voice from St. Christopher's graveyard, but I was all alone here. Not a living soul…

I hurried back to my car, tripping more than once, snagging my jeans on brambles, narrowly avoiding plunging headlong into a clump of thistles.

Breathing a deep sigh of relief, I climbed into my car and locked the doors. From this distance, the building looked forlorn and benign, but what I had felt in its presence was frightening. Evil.

The smell of burning had followed me, and I struggled out of my jacket. I sniffed it. A distinctive odor of bonfires. My mouth felt dry and parched, and I had the strongest taste of smoke. Anxious to get out of there, I fired the engine and returned to Barton Longhope.

I gave the shop a wide berth and settled for the pub instead. The Christie Arms offered a range of real ales and ciders, but I plumped for a large glass of lemonade instead. There were a couple of men at the bar, clearly regulars. They nodded and smiled as I hoisted myself onto a stool.

"Haven't seen you before." The barman handed me my drink.

"Thanks. No, I'm here doing a bit of research into Euphemia Christie." The two men paused in their conversation and stared at me, their smiles a thing of history. "She seems to be a controversial figure."

The barman wetted his lips. "You'll have heard about the fire?"

I nodded. "Yes, I was able to find that out, but are any of her relatives still around?"

The two men drained their glasses and left without uttering another word.

"That's the effect she has around here, even after all these years," the barman said, nodding toward their retreating backs.

"I could understand it if it had happened…oh, I don't know…ten years ago…twenty maybe, but all this reaction after more than a hundred years?"

The barman smiled. "That's how it is around here. We may only be a few miles from town, but Barton Longhope is a village in a time-warp. I've been here twenty-seven years and the locals still think of me as an incomer. Some even refer to me as the new landlord. As for Euphemia Christie and that fire…It was a huge scandal and the village tended to divide into two camps, along family lines mostly. There are those who believed she started the fire deliberately as a way of getting back at her husband. He's supposed to have fathered two children with Euphemia's identical twin sister who lived some miles away. Those who insist on her innocence won't hear a word against her and say she was staying with her sister when the fire broke out. Others say she was seen running away from the scene. Back then it seems you either loved her or loathed her, and nothing much has changed since her death. The stories have been handed down from generation to generation and it doesn't help that she's rumored to haunt the ruins of the Old Manse. Periodically, something happens and the old animosities bubble up to the surface. It's funny you should turn up now, actually. It had all gone quiet up there but, recently, people have been reporting strange smells."

"Like burning?" I asked.

"Yes, and other things. Perfume for some reason and other less pleasant things. As if something had died and been left to rot." His gaze intensified, and I realized it wasn't me he was looking at, but something over my shoulder.

Following his gaze, I saw a small portrait of a woman hanging over the mantelshelf. I slid down off the stool and followed the barman over to it.

"You have a slight look of her," he said. "There's something about the nose and mouth. Especially the way you're standing now—next to her portrait, both of you in profile."

"Really?" I stared hard, trying to see a resemblance, and failing. "So that's her? That's Euphemia Christie?"

He nodded. "You two could be related."

"But her family was wiped out in the fire."

"There was still her sister. Grace, I think her name was. She had those children, whoever the father really was."

I studied the portrait more closely. The woman faced to her left, her chestnut colored hair elaborately styled and entwined with pearls, while her heavy-lidded eyes appeared sad and preoccupied. Her lips set in a firm line as if trying to contain some deeply felt emotion. Around her neck, three strands of pearls and a pendant consisting of a large ruby surrounded by diamonds and pearls gleamed at her throat. Her dress, with its 'V' neckline, seemed to be of brown velvet with a coffee colored lace collar, and she wore a large brooch of many diamonds at her breast.

"Did anyone ever call Euphemia Effie, do you know?"

The barman laughed as he returned to his place behind his bar. "I very much doubt it. No, no, much too grand for that. She had been the Honorable Euphemia Montgomery before she married. Came from old money."

With a final glance, I tore myself away from the picture and returned to the bar. The lemonade slaked my thirst and soothed my throat. When I left, a few minutes later, I knew I had to go back to the ruined house. What I couldn't fathom was why, when every instinct I possessed urged me to go home. I simply couldn't resist the mystery, I suppose, especially one that caused so much violent reaction this many years later.

I had been away from the Old Manse no more than half an hour, probably less, but in that time, the smell of burning had intensified. My nerves tightened and a voice screamed inside my head, warning me to stop. Not to do what I was about to. But another voice pressed me on, and I stepped once more over the threshold.

It seemed an unseen resistance was bent on stopping me from going farther, and I had to force my way through an invisible barrier. My legs moved as if trapped in quicksand. I don't know why I kept fighting it, only that I had to. Something in my head drove me forward.

That's when the weeping started.

Somewhere in there a woman sobbed.

I called out to her. "Hello?"

The sobbing ceased, but only for a few seconds before resuming with renewed force. Someone wept as if their heart was broken.

"Please tell me where you are. Maybe I can help you." I moved a little easier now. Whatever had been holding me back relented, and I stepped over rubble and undergrowth, through an empty doorway and into a room, once again with no ceiling but which at least had three walls still standing. In the corner, a grand piano leaned precariously, its lid shattered and one leg buckled. A thick layer of plaster and dust gave it a ghostly, ethereal air.

The sobbing grew louder. My heart thumped, and I ran my tongue over dry lips. I could see no one, but I was getting closer to the source of the noise.

"Please tell me where you are."

The woman's voice startled me. "They're all dead. There's no hope…"

Still I could see no one. The weeping began again before fading away to nothing. A sudden gust of wind blew debris, sending it swirling around the floor, coating my shoes. The taste of dust filled my mouth.

I don't know how long I stood there, trying to rationalize what had just happened. That I had encountered the ghost of a grieving Euphemia Christie, I was certain. The depth of her despair led me to one inescapable conclusion. She was innocent of any involvement in the deaths of her husband and children.

"Rest in peace, Euphemia," I said, and felt a slight breath on my cheek. As if someone had brushed their lips across my skin. For some reason, it calmed me, and I left the Old Manse with a lighter heart than when I arrived. Maybe all she had needed was for someone to give her a kind thought or word. Perhaps now she could find eternal peace. I wanted to believe that but something wouldn't let me.

At home the following night, I remembered the photographs I had taken in St. Christopher's graveyard and uploaded them onto my laptop. When I arrived at the ones of Euphemia Christie's gravestone, the hairs on my arms bristled. I looked closer. No, I wasn't mistaken. On every single one, a white mist hovered just behind and to the right of the stone itself, casting a ghostly pall. Too excited to be scared, I called Fran.

She sounded tired and worried. "Where were you? Crabby's on your case. She asked me if I'd seen you, and I told her last time I had I thought you looked a bit pale so maybe you weren't well, but she said you hadn't called in sick and hadn't replied to a number of emails she had sent you this past few days. On top of that, you've missed three lectures. You're in deep shit, Marie. Are you at least going to hand in your work by Wednesday?"

I hadn't checked my student account for days and had broken a cardinal rule by not communicating my absence. I had no doubt that a couple of these unanswered emails contained official disciplinary warnings. If I didn't submit my work on time, I would incur penalties or even worse. So, why didn't it matter to me? I had worked so hard to achieve my first degree and had started my Master's all fired up and keen to get on with it. Now, because of one gravestone, it couldn't have mattered less.

"Don't keep on, Fran. I'll get it done, but I need to show you something crazy. You won't believe it." I told her about the mist on the pictures. On the previous evening, I'd already regaled her with my experiences in Barton Longhope, right before I promised to see her today at lectures, and now I was in trouble with the course tutor and probably the Head of School. Did I care?

I rattled on about the mist, its amorphous density, indeterminate shape. Finally, I ended by suggesting we meet, right then.

"Have you any idea what time it is?" Fran asked.

I hadn't.

"It's after two in the morning, and you woke me. I have to be up at seven."

She didn't seem mollified by my mumbled apology, and we ended the call on a decidedly frosty note.

No way could I sleep that night. Six o'clock saw me dressing in jeans and a hoodie emblazoned with the university logo. Remembering the tangled undergrowth, I chose trainers rather than the flat shoes I had worn on my previous visit. I cast aside any thought of the lecture I was due to attend at eleven and the unwritten essay was equally forgotten.

In half an hour, I was back in Barton Longhope.

A blackbird chirped, and a thrush trilled. The sun had begun warming the trees, and an aroma of sap rose from the ground. No smell of burning today. Nor was I alone.

I recognized him straight away. The man from St. Christopher's cemetery stood a little way off and, although he was puffing away at a pipe, releasing small clouds of smoke, I could smell no tobacco. He reminded me of my great grandfather, who I had never known but whose photographs were scattered throughout the pages of an album my mother had inherited.

The man looked directly at me, and I moved a little closer, intrigued rather than perturbed. He removed his pipe from his mouth.

"You have the look of her."

"Who? Euphemia Christie?"

"And her sister. Grace."

"I've seen you before, haven't I?"

"You have. And, doubtless, you'll see me again."

"Who are you? What's your name?"

"You don't need to know that." He puffed on his pipe again. "She's coming. You should take care. She knows you, and she won't——"

A rush of wind knocked me off my feet, and I sprawled on the ground, my face buried in dewy grass. When I struggled to my feet, the man had gone.

There was no more wind, and I was left feeling perplexed and scared. How could Euphemia Christie know me?

I sat in the car and called my mother. After skirting around pleasantries and awkward questions about university, I plunged in. "Does the name Euphemia Christie mean anything to you?"

The silence at the other end of the phone lasted an uncomfortable amount of time before a sigh reached my ear. "She was the sister of your Great-Great Grandmother Grace."

"What? Why have I never heard of any of this? I never even knew I had a relative called Grace until now, and I've certainly never heard of Euphemia being in the family."

"Because it all happened so long ago. It was a terrible scandal at the time, but this is well over a hundred years ago."

"Scandal? Tragedy, more like. Those children and the husband dying in that fire."

"The fire? Oh yes, that."

"You're confusing me, Mum."

"Well the fire... Of course, it was a terrible thing to happen, but I'm not talking about that. I'm talking about the affair Grace had with Euphemia's husband. It went on for years. They had two children. Your real great-great grandfather was Raymond Christie."

"*What?*"

"It's true. When Euphemia found out, she was beside herself with rage. She caught the first train to her sister's to have it out with her. That was the day the fire broke out, or maybe the day after. I'm not sure. Grace's poor husband—who we knew as your Great-Great

Granddad Henry—hadn't a clue what had been happening and thought the children he had been bringing up were his. He never got over it apparently. Took to drink. By all accounts, he was a decent man and had been a successful barrister. After this happened, he gave up the law and spent all his sober hours in the garden growing vegetables and dressed like some old tramp. There's a photograph of him somewhere, puffing on his pipe. Euphemia Christie passed away only a few days after the fire. I was told she was inconsolable and died of a broken heart."

"She's buried in St. Christopher's Cemetery a few miles from here."

"I never knew that."

"Mum, would you be able to scan that photograph of Henry and email it to me?"

"Yes, of course, dear, but why all these questions?"

"Oh…it's some research I'm doing. Family history. This scandal will be just the thing. But what about the children? My great grandfather?"

"Grace and Henry stayed together but Granddad told my father he rarely saw either of them. They employed a nanny who became more like a mother to him than his own. He said Grace was never the same after her sister died."

I drove home with thoughts racing around my head. Now it made sense why I had been so attracted to Euphemia's gravestone. The family connection had somehow triggered something in my brain.

When I logged onto my email account, there was the photograph. I opened it and stared. Of course, it was him. The man from the Old Manse and the cemetery. No longer my great-great grandfather, not even a blood relative anymore.

My course work continued to lay forgotten and my student emails unopened. At night, my dreams took me back to the Old Manse as it might have looked in the days of its former glory, and where my unconscious mind wandered around sumptuous rooms and heard someone play Mozart on the grand piano.

All my waking thoughts were occupied with Euphemia Christie. I yearned to clear her name with those who believed her guilty. She had been so sorely wronged, no wonder her spirit could find no rest. For the next three days, I hid away in the university library, reading and researching anything I could find on our shared heritage of Christies and Montgomerys. The deadline for submitting my essay came and went. On Thursday, I counted twenty unanswered calls from Fran and when the doorbell rang, I ignored it.

Early the following morning, I returned to Barton Longhope once again, with no clear plan. All my research had achieved was to create yet more questions. But some part of me knew the only way I would answer them was to return to the source.

When I arrived, there wasn't a soul about. Just me, a gloriously crisp, sunny day, and the ruined Old Manse.

I lost no time in negotiating my way to the entrance. The sobbing started as soon as my feet touched the floor of the entrance hall, and I followed the sound into the front room with the ruined piano. A breeze through the charred and shattered window fluttered my hair and froze my neck.

In the corner, a shadowy figure moved. It uncurled from a fetal position as it began to take female form. She grew until she stood at full height, a little shorter than me. I recognized her straightaway from the picture in the Christie Arms. A luminous glow surrounded her, and I felt a sense that she was here and yet not here. She slowly turned to face me full on, her hands clasped.

"I am so sorry," I said. "You suffered too much."

I knew she had heard me even though her face registered nothing and she did not speak.

Behind me, something moved. I spun around. Outside, a few yards from where I stood, the man watched us.

His sad voice echoed around me as if we were together in the empty room. "If only you had stayed where you belong. If only you hadn't come back here."

"I don't understand." I turned back to Euphemia. "I want to help you find peace."

She blinked. Her mouth opened and kept on opening wider and wider. Impossibly. Skin sloughed off her face and hands. A stench of rot and decay poured off her, and I retched. How could this be the sobbing woman I had taken pity on?

The rotted, hideous thing in front of me threw her skeletal arms wide. Her evil turned the room dark and gripped me in an iron embrace. I must escape but I couldn't move. A cacophony of voices crowded into my head, filling my brain with her venom, spewing their poison into my veins. Her hatred of who I was overwhelmed me and, in a second, I had the answers I had craved so much. How I wished I hadn't.

I was Grace and Raymond's descendant. I had come here and, by doing so, enabled Euphemia to wreak her eternal vengeance on me as she had on him, yet her own children had perished in the process. The woman's jealousy had turned her insane in life and had grown infinitely in death.

Screams echoed all around me. I had no awareness of uttering a sound. But I knew they were mine.

Flames shot up. Through a wall of fire, I saw the man and cried out to him for help.

"I cannot cross into that place. There is nothing I can do. You are hers now."

The flames crawled closer. A few more seconds and they would reach me. I struggled, but her hold was too strong. A shard of pain seared through me as fire licked my feet.

And then I heard them. Fire engine sirens. My last conscious memory.

Too late.

So here I stay. I cannot leave this place and wander endlessly through the lavish rooms. Oh yes, to me this place is as it once must have been, elegantly furnished. A thing of beauty, but soulless and empty. Mozart plays on the piano, although I have never seen the player. I see no one. Not even *her*. I brought it all on myself. If I had never stopped by her gravestone, I would have been spared. She could not have found me.

Now I know the meaning of the inscription on that gravestone. After murdering her husband and children, Euphemia left Barton Longhope and changed her identity. You see, there was another murder. Euphemia couldn't allow Grace to live. She killed her sister and took her place by Henry's side. He went along with it because he was terrified of her and, even though he now knew they weren't his, he loved those children. He was sure if he betrayed Euphemia's guilt she would take their lives. As a result, I had him to thank for my very existence.

It was he who added the inscription, 'She died as she had lived' after Euphemia's real death some years later.

It is Grace who lies in Euphemia's grave, and her mist that shrouds it. Her weeping comes to me in spirit, and I feel the weight of her sorrow. Like me, she is tied to the evil woman who will not let us go. As for Euphemia, her corpse lies under the plain, unloved stone in St. Christopher's graveyard under her assumed name. 'Grace Farmer'.

I think Grace's husband has passed over into the light. Euphemia could no longer hold him after I arrived. It's my turn to try and warn off any relative foolish enough to come here. So far, there's been no one.

I can only pray there never will be.

Justin's Favorite

By Jeremy Hepler

"You know you're my favorite, right?" Justin asked.

Kim simpered as she handed him the thermos she'd filled with coffee for his trip. She liked the sound of that word. Favorite.

"Oh, really. Favorite, huh?"

The intimate way he searched her with his eyes compelled her to step out onto the front porch, rise onto her tiptoes, and kiss him long and hard.

When their lips parted, she adjusted the collar of his jacket. "Promise me you'll pull over if you get too tired," she said. "And call when you get there."

He had a three-hundred-and-fifty-mile drive ahead of him, five hours of monotonous, open-landscape solitude, and he hadn't slept a wink in the last twenty-four hours. Neither of them had. They'd spent their first night in their new home in their pajamas, listening to Pandora, laughing, unpacking boxes, and sharing childhood stories while they sipped wine. They'd also christened their first shared mattress on the floor of their first shared bedroom more than once. Justin's phone had rung about an hour earlier, shortly after their second go around. His boss, the IT manager for the Whole Foods southern region, told Justin he was needed in Dallas. One of the store's computer networks had failed due to a virus, and they needed to get the store back up and running as quickly as possible, which could take a couple of days.

"I will. I promise." Justin gave her a quick peck on the cheek. "Love you."

"Love you, too."

As he crossed the snow-covered yard, Kim walked to the edge of the porch where a crisp breeze slapped her cheeks and whipped her bedhead bob around. Her over-sized flannel pajamas, Justin's pajama's actually, flapped against her small frame. A cold front had blown in overnight, and temperatures were predicted to remain below freezing for a couple of days. The sun had risen but was lost behind a rolling blanket of gray. She pinched her thighs together, crossed her arms over her chest, and watched the Land Rover pull away from the house. Justin honked twice, then threw his hand out the window and waved just before he turned off of Hillcrest Drive, his typical parting gesture.

Kim raised her hand to wave back but jerked it back down when the front door slammed closed behind her with an alarming smack. She gasped, spun around, and stared at the door long enough for her startled nerves to subside, long enough for logic to convince her that the heater must've kicked on and sucked the oak behemoth shut, before chuckling to herself and heading inside.

The house seemed daunting without Justin. Almost unwelcoming, which Kim chalked up to the newness of the place as well as her own past. She was used to small, meager spaces.

She'd lived in either trailers or apartments her entire life, never a real house. Never in a nice neighborhood. Never anywhere larger than nine hundred square feet, and never anywhere with stairs and a fireplace, a kitchen island and a garage. This two-story, twenty-four-hundred square foot brick house *was* in a nice neighborhood and had all of that. She wouldn't have minded buying a smaller house, or even renting one, but Justin insisted if they were going to move in together, going to get married and share a future, they needed to have a house big enough for a family someday. He'd been single for six years before meeting Kim five months earlier, and he'd stockpiled a fairly large savings. Enough to put thirty-thousand down on the house.

Kim's dad had always said the only way to get past a bad situation was to keep moving forward. Of course, this wasn't a bad situation, not even close, but the sentiment was the same. To become comfortable with the house, to push past the awkwardness of the unfamiliar, she had to keep moving. She made her way to the kitchen, grabbed her phone off the island, then went upstairs to continue unpacking.

Boxes littered the large open area at the top of the stairs, the area they planned to use as office space. When they'd unpacked the U-Haul, they'd piled all the boxes for the upstairs bedrooms and bathroom here. Some of the boxes were empty, some partially unpacked, others still sealed. Kim opened Pandora on her phone and found her INXS station. She lowered the volume to a level where she'd be able to talk to herself, a habit she'd picked up in junior college. Her English 101: Rhetoric and Composition professor, who was also the speech professor, had suggested the technique when trying to work through a thesis. The technique proved beneficial to Kim, annoying to her roommates.

She'd only emptied half of a box labeled BATHROOM, telling herself where exactly to place each item on the counter, in which drawer, when a strange noise found her ears. The scratching came from overhead, the attic. She angled her eyes upward, listening. It sounded like little feet, perhaps rat feet, or squirrel feet, or racoon ones, and they seemed to be right above her head. Scratching and clawing at the sheetrock.

She turned off Pandora, stood, and followed the sound with her eyes as it moved in circles. "What's it doing?"

"Trying to get warm, maybe? Build a bed in the insulation?"

The scratching grew louder, more intense, the circles wider. Then it suddenly stopped. Kim kept her eyes on the ceiling. "Where did—"

She cut her eyes down the hallway when a crash rang out in the spare bedroom at the end of the hall. Slow, silent seconds ticked by. The furnace kicked on and whooshed warm air across her face. She held steady, focusing her attention on the open doorway.

"What if it fell through the ceiling?" she whispered. "Or got into the vents. Could that even—?"

Her heart leapt into her throat, clogging up her words, when a pounding came from the opposite end of the hall. Four quick, solid knocks. Deliberate knocks to her ears. She turned on her heels and looked that way. The master bedroom door was open, but nothing appeared amiss as far as she could see. No animal or person visible. She glanced back at the spare bedroom, back at the master. Now she saw something. Or thought she did. A wispy cloud of a thing with a rough human outline, transparent but slightly rust-colored, standing in the doorway. She watched and waited, her shoulders rising, tensing.

"You're just freaking yourself out," she whispered. "You're not wearing your glasses. It's probably dust motes." She closed her eyes, counted to three, opened them. The image was gone. "Yep. Just dust—"

She stopped when she heard a sliding, scraping noise behind her, like someone rushing up the carpeted stairs. Frightened, she swung around, and her shin slammed into a box. She pitched forward, falling toward the stairs, and threw her hands out in front of her. Her right smacked the wooden handrail, and she clinched it, slowing her fall. Her left hit the second stair, slid off, planted on the third. Her hips hugged the floor on the edge of the landing. She held steady for a moment, then cautiously squirmed backward and sat back on her haunches.

Sucking in a deep breath, she glanced down the staircase. Had she not caught herself, she would've slammed into the wall just below a window, about halfway down at a right turn. She dropped her gaze to the box she'd tripped over. *Or did it slam into you?* her mind conjured.

"That's ridiculous," she voiced. "I'm just exhausted...and clumsy. Always clumsy."

She sighed.

As she ran her hand over the word TOWELS written in Justin's block-letter print on the box and said the word aloud, a slight movement teased her awareness. She looked up and for a brief moment thought she saw the same faint, rust-colored apparition standing beneath the staircase window. But she knew better and blinked the image away. Her fatigued eyes were playing tricks on her again, allowing her imagination too much leeway. She glanced at the master bedroom doorway, at the spare one, up at the ceiling.

"I need to find my glasses."

Downstairs, Kim found her glasses on the coffee table in the living room between her laptop and a stack of mystery paperbacks. The stack was five high, five novels she should've already read. There were twenty or so more in a box on the island. On top of her fulltime job at the Mercy Public Library, she managed a YouTube channel called *Kim's Killer Advice*. Eight thousand people subscribed to her weekly book reviews, but because of the engagement and the move and all that came along with them, she hadn't posted in three weeks. So rather than head back upstairs, Kim decided to read for a bit. Kill two birds with one stone as her mom used to say. Do a little work *and* give her imagination a new, less stressful playground to romp around in for a while.

The lower level of the house was significantly cooler than upstairs, probably a five- or ten-degree difference. After learning that a cold front was expected to arrive over the weekend, she and Justin had fantasized about lighting the fireplace for the first time, cuddling up on the couch under a blanket, eating popcorn and M&Ms and pickles, and watching a movie. Justin had bought a box of Duraflame starter logs as well as a small bundle of real ones. They were on the hearth. Hoping Justin wouldn't mind if she christened the fireplace without him, she placed a starter log and a few regular ones on the center of the rack, opened the flue, lit the fire, and then made her way to the couch behind the coffee table.

The Witch Elm by Tana French was the top book on the stack. Kim grabbed it, slipped on her glasses, kicked her legs up on the cushions, and tucked the throw draped over the back of the couch around them. She watched the paper around the starter log burn away before turning to the first page and diving in.

By the time she glanced over the back of the couch at the clock in the kitchen, thirty minutes had passed. She yawned. The coffee was wearing off, the warmth from the fire weighing down her eyelids.

Sleep tugged at her brain. She curled onto her side, facing the fireplace, and continued reading. Fifteen minutes later, she was softly snoring and dreaming.

She found herself running through a chain of rooms, one after the other, darkness chasing her, gaining on her. The rooms were dimly lit, no windows, one door that led into the next room. The darkness was ten feet away. Five. She stopped when it swallowed her. A coldness accompanied the blackness. She couldn't see anything, so she twisted in circles with her arms outstretched, screaming Justin's name. Her screams turned to horrified shrieks when she felt hands grabbing at her calves and thighs, arms and torso. Hands she couldn't see, only feel, pinching, pulling, wanting. She tried to hit them away, to run, but there were too many, a hand-wall on all sides of her, surrounding her…

The loud clang of the flue closing woke her with a start. Her eyes popped open, and she shot upright. She felt hands touching her, pressing down, saw the rust-colored, wispy cloud of a human hovering over her, partially on her. In her.

"Fuck!"

She jumped up, darted away from the couch, and scanned her body. There were no hands. She pivoted. There was no rust-colored apparition, either. It was all a dream. A nightmare. Just the remnants of a nightmare. None of it was real. There was the smell of smoke, though, that was real. She looked at the fireplace and saw flames still rippling inside, waves of smoke rolling out the opening, curling up over the mantle.

Panic kick-started her legs, and she rushed toward the fireplace.

Why is the smoke not—

"The flue."

She grabbed the poker off the hearth, and, using the hook end to grab the handle, re-opened the flue. The heat from the flames burned the backside of her hand and fingers. She jerked her hand out, dropped the poker, and as she instinctively shook her hand, the smoke alarm in the kitchen triggered, releasing an ear-piercing wail, an exclamation mark to the pain.

"Shit!"

She hurried to the kitchen, climbed up on the counter, took the alarm off the wall, and removed the battery. When she hopped off the counter, she examined her hand. A misshapen patch of red skin the size of a golf ball marked the top. Smaller burnt areas colored a couple of her knuckles and fingers. Blisters were bound to come, and plenty of pain, but she would be okay. She didn't need to go to the Mercy General emergency room or anything. She glanced at the fireplace, at the smoke still rolling out of the opening. What she needed to do was put out the fire and get the smoke out of the house.

She used the kitchen fire extinguisher to put out what remained of the burning logs and coals quickly closed the glass fireplace doors to prevent more smoke from coming out, and then moved from room to room, upstairs and down, talking out loud to herself, trying to make sense of what had happened, trying to keep from freaking out, as she opened all the doors and windows.

The strong, frigid wind flushed most of the smoke out quickly, within thirty minutes, but it also dropped the temperature a good twenty degrees. After slathering her burns with aloe, Kim slipped on a wool overcoat before circling back through the house and closing all the doors and windows. She was in the hallway, on her way to the thermostat to crank up the heater, when three loud knocks stopped her in her tracks.

Solid knocks. Deliberate knocks. Like the ones upstairs earlier.

Her heart hammered. She held her breath.

Three more knocks, louder and faster. From the front of the house. Not upstairs.

The front door.

Through the peephole she saw her co-worker, Heather Jackson, standing on the porch, holding a small bamboo plant in a terra cotta pot. Her heart slowed as she opened the door and greeted her friend with a hug. They'd worked together at Mercy Public Library for nearly three years. They shared a love of reading, sarcasm, eighties fashion, and Asian food. Kim had always thought of Heather, who was twenty years her senior and a single mother to one, as not only a good friend, but also a mentor, the big sister she didn't have.

"What are you doing here?" Kim asked. "I thought you worked today."

"I do, but I wanted to drop off this house warming gift first." She handed the bamboo plant to Kim. "They're supposed to bring good luck."

Kim smiled. "Thank you. I love it. Do you want to come inside?"

"Sure. I have about thirty minutes until I have to be there."

"Great. But let me warn you, I had an issue with the fireplace earlier and just finished airing out the house. It's still pretty chilly in there and smells like smoke. A lot."

"I was wondering why you were wearing that coat." Heather playfully crinkled her nose and waved her hand in front of her face. "And why you smelled like a campfire. What the heck happened?"

"I'm not exactly sure."

Inside, they made their way to the kitchen where they sat on stools in front of the island, and Kim told Heather everything that had happened in the two days since they'd last talked. Unloading the U-Haul, the sleepless night of laughter and sex, Justin being sent to Dallas for work, the noises upstairs, tripping, the rust-colored weirdness, the fireplace incident, all of it.

As always, Heather listened attentively and offered opinions and suggestions at the right moments, without judgement. She agreed the noises upstairs were probably an animal, saying she'd had troubles with "stupid critters" invading her attic and scaring the shit out of her last winter, too. She also agreed the rust-colored weirdness was a symptom of fatigue, a lack of sleep, light and reflections playing tricks on tired eyes. About the fireplace incident, Heather suggested that maybe the flue was old, had been heated and cooled too much over the years, and the heat had loosened the latch just enough for it to slip closed, which sounded plausible to Kim. She'd seen drastic changes in temperature affect metal before.

Kim thanked Heather for listening and making her feel better, then asked, "Would you like some tea?" She retrieved a tin filled with packets of green tea from a box on the floor and held it head-high, like a model from *The Price is Right*, displaying an item for the contestants. "I've got your favorite."

Heather arched an eyebrow. "Girl, you know I can't say no to green tea."

As Kim filled two mugs with water, Heather reached for a small photo album sitting on the far end of the island. A cap, baseball bat, and baseball were painted on the leather cover. "Is this Justin's?"

Kim glanced back over her shoulder, her eyes landing on the album. "Yep. It has all his childhood pictures in it." She set the cups in the microwave, turned it on, and stepped up behind Heather who was opening the one-picture-per-a-page album.

"Is this his sister who had cancer?" Heather tapped her long, bright pink fingernail on the little girl in the first picture.

"Yeah. That's Lucy." In the picture, Lucy was sitting on a hospital bed, Justin snuggled up beside her, a book in his hand, reading to her. Her hair was only stubble, her skin like wet paper, thin and pale enough to expose veins. She had no meat on her body and a frail smile on her face, a smile aimed at her big brother. "That was taken a week before she died."

Heather flipped the page, revealing a second picture of Lucy. This one a school headshot of the eleven-year-old taken only six months before the hospital one but appearing to have been taken a lifetime earlier. Her cheeks were plump and full of color, her hair thick and wavy and shoulder-length. Eyes bright and green, smile unbreakable.

"That's the one Justin has tattooed on his arm," Kim said.

Heather lingered on the page. "It's so horrible. Cancer. What it can do and how fast it can do it. How it doesn't discriminate."

The microwave beeped, and Kim went to get the mugs of tea. When she returned, she set one in front of Heather. "Be careful. I think I heated them up too long."

Heather blew at the steam rising from the mug, then continued to flip pages. She stopped on picture of Justin when he was about three, clinging to the leg of tall woman with curves in all the right places. "This must be his mom. She has the same eyes and smile as Lucy." She glanced at Kim, and Kim nodded.

"That's the only picture of her he has."

"How long has it been now, since he's seen her?"

Justin's mom disappeared about four months after Lucy died. One day, he came home from school—he was a senior at the time—and she was just gone. No goodbye. No note. Never a phone call or letter or email. Nothing.

"Seven years," Kim said.

Lightly shaking her head, Heather turned the page. "I can't imagine how someone could abandon their kid like that. I mean, I understand she must've been devasted, with what happened to Lucy and all." She met eyes with Kim. "I honestly can't say what I'd do if cancer took my Genevieve, but I'd like to think I wouldn't abandon my other kid if I had one. It'd be like driving a knife into their heart."

Kim nodded. She had no sympathy for Linda Patterson. Not only had Linda abandoned Justin, she'd also pretty much abandoned Lucy. Justin said the sicker Lucy got, the more she needed her mom, the less Linda visited, the less she hugged, the more she drank and smoked and snorted. The more she left to Justin. She wasn't there with Justin when Lucy died, and she was late to the funeral he'd organized. A couple weeks before she high-tailed it, he said she tried to apologize, make amends, promising she'd sober up and be a better mom. But that never happened.

"It was definitely rough on Justin. He experienced more pain in six months than some people will in a lifetime. First Lucy, then his mom...then Renee."

"Who's Renee?"

"I didn't tell you about her?"

Heather shook her head.

"Well, Justin moved in with her after his mom vanished. She was his girlfriend at the time. She was a year older than him and had an apartment over on 45th. The Newport, I think. Anyway, she was from a broken family like him. Neither knew their dad, and both hated their mom. One night, a few weeks after he'd moved in, he came home from the laundromat, and she wasn't there. They lived on the third floor, and, as he was walking out onto the balcony for a smoke, he dialed her cell number." Kim pushed out a breath. "Then he heard her Darth Vader ringtone, somewhere below the deck, and when he looked over, he saw her. Facedown on the cement sidewalk below."

"Oh my." Heather brought her hand up to hollow of her throat. "That's... How did she..."

"It was ruled undetermined. There were no signs of a struggle or foul play, but there was also no way to call it a definite accident or suicide. She had struggled with bi-polar disorder and threatened suicide in the past, but according to Justin, she also liked to sit on the balcony rail when she was on her phone or smoking. I don't know."

"Damn." Heather closed the photo album. "What a shitstorm of loss for that poor boy."

Kim nodded and swallowed, forcing the ball of emotion swelling in her throat back down. Thinking about all Justin endured back then always squeezed her heart. She needed to steer the conversation in a different direction before the tears started. "What do you say I give you a quick tour of the house before you go?"

Heather beamed, seemingly eager to change directions, too. "Absolutely. I'd love a tour of Castle Patterson."

Sipping tea, they visited every room, talking about furniture layouts, paint colors, carpet upgrades, and other decorating ideas. The tour ended at the front door where Kim took Heather's empty mug, hugged her, and thanked her again for the plant.

"My pleasure," Heather said. "I'll give you a call when I get off to make sure you haven't tried to burn the place down again."

A smile touched Kim's weary eyes.

In the kitchen, Kim put the mugs in the sink and shrugged off her overcoat. The house was finally back to a comfortable temperature. But it still stank. She stank. Her clothes stank. She checked her phone to make sure Justin hadn't called or texted before she headed upstairs to the master bathroom.

She lit the two vanilla candles on the bathroom counter and turned the hot water on full blast, filling the room with steam. She grabbed a fresh change of clothes from a box in her bedroom, and two towels from the box labeled TOWELS that she'd tripped over earlier. One towel was to dry herself, the other to drape over the edge of the tub, to rest her arm on. Submerging her burned hand in hot water was not an option. The pain was already demanding enough. She washed down four Tylenol with a handful of water to temper the sting, undressed, and climbed into the clawfoot tub.

The whooshing of the furnace supplied a steady, hypnotizing white noise. The vanilla scent dominated the room, a welcome change to her smoke-weary nostrils. The hot water turned her muscles to putty. She found it hard to move. Hard to think. Hard to anything but lie there and breathe. She leaned her head back against the tub and closed her eyes, giving in to relaxation.

When the furnace cut off, her eyes popped open, and she stared up at the ceiling for a dazed moment. "I cannot fall asleep in here," she said, lifting her head up.

She held her burned hand high, then closed her eyes and slid forward, fully submerging her torso and head in the warm water. She was combing her other hand through her short hair, breaking up the tangles, when she felt something press down on her shoulders, hard, pinning her to the bottom of the tub. Startled, she twitched and tried to rise up but couldn't. Her eyes shot open.

Blurry, above the water, six inches from her face, the rust-colored thing lingered. There appeared to be a head with long hair attached to a neck, the neck to shoulders, the shoulders to arms that cut through the water and held her down. She tried to grab at the arms, wanted to pry them loose, but her hands passed through the water like they weren't there. She twisted and writhed. Water sloshed and splashed. She gasped and sucked a gulp of water down the wrong pipe. Her chest tightened. The rust thing remained.

She thrust her hips and flailed her legs, tangling her foot in the stopper chain.

The drain!

She kicked her tangled foot, ripping the stopper loose. As the water began to drain, and she continued to struggle, breathing in more liquid, the rust ghost vanished, and the pressure on her shoulders with it. She sat up and frantically crawled out of the tub, coughing, spewing bath water, struggling for air. Her eyes darted around the room, searching for the rust ghost. It wasn't there.

She scraped up her clothes and stumbled out of the room, down the stairs, into the kitchen where she'd left her phone, where her car keys dangled on a hook on the wall.

With her keys in hand, she fumbled to slip on her sweat pants, her eyes paranoid, moving, on alert. When she popped her head through the top of her T-shirt, she saw the rust ghost between the coffee table and fireplace. Its feet floated an inch off the floor, and it appeared to be pulsing, a mirage rippling in the heat. And definitely female, a short petite female. It had long hair and wore what appeared to be a dress, or a skirt. The exact facial features were indiscernible, but where the eyes should've been, there were two black holes.

A terror bomb exploded in Kim's chest. She reached for her cell phone on the corner of the island as the ghost rushed at her, mouth open, screaming in a shrill voice. The same two words over and over and over.

"You can't! You can't! You can't!"

As it passed through the coffee table and couch, books, cushions, blankets, and her laptop flew into the air. When it penetrated the island, everything jettisoned off, flying toward Kim. Pots and books, Justin's photo album and silverware, her cell phone, all of it, a barrage of debris, slammed into her backside and the wall behind her as she ran.

She didn't look back when she reached the front door.

She didn't look back as she sprinted across the snow-covered yard.

She didn't look back as she jumped into her '87 Firebird and peeled out of the driveway.

She barely slowed as she careened around a corner off of Hillcrest Drive, heading for her mom's house. The sun was still trapped behind a featureless wall of gray clouds. Snakes of wind-driven snow slithered along the surface of the frozen roads.

Tears streamed from Kim's eyes as she sped down Cedar Street, blowing through a stop sign, almost hitting two parked cars. "It's going to be okay," she uttered. "I just need to—"

"You can't be his favorite!"

Kim screamed and jerked her head to the right. The rust ghost's face was inches away from her own. Kim's eyes widened with terrified recognition. Without distance, without the distortion of being underwater, the identity was clear. The ghost was the spitting image of the tattoo on Justin's upper arm.

Twelve-year-old Lucy Patterson.

But this Lucy, rust-colored ghost Lucy, had black holes for eyes, not bright green ones. And rather than an easy, big-toothed smile, she presented a fierce grimace.

"I'm his favorite!" Lucy screamed as she lunged toward the steering wheel. "*Me!* Not *you!* Not *Mom!* Not *Renee!*"

Kim tried to see the road through the blur of rust, tried to fight against the wheel when it jerked right, tried to keep her bare foot from pushing the gas pedal all the way to the floor. But she couldn't. The

Firebird jumped the curb and sped into Keeler Park at forty miles per hour.

"I'll always be his favorite! His *favorite* favorite!"

By the time it accelerated across two soccer fields and slammed into the massive oak tree shading the playground, it had reached a fatal speed of sixty-five.

Holes in the Fabric

by Todd Keisling

-1983-
Outside Stauford, Kentucky

Norma Leifthauser stood behind the volunteers while the county fire marshal went over the disposal procedures. The other men snickered and cracked jokes under their breath, half-hearted attempts at hiding the nervousness among them, the anxiety in the air. Norma tasted that anxiety now as she waited in the shadows of the poplar trees. Ash, copper, grass, smoke. The smell of death had yet to overwhelm the forest clearing. That would come much later.

"Any questions?" The fire marshal, a stout man named Gary Kissinger, surveyed the row of volunteers culled from the neighboring towns. His eyes fell upon Norma, the only woman in the group, and lingered for a few seconds before moving on.

A lanky fellow in the front raised his hand. "How're we s'posed to get the bodies back to the road?" He gestured to the trail behind them, a beaten path swallowed by the overgrowth. "You don't expect us to carry 'em back through that shithole village, do ya Gary?"

"Yeah, Eugene, I do." Gary looked to the rest. "I expect all of you to help, and I expect you all do this as respectfully as possible. These people had families just like you 'n me."

Someone scoffed.

Another man piped up from the far end. "We should just stack 'em up there with the rest of their church and watch 'em burn. Fuckin' Satanists is all they were."

Murmurs erupted among the group, and Norma counted ten nodding heads. Gary's face reddened. He stomped over to the dissenter and leaned into the man's face.

"You so much as look at them ruins and I'll make sure you spend a week in lockup. Chief Bell and I go way back. Don't test me, son."

Norma watched the exchange, transferring her weight from one foot to the other. Contrasting scents of ash and blood filled her nose and stained her tongue with an awful taste. Coming here was a mistake. She shouldn't have volunteered.

But the money...

She thought of her son, Johnny, and of her landlord, Mrs. Pennington, and how she was already three weeks past due on the rent. Her jobs at Ron's Department Store and Garvey's Gas 'n Go were barely keeping a roof over their heads; every month was a game of hot potato with the bills, juggling which would get paid on time and which wouldn't. Mrs. Pennington was kind enough, but she had her own bills to pay, and Norma hated being a burden to anyone. The extra $250 promised to volunteers would go a long way in keeping them off the street.

"—Gonna keep up, missy?"

Gary's voice ripped her from her thoughts. Norma lifted her chin and met the man's stare.

"Sorry, didn't catch that."

A few of the other men laughed. Even Gary had a dumb smile on his face. "I said it's gonna be a long day, are you sure you're gonna keep up?" He paused, listening to the muffled laughter. "Ain't too late to back out if you wanna go back home."

Norma's cheeks flushed, but she clenched her teeth and forced a smile. She broke through the line of men and stood in front of the fire marshal. "I'll keep up." She reached for the work gloves in her back pocket and slipped them on. "Can you?"

The men broke into a fit of laughter this time. Gary stared, sizing her up, a crooked smile on his face. He nodded. "That's the kind of grit we're lookin' for."

"Good," Norma said. "It's the only kind you're gonna get from me."

She patted Gary's shoulder and started up the hillside.

Late morning light broke through the forest canopy and drove away the shadows crawling along the side of Calvary Hill. They'd managed to move half the bodies in a couple hours, but the day was warming up and the flies were beginning to amass.

Norma snuffed out her cigarette and watched a pair of men carry another body to the pile. There were twenty or so now, stacked like a cord of firewood along the perimeter of the clearing, each one tied in thick plastic sheeting. Dark trails striped the hillside from where the congregants took their lives, overshadowed by the charred remains of the old church, its timbers still smoldering.

She thought about what the man said earlier that morning. *Fuckin' Satanists is all they were.* Norma knew that wasn't true, of course. They might've been crazy—their minister, Jacob, certainly was—but they weren't Satanists. There were no pentagrams here, no mockery of the trinity. She'd grown up hearing about the crazy cult out in the woods near Devil's Creek, heard the old tales of voices on the wind and living shadows creeping among the trees.

Norma looked around the clearing, at the groups of men dragging bodies from around the curve of the hill. The sun shone down on them all from a clear blue sky. She might as well have been on a nature hike.

$250 for this? Easiest money I've ever made.

She'd heard the call for volunteers on the radio the prior morning on her way to work. The county was offering cash money since no one was willing to do it for free. And why would they? Everyone else her age had heard the same stories, the same gossip about the crazy Masters cult near Devil's Creek Road. The woods were haunted, of course. Ghosts of the damned everywhere. Everyone knew someone who'd driven out here to get a look at the strange compound the cult built in the woods. *Everyone* had a story about this place.

Now that she was here, she realized she'd have a story of her own. And what a story it would be. Fifty-plus bodies all dead from self-inflicted wounds, the smoldering ruins of a church, twenty macho guys trying to impress the single lady in their presence—maybe she'd write a novel and make a fortune like that guy in Maine.

Or maybe you could stop daydreaming and get back to work.

Smiling, Norma wiped sweat from her brow and put on her gloves. She was three steps into the clearing when a voice called out to her from the woods.

Norma Jean Lefty. You ain't aged a day.

The voice was familiar, a singsong lilt she'd not heard since high school. No one called her Norma Jean Lefty except Molly Croner, and she'd not seen Molly since—

Norma stopped, pivoted on her heel and searched the perimeter. Weeds and wildflowers and tree limbs swayed in the breeze. Clouds rolled in front of the sun, blanketing the clearing in shadow, and a slow chill crept along her arms. Elsewhere, Gary barked orders about the remaining bodies.

"Molly Jane Croner," she whispered, "you're dead with the rest of them." She turned back toward the hill and shrugged off the chill. "Dead as a doornail, darlin'. You and Robby and Mr. Marley, too."

Molly Croner's body lay near the remains of the church entrance, her hand still clutching the knife she'd thrust into her own throat. Norma hesitated before covering her old friend in plastic. The pained expression on Molly's face spoke for her in the absence of life, a determined rictus of agony and contempt and defiance, with cloudy eyes gazing upward at some unseen paradise.

Gary had told them they might see familiar faces, told them to push through it and remember these lost souls made their choices. And what a choice Molly had made. Norma unfolded the plastic shroud beside her dead friend and struggled to remember when they'd last spoken.

You ain't aged a day.

But she had, and the years between them had not been kind. Five, maybe six years now, long before Johnny was born. Molly and her husband Robby stood up among the congregation of First Baptist, professed their devotion to the one true higher power, and marched down the aisle amidst mumbled protests and gossip. Months later, Norma heard rumors that her friend had joined the cult outside of town, right around the time allegations of child abuse surfaced against the Reverend Jacob Masters. No charges ever materialized, however, and the murmurs of Stauford's dirty secret out here in the woods slowly faded in the months to follow.

Time ebbed and flowed. Norma met a man, had a child, and lost that man in the span of a year. She struggled to keep that boy fed, struggled to keep herself fed for that matter, and now after all these years, here she was staring down at her friend's pallid face.

Norma rolled Molly's body onto the plastic sheet. *Like stacking logs. Firewood. It's not her anymore, Norma Jean. The body's just a vessel. A temple. Remember that—you're just moving an empty temple.*

Something gurgled within her friend's corpse. The body uttered a guttural belch from its orifices, an expulsion of gases and decay, and the smell hit Norma like a rotten wall. She turned away and retched.

"Hold your cookies, missy!"

Gary's voice echoed across the clearing, followed by a chorus of laughter. Norma shook her head, wiped her mouth, and gave her audience the finger.

It's like that time everyone in school laughed at you when you slipped in dog shit at the playground.

Norma's breath hitched. She wheeled around, expecting to find her friend there, grinning. Molly Croner's body lay face down on the plastic. Flies danced across her matted hair, tasting the blood soaked into her scalp. Norma removed a glove and wiped the sweat from her face. Had to be the heat. She thought about taking a break after pulling her dead friend down the hill, but the longer she stood there deliberating, the more she felt lightheaded.

Water. Rest. Molly ain't going anywhere.

Twenty minutes later, after slaking her thirst and shrugging off the smartass quips of her coworkers, Norma returned to the summit and discovered Molly's body missing. The plastic shroud was gone.

"The hell?"

She turned, looking for someone dragging her friend's body, looking at the stack of dead cult members near the trailhead. Members of the cleanup crew were farther down the hillside, wrapping bodies in plastic shrouds like morbid gifts. She called out to one of them, and he looked up from his task. The scrawny guy from earlier. The whiner.

"What's that?"

Norma cleared her throat. "I had a body here. Did someone take it?"

"Wasn't me. Maybe it walked away." He let loose a wild howl of laughter, revealing a mouth of missing teeth. Norma rolled her eyes and turned away. *No one's taking this seriously. These people killed themselves. Ain't there no respect for the dead?*

Confused, she made her way back down the hill, intending to investigate the stacks of bodies, but something else caught her eye. Something on the far side of the clearing, shielded from the beating sun by a shadowed canopy of trees. A flash of blue. A figure sheathed in white. Red splotches blossomed on the fabric.

Norma Jean Lefty. Over here, darling.

Molly's voice carried on the breeze, teasing Norma's ears.

"Can't be…" She turned back to the lanky fellow, but he was dragging a body down the hill. Several other men, Gary included, were doing the same. The rest were huddled in the shade near the trailhead, their voices and laughter muffled by the distance.

Laughter. Of course. They were playing a joke on her. Mocking her. *Bunch of fuckin' frat boys.*

When she turned back, the figure was still there. It raised its hand to her in offering.

I want to show you something, honey. It's the most beautiful thing you'll ever see.

More laughter erupted from down the hill. Norma sucked in her breath, swallowed back the agitation, the anger. Enough was enough, but then again, maybe she'd play along, confront this joker head on.

Defiant, she walked down the hill toward the trees.

She'd walked a few yards into the brush before reconsidering. This was foolish. She had nothing to prove to those macho assholes. The figure she'd glimpsed from the top of the hill was nowhere to be seen. An expanse of trees, ferns, weeds, and shadows stretched before her. Fallen logs lay rotting in the overgrowth. Gnats buzzed about her head and she swatted at them absently.

A light breeze whispered through the trees. She closed her eyes, relishing the cool air in the shade. Molly was dead. She'd seen her friend's body with her own eyes, wrapped her in plastic with her own hands, and now a bunch of good ol' boys were having a laugh at Norma's expense.

"This is stupid, Norma Jean. Just a prank."

I'm here, Norma. Come walk with me.

She opened her eyes and froze. A lone figure stood amongst the trees twenty yards ahead. Molly was unmistakable, still draped in her blood-soaked robe, the wound in her throat wide open and grinning.

"This is impossible." The words left her in a whisper, barely audible even to Norma's ears, but Molly heard. *She heard.* And she responded.

My lord makes anything possible, Norma Jean. Come with me. I want to show you something.

"You're dead, Molly."

I live forever in the womb of my lord, Norma.

"I saw your body. You…" Norma's breath hitched as she stifled a sob. Her vision clouded with tears. "…Molly, you killed yourself."

Sunlight filtering through the forest canopy caught Molly's eyes, reflecting a deep cerulean blue so bright they seemed to glow. Did Molly have such blue eyes? Norma couldn't remember, and it didn't matter anyway because this was a horrible joke. It wasn't Molly, but someone else. One of the men—probably Gary, that asshole—had talked his wife into driving out here to play a prank.

Shit, was Gary even married? Had they known Molly? And how did this impostor sound so much like her?

Her mind raced, circling a deep, thudding ache buried in the back of her skull. Every part of her body was overheated, her throat parched, and a tidal wave of nausea crashed in her belly. *I should go back. This was a mistake. I should've stayed home. I'll find the money some other way—*

A branch snapped as Molly turned and walked beyond a pair of trees.

My lord can help you with the money, Norma.

Confused, Norma defied the voice screaming in her head, screaming for her to turn around, run, quit on the spot and leave this awful place. The forest around Devil's Creek was truly haunted. She understood that now, understood the stories were all true—

But the money. God, she needed the money. What if she wasn't hallucinating? What if her friend was a messenger from the Lord, and there was real salvation out here in the woods?

Head swimming, Norma wandered forward into the forest, crunching fallen leaves and twigs underfoot as she followed the voice of her dead friend. Part of her knew this was silly, chasing a ghost into a supposedly haunted forest, but that inner voice of reason took a backseat to her want of understanding. Molly and Robby disappeared when they were in their early thirties, gave up good lives to live out here in the wilderness with a bizarre family of fanatics.

Do you remember when we were little girls, how we used to play in the woods behind my house?

Every weekend after church, when their families came together for an early dinner, and every afternoon in the summertime. They made up stories for their adventures, the two girls always intrepid explorers diving deep into the uncharted wilderness on the outskirts of Stauford. Even when their parents cautioned them about doing so, suggesting little girls play with their dolls or play house, Molly and Norma insisted they chart the vast thicket of trees behind Molly's house.

"We made a map of every tree, every gully, even the dried creek bed."

Remember our fort?

"I do, but there wasn't much to it. Just some old pallets we found near the road and some fallen branches covered in leaves. The day we built it, I went home and found two ticks on my leg. My daddy had to burn 'em off with a match."

Remember the last time we went there?

Norma stopped, sucked in her breath. The forest was silent now, except for the faint trickling of water. Devil's Creek wasn't far from here. Molly appeared from behind a tree and smiled.

Remember when I kissed you? When you kissed me back? Remember when you said you loved me?

Her cheeks flushed. Reluctant, Norma nodded. She remembered, had thought about it every day since. They were teenagers then, nearly out of high school, inseparable even when their peers pressured them to stay within their social classes.

"Your little brother had followed us into the woods and saw us. Told your dad. God, I thought he was going to explode when we got back."

The kiss wasn't expected, nor was it surprising. She'd adored Molly for years, but only when they reached high school did her feelings intensify. That Molly made the first move only reinforced what Norma felt in her heart—which made what happened between their parents more painful. Accusations between families flew for weeks, culminating in Molly's parents sending her away to a special

Christian camp shortly before graduation. Norma's mom and dad couldn't afford such things; instead, they grounded their daughter and forbade her from seeing Molly again.

And she didn't—not until several years later, when Molly returned home after college. By then, Norma was on her own, working two part-time jobs and dating the man who would become Johnny's father.

"I thought you'd moved on. You *did* move on. And I..."

Just stood in place, she wanted to say, but her words were drowned by the tears spilling down her cheeks. When she wiped her face, she spotted Molly in the distance, framed between the hollowed trunks of two fallen trees. The glow of her eyes pierced the shadows and cast the forest in a blue haze.

We can make up for lost time, Norma. Come with me now. It's just a bit further.

"I never understood why you never talked to me again. Even after you came home, after you graduated and moved out on your own, you never tried to talk to me. Like I didn't exist anymore. What did they do to you at that camp?"

Silence but for the rustling of the trees and weeds in the breeze. Molly's phantom was gone. Norma held her breath, waiting for her friend to reply, but there was only the whine of gnats in her ear and the chirping of birds overhead. She'd gone so far into the forest that she couldn't hear the rest of the cleanup crew. She wondered if they'd noticed she was missing. The thought of Gary's red face emboldened her.

Norma Jean Lefty...this way.

Her aching heart fluttered at the sound of Molly's voice. Norma pushed forward into the brush.

She followed her friend's apparition until they came to Devil's Creek; from there, Molly turned north toward the creek's watershed, the Cumberland River. Norma walked in silence, wrestling with the knotted thoughts tumbling through her head. All of this felt like a dream, and she half-wondered if that was true, that she'd fainted from the heat back at Calvary Hill.

Twice she pinched herself in the soft flesh between thumb and forefinger.

Twice she winced at the pain.

She wasn't dreaming. This was real. Her friend's spirit was here, walking along the surface of the creek's babbling waters like Jesus, and she was following like a true disciple would. Her world and worries seemed a universe away, lost in the back of her mind in a heavy fog. Molly was here, Molly was real, and somehow this would all work out. She'd go home, introduce Molly to Johnny, and together they'd be a family—

Except that wouldn't happen. *Couldn't* happen.

Molly's dead, she told herself. *You saw her wound and all that blood. You pulled the blade from her throat. There's no comin' back from that.*

And yet Molly was here, mere feet away, upright and walking and talking and saying things only Molly would know. Molly Croner was dead and yet very much alive, and goddammit, that had to mean something.

Molly looked over her shoulder and smiled. Her eyes painted the forest in shimmering blue light.

This is the power of my lord, Norma. I am given everlasting life in the womb of my lord. Father Jacob promised me immortality, and I have been delivered this most holy gift.

"All this time you were out here worshiping God?"

Not any god. Not the god of the deceivers. Not the god of the false messiah. The one true God. Can't you see we're among His angels here in the garden?

Molly lifted her hands to the trees as if in prayer, motioning to the shadows clinging to their trunks like rich oil. And then the shadows opened their piercing blue eyes and peeled themselves away, stretching their bodies until they stood upon the forest floor with impossible legs.

Norma stared in terror, unable to believe what she was seeing. She'd heard the stories of living shadows in these woods. Shadows with eyes that whispered and sang with a chorus of different voices. Molly's angels in this unlikely Eden.

Come, my love. They will usher us into the waters of your baptism.

"My baptism?"

So that you may see with our eyes, hear with our ears, and speak with our many tongues. The Old Ways demand it.

Norma had been raised in the church, attending First Baptist in downtown Stauford just like everyone else, but she'd never believed it. People who picked on her at school were nice to her at church, and she'd learned early on that masks were a part of everyone's Sunday best. She'd never conformed to that ritual of hypocrisy, much to her parents' disappointment, and the thought of pledging herself to a faith with a ceremonial cleanse had always seemed wrong to her.

But now, as they neared the river, Molly's suggestion of baptism was almost pleasant, peaceful. Why not shrug off the worries of the world and devote herself to something greater? Eternal life in the womb of Molly's lord sounded just fine with her if it meant she could be with Molly for all time. And Johnny, he would serve his new lord in another way, for the Old Ways demanded flesh, demanded a sacrifice as a means of devotion. Little Johnny would become a vessel for the nameless god, his skin the pages of a new gospel, writ in blood and scars. For the lord demanded youth and vitality for sustenance, and little Johnny—

A voice screamed from the back of her mind, its sound a furious cry of rage so intense it swept through her in a singular convulsion: *NO!*

Norma snapped back to the present, cognizant of the change in her surroundings. The rushing waters of the Cumberland River were in sight, babbling across a small delta of sediment and feeding the creek. A crow cawed overhead. Somewhere along the shore, a bullfrog barked before diving into the murky water with a solid *plunk*.

Molly and her angels were gone.

Johnny, she thought, looking up at the sky. The sun was past its midpoint overhead. The cleanup crew would be finished by now. Hell, they'd probably left without her, and she suspected Gary had taken pleasure in it. She turned, peered into the mouth of the forest. Devil's Creek Road was miles back. If she followed the creek, she'd reach the road by sundown; from there, she had a long walk back to civilization. Johnny would be fine with his grandma, but Norma knew she'd never hear the end of this from her mother.

God, what the hell was she thinking, wandering this deep into the forest?

She made for the woods, intent on retracing her steps alongside the stream, but slipped on a collection of rocks and splashed down in the creek. The cold water stole her breath as it ran over her hands and soaked her jeans, but she welcomed its relief from the heat. She remained there in the creek for a time, watching the water wash over her calloused hands as she buried her fingers in the silt.

Baptism. She'd been daydreaming of baptism and Molly Croner and...something else. A primal thing, its voice a jarring echo of forbidden song and scripture deep in her head. Its reach was immeasurable in body and spirit, a nameless thing of shadow and earth and stars and so many eyes. Eyes she now felt bearing down upon her.

Our Lord sees you now, child.

Molly stood at the mouth of the forest, coated in shadow and eyes alight in blue fire. Others joined her now, robed figures coated in their precious lifeblood. There was Robby Croner, one of the first to be wrapped in plastic and heaved down the hillside. He floated to his wife's side and smiled. The rest she didn't know, but she did recognize their pale, lifeless faces. She'd wrapped some of them in plastic herself.

The victims of the suicide cult emerged from the forest. An army of blue eyes, gory robes, and mutilated throats marching—*floating*—toward her. Fear chilled her blood as she struggled to reconcile the impossibilities before her. She closed her eyes, shook her head to wake up from this nightmare.

The figures were still there when she opened her eyes again. Smiling from mouth and wound. God, there was so much blood, pouring dark and rich from their throats and collecting in the stream below them. Dark tendrils formed in the water, entwining with one another as they snaked their way against the current. Norma watched in a frozen stupor as the dark substance coiled around her fingers and wrists.

"Oh, Jesus, gross—"

The tendrils hardened as they pulled her down toward the water. Norma braced herself, digging her heels into the mud as she pulled against her bindings. Laughter erupted among her ghostly audience as she struggled, filling her mind with a new surge of fear, and she tried to block them out. The tendrils were more like roots now—perhaps they'd always been—dark skeletal fingers reaching from the earth to ensnare her. They rubbed her skin raw as she fought to pull herself free.

"No, let me go, let me go!" Norma wrenched herself upright, stamped her shoe against the gnarled roots, and yanked backward as hard as she could. *"LET—ME—GO!"*

The roots snapped, and she fell backward across the delta of mud and stones, splashing down on the river shore.

The time of your baptism is here, Norma Jean.

Stunned by the fall, Norma scrambled to regain her footing. The congregation of spirits barred her way into the forest. No matter, she'd swim if she had to. Anything to get away from this cursed place.

She turned and gasped.

Children. Dozens by the look of them. Maybe hundreds. Each one draped in bloody robes, pale-faced with bright blue eyes, hovering like lifeless dolls above the churning river current.

Norma had no time to rethink her plan. Something erupted from the water to her right and was upon her in an instant. The last thing she felt was a coarse fabric pressing into her face—and something rancid and cold forcing its way into her mouth.

The shroud pulled over her face stung her skin with its coarse texture. Whatever held her down beneath the surface had wrapped her face tight in the cloth, and she beat her hands against the attacker while fighting the urge to breathe.

Tighter, the shroud dug into her skin, tearing a trench across the lower half of her face. Panicked, she opened her eyes to the cold, wet darkness. There were holes in the fabric, and through them she saw shadows, shapes in her violent drowning—

—darkly impossible things with too many eyes and so many mouths, each needle-like tooth a spike on which parts of children were impaled and oozing the blood of many while thick ropes of viscous sludge coiled and contracted in the gaps between, and the cold, God, the cold was beyond anything she'd ever experienced, a frigid blanket of air oppressing her body and lungs and heart and numbing her soul to the point of willful oblivion, a cold so vast and deep it cracked her mind, deep canyons in the folds of her brain now overflowing with the knowledge of what is and should not be, a place beyond death where her friend Molly now existed and where the dead were slaves to something far greater than themselves, something seen and yet unseen, an absence of logic and reason in the scope of human understanding, an entity so vast it lacked distinguishable form tucked away in the folds beneath continental shelves watching the human parasites walk upon the surface with a thousand eyes poised outward, inward,

through the fabric of time and space, a being so infinite and yet now, here, held beneath the waves like an insect washed out to sea, it saw her, Norma Jean Leifthauser, mother of little Johnny, her only legacy to a cold and callous world from a lifetime of disappointment and hardship, it saw her with all its eyes, it tasted the salt of her skin with all its many tongues, and in those impenetrable moments when time ceased and she glimpsed the impossible through the shroud, the nameless void infected her mind to make her one of its own, gifting her with but a grain of knowledge from the sands of an infinite shore and taking from her the essence that was her soul on which to feed upon later, and in that fraction of time it whispered its desire, its deep and guttural wanting, a primal need of the tender flesh of human youth, and if she would give up her only son as so many others have before her then she would be gifted eternal life in the womb of this divine creature as they awaited the coming of their savior from the depths of the earth—

—and through the violent churning of waves, she heard a voice whisper in her head with the sweet innocence of all those sacrificed children: *Do you accept this blessing in exchange for the flesh of your son?*

Norma shook her head to free herself from her captor. Colors swirled before her eyes as her lungs yearned for one more breath. Desperate, she thrashed the air and planted her feet, found solid ground, and forced herself upright through the water's surface.

She gasped for air, swallowed water, and doubled over in a coughing fit. The fabric shroud clung to her head, and she tore it free once she regained her composure.

Molly and the other suicides were gone. The children were gone, too, and as she surveyed her surroundings, Norma began to wonder if they were ever there in the first place.

She stood in the shallows of the river. Overhead, the sun was slowly setting below the forest canopy. Her head and chest ached, and when she returned to shore, a violent pain tore through her gut. Her knees buckled, and down she went, splashing into the mud once again.

"Get out of my head." Her voice little more than a whimper, barely audible against the sound of the river current. "Stop telling me. I won't—I can't—"

When the pain subsided, she gathered her strength and found her footing. Norma gripped the fabric in her hands and examined it. Her baptismal shroud was a torn section of white cloth marked with holes and bloodstains. On one side, a series of faded words read "Property of Molly C."

A piece of her dead friend's robe. Had Molly been the one to hold her down beneath the waves? Had it really happened?

The new voices in her head said so.

Gary Kissinger found the woman walking alongside Devil's Creek Road. It had been hours since they'd packed up the last of the bodies and left that awful place, but when all was accounted for, he was missing one body: the proud little thing from that morning with the nice figure and tired eyes. Back at the station in town, none of the men could recall seeing her, not since earlier that afternoon. Not since they'd teased her about tossing her cookies.

He didn't want to be the one to tell Chief Bell there was a woman lost out here in the woods. After all the men had gone their separate ways, Gary hopped into his pickup and drove back to the wilderness beyond Stauford. He spotted her just beyond a fork in the road.

"I'll be goddammed..." He slowed the truck and pulled alongside the woman, lowering his window to talk to her. "Missed your ride, huh?"

She said nothing, kept on walking. The blank look on her face made him uneasy. Maybe it was sunstroke. Or maybe she'd seen something out there in the woods. Maybe she'd seen one of those shadowy ghosts all the old-timers used to talk about when he was a boy.

"Missy? Let's get you home, whaddya say?"

No response. Frowning, Gary parked the truck and climbed out. He walked up to her, put his hand on her shoulder. "Miss—"

The young woman slowed to a stop and turned. Tears streaked her dirty face. Gary Kissinger didn't say another word. He took her hand and led her back to the truck.

On the drive back into town, he asked her what had happened, and finally she spoke.

"I saw..." She stopped, eyed him with caution, and then turned toward the window. "I got lost. Couldn't find my way back."

"Aw hell, there ain't no shame in that. Happens to the best of us. Shit, this one time—"

"Am I still going to be paid?"

He swallowed his words, gave her a once-over as they parked at the fire station. He had half a mind not to pay her a dime, especially since she wasn't around to help carry the bodies back to the trucks, but there was something about the look of her, a desperation he couldn't place. A desperation that wasn't there this morning. Whatever had happened to her had bled the confidence right out of her. All he saw now was a scared woman who'd been through something she didn't want to talk about.

"Yeah. Come back in the morning and pick up your pay. $250 as agreed."

She offered him a timid smile as she opened the door. The dome light reflected in her eye, filling them with an odd blue glow. He'd never seen such blue eyes before, and he found himself staring too long. He looked away, embarrassed.

"You'll be okay?"

"Yes," she said, climbing out of the truck. "Thank you for the ride. Have a good night."

He watched her walk to her car and waited until she was gone to leave himself. The whole ride home he thought about her eyes and how he couldn't remember if they were blue that morning.

Johnny was asleep when she arrived at her mom's house. Her mother attempted to start an argument, but Norma said nothing in reply. She gathered her son's things and carried the sleeping boy to her car. She'd deal with her mother in the morning.

Back home, Norma tucked Johnny into bed. When she was done, she sat at the edge of his bed and watched the child sleep. The voices in her head told her to do her lord's will, but she hesitated, wringing the piece of Molly's robe in her hands instead of acting on those foreign urges.

"I won't. I didn't—I refuse. You put this inside me. It's not my will. *It's not my will.*"

Her son stirred, rolled over, opened his eyes in a squint. "Mama? Are we home?"

"Shh. It's all right, love. Go back to sleep."

Johnny was satisfied with this. He smiled softly before closing his eyes, and within minutes, he was fast asleep once again. Norma wanted so badly to join him in slumber, but every time she closed her eyes, she saw the dead faces of the cultists staring back at her, saw the unblinking eyes of a nameless void staring into her soul.

They begged her to end her son's life. Begged to give him over to the one true god deep below the earth.

Norma Leifthauser curled up with her son and watched him sleep, vigilant against the forces inside her which demanded his life. She knew she couldn't avoid sleep forever, knew those ghosts in her head were persuasive. The impossible things she'd glimpsed through the holes in the fabric, the impossible things which had stared back into her, would be there waiting for her in the dark.

She'd face them then, for as long as she could fight. It was the only sort of grit they were going to get from her.

Dog Days

by Kenneth W. Cain

January 3rd, 1979 (Found September 4th, 2018 in the attic of Nelson Contreras' house on Dovetail Drive)

Somehow, I've ended up trapped in my dusty attic. The distinct aroma of mold fills my sinuses. A haunting wind whistles through the vent. Despite my surroundings, I'm only trying to survive, writing this letter to maintain my sanity more than anything. Truthfully, I'm not sure why I bother. I doubt anyone will find it. Hopefully, if someone does, by that time I've made it through this madness unharmed. That's all I want; to live.

It started three days ago when my dog, Honey, was out back and started barking like crazy. At first, I ignored her. Being a beagle, she gets to hooting and howling most nights. But something about that night got her worked up, and it was late, so I wanted to get her inside before any of my neighbors complained.

Speaking of neighbors, I have seen none for weeks. I'm unsure if that's a sign of what happened to them—what might happen to me. My sole focus was to get Honey inside before she made too much of a ruckus. Now I wish I had left her outside.

I don't know what Honey got into out there, but she dug in good, yapping and yapping, refusing to come when I called. I'd thought she cornered a possum or a skunk. Whatever she got into out in the woods behind my house, it couldn't have been any regular creature. Not after the way she's been acting ever since.

By the time I got her inside, Honey had changed. Not outwardly but something in her eyes. Not that I thought her rabid or sick; this was something different. Honey looked *off*, like she wasn't altogether there. And though I felt bad for my pup, I decided I couldn't take any chances. So I locked Honey up in the laundry room, until morning, when I could take her to the vet. Just my luck, I never got the chance.

When morning came around and I looked out the front door, I noticed a change in our little rural neighborhood. Several dogs roamed freely about the streets, none of them with their owners. I saw a couple I recognized over the next few hours looking out the front window—the Smiths' dog and Gregor from down the road—but most of them weren't familiar. Worse yet, all these dogs—and I mean every last one—had that same mad look in their eyes Honey displayed prior to me locking her up. One of the other dogs—a dark-haired husky—saw me in the window and ran up barking and foaming at the mouth. I knew then I had to call the police.

What scared me most was finding my phone dead. My luck couldn't have been any worse. No way was I heading outside to face those dogs. Sure, I'd considered it, and maybe I would have if it hadn't been for Honey. I'd gone to feed her, filling a couple Tupperware bowls with food and water and opening the door enough to slide them in. When I opened that door, Honey attacked, clawing at the bowls, sloshing the water all over the floor in her attempts to get at me. Her ferociousness worsened by the hour too, until I feared I would have no choice but to put her down.

My heart breaks just thinking about it. I never thought I could bring myself to hurt Honey. Even writing about it now brings a tear to my eye, remembering when I bought her as a pup, her snuggling beside me each night while watching TV. No way I could put her down, so I'd thought. Heck, I don't even own a gun. Never have. Just wasn't my thing. Now I regret my reluctance to arm myself, forced to resort to wielding two of the biggest knives I have as if they could fend off any dog. And that's exactly what I needed, protection. Because right then, after I'd made one of the hardest decisions of my life, Honey escaped the laundry room.

I've no idea how she got out, but I took off like a bat out of hell. Maybe she chewed her way through a wall into the foyer bathroom. I'd been spending a lot of time upstairs, trying to spy another living human through some binoculars I kept in my nightstand. Honey had been making plenty of noise all along, so I hadn't paid her much mind.

When I went to go back down and saw her standing there at the foot of the stairs, I nearly pissed myself. She came barreling up the stairs, and I had to think fast. Like an idiot, I chose the attic, barely escaping as I climbed the wooden ladder. When I spun to draw up the stairs, Honey kept trying to bite my hands, clawing and snapping her ferocious jaws. That was my Honey, my dog, my best friend, trying to hurt me. It was an hour after I got those stairs up before I stopped crying.

Up here, there's no food. And Honey's a smart dog. She knows I need to eat. If only I could trap one of these mice, or even a squirrel, anything. I swear, I'd eat it raw. Because I *have* to eat. How many days can someone go without eating? What is it, three weeks? I'm uncertain, as it's only been a little over two, and I'm feeling desperate.

The only way out of this attic is down those stairs. I can hear Honey pacing up and down the hallway. Either that or I have to make my way out through the vent. Then, it's a three-story drop, straight down. If I had wings, that wouldn't be far, but as a human, a fall like that would probably kill me. Even if it didn't, I'd break every bone in my body, and I'd have to face off against those dogs out there. With some good fortune, maybe I could make it to safety, but I'm not lucky often. It's more probable those dogs would claw me down as I hobbled toward safety. They'd end me for sure.

Still, I can't face Honey. I'm not sure which option is better; starving or jumping to my death. I suppose once I get desperate enough, we'll find out.

Ellen Furlong

June 22nd, 2001 (Recording found September 4th, 2018 in the kitchen drawer. Also found, two printed photos of an ordinary hand.)

Note to self, call my lawyer as soon as possible. I'm recording this as documentation for a potential lawsuit. There are three dogs, maybe more, outside my house. I'm unsure whose dogs they are, as I've only just moved here within the last few weeks, but whoever owns them, either they aren't aware of the leash law or they don't care. Whatever the case, I plan to sue the pants off them once I find out whom these mutts belong to. I'm too damn old to get accosted by these numbskull neighbors' dogs without getting something out of it.

On the way into my house, they came after me; all of them at once. One nipped my hand. It took a full hour to stop the bleeding. I've taken photos with my digital camera and printed them out as evidence. Worse yet, I have a fever now I can't seem to shake. No doubt this is something I caught from that mutt. Now my arthritis is flaring up, and there's a stabbing pain in my hip from running so damn hard at my age.

Going to the doctor soon. I've got my handgun, and I'll shoot to kill if one of those mongrels comes at me. I wish this house had a garage. Who builds a house like this without a garage? Maybe I can find out who the builder was and sue them too. All these kids nowadays, so lazy, always doing things the wrong way. They have it coming to them.

Unknown

October 10th, 1962 (Found September 4th, 2018 beneath the kitchen cabinets)

Dearest Gary,

Should you find this letter, please help. You might not believe this, but Kipper tried to bite me today. You've been on the road for work, so I was preparing dinner for myself when Kipper came at me. I hurried to the basement, threw the door open, and ducked into the darkness below. When I turned to close to the door, there, standing in the doorway, was our Kipper. He growled at me like he didn't know who I was anymore. It frightened me, the way his eyes caught the light and glowed that strange green color like they do. I shooed him away, but Kipper only snapped at my hand when I did, growling even louder and acting like a crazy dog. Before he could push his way through, I tried to close the door but didn't get it shut in time. He got his upper half through, each of us fighting against one another for ground. If he hadn't lost his footing, I might not be writing this letter now. That's how bad it's gotten. I quickly slammed the door shut, and Kipper's been whining and moaning and clawing at the door ever since.

Something about that dog isn't right, not any longer. You aren't due home until tomorrow, and I'm afraid what could happen in that span of time. I pray someone else comes to check on me before then, maybe my mother or one of our close friends. Anyone would be a godsend. I'm worried about our dog, but most of all, I'm concerned for my safety. I think Kipper's gone mad.

From time to time, he settles. When he does, I watch beneath the door, waiting until he gets back up and starts pacing back and forth. It's like he refuses to give up. I've never seen our happy dog so determined. That's why I know I can't escape through the kitchen. I have to find another way out.

The windows in the basement are small. I'm thin but likely not skinny enough to squeeze through the opening. Regardless, I'm not sure I have any choice but to try. That might be my only way out of this basement. If I can free myself, I'll run to the neighbor's and call the police. Maybe they can help with Kipper.

Anyway, if you find this letter, I love you. I'll likely be at the Nelson's. Just know that I'm scared. I need my husband. Gary, please come as soon as you get home.

Farah

October 13th, 1962 (Found September 4th, 2018 lodged behind the basement window sill)

To whom it may concern,

When I slid my last letter under the basement door, our dog Kipper wasn't around. But the second I slid that letter through, he started making an awful fuss. Stooped over on my hands and knees, my face planted against the cold wood of the top stair, looking under the door, I saw his shadow come into view. It all happened so fast. Kipper tried to nip my nose which startled me so badly, I nearly fell down the stairs when I leaped back.

Once I recovered, I made my way back up, trying to determine whether my letter could be seen. And the more I tried to see, the more Kipper acted up, gnawing on the wood, tearing away thin strips and chewing on them before spitting them to the floor. It's almost like he's rabid. Dear God, I hope that's not the case.

Anyway, seeing him like that, I made my way to the lone basement window, where I tore down the blinds and cracked the window. The glass only opens so far, maybe twelve inches at most. It looks rather tight for a woman my size. I could break it, but I wouldn't want to do that unless it's necessary, given the cost of repairing a window. Either way, I'm glad I didn't.

Upon readying to climb through the window, the most ferocious face greeted me. I didn't recognize the snarling dog, perhaps a stray. If it wasn't for me shutting the window, surely that dog would have broken through. This dog is far more disturbed than Kipper. It never leaves the window, standing there with its nose pressed against the pane, hackles up, constantly growling at me. Whenever I make the slightest move, the dog barks and scratches the window. All I can do is watch as its nose follows me around the basement, leaving a smear of snot and blood and foam.

There must be something going around. I'm not sure if it's rabies or something worse, but I wish someone would come and put this dog down. I'm more afraid of it than I am Kipper, and I'm not attached to this one. Regardless of either dog's state of being, I have to escape. I need to find a way out of this house, so I can seek refuge elsewhere. Someplace where I can get a meal, because I'm famished. Even the crickets look good at this point. I've considered trapping a juicy one, to see if I can stomach it, but there are other concerns that haunt my thoughts, nagging me to just give up.

My husband, Gary, should have arrived home this morning, but he's long overdue. I've screamed all day at the top of my lungs despite the crazed dog at the window, and not a single person has come for me. My voice has gone hoarse from yelling, and surely, if there was anyone out there, they would have heard me by now. I would have seen someone stroll by, but I've not seen a single soul.

My desperation has me not thinking straight, but should the dog at the window let down its guard, I'll make my move. If someone finds this letter, please get word to my Gary, so he knows where I am. I'll wait until tonight when the dog is sleeping, which it rarely does. Wish me luck.

Farah Antwerp

March 13th, 1988 (Found September 4th, 2018 in the bedroom closet)

Why am I even writing this stupid letter? And who is it even to? I think I've just got to get this out of my head, try to sort through what just happened. I feel like I'm losing my mind, and if I can't get my thoughts straight, I might do something irrational. Then again, maybe that's exactly what I should do. I'm pissed, and some fucker has to pay for this.

My neighbor's dog attacked me when I got home from work. I ran into the house, but unfortunately, I wasn't quick enough to get the door shut. That bastard got in and next thing I know, I'm on the floor grappling for my life. No way I can shake that image from my thoughts now. Every time I close my eyes, I see it standing over me, its jaws snapping again and again. Its bloodshot eyes squinted. Lips drawn back in a snarl. Foam and spit and blood dripping onto my face. Something about its breath wasn't right. And if I hadn't been within reach of my umbrella, which luckily had fallen from my coat rack when we knocked it over, I might not have escaped. I had to beat that thing off me, and even then, that took longer than I would have expected.

I've no idea what sort of damage I did. I took off upstairs to the bathroom before I could get a look. Not that it mattered. I heard that bastard scrambling up the stairs behind me, and it's been clawing at the door ever since. You'd think it would get tired, figure out there's no way in and move on to some easier prey. But no, that fucking dog's still out there, whining, making all sorts of noise. If I owned a gun, I'd blow a hole the size of Texas through that thing and put it out of its misery. God knows it's got rabies or some shit like that, and it's attacked me, so I wouldn't be in the wrong. The damned thing is crazy mad.

One thing's for sure, I will have to take it out myself. I tried to call the police, but my line is deader than a doornail. There's only two ways out; through the window or the door. If I take the door, I have to face off against that dog. The window might get me to the roof. From there, maybe I can take a tree down to the ground and hustle over to a neighbor's house. The latter is likely my best bet.

Anyway, I figure I'd best leave a note just in case something happens and I end up breaking my neck climbing down from the roof. I'm probably just being silly and making a big deal out of nothing.

November 29th, 2009 (Found September 4th, 2018 carved into the foyer closet wall)

Fucking dogs! Goddamned dogs! Kill. Kill. Kill. Dogs suck. Do

September 4th, 2018 text message to Ella Taylor, Nelson's fiancé.

Ella, I found all these letters about dogs around the house

So?

It's just messed up. I think these people died

What? What are you talking about?

Well, one of the neighbors said this house was all F'd up
That people went crazy here talking about rabid dogs

Hmm, WTF

Right? Thing is, no one ever found any bodies according to him
And a lot of these peeps claim no one else was around
This guy, though, says that wasn't true
Their neighbors were home all along
I found the first letter shortly after talking to him

I'll have to check them out when I get off work

> Yep, it's messed up AF
> You think it's anything to worry about?

What? Don't be silly
I've not even seen any dogs around that neighborhood since we
started looking
Don't be silly :)

> It's just that
> Wait
> You said there weren't any dogs, right?

YES

> Then whose dog is outside?

Stop kidding around
That's not funny

> I wasn't trying to be
> I'm not kidding
> There's a fucking dog outside!

Well, leave it alone
Stay inside!

> I will
> Don't worry
> I'll call the

Nelson?
Nelson?

Stop fucking around!
NELSON?????
WTF
Stop it now!
Nelson?

September 5th, 2018 from The Daily Boast

A couple who only recently moved to Reeseville, Maryland found themselves in a dire situation yesterday when one Nelson Contreras texted his fiancé about some letters he found regarding the history surrounding the property at 346 Dovetail Drive. Sources say Nelson could not be located upon his fiancé arriving home and that no such letters were found at the residence. Foul play is not suspected at this time, though Nelson's fiancé has filed a missing persons report. Anyone having any knowledge of Nelson's current location should contact the state police. Reward offered.

Drown

by Hunter Shea

"You can take your blindfold off now," Eddie said, the brakes squealing slightly as he pulled the car to the curb. Motes of dirt and dust swirled around the black Jeep Wrangler. It had been an exceptionally dry June with no sign of rain coming soon.

The early summer sun brought out the deep reds and purples in Jessica's hair. Her friend Angela had given her a birthday gift certificate to Jess's favorite salon and Eddie's girlfriend had wasted no time changing her look. Impulsivity was her middle name.

Jessica pulled her eye mask down and squinted against the glare. She'd been in the dark for the past hour and her eyes needed to adjust. Her vintage Cinderella 1988 concert tour shirt pulled tight against her chest as she stretched. Blinking back a tear, she looked out the front window and scowled. "Is that what I think it is?"

Eddie grinned. "It depends what you think it is."

"You know how much I hate bed and breakfasts."

He curled his hand behind her neck and massaged the spot just behind her earlobe. "I sure do. Hence the blindfold. Plus, I wanted to keep your mind clear and fresh."

She pulled the eye mask off her head and tossed it on the dashboard. "Really? You brought me to a haunted B&B for our anniversary?" She made air quotes when she said the word *haunted*.

"Call it a working vacation." A year into their relationship, Eddie was well aware how saying or doing the wrong thing could lead to his doom. Part of his charm, at least he thought, was that he tromped through her landmines without a care in the world. They'd been through too much not to be direct with one another.

"Who says I want to work? I just wanted a vacation." She pulled away from him with her arms crossed over her chest.

Jessica turned to look at the old Victorian home. The wood carved sign above the door read: SUMMER HOUSE. The looming structure looked to have been freshly painted a canary yellow with a purple wraparound porch and shutters. This place couldn't have been missed from space.

"I promise you, it's really nice inside," he said.

"I hate being sequestered to a room and sharing a bathroom and listening to other people screw right next to me. And don't get me started on having to eat what someone arbitrarily decides constitutes a delightful breakfast. Just gross."

Eddie tried not to sigh out loud. "You have made all of those points crystal clear to me before. Would it make you feel better to know we're the only people booked for the weekend?"

She bit her lip. "Slightly."

Ah, the ice was breaking! "And that I know for a fact there is a McDonald's nearby where I intend to buy your breakfast, which I will serve to you in bed? Extra biscuits, of course." Her love of Mickey D's pancakes, eggs, sausage and biscuits would never cease to confound him.

Her arms fell to her sides and her face softened. "You're getting warmer."

"And that I love you fiercely and only want the best for you?" That brought down the whole ice wall, castle and all.

"You jerk," Jessica said, pulling him in for a passionate kiss. "I love you, too."

Stroking her hair, Eddie asked, "All is forgiven?"

"You can be cautiously optimistic. I'm not even worried about the whole getting back to work thing because we both know that these B&Bs only pretend they're haunted to drum up business."

"This one's different." He got out of the Jeep, jogged around the back, and opened the door for her. "The owners of this particular B&B want people to *stop* saying it's haunted. Or, if it's truly haunted, they want their resident EBs to take a hike."

Jessica never used the terms ghost or spirits. Instead, she called them EBs, or Energy Beings, since that was the core of their makeup. A core that couldn't be destroyed, simply altered.

"And that's where I come in," she said. "It's nice to think the owners aren't con artists, but I still have no desire to go chasing EBs away. Besides, they've been steering pretty clear of me lately."

"Part of my anniversary gift is to make sure you get back to using your gift. You have it for a reason. Just like I had mine for a reason." Which, he knew, was to save her back on an island haunted by over a hundred dead children and the spirits of a mad family of monsters. That night had literally burned out his psychic powers. He'd left Ormsby Island a shell of his former self. He was still coming to grips with being a 'normal' person. "You ready for this?"

"No, but I'm too happy to be a bitch."

He got their bags out of the trunk and slipped his arm around her waist as they walked onto the porch. "That's the spirit."

The old B&B was exactly like every other, with plush, worn chairs and couches, a ticking clock on the wall, much-used board games stacked on a shelf, doilies on the end tables and long flowing curtains hanging from the windows. It smelled like potpourri and a decade of bacon and fresh-made hot cakes.

They stopped at a raised table with a bell on it, along with a sign that read: Ring the bell to begin your break from the rat race.

"Care to do the honors?" Eddie asked Jessica.

"Why not." No sooner had her palm hit the bell than a couple in their late sixties popped out from a door that neither Eddie nor Jessica had noticed. It gave them both a start.

"You must be Eddie and Jessica," the matronly woman said. She had short gray hair and chubby cheeks that matched her hips. Her little green eyes twinkled and her smile made Eddie wish he had a grandmother he could hug. Beads of sweat dotted her forehead and upper lip.

"You have a beautiful place," Eddie said, shaking her damp hand.

"We're not charting new territory, but it is cozy," her husband said. He was tall and lanky with a long jaw and a white beard that touched his chest. Eddie couldn't help thinking, *He's a skinny Santa!* His shirt was darkened by perspiration.

"And aren't you both adorable. My name is Claire Judson and this is my husband, Jet."

"Jet?" Jessica said.

The old man's face reddened. "It's short for Jethro. She was a real southern belle, my mother. Unfortunately for me, I was born in the north. Not many Jethros in my time."

Claire clasped Jessica's hand and asked, "So, do you see or feel anything?" Her eyes darted around the living room.

Jessica took a moment and then replied, "Just your hospitality."

That brought a world-class smile to Claire's face. Jessica could be a charmer.

"You didn't need to book all of the rooms this weekend," Jet said. "We would have just told folks they were already booked. The fact that you're helping us is more than enough. If we can get these ghost hunters out of here, we can go back to living a peaceful life. We didn't buy a little B&B at our age to work eighty hours a week with all this ghost nonsense."

Claire slapped his arm with the back of her hand. "He didn't mean to offend you."

"No worries, we're not ghost hunters," Eddie said. "We don't even call them ghosts."

Claire looked relieved. "Relative peace and quiet is all we're looking for."

Jessica asked, "When did the activity start to pick up?"

Claire and Jet gave each other a look. "About the time we settled in," Jet said. He wiped his brow with a hanky from his back pocket.

"And that would be when?"

"Oh, a couple of months ago," Claire said.

"A couple of months?" Jessica said. "That's not a lot of time to get so much buzz going."

Jet winked. "You'll see for yourself. What goes on in Summer House is pretty, well, unique, I would say. I'll leave it at that."

"We're pretty good when it comes to working with the unique," Eddie said. The couple stared at one another uncomfortably for a bit, then Jet said, "I'll show you to your room. Rooms, actually." He handed Eddie a key ring. "You'll have the run of the place. Eddie already said you won't be needing our cooking services." He looked slightly insulted.

Eddie jangled the keys and said, "We have strange hours. It wouldn't be fair to you to work around our schedule."

"Well, let me give you the ten-cent tour then."

Jet and Claire showed them around, giving a little history of the century-old house, town, and how they came to be B&B owners. They were then led upstairs and given the choice between three rooms where they wanted to set their things.

"We'll stay with…friends…to keep out of your hair," Claire said. With a hand to her considerable chest, she added, "I just know you're the answer to our prayers."

Jessica touched her lightly on the elbow. "We'll do our best."

Jet and Claire shuffled downstairs. When the front door clicked shut, Jessica dropped on the bed and pushed out a huge sigh. "Oh my God. Are they the sweetest couple ever? I want to hug them both like puppies."

"It's why I picked them out of everybody. Your website's inbox is pretty full. When you went with Eve for that weekend in Montauk, I spent the time reading through the requests. Jet and Claire sounded sincere. And they need help. Your kind of help."

It had been a year since Jessica had sent an EB packing. A year since she'd even mentioned sensing one. Maybe she'd been tapped out just as he had.

But it also meant she could no longer communicate with her deceased father, a fact that devastated her. For that reason alone, Eddie had to get her back in the thick of things to see if her powers could be revived. This weekend would be the perfect setting. A potentially benign haunting in a nice B&B. If nothing happened on the supernatural side, they'd have a great getaway. However, if it worked…

"Do you want to get naked now or later?" Jessica asked, pulling him from his thoughts.

"Now," he said, grinning. "And later. And maybe a little later after that."

She tugged her shirt over her head and unsnapped her bra, tossing it at him. "We'll see if you can handle this much first."

Jessica woke up gasping.

It wasn't from a nightmare or sensing a presence in the room. Sitting up quickly, she coughed into her fist until a speck of peanut landed on her hand.

"That's what happens when you snack before bed and don't brush your teeth," she whispered, happy to see Eddie was still asleep.

Water. She slipped out of bed, nude, her flesh covered in goosebumps from the air conditioning, and into the bathroom to pour a glass of water. She kept the lights off, savoring the chill and darkness, the sound of Eddie's light snores.

Jessica closed her eyes and calmed her mind. Nothing. This place was as empty as a dry well.

Or maybe there was an EB in the bathroom with her and she just couldn't access it anymore. In the past, Energy Beings were drawn to her like a flame. Something about her gave them power, at least until she sent them back to where they belonged. She didn't believe in Heaven or Hell, but she knew for sure there was a place, another plane, where people went when they died. She'd sent her fair share to that mysterious place to know there was more to life and death than a beginning and an end. Her father spoke to her from that place. Or, he used to.

Looking at herself in the mirror, she said, "Yep, you're broken."

She hadn't missed her abilities most of the time. Life was far less complicated, maybe bordering on dull, but dull was better than nearly getting killed by the paranormal. Here, in this place, she suddenly wished she could get back to some semblance of her old self.

Damn Eddie. He knew her better than she knew herself.

Eddie had clued her in to the main attraction and she could see why ghost hunters great and small had swarmed Summer House.

Apparently, there were numerous reports of the tubs suddenly turning on at six in the morning on the dot. When guests ran into the bathroom to see what had happened, they would witness the water in the tub taking the shape of a sexless person, their legs kicking about, water sloshing over the edge. The apparition struggled in the water until 6:01 and then disappeared. Possible poltergeist? A full-bodied apparition? Tantalizing stuff for the paranormalites.

Jessica sat on the toilet, her hands smoothing over the cool edge of the tub. She'd already set her alarm for 5:55. If normies could see it, perhaps she could, too.

A cold shiver ran through her. Used to be, Jessica was never scared of EBs, even the ones that lashed out at her.

The past couple of years had shown her there was much to be feared, much more than jumping at shadows or busy poltergeists or whispered disembodied voices. She had almost lost her life more than once at the hands of an EB. It had changed her. It had definitely knocked the cocksure attitude out of her.

The floorboard creaked as she shifted her weight. The sharp noise made her heart flutter.

I'm afraid, she thought.

Was it that fear that kept her powers locked away? Had it been the barrier that had hidden her abilities? Thinking about it, she had a sudden desire to turn on the lights. Safely bathed in a fluorescent glow, Jessica stared at the tub, waiting.

The next thing she knew, Eddie was standing over her saying, "Jess, did you sleep in here all night?"

Her back crackled when she pulled her head up from her folded arms. The pain woke her right up. "I can't believe I fell asleep on the toilet. I haven't done that since I was three."

Her phone was in his hand. "Your alarm woke me up. The bed was quite comfortable, by the way." She playfully flipped him the bird when he grinned.

"What time is it?" she asked.

"T-minus one minute."

"You know nothing is going to happen."

"That would be music to Claire and Jet's ears."

"Or it could mean we're past our sell-by date."

Eddie kissed the top of her head and rubbed her back. "My money is on only one of us being spoiled milk. And that one isn't you."

"Yeah, well, we'll see." She ran her tongue over her teeth. "I need to brush, bad."

She was reaching for her toothbrush when the cold water handle emitted a tiny, metallic squeak. Jessica and Eddie froze, eyes locked on the faucet. A single drop of water plopped from the spout. The pipes groaned within the tiled wall.

"Pressure building up overnight?" Jessica said.

"Shhh."

The knob turned, slowly at first. Water dribbled, then flowed in a steady torrent.

Normally, when an EB made its appearance known, Jessica could feel it on her skin, in her bones and even through to the tips of her hair. This time, she felt nothing, other than fascination.

The tub quickly filled to the halfway point. Jessica and Eddie leaned closer.

The faucet snapped shut with a sudden twist.

They waited for a moment. Jessica went to dip her hand in the icy water. Eddie whispered, "Don't."

When Jessica saw the figure start to take shape in the tub, the water churning and oozing, searching for solidity, her heart banged against her chest.

A thin torso, followed by arms and legs comprised of funnels of water, rapidly took shape. A neck stretched from the top of the writing trunk, ending in a bulbous head that filled like a water balloon. The arms and legs beat against the sides of the tub.

Thumpthumpthumpthumpthump.

Jessica felt Eddie's hand on her shoulder, squeezing harder as the figure struggled more and more. Water splashed on their feet, sprayed Jessica in the face. It was so cold, it felt like being punctured by tiny darts.

A depression opened in the center of the featureless head.

"Aaaahhhhhhhhh!"

Water shot out from the oval maw, pelting the opposite wall. The gurgling, desperate cry made Jessica flinch.

The alarm announcing it was 6:01 on her phone chimed. An instant later, the figure dissipated, the water settling, though still undulating.

"What the fuck was that?" Jessica said, breathless.

Eddie handed her a towel. Her face and hair were soaked. "I think we just watched someone drown."

Now Jessica plunged her hand in the water. The sharp chill had begun to subside. It was still cold, but not so that it would freeze the marrow in her bones.

"Did you feel anything?" Eddie asked.

Jessica shook her head. Her shock had given way to anger. There hadn't been reports of the water EB screaming before. That was proof she was still giving off some kind of energy that could be manipulated. So why were the rest of her strange powers still dead or dormant?

"I'm sure you checked to see if anyone was drowned or murdered here and in the neighboring houses," she said. She tossed him the towel, and he dried his feet.

"This isn't my first rodeo."

"That doesn't mean there wasn't an unreported murder. You didn't get any connection either?"

"Not a thing." He rapped his knuckles on the side of his head and shrugged.

Jessica wanted to know the story of this EB, a story the old Eddie would have been able to glean in seconds. In another way, she was grateful nothing had come to him, because she knew the price he paid for using his gifts.

"Claire and Jet aren't gonna like this," she said. "Unless I can somehow miraculously make it disappear."

"Let's get dressed," Eddie said, heading into the bedroom. "We have work to do."

After a quick breakfast at McDonald's—Jessica scarfing down three sausage and egg biscuits in minutes—they headed back to the empty B&B.

"I will never get over how you can eat and not gain an ounce," Eddie said. They sat in the living room, waiting for what, they weren't entirely sure.

"I'll enjoy this metabolism while I have it." Jessica sat on a chaise lounge with her eyes shut. *I'm sure that will change after I have a kid,* she thought. She cleared her mind, leaving herself open for the EB residing in the house. Eddie sat on a love seat across from her, a pen and pad in his hands, ready to record any out of the ordinary instances.

Over the past year, Jessica had been immersing herself in meditation for a bevy of reasons. Her near-miss with death on Ormsby Island had necessitated a change in thinking. She quickly lost herself in her breaths, the passage of time unknowable and immaterial.

She acknowledged the groaning and pop of wood and shifted her mind away, confident Eddie would handle the details. It was a system they had talked about working on before they both realized they had been shut out of the paranormal game.

Something dropped on the floor above her.

Dropping, she thought, acknowledging the sound but not lingering on it.

There was a soft bang from one of the other rooms next to them.

Banging.

It went like that for several more intrusive noises, the intervals between each growing shorter and shorter, like contractions before a birth.

Scribbling.

She could hear Eddie writing on the paper, hopefully recording the type of noise, potential source, and time it happened.

It was getting harder to simply breathe and focus on her breath. The B&B was coming alive.

Because it's full of the dead, she thought.

She felt her hold on her meditative state wobble, slipping away with each passing thought that refused to be shuffled off.

A pipe banged against the wall and there was a rush of water in the kitchen. Jessica's eyes flew open. Eddie was bent over his book, stealing glances at the timer on his cell phone that he'd placed on his left knee.

"You coming?" Jessica asked as she sprinted to the kitchen.

"Right behind you."

The sink faucet was on full blast, the water hitting the bottom of the sink so hard it coned upwards like an erupting Old Faithful. There was no figure struggling to take form in the water. Jessica went to turn the knobs but they wouldn't budge.

"Find some towels," she said, opening drawers. The Judsons were going to have some serious water damage if she and Eddie didn't stop it from overflowing. Eddie ran upstairs and came back with an armful of fluffy yellow towels. Jessica tossed every tea towel she could find onto the floor. "It won't turn off."

"Let me give it a try." Eddie worked the hot water knob until his face flushed red and his wrist popped. The water kept flowing.

They both looked to the ceiling at the sound of the faucets in the upstairs bathrooms going on at the same time.

"Fucking great," Jessica said. "They wanted us to help them, not destroy their house."

Eddie dropped the towels on the floor and moved them around with his foot to sop up the water. "Jess, don't take this the wrong way, but you need to get the hell out of here."

"You can't do this alone."

"I can if you get as far away from here as fast as you can."

She was about to ask him what he was going on about when their eyes met and she felt stupid for not putting two and two together.

Eddie said, "Catch."

She snatched the keys out of the air. "You sure about this?"

"Yes." He tried the knob again and almost slipped and fell. "Kinda. Go!"

Fighting against her nature, Jessica ran out the back door, jumped in the Jeep, and sped down the street. She had to unplug the battery that was powering the EB. Which meant she had to unplug herself and not look back.

Jessica knew it was time to ease her foot off the gas when she leaned into a hairpin turn, tires wailing, and almost hit a mother pushing a stroller. Too ashamed to say she was sorry, she slowed down the one-way street, avoiding the mother's angry gaze, low branches on the trees lining both sides of the road almost touching the top of her Jeep.

She drove without direction, making rights and lefts, eyeing her phone, waiting for Eddie to tell her everything was all right.

I shouldn't have left him.

She swallowed her guilt like a spoonful of fish oil. He was right. Her presence was like a steroid shot for the EB.

Ascending a steep hill, Jessica blasted Poison's first album, *Look What the Cat Dragged In*, hoping some 80s hair metal would get her back to normal.

When she crested the hill, she stomped the brake pedal with both feet. The car rocked and she just missed slamming her head against the windshield.

The bronze sign read: *Kenner Dam, circa 1953.* A stone wall spanned the road in both directions.

She turned the stereo down, creeping along the road until she found a place to pull over. A hot breeze kissed her face as she walked to the wall.

"Water."

Resting her palms on the warm stone, sparkles of quartz pierced her vision. She turned her gaze to the placid water of Kenner Dam.

The church steeple in the center of the reservoir was an unexpected sight. As were the sodden rooftops of several buildings. She even spotted a half dozen rusted streetlights, onyx crows sitting atop them, basking in the sun.

The reappearance of the sunken town told the story of the drought that had been steadily draining the reservoir. She was aware that towns had been sacrificed to the gods of science working to devise ways to keep a growing population in life-giving water. But weren't the structures usually razed before being flooded? Maybe there just wasn't money in the budget for this place.

Her phone chimed and she read Eddie's text.

All good. A little wet, but good. Maybe it's better we leave. Sorry, I wasn't expecting this.

She tapped her reply.

You ok?

Yep. Should have worn my bathing suit.

Her thumb hovered over the green phone icon to call him when every short hair on her body rose, each tiny fiber pointing toward the reservoir.

Jessica looked up.

The crows flew away in cackling unison.

The water remained still, the steeple straight and silent.

Despite the appearance of emptiness and serenity, something was coming. Jessica's heart seized, and she doubled over with pain. It felt as if someone had hit her in the gut with the stock of a double barrel shotgun. Her vomit hit the top of the wall, spraying into the reservoir's dwindling store of water.

Sweat stung her eyes and bile needled her throat. She blinked away tears, a thin line of sunlight glinting off the water like a lance running through her brain.

"Christ, what the fuck is…happening to me?"

Just like that, the pain and nausea passed. She was left staggered and weak, leaning on the wall.

The water rippled as if something were rising from its dark depths. Individual whirlpools broke out like hives on the skin of the water. They flowed across the surface, all heading in one direction.

Toward Jessica.

After a year of silence, a year of emptiness and a bitter-sweet year of powerlessness, her brain and body were suddenly filled to the point of bursting.

"They left them there. My God, they left them there."

The whirlpools picked up speed. They would come to the shoreline beneath the wall sooner than she'd like.

Jessica felt their collective energy bubbling through her.

Lightheaded, Jessica peeled herself away from the wall, stumbling to the Jeep. She heard the splash of water like waves against a rocky shore. Her hands were numb, useless blocks of wood. Getting the key in the ignition was like trying to put her elbow in her ear. A plume of water sloshed over the wall.

"Come on, come on, come on, you son of a bitch!"

She jammed the key in the ignition with the palm of her hand. The Jeep roared to life, and she managed to slam the car in drive. The back end fishtailed and she almost lost control. She had to call Eddie. Jessica looked down. Shit! She'd left her phone on the wall. Speeding from the B&B, she hadn't bothered to take note of the streets she was passing. Her phone's GPS could always take her back.

Just drive.

The feeling in her extremities came back, but there was a deep pressure at her back. The EBs had attached themselves to her. No matter how fast she drove, they were close behind, growing in strength. Her heart pounded in her ears. Her vision swam and she felt close to passing out.

Could a person die from terror?

She could think of only one thing.

Eddie.

She had to get back to Eddie.

Eddie dropped a towel made leaden from sopping up so much water at the sound of screeching tires. The front door banged open.

"Eddie!"

Jessica looked like she was on the verge of a panic attack. He almost fell backward when she flew into his arms.

"What is it? What's wrong?"

"Water. I...I found a reservoir not far from here. There are EBs trapped in the water. But the...the reservoir is drying up, and they're coming for me."

He smoothed her sweaty hair away from her face. "What do you mean they're coming for you?" He didn't dare voice his concern that her return would amp up the EB in the house.

"I can feel them," she said breathlessly. "They followed me here."

He was about to ask her how she could know such a thing when he heard the splish-splash of what sounded like wet footsteps on hardwood floors. He peered over Jessica's shoulder. Multiple wet footprints appeared to be entering the house.

"Let's go," he said, pulling her into the kitchen. No sooner had they walked in the door than the sink faucet suddenly opened, water roaring out of the old pipes once again. Every faucet in the house went on full blast.

They went out the back door and into the yard.

"We can't run forever," Jessica said, though her eyes told him she was willing to give it a try.

"Send them away," he said.

"I...I can't!"

"Yes, you can."

The back door blew off its hinges. Water cascaded down the steps into the grass.

Jessica froze, her grip like a vice.

Eddie had never seen her like this before and never imagined he would.

"Fight through it, Jess."

Her mouth trembled. A tear squirmed from the corner of her eye.

He'd never felt so useless in his life. "The car."

He took one step to the pathway leading to the street when a splash of water doused his back. He fell to his knees and his eyes rolled up in his head.

Then he saw them.

Men, women and children. Their faces were bloated and misshapen. They wore clothes from another era, but not all that far removed from modern day.

Jessica tugged his arm and shouted something, but he couldn't hear her over the frantic ramblings of the dead. They knew he could see and hear them and they bombarded him with desperate pleas.

"Stop talking all at once!" he screamed, holding his head.

"You can hear them?" Jessica asked, her voice rising above the others. All he could do was nod.

They had been murdered. Several families had fought the building of the dam. The developers took them to court, but they still refused to relinquish their homes, houses that had been with their families for generations. These people ignorant to change had cost the company and their less than savory investors time and money. On the day when the town was to be flooded, they had been beaten and locked in their homes by paid ruffians and left to drown.

Eddie felt their suffering, their last gasps before cold, cold water filled their lungs, their bodies jerking in painful spasms.

"No."

His eyes flew open. Jessica was practically nose-to-nose with him.

"Don't be afraid," he said, absorbing their terror lest Jessica feel or sense it. "Give them peace. They deserve it."

She shook her head. "I don't know if I can."

"They need your help. They don't want to hurt you. Try, Jess. Some of them...some of them are just little kids."

Jessica rocked back on her heels. "Kids?"

The smaller water figures reached out with pleading hands.

She stepped away from Eddie. The square set of her jaw, the balled fists, the flickering fire in her gaze, the woman Eddie had fallen in love with had returned.

"You can go now," she said. Her body shook and for a moment, Eddie thought she would fall. He saw two EBs, a man and a young girl, fade into nothing.

"It's working," he said. "Keep going."

"Find peace," Jessica said. "There's nothing for you here...anymore."

Eddie watched a woman mouth, *thank you*, before flickering out.

Moments later, they were gone.

Jessica swooned but kept to her feet. "Did I do it?"

He managed to smile through the agony in his head. It seemed even his abilities still had a little left in the tank. "Yeah, you did it."

Jessica packed while Eddie was in the bathroom shaving. She felt good. She felt whole for the first time in a long while.

"*You don't know what you got, 'til it's gone*," she sang, trying her best to imitate the guttural growl of Cinderella's lead singer.

She'd thought she was happy never encountering an EB again, but she'd been wrong. She'd forgotten that not every EB was out to harm her. Thank God some of Eddie's incredible power had been restored as well so he could teach her that lesson.

They'd talked for hours after she sent the EBs to where they'd belonged. Eddie recounted the stories they'd projected to him and it wasn't pretty. How could someone willfully drown whole families? As more of the town became exposed from the drought, the EBs sought the light, escaping their dank, watery grave.

The door opened downstairs, followed by Claire Judson's singsong, "Hello, it's just us!"

Jessica stepped to the open doorway and called out, "We'll be down in a minute."

"Take your time," Jet replied.

Eddie emerged from the bathroom toweling bits of shaving cream off his face. "They sound happy."

"We just lessened their workloads. They should be."

"We good to go?"

She snapped their suitcase shut and kissed him. "Thank you."

Eddie hugged her tight. "We have each other to thank."

"Back in the saddle."

They walked downstairs holding hands. Claire and Jet Judson were sitting at the dining table, steaming mugs of coffee in their hands. "I'll get some coffee for you kids," Claire said, hustling into the kitchen.

Eddie and Jessica sat across from a smiling Jet. "Are you sure whatever was here is gone?" he asked.

"Gone and hopefully happy and at peace," Jessica said.

He arched a bushy eyebrow. "How can you be sure?"

Jessica patted Eddie's hand on the table. "Let's just say we're uniquely qualified to do what we do."

Claire returned with their coffee.

Eddie grabbed Jessica's hand.

"How do you...I don't know, send a ghost away?" Claire inquired. She sat next to Jet on the padded bench.

Jessica took a tiny sip. "I just tell them they can go."

"Just like that?" Jet said.

"Pretty much. Even I'm not entirely sure how it works."

"Jess," Eddie hissed.

His grip tightened until it hurt.

"Ow. What's wrong with you?"

Jet set his coffee down. "Could you show us how you do it?"

"You're inside them," Eddie said.

Claire's smile vanished. Her jaw went slack and her eyes deadened. "We don't want to be. Not anymore. Now that you're here."

Jessica looked at Jet and Claire, shocked by their transformation, and whipped her head back to Eddie. "What's going on here?"

"They needed to find a way for us to set them free," Eddie said.

Jessica was confused. "Us? They don't even know us?"

"We all know who and what you are," Claire and Jet said in eerie unison. "Now show us."

This time, Jessica wasn't frightened. She'd never encountered an EB that had taken full possession of a living person before, but she was wise enough to know she hadn't come close to seeing everything this world, and the next, had to offer.

"Show us now," Jet said, a rough edge to his voice.

"Are you one of them?" Jessica asked. "From the dam?"

They nodded slowly. Tears leaked from their eyes. Drool spilled from their parted lips.

Jessica's heart broke. "I'm so sorry. I can stop your suffering."

"Please," the EB within Claire said.

Jessica closed her eyes and said, "Leave now and find true peace." She felt the familiar tingle ripple through her body.

Eddie jumped from his chair and shouted "Don't!"

But it was too late.

"I can't sense them," Eddie said, rushing to the other side of the table.

"Who?"

"The real Jet and Claire. They're not here. And if there isn't another spirit to take over their bodies…"

Jet and Claire's eyes rolled up until they were bulging, hardboiled eggs. Their heads jerked backwards and their bodies began to quake.

Jessica pushed away from the table. "What's happening to them?"

Ugly gargling noises emanated from their throats. Water flowed from their mouths, running down their necks.

Eddie pulled Jessica close. "The EBs are separating, leaving them…empty."

Jessica slid over the table and straightened Claire's neck, pointing her head down so the water could run free. Her body shivered and shook, racked with wet coughs and slippery inhalations. Eddie took her cue and did the same with Jet.

"Come on, just breathe," Jessica said. Claire started flopping so wildly, Jessica was thrown sideways as if being tossed off a bucking bull.

Claire and Jet gasped once and then fell over backwards. Jessica fumbled to find a pulse on Claire's neck and wrist. Tiny bubbles popped within the froth on the old woman's lips. Jessica started doing chest compressions. "No, no, no!"

She kept at it until Eddie pulled her off. "They're gone."

"But what about the real Claire and Jet?"

"I don't know. I can't sense them."

Jessica chewed at her thumbnail. "I…I just killed them."

"They were already dead."

"The police won't see it that way."

The sound of water slowly dripping into a pan in the kitchen sink rang like gunshots in the suddenly still house.

Those Who Are Terrified

by Elizabeth Massie

My sisters Carol, Connie, and I didn't like our grandfather. He was a large man, not tall, not quite fat, but big. Thick white hair, caterpillar brows, face like a potato and a voice that could crack concrete. His name was Harry Franklin. Our father's father. He was a successful real estate broker who owned several buildings in our town. Adults liked him. They called him "Pops" and even elected him mayor for two terms. We called our grandfather "Sir." He ignored us because he didn't like us much, either.

Our grandmother was the opposite of Sir. She was tall but small, and very quiet. Her hair was gray and thin. She stayed at home most of the time, cooking, watching her "shows," and tending her hydrangea bushes. She got out to church three times a week; on Tuesdays and Thursdays for the garden club meetings and Sundays for the worship service. We called our grandmother "Nannie." She wasn't as bad as Sir but wasn't all that nice. She didn't say anything the few times Sir noticed us and yelled at us. Nannie mostly ignored us, too. Maybe she was tired. Or just old.

It was July, 1961. Our parents had gone to Florida on what Sir called an "extended vacation" because they needed a break. We missed Mom and Daddy, but staying at our grandparents' house wasn't too bad. Except for Tuesdays, Thursdays, and Sundays.

Bossy Carol was eight. I was seven. Little Connie was five. We were too young to stay at the house alone, so Tuesday, Thursday, and Sunday mornings, we had to go with Sir to his work. Connie and I would pile in the back of Sir's white Cadillac. Carol sat in front. Nobody talked except for Sir, who would ramble on in his concrete-cracking voice, talking to himself. This morning, he was angry about a man and woman who'd been shown a Victorian house at the edge of town.

"Ninnies!" he swore around his smoldering Lucky Strike as his hands tightened on the steering wheel. "Spent a whole damned hour with 'em, walking through all the rooms, answering all their blasted questions. And then the husband says, 'Oh, sorry, we can't buy. We'd be absolutely terrified to go into debt right now. Ha ha!' Low-lifes! Well, those who are terrified deserve to be terrified." This was one of Sir's favorite claims. Connie and I exchanged glances and were glad when we reached Sir's office and were able to crawl free of the car and the close proximity of the old man.

Sir's real estate office was located in a building atop a rise on Main Street, a building called "Hillcrest Hall." It was three stories, faded red brick, and had originally served as the town's first and only hospital from 1911 to autumn 1960 when the new, larger county hospital was constructed. Hillcrest Hall was empty a few months until Sir snapped it up, buying it from his best friend, old Doctor Erhard Adelmann, who'd been the hospital administrator and property owner for thirteen years and had died soon after.

The third floor and second floors of the building consisted of empty office space that Sir planned on renovating to rent. The whole first floor was Sir's office, even though he was his only employee. Rooms full of books and maps and rolled up papers and dark green file cabinets. Sir had a secretary once, a sweet lady named Mary Root, who sat in the front foyer at her desk and gave us hard butterscotch candy. But she moved away. The bowl of butterscotch was long empty but the big butterscotch bag remained inside her desk. We would sneak a piece when Sir wasn't in the room. It didn't have much taste, but it was okay.

Butterscotch from Mary Root's desk and the Hillcrest basement were the only two good things about going to work with Sir. We never told Sir we played in the basement. My sisters and I always said we were going outside to play. Of course, he didn't care enough to wonder where we were.

The basement was accessible three ways. Down a narrow flight of steps. By way of a service elevator in the back hall. And through a heavy, garage-type door outside at the back of the building, down where the hill sloped away and a well-worn gravel alleyway came up.

We couldn't get down the steps because they were blocked by two of Sir's file cabinets. We couldn't play in the service elevator because the desk in Sir's main room faced down the hall, and he would see us in a second. That left the garage-type door on the outside.

This door was heavy and rusted in its tracks, but when Carol and I pulled on the handle together, we could get it to go up high enough for us to roll under and in.

And oh, the basement!

It was a vast, cavernous space over-packed with fascinating things. Flipping the light switch beside the door did little to cut the shadows, as there were only two bulbs overhead that worked. That made it more fun, because it was easier to hide from each other. Connie sometimes cried but Carol, in her bossy tone, told her not to be a baby. "If you're scared, you deserved to be scared," she'd say, paraphrasing Sir.

We spent our time in the basement away from Sir, climbing, digging, crawling. There were myriad pieces of furniture–beds, dressers, tables standing upright and some on their sides, chairs stacked neatly or piled up like a bonfire waiting to be lit. There were appliances–stoves, refrigerators, freezers. There were toilets and sinks. There were lengths of lumber, car fenders, trunks, lawnmowers, bookshelves, and columns of cardboard boxes that leaned precariously this way and that. Sir had collected these things from the various homes and businesses he'd bought and put on the market. He said he would have a big auction sale someday and make a lot of money on the side.

This particular Tuesday, after we sneaked our butterscotch, we headed outside, around the building, and down the grassy slope to the basement door. Connie slipped and tore the seat out of her shorts. She thought it was funny, though, the way her now green grass-stained underpants showed through the hole.

Carol and I pulled the door up as far as we could and the three of us scooched inside. It was dark as the bottom of a well and smelled like mouse poo. I reached along the wall and turned on the switch.

Yellow light drifted down from the center of the ceiling. Carol raced off into the shadows, footfalls echoing. As she rounded a tall stack of crates, she called out, "Can't catch me, I'm the gingerbread man!"

This was the signal to count to twenty then go looking. Connie and I counted. Then I took off to the right; Connie took off to the left. I clambered over a heap of old mattresses, under a kitchen table, and squeezed through a narrow passage between chairs and a ceiling-high column of boxes. A mouse darted out in front of me then ran under a stack of old paintings. In the past, Carol had hidden inside the wardrobe with a broken door, under some of the stinking mattresses, and behind a clothes rod that held old fur coats and evening dresses. She would never hide in the same place twice.

"Here I am!" Carol called from somewhere deep in the basement. I stumbled over some lumber and pushed my way around a splintering chifforobe. My reflection flashed in a full-length mirror I passed by and it startled me. I knew it was there. I'd seen it before, but it always caught me by surprise.

"Can't find me!" called Carol.

Her voice was closer now, and my eyes were fairly well adjusted to the dim light. Around an old typewriter stand I hurried, and up over a sloppy pile of cracked and stacked wicker baskets, where I lost my balance, toppled forward, and slammed onto the floor on my face.

"Oww!" I said. I'd bit my lip.

"What happened?" This was Connie, not far away.

I flipped over onto my back. "I tripped! I bit my lip!"

"Idiot!" Carol laughed.

"Not funny!" I said. I touched my lip and there was a small dot of blood. It stung like crazy.

"It's kinda funny," said Carol.

"If it was you, you wouldn't think so!"

There was silence. Then Carol said, "You okay?"

I held still waiting to see if anything else hurt. It didn't.

"I guess," I said. I pulled up my knees, ready to get back up. Then I saw it, tucked up underneath the wooden desk beside me.

A wooden leg with a man's shoe.

"Ew!"

I quickly hopped to my feet and stared at the desk, knowing what was underneath it.

"Ew, what?" called Carol. "Where are you? I want to see what's ew!"

"Where are you?" This was Connie, a bit farther away.

"Here. Beside the wicker baskets."

"I don't remember where they are!" said Carol.

"Me, either!" said Connie.

"Just keep looking!"

I gathered my courage and knelt down to look under the desk again. There it was. The wooden leg. Covered in peeling pinkish paint that might have been another color ten years ago. The shoe was cracked leather coated with green mold. An equally green, molded leather harness was attached to both sides by rusty rivets. There had been a sock once, but it was chewed to a few threads by mice. The leg was hollowed from the top several inches, where a stubby leg would go. Carved into the wood were initials. "LAC."

Carol came crashing over the pile of wicker baskets. Little Connie was close behind.

"What's wrong?" asked Connie. Even in the shadows, her chubby little face was clearly worried.

"It's a leg," I said, putting my hands on my hips. I wasn't going to let my little sister think I was scared. And I wasn't. Not exactly.

"Nuh-uh!" said Carol.

"Oh, no? Look at this." I steeled myself and grabbed the leg by the shoe. I pulled it out. Connie gasped in fear. Carol gasped in delight.

"Wow!" Carol yanked the leg from me. "I wonder who wore this?"

"Hop-Along Cassidy," I offered.

"Or maybe Limp-Along Cassidy?" said Carol, always the smart ass. "Those initials would fit." Carol stuck her knee down into the hollow of the leg. She leaned into it. "Too big."

"'Course it's too big," I said. "It's got a man shoe."

"I like it," said Carol. "Let's keep it!"

"I don't like it," said Connie.

"Where do we put it?" I asked. "Sir won't let us take it home."

"We'll keep it here so we can play with it. We can take turns trying to walk it in!"

"Yeah," I said, still a little unnerved by the leg. "We can do that."

Connie clutched my arm. "I don't like it, Cathy. I really don't want to–"

Then the overhead bulbs winked out.

Connie's fingers dug more deeply into my arm.

"Oh, no!" said Connie. "Too dark! Too dark!"

And we saw it.

We saw *him*.

Hovering above cardboard boxes, glowing silver like the moon. Eyes red as campfire coals. Skin on his face stretched tight against the bone revealing every detail of the skull. Piss-colored teeth protruding like broken seashells.

One leg dangled freely. The other was missing at the knee. The stump paddled madly against the air.

We screamed.

Carol flung the wooden leg away and dove back over the wicker baskets. I grabbed Connie's hand and tossed her after Carol. The tear in Connie's shorts flapped like a bird's wing. I scrambled behind, my heart banging. My brain cried out, *Jesus God help us, help us!* but fear locked my voice in place.

Banging knees and elbows and shoulders on the furniture and appliances and boxes, we raced toward the garage door.

Help us help us HELP US!

I knocked over a bin filled with slimy clothes and tripped on a coat. I whirled my arms, kept upright, and pushed on.

HELP HELP HELP!

There! The slice of sunlight along the floor!

We slammed into the garage door...*thump thump thump!* ...then dropped to our bellies and dragged ourselves out into the day.

"What was that?" cried Connie as she stood up, blinking against the hard sunlight. "Cathy! What was that?"

I had no answer.

Carol stared at the space under the door. She was breathing as heavily as we were, but I could see she was also thinking.

And then through chattering teeth she said, "It was nothing."

"Was, too!" Connie said, weeping and leaning against me. "You saw it, Carol!"

"I said it was nothing," said Carol. "And I'm right. I read a lot. I know a lot. So shut up. It was a dummy, a stupid old dummy hanging from the ceiling."

"We never saw a dummy in there before!" said Connie.

"We never saw a wooden leg, either," said Carol.

Carol, Connie, and I stared at each other and at the opening beneath the door.

Then Carol said, "We're going back in. I'll prove it."

I said what I'd heard Sir say lots of times. "The hell I am!"

"Oh, yeah?" said Carol, leaning in close to both Connie and me. "Then I'm going to tell Sir that you two stole stuff from Sir's office."

I stared. "I never stole anything, you brat!"

"Carol, don't!" said Connie. Her face was slick with tears and snot. "I don't want Sir mad at me! He scares me!"

"I'm gonna tell him you two stole and tore up some of his important papers. He'll believe me 'cause I'm the oldest and never tell lies."

"I don't want to go back in!"

Carol snorted. "Who you more scared of, Connie? The thing in the basement or Sir?"

"Both!"

"Don't forget, Connie," said Carol with a haughty arch of her eyebrow. "Those who are terrified deserve to be terrified."

Connie cried even louder. I glared at my older sister.

"Suit yourselves," said Carol. "I'm going in. Stay out here if you're too baby to come with me. Then you'll get in trouble with Sir for what I'm gonna tell him! He never whipped you but you can bet he will if I tell him you stole his papers."

Carol got down and crawled into the basement.

"I don't wanna get in trouble with Sir!" bawled Connie. "And I don't wanna see that thing!"

Neither did I.

I clenched my jaw. "We'll keep our eyes closed. Okay?"

Connie shook her head but didn't resist.

We crawled back into the darkness and shut our eyes.

Carol held my hand. I held Connie's. Single file, Carol led us through the musty hoard in the direction of the silvery thing with the red eyes and flapping stump. My mind raced, thoughts bumping off each other as I bumped into the things around me. I would not open my eyes. I wouldn't look. Unless Carol could absolutely for-sure promise it was just a dummy.

My cut lip burned. My ears buzzed. Connie's crying faded to a whimper.

We reached the baskets. We crawled over.

Then Carol said, "Well, it's gone."

"Good!" said Connie.

"Good?" I said. I opened my eyes to slits. "That's not good! If it was a dummy, it would still be there! Dummies can't move!"

"Oh," said Carol. She hadn't thought of that.

"Where is it, Carol?" I demanded.

Then it rushed up from the floor in front of us, springing toward the ceiling like a horrific jack-in-the-box, arms out, fingers clawing at the air, red eyes glaring, stubbed leg flailing. Sprigs of hair coiled up from the head like seaweed. One arm shot out and a finger was aimed in our direction.

"YOU!" it wailed.

All three of us dropped to the floor on our knees, our hands over our heads.

"YOU!" the thing screeched again. I could feel the frigid air that encircled it. I knew we were going to die.

"YOU!"

Connie whined like a puppy in a trap.

Carol yelled into the floor, "Go away! I mean it! You'll...you'll be sorry!"

We were going to be killed, snatched up by bony hands and chewed down by seashell teeth. We'd never see our parents whenever they came back from Florida. I'd never go to second grade.

I sobbed, waiting for it to happen. Waiting for the pain. There was nothing else I could do. Would I go to Hell for cussing? Would Carol go to Hell for being bossy?

I waited.

Connie panted. Carol shouted another tattered threat. Cold air played with my hair.

I waited.

I did not die.

I waited.

I still did not die.

I moved my hands from my head. I slowly angled my head to look at Connie on one side of me and Carol on the other.

Finally, I looked up at it. At *him*, hanging mid-air, drifting back and forth. His teeth still chattered. His fingers still clutched. His half-leg still wagged back and forth. But the bright red eyes looked....

Sad?

Hopeful?

"YOU!" he wailed, pointing at me.

I didn't think I would say anything, but my mouth fell open and I squeaked, "Cathy. I'm Cathy."

He nodded. He shivered there, all silvery and dreadful and sad.

Carol punched my shoulder, looking at me but not at him. "Don't talk to it!"

I pushed her away. She hit me again. "Stop it!" I said then looked back up.

"Cathy," he said, his voice sliding down from a wail to a bone-dry whisper. "You found me."

"I just found your leg," I said.

"Yes. So soon, I can go."

"Go where?"

"Cathy," whispered little Connie. "I think he's a ghost," She was looking up now, too.

A ghost. Yes, I knew that. Before Connie had uttered the word, I knew it. He was a ghost. The ghost of a man who'd had a wooden leg.

"What's your name?" I asked.

The red eyes winked, glowed. The silvery body hovered up and down between the ceiling and the floor. "Lonnie Conyers."

"Why're you stuck in the Hillcrest basement?"

"Because no one knows what happened to me."

"What do you mean?"

"Find the box."

"What box?" This was Carol.

The ghostly arm stretched out, silvery strands following the wake of the motion, and pointed to the far corner of the basement. "The answers are in the box."

I looked at Carol. Carol looked at me. Connie wiped her sticky nose and sniffed.

"He's not a bad ghost," Connie said.

"I don't think he is," I answered.

Carol wasn't having it. "There aren't any good ghosts!"

"Casper's good," said Connie.

"It isn't goddamn Casper!"

I ignored Carol. I stood and followed the ghost to the box in the corner. It was a tall, green, metal file cabinet like the ones upstairs in Sir's offices. It was covered in a blanket and laced with cobwebs. No wonder we hadn't noticed it before.

"Open it," said the ghost.

I touched the handle of the top drawer and tugged. "I think it's locked."

"Open it."

I tugged again and felt a latch inside snap. The drawer came open with a gritty rattle.

Carol and Connie were close behind me now, watching.

There were age-stained folders inside the file box. I pulled one out. Printed in black ink on the front was, the name of our town, "Rallytown," and another word I knew, "Hospital." Stamped in red ink was "Deceased." On the little folder tab was written, "Mason, Jennifer."

"What's 'deceased' mean?" I asked.

"It means dead," said Carol.

I put the folder back and flipped through several more. They were all printed the same on the front, but with different names on the tabs.

"These are all files for dead people?"

"Yes," said the ghost.

"People that died in the hospital?"

"No. These are files of people who died somewhere else. They were brought here, to the hospital basement. Their bodies were burned to ash and taken to the town dump."

My heart pounded against my ribs. "Are you...in here?"

"My file is there."

"But why are you a ghost?" interrupted Carol. "Why didn't you go to wherever other dead people go? Like Heaven or Hell?"

"I can't be released to the Final After until someone living knows the truth about me. That will allow me to remember the truth, too. In the meanwhile, I can visit some places that were important to me. My home. The bar where I went with my friends."

"Do you scare them?" I asked. "Being as you're a ghost?"

"I don't let them see me. Those of us who are in the Realm are only seen when we want to be seen."

"Oh," said Connie.

"And sometimes, even when the truth is known, a ghost will stay around because there's unfinished business."

"Do you have unfinished business?"

"No. I just want to go. Please. Find my folder."

I carefully flipped through the folders, reading the names on the tabs as best I could. Names I didn't know, couldn't have known. Then, in the back, I saw the name "Lonnie Aaron Conyers." I pulled it out.

"Don't open it!" said Carol.

"Shut up, Carol." I opened the folder.

There was a typed page that I couldn't read much of, except for a name –"Dr. Erhard Adelmann" and initials–"HBF." Behind the page were two black and white photos. One of a tall man, smiling beside a tree. He had one wooden leg. The second photo showed the same man, dead on a cot in what looked like this basement. There was a big hole in his forehead, with blood smeared down his face and one eye popped out.

I dropped the folder. I thought I was going to throw up. "Somebody killed you!"

The ghost sighed, emitting a blast of cold air that gave my arms chill bumps. "I remember now."

"Somebody shot you in the head!"

"It was Erhard Adelmann."

"Who?"

"The doctor who ran the hospital."

I shivered. The image of the bloodied head stayed in my mind. I felt weak in the legs and grabbed the edge of the cabinet.

"Why...why did he shoot you?"

"A child doesn't need to know. Put the folder back."

I slid the folder back into the drawer. I could see Connie and Carol's faces out of the corner of my eye. Their eyes were wide, their lips trembling. Little Connie seemed to reflect the silver from the ghost.

"Now a living soul knows I was murdered," said Lonnie Conyers. "So now I remember. And I'm free. Thank you."

I didn't know if I should say, 'You're welcome.' I said nothing.

"The box has other secrets," said the ghost as he began to fade. "Find them. Read them aloud. Know their truth. Free them." And then as quietly as a breeze, he disappeared.

"But I can't read good!" I called after him.

Carol said softly, "I read good, Cathy."

And she did.

There were two drawers in the cabinet. We started with the top. I took out one file at a time–14 in all–and Carol read aloud the name and the details. Several were typed. Others were written in ink. Some of the people had been killed. Others, wounded or sick, had been left to die at home for the purpose of, according to the record, "...to see how long this patient would survive without treatment." Each file had photos of the person alive and then the person dead, photos I didn't want to see but couldn't help but see.

All the files were signed, "Dr. Erhard Adelmann." and initialed "HBF."

As Carol read and Connie wrung her hands, there was rustling amid the furniture, the mattresses, and the boxes throughout the basement. And one at a time, horrible, silvery, red-eyed, glowing specters rose up, wavered, then vanished like sparks from a campfire. Some voiced "thank you" as they went. Others were silent. Connie and I sat, listening to Carol and watching the ghosts come then go away.

"Doctor Adelmann was a murderer!" said Carol.

"So awful!" I said. "Why do you think he killed all those people? And kept folders?"

"Maybe he was a Nazi," said Carol. "I read all about them. They killed people they didn't like and killed people for fun. They kept folders on all the bad stuff they did to people."

I cringed. I shut the top drawer and opened the bottom. I handed Carol a file. She opened it then immediately slammed it shut. She shoved it back into the cabinet.

"What's wrong?" I asked.

"We've been down here too long!" she said. "Sir's going to wonder where we are! We have to leave!"

She was right. We hurried back to the garage door, squeezed out into the daylight, and clambered up the grassy slope to the road. We climbed in Sir's car and waited for him to come out and take us back to the house.

We hung out with Nannie on Wednesday, watching her bake cream puffs, enduring her boring "stories" on the television. We played outside in the bushes in the yard and tried to catch the chickens that escaped from the next-door neighbor's pen. I thought about the ghosts in the old hospital basement. I wanted to talk about it, but could tell Carol didn't. She would look at me and then look away, like she was angry that we shared such a dark secret. Connie, on the other hand, seemed happy; could be she was just pretending none of it had happened. She was good at that.

Night came. As Sir and Nannie watched late-night television, we put ourselves to bed.

Carol and I shared a bed. Connie had a cot in the same room. Usually we whispered and made up songs until we fell asleep. This night we lay awake, staring at the ceiling. Until Carol said flatly, "They're dead."

I turned to her in the darkness. "Who?"

"Mom and Daddy."

Connie screeched. "Don't say that! What a mean trick to play on us!"

"Shut up, Connie," said Carol. "It's true."

My heart squeezed like a dry sponge. "Why are you saying that?"

"I saw Daddy's file. It's in the cabinet."

"No, it's not!"

"And if he's dead, so's Mom. They're never coming back from Florida. They aren't in Florida."

"NO! Shut up!"

"It's true."

"*Shut up!*"

I curled up and pounded my chest with my fists. This was impossible! Of course Carol was lying! She could be the meanest person on Earth. Mom and Daddy were on vacation in Florida! Sir said so!

"I'll show you tomorrow," said Carol. "You'll see."

And then I knew she was telling the truth.

Throughout the night, Connie and I cried and Carol just lay in bed, staring into the blackness.

Thursday, we went to the Hillcrest Hall with Sir. I didn't want to go. Connie didn't want to go. But we had to go. Sir ignored us as he always did, let us go wherever, he had business to take care of. Connie and I didn't want any butterscotch candy. We didn't want to go back down to the basement, either, but we had to.

The garage door was still open at the bottom.

We stared at the opening. My arms shook.

"Those who are terrified deserved to be terrified," said Carol. Her head was cocked; her face tight.

"I hate you," I said.

We went in. We pushed our way around to the terrible file box in the back corner. Carol knelt by the cabinet. I sat beside her. Connie lay down again, arms over her head, face toward the floor. Carol opened the bottom drawer and drew out the folder she'd shoved back in.

"This is it," she said. She opened it. I didn't look. I knew there would be photos.

Carol read, "Mitchell Avery Franklin. Age 34. Drowned. Rallytown Lake. May 6, 1960…"

"That's more than a year ago!" I said. "It can't be true!"

"…along with his wife, Julia Mason Franklin…"

"Stop it!"

Carol lifted another folder from the cabinet. It was marked "Julia Mason Franklin." She shoved it at me. The folder flopped open. I glimpsed the photos before batting them away. They'd shown Mom standing by our house, arm around Daddy. Mom on a cot in the basement of the Hillcrest building, eyes open and white as a dead fish, hair plastered down, lips swollen.

"See?" said Carol.

"It's true."

The deep, quavering voice came from behind us. Carol and I spun around to see two ghosts rising up from the hoarded mess of Sir's collection. Connie looked up, her eyes bugging.

Daddy, skull-faced and silvery-green, with huge, scarlet eyes. Mom holding onto Daddy, her face bloated, her hair drifting like seaweed. I wanted to rush to them and hug them. I wanted to set fire to them and have them gone.

"Dearests," said Daddy. "Now you know. And now we remember."

"You aren't dead!" I cried. "You went to Florida!"

"No," said Daddy.

"Your father and I saw him with her," said Mom.

"Yes, we saw them together. He knew we saw," said Daddy.

"Oh, he was so angry!" said Daddy. "He thought we would tell on him and ruin his reputation. We went camping at the lake. He and his friend Doctor Adelmann came to us at night. Threw us into the boat, cracked our skulls, tossed us into the water. I'm sorry, dearests, but the truth must be known. How we've missed you!"

"But who's he?" I asked around my tears.

"Sir," Carol answered. "Harry Barnes Franklin. HBF."

"*Sir* killed you, Mom? Daddy?" I asked.

Mom's dreadful, skeletal, silvery head nodded. "There is more to know. Find it." Carol, Connie, and I stared at our ghastly, loving parents. They looked down at us. It made no sense. How could they have been dead so long and we didn't know? How could Sir have done what he did?

Our parents' ghosts began to fade away.

"Don't go!" Connie cried. "Mommy! Daddy!"

"More to find," said the faint outline that had been Mom. Then they were gone.

I didn't want to know any more. I wanted to go home to Nannie. No, I wanted to go home to *our* house! I wanted Mom and Daddy back!

With furious fingers, Carol pawed through the other folders.

I shoved her. "Don't, Carol, please!"

Carol pulled out a folder. The tab read, "Mary Root."

"Mary Root can't be dead!" I said. "She moved away!"

As Connie cried, Carol showed me the photos. Smiling Mary Root at her office desk. Battered and bloodied Mary Root, lying in the basement on top of an old mattress.

"She's for sure dead, Cathy," said Carol.

"Ahhh!" came a wail. We looked over to see Mary Root's silvered ghost glide from behind a stack of crates. Her head lolled on her neck as if it might fall off. Her eyes were black hollows with pin points of bright red. "You saw the truth," she muttered. "Now I remember what happened. I was pregnant. He said he'd marry me. Your parents found out. He beat me to death to have me gone."

"No! You moved away!" said Connie. "You left your butterscotch behind!"

Mary Root shook her head. "The truth is known. Now I can go. Thank you."

Her head flopped back, forth, and then she disappeared.

"Sir killed Mom!" I said. "Sir killed Daddy! Sir killed Mary Root! I am going to kill Sir!"

"We can't!" cried Connie. "We're kids!"

I grabbed Carol's arm. She didn't pull away, even as my fingers dug into her flesh. I could tell she agreed with me. "Then I'm running away! Let's run away and never, ever come back!"

Connie and Carol agreed. We hurried out of the garage. Instead of climbing up to the road, we skittered down to the alley below.

"Where are we going?" asked Connie.

"I don't know. It doesn't matter," I said. "We just have to go!"

We marched along the alley. I was crying. So was Connie.

Then Carol drew up short.

She turned to looked back up the alley at the rear of the old hospital. Connie and I stopped, too.

"They wouldn't camp without us," Carol said.

I didn't know what Carol was talking about. I didn't want to be stopped. I tried to move around her but she blocked my way with her leg.

"Did you hear me?" she said. "Mom and Daddy wouldn't go camping without us! We always went camping together!"

She took off, back up the alley. Connie and I raced after her. We went back to the garage-type door of the Hillcrest basement. Carol crawled in while Connie and I stood, confused and distraught. A minute later, Carol was back with a folder.

A single folder. She held it up.

"I don't want to see!" said Connie, burying her face in the neck of her shirt.

I looked at the tab on the folder. I whispered the name. "Connie Jennifer Franklin."

Connie screamed.

"Open it," said Carol.

I shook my head.

Carol opened the folder. She read: "Connie Jennifer Franklin. Age 5. Drowned. Rallytown Lake. May 6, 1960."

"*No!*" said Connie.

"This is wrong!" I said, shoving Carol so that she almost lost her footing. "Connie didn't drown! She's right here!"

I looked over at Connie. She was changing. The sweet child's face was morphing into a sunken child's skull. He arms and legs withered into silvery appendages and her blue eyes turned bright red.

Then Connie cried, "I remember! Oh! I was camping with Mommy and Daddy! Sir and the doctor came into our tent! They took us out on the lake. They drowned us! I'm a ghost! I don't want to be a ghost!"

"But you can't be!" I said. "You've been here all the time! With us!"

Connie's gruesome face was folded with grief and fear. "Lonnie said ghosts can go where they want! Remember? They can let people see them if they want! I let you and Carol see me. I didn't know I was doing it, but I was!"

My breath snagged until I thought I would faint.

Then Carol said, "Shit oh shit! I remember, too!" She spun me around. "We were at Brownie Camp last year when they went to the lake! Sir told us Mom and Daddy went to Florida. He said Connie went, too, but we thought he was just playing a stupid joke because Connie was still with us!"

The three of us stood in a tiny circle... two girls, one ghost.

Then I said, "I don't want to run away. I want to kill Sir."

"Me, too," said Carol

"Me, too," said Connie. "I think Lonnie called it unfinished business."

Sir was at his desk, rifling through papers, chewing on a pen. His bushy brows nearly obscured his eyes. He growled to himself as he sought something or other.

"Sir," I said, standing in the doorway beside Carol.

Sir looked up. His brows remained down. "What do you want?"

"There's a body in the basement," I said.

I'd never seen Sir looked scared before. Though the scared look quickly changed to fury.

"What?"

"We found a body in the basement," said Carol.

"You were in the basement!"

"You never care where we go," I said. White-hot anger gave me courage. "Now you're mad 'cause we were in the stupid basement?"

Sir stood up, slamming his chair back. It looked like he would choke us. But then he said, "There certainly is no body in the basement."

He wants to kill us like he killed Mom, Daddy, and Connie, I thought. *Like he killed Mary Root.*

Sir stormed out the door past Carol and me. Connie was in the hall against the wall, invisible to our grandfather. We thought he would go outside and down to the heavy basement door. Our plan was to trap and crush him as he tried to crawl inside. We would tell everyone it was an accident.

But instead, he went along the back hall to the service elevator. He reached down for the handle and yanked the door up. The elevator wasn't there. He leaned forward a bit and looked up. We looked up, too. The elevator was stuck on the third floor. That seemed to please him, though.

"Are you a Nazi like Doctor Adelmann?" asked Carol.

Sir turned to us and grabbed our arms.

"Children die so easily when they fall on their heads!" he laughed. "Down you go, you brats! Such a sad accident!"

Then Connie appeared, drifting in the elevator shaft. She said, "Sir!"

Sir let go of us and turned on his toes.

Connie was in her terrible glory—yellow seashell teeth, gangly arms flapping, skull-face wobbling back and forth, red eyes glaring.

Sir uttered a piercing, animal-like scream.

"Those who are terrified deserve to be terrified," said Carol. We rushed forward and struck him from behind. His foot caught the edge of the shaft and he flipped, head first, down to the basement where he struck the concrete floor.

The sound of his snapping neck wasn't as loud as I would have hoped. But it was satisfying enough.

Carol and I stared down at the dead man. When we looked back, Connie was gone. Released. Free.

We would miss her.

Now, to tell Nannie.

Poor old Nannie. She didn't deserve to be terrified.

Or maybe she did.

Cool for Cats

by William Meikle

Wendy Miller cried at the funeral, and all who saw her remarked on her obvious distress and at her loyalty to the old woman they were burying that damp day on the hillside above Loch Awe. But Wendy knew the truth; her tears were not of sadness or grief. She cried, not for the bereaved, but for herself. She had given ten years of first housemaid then nursemaid service to Mrs. McKay; a decade in the hope of getting a comfortable pension out of the will or just a nice tidy lump sum to see her over the next few years.

And what did I get? A bit of manky costume jewelry and a 'thank you for your service' letter. Bloody old cat-lady bitch!

So she cried over the grave, bitter tears of anger. She was still there, head bowed, after everyone else had moved away from the graveside. It was only then that she spoke.

"I killed your cats after the reading of the will," she said softly and with some relish. "All of them. Just a wee drink of the milk with some special sauce added. They lapped it up just fine, then I put them in plastic bags, and they got taken away with the garbage. I just wanted you to know that."

She smiled thinly. It was a small victory, but the only one she was going to get. She was about to turn to leave when she felt a hand on her shoulder.

"I know it's hard, lass," a soft voice said. "But she's gone to a better place."

She expected to see the Presbyterian minister who'd officiated at the service, but turned to see a small, wiry, somewhat disheveled man, gray haired, moist eyed and wearing a heavy tweed suit that had seen its best days before Wendy had taken up in Mrs. McKay's service.

"I'm sorry," she said, "do I know you?"

"No, lass," he said. "She sent me to fetch you."

He nodded towards the open grave.

"You know who I mean. You can see her again, if you'd like."

Wendy had been scheming on her own behalf for long enough to spot a con job when she saw one. She also knew that when you spotted a con, there was usually a way to swing it to your advantage if you played it right. She stayed in character, the bereaved nursemaid looking for comfort, and let the man leave his hand on her shoulder, even leaning slightly in towards him, giving him the impression that more contact might be available if he wanted it. The man looked like he might want it so she gave him a pathetic, near to fainting flutter of the eyes and that did the trick just fine.

"Can I get you a cup of tea, lass?" he said. "You look like you could do with one. The house is just over the other side of the cemetery. Say you'll come? It would give me a chance to explain myself."

Before she could answer, he sneezed and took his hand from her shoulder.

"Sorry, allergies," he said. "You must have a cat."

More cats than I ever wanted, she thought. *And now that they're gone, I wouldn't care if I never saw another one in my life.*

She let the man lead her away as the groundskeepers moved to start filling the grave. She never looked back.

The house he showed her to was one of the old two storey Victorian sandstone buildings that lined the shore along the lochside. Its imposing gray frontage had been built to stand up to the inclement weather that washed off the loch three seasons of the year. The front window of a sitting room looked out over the loch itself, but the man led Wendy through the back to a dining room. A large bay window looked up the hill at the old cemetery they had just left.

She could just make out the red and yellow flowers waiting to be laid on the grave when the diggers had filled over the coffin with earth and sod. He left her with the view and went through a door to the kitchen, where she heard water running, cups rattling, and him sneezing.

He's making sure I have a good long look at the grave. This is another part of the con.

"Sorry," he said again when he finally returned with a tray, a teapot, two cups and a small plate of chocolate biscuits. "You must think I'm awful, accosting you at the graveside like that. But she's coming through very strong, you see?"

He sneezed again at that. His head tilted to one side, as if listening.

"She says it's just fat old George," he said. "She says he's always molting."

He's good, Wendy thought. *He'll be asking for money soon.*

She fed him what she thought he'd expect to hear.

"She always was very fond of her cats."

"Yes, that's why she left all her money to the charity. She says she knew you would understand."

Wendy almost choked on her tea at that but managed to regain her composure.

He hasn't done his research as well as he thought. Firstly, I'm not an easy mark, and secondly, I understand just fine...I understand the old bitch is exactly where she deserves to be...and so are her cats.

Even while she was thinking it, the man across the table sneezed again, just as something warm and hairy brushed past Wendy's ankle. She looked around for a cat but there was no sign of one. The gray-haired man smiled.

"I told you she was coming through strong."

Wendy wasn't sure now whether she actually had the upper hand here. The man was just sitting, sipping tea, and smiling at her. He hadn't asked for money, and the trick with the cat brushing her leg was so good she couldn't see how he'd done it. She decided to drop the subterfuge.

"Look," she said, "thanks for the tea and all that. But I don't know what your game is here. I do know that you won't get a penny out of me."

He smiled across the table at her and opened his hands, showing her his empty palms.

Look, there's nothing up my sleeves. He's either very good or I'm losing my touch.

"I don't want your money, lass," the man said. "I don't want anything from you. She does, though, if you'll talk to her. She's upstairs in the back bedroom, and she wants a word."

"Who wants a word?"

"You know who it is that I'm talking about," he said. "And I think there are things you want to say to her, aren't there? Things that have been left unspoken?"

I said all I have to say at the graveside, thank you very much.

"What are you, some kind of wee pretendy medium?"

He smiled again.

"I'm not a wee pretendy anything, lass," he said. "I'm just the housekeeper. The house itself is in charge here."

She couldn't make much sense of that. Now she was thinking it wasn't a con at all, that the small man was clearly insane and she'd allowed herself to walk into his delusion. But, as she stood to leave, a voice she could never forget called out from somewhere upstairs.

"Wendy, darling? Is that you? Fetch me my glass of warm milk would you, there's a dear."

"Okay, that's quite enough of this bullshit," Wendy said to the man across the table. "It's a very good trick, I'll give you that much. But I've told you, you won't get a penny out of me."

He just smiled and showed her his open palms again.

"It's not me you should be telling, lass" he said. "I just look after the house."

She turned and left the room, meaning to head for the front door, but stopped at the foot of the stairs, listening. She heard two soft thumps and knew exactly what she had just heard—two cats, probably her pride and joy, the leaders of the pack, George and Mildred, jumping down off the bed where their mistress sat up reading a Mills and Boon romance.

"Wendy?" the voice shouted again, muffled as if coming through a shut door. She'd been obeying that voice for too long to ignore it now. Without any real conscious thought, she made her way quickly upstairs to the landing at the top. There were four doors off, but only one was shut. A shadow moved in the small gap between door and floor, something low and squat and fat—George again. A radio played softly on the other side of the door, Paul Anka, one of Mrs. McKay's favorites.

"Well don't just stand there, girl. Fetch me my milk," the voice demanded.

I've come too far not to look. But it's a trick. It has to be.

Before she could talk herself out of it, she stepped forward, turned the door handle, and pushed the door open.

The room was totally empty, bare floorboards, an uncovered light bulb covered in spider webs hanging from a ceiling, no curtains on the window that overlooked the graveyard and the long cold remnants of a fire behind an old wrought iron grate.

Something warm and furry brushed against Wendy's leg.

Mrs. McKay whispered, right beside her ear, "Where's my milk?"

Ten seconds later, she was back down at the table across from the gray-haired man, letting him pour her a stiff measure of scotch that she took with trembling hands.

"It was her. It was really her," she said.

"Yes," was all the man said.

But it can't be. I killed her, killed her dead, and she didn't even leave me a penny.

She spoke, mainly to give herself time to recover her nerve.

"So what's the deal? What's going on here?"

He poured himself a stiff drink before starting.

"I'll have to give you the speech. Everybody gets the speech," he said, then spoke as if reciting by rote.

"There are houses like this all over the world. Most people only know of them from whispered stories over campfires; tall tales told to scare the unwary," he went on. "But some of us, those who suffer…some of us know better. We are drawn to the places, the loci if you like, where what ails us can be eased. Yes, dead is dead, as it was and always will be. But there are other worlds than these, other possibilities. And if we have the will, the fortitude, we can peer into another life where the dead are not gone, where we can see that they thrive and go on. And as we watch, we can, sometimes, gain enough peace for ourselves that we too can thrive, and go on.

"You will want to know more than why. You will want to know how. I cannot tell you that. None of us has ever known, only that the houses are the sources of the powers that flow through them. That is the constant here."

"But I heard her!"

"See her, hear her, whatever the house chooses to give to you, you will receive. You have only had the first taste. But before you can delve farther into the mysteries, there's something else."

Ah, I knew he was going to ask for money.

But he surprised her again.

"If you want to come back, you need to bring a totem, something that connects you to the departed. And you'll need to get a sigil," he said. He rolled up his sleeve to show her a small, perfectly detailed rose on his inner arm. "It has to be something meaningful to the both of you. For proper contact to be established here in this place, you need to get inked."

"And what happens if I don't?"

"Then you'll never make full contact. You need the totem and the ink, the sigil. Those are the house rules. Without both, the house will not accept you as a guest."

Maybe I don't accept the house? But this doesn't feel like a con, is there anything in it for me?

"Do you get many people coming 'round for this…service? Is it a service?" Wendy asked.

"More than a few, less than a lot," he said. "Some regulars only come for an hour or so at a time, just to replenish cherished memories. Some others take a room for a night, a week, even months at a stretch. The house provides."

"And you don't charge for this?"

He showed her his empty palms again.

"I'm just the housekeeper."

Wendy was starting to get an inkling of an idea.

Maybe there is something here for me after all.

It took her several months to put the complete plan into action. Of course, she didn't get a tattoo; the very thought of getting permanently marked in pursuit of a con was repugnant to her. She faked it and got a decal of a cat, one that could be washed off easily after she'd showed it, quickly, so fast he couldn't tell it wasn't inked, to the man in the house. She also took along the cheap necklace Mrs. McKay left to her as her so-called totem.

"I want you to cherish it. It belonged to my mum," the old lady had said, but to Wendy's eye it looked like something that might have come from Woolworth in the sixties.

The man thought it to be appropriate though. She found out his name—Graeme Barclay—on that same second visit and started her seduction there and then.

Over the coming weeks, she made regular trips to the house but always avoided going back upstairs.

"I'm not ready yet," she would plead. "I want to be sure everything is right."

Every so often, she'd feel a non-existent cat brush her legs or hear a voice call from above, but such things were easy to ignore. She had her mind on a higher purpose.

Graeme Barclay proved to be a soft touch, malleable to her every wile. She didn't even have to take him to her bed—he was old fashioned enough to want to save all that stuff for marriage, and that was a topic they hadn't got around to—yet. By the end of the second month of her campaign, she had him wound around her little finger.

"Darling," she would say when a new 'guest' was being introduced to the house's secrets. "Can I sit in?"

At first, and for a few weeks afterwards, he refused her, but she was nothing if not persistent and eventually he came around—he even came to think of it as his idea, such were her powers of persuasion. She learned 'the speech', learned how to appear properly solemn and although Graeme was genuinely empathetic towards the house's guests, she was able to fake it so well that none of them ever noticed.

The only thing he balked at was her request to start charging the guests for their visits. She suggested a sliding scale from an hour to months that would be on a level similar to a hotel stay of equal length.

"But we're not a hotel, dear," he would say as if explaining it to a child. "We are not even a boarding house. We're just housekeepers. You said it yourself that first day. We are providing a service. But I see it more as a calling, a ministry. I couldn't possibly debase that by asking for payment."

Well, I see it as a cash cow going to waste, she thought but never said. She bided her time.

Her plan came to near completion when Graeme proposed marriage; he also thought that was his idea. Their trip to the registry office took place four months to the day from their meeting in the graveyard. There was no honeymoon; the house needed its keeper on a full-time basis, but they consummated their vows that same night. Wendy insisted on keeping the lights off and traditionalist Graeme did not quibble, although he might have had he been given enough light to see that there was no sign of a tattoo on his new wife's arm.

After that it was a matter of taking things slow and easy; the hard part was done. Every night she brought Graeme a drink of warm milk and whisky, and if there was a little bit of something extra in it every night, he neither noticed nor complained. The part of old lady McKay that lived upstairs got increasingly noisy, and it sometimes sounded like there was a whole herd of cats up there with her, but that was all mere background. Wendy never went up into the back room. Graeme had his house and a new wife, and if he was happy, she would pretend to be happy with him...for however long he had left.

Guests kept arriving; some stayed a few nights, some left happy after only a couple of hours. None of them paid and that rankled sore with Wendy, although she never let it show because it was obvious to anyone with eyes to see that Graeme was not long for this world. His health had started to downturn as autumn turned to winter, and by the time the first ice of the year stretched across the loch, he was a pale shadow of the man he had been the previous summer.

"Don't you dare drink my milk," Mrs. McKay shouted from upstairs, and a thunder of tiny feet echoed above as the spectral cats ran amok. Wendy and Graeme were so used to the noise from the back room that neither of them paid it any heed.

"I think I need to see a doctor," Graeme said one day in January.

"Whatever you think best, dear," Wendy said. "It's probably just a virus. There's one going 'round."

The doctors found Graeme's blood wasn't thick enough to sustain him and put him on an ever-strengthening regime of medication but all to no avail. Wendy could have told them they needed to look at what was lurking in his nightly milk, the stuff you use to keep the rats down, but she kept that to herself behind eyes she ensured looked increasingly concerned.

Knowing that he was gravely ill, Graeme insisted the house deeds be redrawn with her name added. He gave her similar access to his bank accounts, which were much better appointed than she could even have hoped. Indeed, she wouldn't need the money that might come in from charging guests. But her plan was too far along, Graeme too far gone, to back down now.

Besides, extra cash is extra cash, whichever way it comes.

Near the end, Graeme had one last wish of her.

"Bury me in the cemetery, darling," he said. "Bury me where you can see me from the window and I can watch over you."

She agreed, willingly. It was a small price to pay for what was coming to her.

He reached into his waistcoat pocket, took out a small, thin, gold ring, and put it on her left middle finger.

"This was my grandmother's," he said. "And it's your token for me. With this and your tattoo together, they will ensure I'll be here in the house, always with you."

She left it on—it looked good on her finger.

For now. I can always hock it later. It looks antique. It's worth more than old lady McKay's manky costume jewelry in any case.

The old lady called out for more milk from upstairs, the cats continued their berserk running in circles on the floor above, and Wendy smiled sadly at a husband who barely had the energy to smile back.

It won't be long now.

Graeme passed away peacefully in hospital in late February with Wendy at his bedside, holding his hand. She took herself away shopping in Edinburgh between his death and the funeral and didn't intend to return to the house until after the small, quiet ceremony in the cemetery above the loch.

She looked down at the coffin while the minister droned on, only looking up once, straight at the house, then looking away quickly. There had been movement at the upstairs window, a pale, round face smiling out at her. She lowered her gaze to the lower room window, half-expecting to see Graeme waiting for her to come home, but, thankfully, the downstairs looked empty and quiet.

I can only hope it stays that way.

Some of the house's guests came up to her to pay their respects, and Wendy kept up her grieving widow act for their benefit, knowing full well the next time she saw them, she would be asking them for money. She spent the short walk back adding up figures in her head as to how much extra per month she would be able to squeeze out of the house's 'services.' That prospect meant she had a small smile on her face as she strode down to the lochside and into the house.

Something didn't feel right; she knew that as soon as she stepped through the door. She heard a clattering of cups, a rush of running water from through in the kitchen. The thin gold ring Graeme had given her felt warm on her finger, but when she tried, she couldn't pull the thing off. The distinctive whistle of a boiling kettle echoed throughout the downstairs area.

"Hello?" she said, aware of the tremor in her voice. "Is somebody there?"

A sneeze joined the sound of the whistling kettle, and Wendy felt something warm and furry move against her leg.

"Graeme?"

She knew what she was going to see as soon as she entered the kitchen; Graeme, her dead husband Graeme, stood at the cooker, pouring boiling water into a teapot.

"I buried you," she whispered.

Upstairs, old lady McKay cackled loudly and shouted, "Don't forget the milk."

"Graeme," she whispered as the man put the teapot down on the work surface and turned towards her. The gold ring on her finger flared in heat, but she only had eyes for the man across the room. He opened his hands, palms outwards in the well-known gesture, and pulled up his sleeve to show her the rose tattooed there. She saw the query in his eyes.

I've showed you mine. Now you show me yours.

As he stepped forward, she turned and fled.

His shout followed her out to hallway. "The house will not accept you as a guest."

Her only thought was to reach the front door and flee out into the road, but when she touched the handle, it flared in red heat, scorching her palm. The thin gold ring on her finger gave out a blazing light as it too flared, growing too warm, burning her skin until it smoked, scorched black around the base of the finger and up to the first knuckle. Wendy whimpered, reached for the door again, but it was too hot to touch.

Something slammed, hard, upstairs shaking the whole house, and she knew immediately what it was.

The upstairs door's open.

"Wendy? What in blazes has got into you, girl. Where's my damned milk?"

Old lady McKay appeared at the top of the stairs, her white nightgown billowing as if in a strong wind. Wendy's brain was close to shutting down by this point, but she had enough sense left to see that the old woman floated six inches above the top step. Her cats crowded, a furry, squirming pile at her back, fat George's wet smile leering down from between her legs, Mildred licking her lips beside him.

"Where's my bloody milk!" Mrs. McKay shouted.

"Graeme," Wendy whispered as her husband came out of the kitchen into the hall. "Do something. Do something, please?"

He showed her his palms again.

"What can I do? I'm just the housekeeper, and you're not even a guest."

"Where's my bloody milk!" Mrs. McKay bellowed again, and came floating down the stairs.

Wendy pressed her back to the door trying to wish herself to freedom on the other side, but there was nowhere to go, no way to escape as the cats came down in a flood alongside their mistress.

She quickly found out they were all, cats and mistress and housekeeper, very hungry.

Russian Dollhouse

by Jason Parent

Kit glared at her brother. She couldn't see through the mesh eyes of his Power Ranger mask, but she knew he was glaring right back at her, ruining everything, just like he always did. Well, like he *sometimes* did.

For the past three years, she'd been stuck taking the little shit trick-or-treating. Okay, she hadn't minded taking Cole—actually Nicola, but their parents, who'd opted to name them Nikita and Nicola in the first place, had tired of having two children respond to the first-syllable nickname, so they'd moved on to the second. In fact, she'd enjoyed dressing up with him, and together, they'd cultivated an entire patch of plastic pumpkins gorged with candy. Kit had taught her brother where all the best houses were, where people gave out the full-sized bars, and where those who gave out crap like Smarties and Fruit Roll-Ups or the dreaded Good & Plenties lived.

But that year, she wouldn't be caught dead in some cheap-ass princess or mermaid costume their smelly grandmother had made. No, a mask would mess up her thick blond hair, which she'd spent hours curling, and cover her cherry-red-lipsticked lips, and she hoped those lips would finally taste Jordan Ballard's before that night was over.

But Jordan would never kiss her with Snot-Nosed-Bug-Face hanging around. She let out a groan, Cole still staring up at her. "All right." She sighed. "Let's get this over with."

"Yay!" Cole bounced and punched at the air, his empty plastic pumpkin swinging on his wrist.

Kit couldn't help but smile. After all, she did love the little shit. She crouched in front of him; her growth spurt had hit hard, and his was still some years away. "All right, ninja man. You know the rules. You don't need to hold my hand, but you've gotta stay close." She stood and put her hands on her hips. "Got it?"

Cole nodded.

"Okay. And make sure you save me a Reese's. A big one, not one of those minis."

Cole nodded again.

Kit smirked. "Well? What are you waiting for?"

She grabbed the back of Cole's costume just before he could dash out into the street. "Stay close," she reminded him, not that he was in any danger. The street was empty of cars but loaded with trick-or-treaters. Halloween's heyday had returned to their neighborhood as new families with young children moved in all around their house.

Her father had lived in the same house his whole life. Kit's parents had bought their home from her live-in grandmother, who knew the comings and goings of the neighborhood for the better part of a century. "Neighborhoods have short memories," Kit's dad had said, recounting how Halloween had died there when he was a kid after some children, the urban-legendary Alderman twins and a couple other kids whose names and genders changed with each telling, went missing.

Kit took in the bustling street. *This might be the busiest Halloween ever.* As she breathed in the cool night air and watched as hordes of dragons and monsters and, of course, enough princesses to make Disney World jealous ran amok, she almost wished she'd allowed Grandma to make her a costume that year, something a little more grown up but still pretty—something Jordan would like.

Jordan. She sighed and checked her cellphone for any missed calls but saw none. By the time she snapped herself away from thoughts of her hopefully soon-to-be boyfriend's dazzling blue eyes, strong arms, and sweet lips she wanted so desperately pressed against hers, Cole was three houses down the road.

She laughed. *He plays to win. I'll give him that.*

By the time she caught up to him, Cole was sprinting across a yard to the next house. They were closing in on Waterford Lane, which had no streetlights and, aside from the homes at the corner of Simon and Waterford, also had no houses. Except for one, set way down the lane and deep into its yard, nestled in woods. No one had lived there since before Kit was born. Her dad couldn't remember anyone actually living there, and her grandma wouldn't speak of the place.

The house, an old colonial, was condemned. Boards covered every window. Caution tape and a notice of condemnation covered its door. Its wood was the color of ash, shaded in such a way that made the house loom darker than the night itself on that unlit lane. Every teenager had seen it. Most had been dared to enter it. But as far as Kit knew, no one ever had. Even the homeless people downtown chose bus shelters and park benches over squatting there. Why the house had never been torn down was anyone's guess, but Kit aligned herself with the theory that it was some kind of historical landmark.

For trick-or-treating purposes, Waterford Lane marked the turn-around point. Kit and Cole would work their way back up the other side of the street then bear left onto Kinsey Road. As they approached the quiet lane, husks of leaves clattered across the pavement, breaking apart in the cold wind. The last streetlight on Simon flickered and hummed, occasionally crackling like a bug zapper. Beyond was a pitch-black landscape under barren pines that stabbed at the sky.

Somewhere behind those dying sticks, somewhere beyond where the lane curved and came to its dead end, the abandoned house squatted in isolation. The thought of it sitting there, somehow conscious of Kit's nearness, sent a shudder through her.

"Rarrrrr!"

Kit yelped, her heart leaping against its cage. She turned and faced a small, rail-thin boy in a rubber werewolf mask. Tilting her head to the side, she said, "Screw you, Pedro."

Pedro pulled off the mask, revealing a smile loaded with metal. "Oh, I got you. I got you good."

"Don't mind him," another boy said, approaching from behind her. "His parents keep him in a cage most of the time, so he doesn't get out much."

Jordan! Kit almost clapped but focused instead on wiping the goofy grin off her face before turning around. She bit into her lower lip and looked up shyly, unable to meet his gaze for long before having to look away. "Hi, Jordan," she said, her voice barely more than a whisper. She swayed her shoulder forward and back as she twisted on her toes.

When she found the nerve to look up again, Jordan was only inches from her. A sophomore and already varsity, he looked clean and beautiful in his yellow-and-black letterman's jacket.

At his elbow stood that bitch Melissa, with all her tats and piercings making her look like a punk band's groupie or a horror-movie reject. She was forever hanging at Kit's man's heels, always trying to steal Jordan away from her.

If she hadn't thrown up a timid wave, Kit might not have noticed Tabby, who was cuter than a mouse and quieter than a dead one, hanging back like she always did. With her glasses and short, straight hair, she looked a lot like Velma from *Scooby-Doo*, and the thick turtleneck she wore did little to distance her from the comparison. She'd been Kit's best friend since kindergarten, but Kit was starting to wonder whether Tabby was holding her back in her quest for freshman-class status and Jordan's undying love.

"What—" Kit's voice squeaked. She cleared her throat. "What are you guys doing here?"

Jordan smiled, his two rows of perfect teeth glistening in the moonlight. "We were headed in your direction and thought we'd surprise you."

"Yeah," Pedro said, pulling his mask back down. "We're seeing what kind of mischief we can get into post-Mischief Night." He held a plastic bag open in front of him, revealing a carton of eggs. "We're going to egg that old house at the end of Waterford."

"Why would you egg *that* house?" Cole asked. "Nobody lives there."

Kit frowned, remembering her charge. How long he'd been standing there, listening, she didn't know.

"See?" Melissa laughed. "Even the little kid's smarter than you, Pedro."

Pedro snatched the plastic pumpkin right out of Cole's hand. "What you got in here, kid? Anything good?"

"Hey!" Cole whined and reached for his pumpkin. "Give that back!"

"Hold on, hold on." Pedro pulled out a Three Musketeers bar. "I'm just gonna take one. Three Musketeers, see? Nobody likes them anyway."

Kit glowered. "They're actually his favorite."

"I'm sorry," Pedro mumbled as he jammed the whole bar into his mouth. He gave the pumpkin back to Cole. "I can't help it. I'm always hungry."

"Maybe you have a tapeworm," Cole said, still sulking and sifting through his candy bowl.

"I don't have a tapeworm."

Kit crossed her arms and studied her classmates. "So, what are you really doing here?"

Jordan pointed at Pedro. "*He's* going to egg that house. We," he said, throwing his thumbs over his shoulders, "just want to check it out. Want to come?" He raised an eyebrow in a way that always made the butterflies in her stomach multiply through mitosis—or was it meiosis?—like she'd learned in biology class. She could feel them fluttering and thought she would die right then and there if they gave her gas. That bitch Melissa would probably tell the whole school.

"I can't." Kit pouted. "I have to watch Bugface."

"I'm not Bugface." Cole raised his fists. "I'm a Power Ranger!"

Kit turned to Tabby. "You're up for that?"

"Not really." Tabby squinted and grinned in a way that made her look as though she were in pain or related to Robert DeNiro. "Just didn't have anything else to do."

She looked at Jordan and raised a finger. "One moment." After ordering her brother to stay put, she shuffled Tabby aside. "Can you take my brother trick or treating? He knows the route. All you have to do is follow him."

Tabby pursed her lips. "I don't know…"

"Come on!" Kit grabbed her by the arms. "My parents love you, sometimes I think more than me. Cole loves you. This is my chance to finally kiss Jordan before Melissa can move in. And you don't *really* want to go to that house."

"I don't, but—"

"Great! Then it's settled." Taking Tabby by the hand, she led her back to the group. "Tabby is going to take Cole trick-or-treating as my stand-in. We'll all meet back at my house after." She bumped Jordan with her shoulder, her hands buried in her pockets. "I'm all yours."

They turned and started walking down Waterford. In only a few steps, Jordan's hand found hers. She knew there was a reason she always loved Halloween.

Behind her, her brother asked, "Where are they going?"

"Just down the street," Tabby answered. "They'll be back in a bit, but in the meantime, you and I are going to fill that pumpkin to the brim."

"Don't worry. I got extras." His voice barely audible, Cole said, "But they shouldn't go that way. Grandma says we should never go down there."

Kit smirked then looked away, a twinge of guilt sprouting as she pawned off her responsibility for her brother. At least she knew Tabby would take good care of him.

They walked in silence under a giant moon, a massive golf ball falling toward an earthen fairway. Kit kicked rocks over the cement, her sweaty fingers interlocked with Jordan's.

Pedro spoiled the moment by sprinting ahead, howling at the moon like the werewolf he purported to be. He ran far ahead, rounded the curve in the lane, and disappeared behind the trees.

Then he fell silent.

"Pedro?" Kit called.

No answer.

"He's just trying to scare us," Melissa said. "It never gets old to him."

"Yeah." Jordan chuckled. "The jerk's got like a hundred hiding places up there. We'll never be able to guess which tree he'll jump out from behind."

Though Kit couldn't say why, Pedro's silence bothered her. She knew Jordan and Melissa were probably right—Pedro was always doing stupid shit. He'd just spent last week in detention for bringing a tarantula to school and nearly giving arachnophobic Mrs. Taylor a heart attack, not to mention Jordan, who'd tried to act tough but apparently suffered from the same affliction. She half expected to hear him break out giggling and howling like a madman as he jumped out at them. But she didn't hear so much as a twig snap up ahead. Then she understood what had unnerved her.

It wasn't that *Pedro* was silent. The entire woods was a vacuum void of sound beyond their footsteps and the sizzle of hot breath on cold air. The world was still, maybe frozen, and it was the first time Kit noticed the cold.

The night darkened, and the trees seeming to jut higher as they neared them, lancing out the light. Moonlight cast the lane in shades of blue that reached over the grass to the tree line, where black swallowed everything.

Kit leaned in closer to Jordan, who let go of her hand and placed his arm around her. She shuddered. "It's cold. Maybe we should head back."

"It's just a little farther." He gave her a squeeze. "Let's let Pedro have his joke, and then we'll head back."

"What's so magical about this house, anyway?" Melissa asked, coming up alongside Jordan.

"I know you just moved here last year, but I'm surprised you never heard about it." Jordan hunched, beckoning the others closer as if what he had to tell was some big secret. "The house is a local legend. Long story short, some kids went missing something like thirty years ago and were supposedly last seen entering this house."

"Do you believe it?" Melissa batted her eyelashes and feigned interest in a way that made Kit want to stab her.

"Nah." Jordan scoffed. "Every old house earns a story if it's allowed to sit empty long enough."

They continued on around the bend where Pedro stood. His back was to them, the long ears of the werewolf mask sticking out like antenna from a mat of black hair. He wasn't moving. A few steps closer, and Kit saw why.

The old abandoned house no longer looked so old or abandoned. It had been done up for Halloween, a spectacle to rival an amusement park attraction. In the long yard before it stood row upon row of gravestones, mechanized zombie arms reaching from several of the graves. Mausoleums stood on each side of the path leading up to the house's front porch. The door to the structure on the left cracked open, and green fingers curled out around it, only to retreat into the darkness as the door slammed shut, the process repeating on a loop. Screams came from the mausoleum on the right. What looked like blood ran down a solitary window. Wilted flowers swayed in the sill beneath it.

On the porch, an empty swing rocked. Yarn cobwebs decorated every crook and corner, and their supposed owners—fat black-rubber spiders the size of bowling balls—yo-yoed on springy string. Skeletons rattled in windows, their jaws slowly unhinging then snapping shut. Holographic bats circled a chimney, from which a small plume of smoke rose. Every so often, a witch would cackle or a chainsaw would buzz from somewhere inside the house. What looked like a real black cat tiptoed across the porch railing.

"What is all this?" Melissa asked. "I thought you said it was abandoned."

"It's so beautiful," Pedro said, dropping his bag. "I don't even want to egg it anymore."

Kit just stared, dumbfounded. Something was all wrong about the house. She hadn't seen any trucks come by, hadn't heard the sounds of renovation. The shape of the house seemed the same, but it was no longer falling apart. It was as though some wizard had made what was old new again with the wave of a wand. *And all the decorations? Why?*

"I've been waiting for someone to show up," a boy called from his seat on the porch swing.

"Where the heck did he come from?" Jordan asked no one in particular. He stared at the boy with what looked like wonder.

Kit hadn't seen the boy before he'd spoken and could have sworn he hadn't been on the swing when she first looked. He wore an orange-and-black letterman's jacket not unlike Jordan's but older and grimier. His features were gaunt and frail, so much so that Kit couldn't picture him playing any sport well.

"I've been waiting here a long time," the boy said. "My friends have already gone in, but I had to wait for the next group. Now that you four are here, though, we all should be able to get in."

"Get into what?" Pedro ran up the steps and passed the boy. He peered into one of the windows. "Is this like some sort of haunted house? How much does it cost?"

The front door swung open, revealing an empty foyer with a polished wooden floor, unadorned except for a large candelabra hanging from the ceiling. Each candle in it emitted a warm orange glow.

"Cost?" The strange boy laughed and waved them into the house. "Well, you don't need any money to get in. Just step inside."

Kit held Jordan's arm a little tighter. "I'm not so sure we should—"

"Chicken," Melissa said, twirling across the threshold with Pedro right on her heels.

"That boy, he... he doesn't look right."

Jordan squeezed her back. "He's just part of the show."

"This isn't right. I mean, what's this place doing out here? Why would someone put a haunted house way out here, and why didn't any of us know about it?"

"Come on," Jordan said, pulling her forward. "This has Pedro written all over it. You know his parents are loaded and basically give him everything he wants." He shrugged. "Anyway, it could be fun."

Jordan escorted her into the house. As she passed the boy at the door, he offered her a worm-lipped grin. Though she didn't hear his footsteps follow her in, she could sense his presence, as heavy as a rain cloud, right behind her.

The door creaked shut. At the sound, Kit spun around and nearly fell atop the boy, who'd been inches from her back. He smelled of dust and something stale, like old sweat but with a metallic undertone. His eyes, deep-navy pools, were looking at her, or maybe through her.

"Dude!" Pedro bounced forward and pointed. "Check it out!"

As if spray-painted by an invisible hand, a circle appeared on the floor, red and running like blood. Spatters dotted the wood inside and outside the circle's sloppy curve. Kit's pulse quickened as the invisible spray painter continued its artwork, drawing within the circle an upside-down star.

Melissa threw back her hair, her mouth agape. "How are they doing it?"

"So cool," Pedro muttered.

Jordan put his arm around Kit and kissed her temple. Even his touch, the very thing she craved more than free period and Chris Hemsworth movies and all the Bruno Mars concerts in the world, went barely noticed as she watched the floor paint itself. The effects looked so real. They looked *too* real.

Smoke rose from the floor beside each point. The numbers one through five, charred and black, etched themselves into the wood, each corresponding to a point of the star.

"I'm number one," Pedro said, rushing for the point in front of him.

"The hell you are," Melissa said, hip-checking him as she raced for same the point. Pedro staggered, his momentum carrying him diagonally so that he nearly fell atop the "2." As his sneaker landed on it, the number lit up in a bright-red glow.

Kit's attention shifted back to Melissa, who was standing on the "1." A bright-red glow illuminated her fishnets.

"I guess that makes us three and four," Jordan said. "Unless…" He turned to the boy, who lingered by the door with arms crossed. "You don't mind, do you?"

He bowed and waved an arm in an extravagant gesture. "By all means."

"Five's closer to the three," Kit said, not wanting to let Jordan go.

"Yeah, but what if we have to pair up at some point?" Jordan smiled. "I'd rather be paired up with you than Walking Dead over there." He glanced over his shoulder. "No offense."

"None taken," the boy said, his thin-lipped smile revealing too much teeth.

After a moment's hesitation, Kit relented. She walked over to the "4" and watched it light up. As Jordan took the third spot, he said to the boy, "Well, if you're going to be joining us, we might as well know who you are. I'm Jordan. That's Kit, Pedro, and Melissa." He pointed at each in turn.

The boy made no response. Instead, he stepped on the "5."

Kit raised an eyebrow and tilted her head at Jordan, who shrugged in response. After a second, he asked the boy, "What's your name?"

The boy's brow furrowed, and he frowned. "Name? I think it was… Billy." He smiled as if he'd just delivered the answer to all life's mysteries. "Yes, Billy. That's what is was."

Kit barely had time to register the oddness of the response, when a whispering voice materialized out of nothing, airy and hissing but somehow as loud as if it spoke directly into her ear.

Your time is fleeting
And odds are slim
Best bet is to leave
For only one can win.

Pedro wiggled his fingers in the air. "Wooooooo. Spooky." He laughed.

Kit caught movement in her peripheral vision. Something rose in the corner behind her. She stepped closer to Jordan. Another something appeared in the corner nearest Pedro. She pointed. "L-L-Look!"

Everyone followed her gaze. Pedro took a step toward the growing shadow.

"There's another one over there,"

Melissa said, pointing to her left. "What are they?"

Kit spun around, spotting a rising shadow, then another and another. "There's one in every corner."

Nobody moved. Nobody said a word. As Kit watched the black mass swell and her own unease swelled with it, she shrank back into the room's center.

The things in the corners emerged out of the walls and floor. Unblinking, Kit watched one take form, two black comets with tails dangling from its head like prongs on a jester's cap. An idea came to mind, and with it, a cry rose in her throat. She swallowed hard to keep it from spewing out. *Antennae.*

At first, Kit thought the creatures might be giant roaches, but their bodies were too wiggly and shapeless. They rose slowly but continuously, reaching a height of over six feet. The one nearest Kit slowly turned. She gripped Jordan's arm a little tighter, her feet frozen to the ground.

Pedro, either the bravest or the dumbest, stepped closer to one of the creatures. It fell onto its belly and moved—no, slithered—like some giant slug or snail or worm or other creature with no business being as big as it was. Pedro inched closer. The creature rose, revealing an orange underside lined with two rows of stubby, conical protrusions that looked like the bottom of an egg carton.

Several of the protrusions leaked a substance resembling snot, none more so than two at the head of the creature, set where Kit imagined the thing's eyes should have been. Aside from the antennae and those two leaking pustules, the caterpillar-snail-thing had no recognizable facial features. Not until it rose over Pedro, and a vertical slit between its running nostrils opened to reveal a shark's maw turned sideways, lined with rows and rows of pointy teeth.

Pedro raised a finger.

"Don't touch it," Kit said, struggling to get the words out.

Pedro didn't listen. He pressed his finger into the creature's belly. "It's spongy." One of the protrusions above his finger gurgled and spat mucus onto his hand. He stepped back and shook it off. "Gross!"

The creature's head reared back. Its top two protrusions were swelling up, the nostrils opening wider.

Kit heard the creak of a door and turned around just in time to see it close. The strange boy was gone. When she looked back at Pedro, the creature in front of him moved backward like a film played in reverse. The others returned to their corners and disappeared.

"That was so cool!" Pedro laughed.

Melissa ran after one and stomped the floor where it had retreated. The sound of solid wood answered. "It's like it was never there at all," she said, trembling with excitement. "Some kind of projection?"

"But I touched it," Pedro said. "Didn't feel real, though. Rubbery, like the stuff they used to make monsters in old movies, before special effects got good. Like *Jaws* and *E.T.* and shit. Still, pretty badass."

"Guys," Kit said, trying to keep her voice from shaking. "Where'd that kid go?"

Pedro sniggered. "Probably got scared and ran off." He scoffed. "Puss."

"What happened to the windows?" Kit asked.

"What?" Jordan squinted at her.

She ignored him and ran to the front door. "There were windows here." She pointed at the wall beside it. She turned around. "Pedro, don't you remember peeking through one?"

"Yeah, but I couldn't see nothing. Now I see why: walled over on the inside. Nice touch. But... wait..." Pedro's mouth dropped open. He stared past Kit. "Wha..."

Kit turned around. The door was gone.

Above, the candelabra brightened, illuminating an empty room without doors or windows. That strange voice echoed off the walls:

To carry on
Your herd must thin
Five to four
But only one can win.
Your chance to leave
Has now departed
The worms must feed
Who'll be discarded?

A door appeared on the opposite wall from where they entered. It slowly opened, revealing a room cloaked in darkness. "I don't like this anymore," Kit said. She ran to the back wall and pushed on it. She might as well have been trying to move a mountain.

"Looks like there's only one way to go," Jordan said, a quaver in his voice, his smile not beaming with its usual confidence.

"This is so cool," Pedro said, rushing through the open doorway and vanishing into black.

Melissa shrugged. "I have to admit: it kinda is." She followed Pedro.

"Come on," Jordan urged. "It doesn't look like we have much choice."

"There's gotta be another exit," Kit pleaded. "It's like a fire hazard or something if there isn't." The irony of expecting a condemned building to be up to code was not lost on her. Still, she stared up at the ceiling, bouncing on her toes. She examined the cracks in the walls for tiny cameras, a secret panel, anything that might reveal the operators of the attraction or the emergency exit. "I want to get out now," she called. "I've had enough."

No one answered.

"Let's just try the next room." He wrapped his arm around her shoulders and smiled. "If any monsters try to bite, I'll kick their asses."

For the most part, Kit's damsel-in-distress act was just that: an act to lure in Jordan. But everything about the house—its overnight remodeling, the better-than-blockbuster-film effects, that creepy boy who had met them outside then just disappeared—wasn't right. She felt like a rat trapped in a maze—or worse, like a human trapped in a social experiment, as though she were in one of those awful "reality" television shows where people had to spend a night in a haunted house.

And velvet worms? That's what those giant slug things were, weren't they? Kit remembered how Pedro had nearly given the normally tough-as-nails Melissa a heart attack by putting one of those worms in her hair during a lesson on ambush predators in third-period biology, but that critter had been smaller than her pinky finger. *And yet Melissa charges forward. Probably not willing to let Pedro know he can get to her, not again anyway.*

Kit sighed. *Yeah, Pedro has gotta be behind all of this.* She nodded and puckered her lips, beginning to feel stupid. The worms, Pedro running up ahead and leading them to that house—maybe it was all just the elaborate prank of some bored rich kid. Kit thought he was stupid, but she had to admire his commitment to his pranks.

Taking the lead, she pulled Jordan into the next room, stepping into a sightless unknown. The door closed behind them. A candelabra alighted above them, shining its light upon a room identical to the one they had just left, albeit a little smaller. The corners came to life.

"This again?" Pedro crossed his arms. "Lame."

Melissa stuck out her tongue. "You think I don't know this is your doing? I've had nightmares about those disgusting worms ever since you put one in my hair." She walked straight toward the corner. "Well, I won't let your dumb friends get the better of me."

"I wish I could take credit for this." Pedro punched Jordan in the shoulder. "Nice work, man."

"Sure, Pedro." Jordan punched him back. "You can stop pretending. We all know you did this."

"Yeah," Melissa said, laughing. "Which one of your dumbass brothers is in this costume? Mark? I bet it's Mark." She kicked the shape emerging from the corner.

The worm sprang up to its full height, shrieking in a way that resembled a dolphin's click but higher pitched. Startled, Melissa stepped back, throwing her arms up in front of her. The worm's head reared back, and it snot-rocketed all over her.

Pedro burst out in laughter. Jordan gave an unsure chuckle. Melissa released a stream of curses. She shook out her arms, whiplashing gooey strips of the mucus-like substance against the wall and floor. "Very funny, Pedro. Very fucking funny."

She raised her fist and tried to lift her foot, but only her heel came up before the mucus suctioned it back to the floor. "Guys, I can't move." She groaned. "This isn't funny, Pe—"

The worm's mouth clamped down on her shoulder. Melissa screamed. Blood spouted from where its teeth punctured her flesh. It attracted the other three worms, which beelined toward Melissa like starved children answering a dinner bell. The one in the corner opposite her pushed between Jordan and Kit, knocking them to the floor. Its mouth severed Melissa's leg at the knee a moment later. The third latched onto her hand and the fourth onto her hip.

Pedro fell on his ass. He scampered away from the creatures on palms and soles. Kit curled into Jordan, who threw up his arm to shield from an attack that wasn't coming.

The slug-things seemed only interested in Melissa. Her screams amplified, her face ashen as she bled out. Kit got up and took a step toward Melissa, part of her aching to help, but she froze when hundreds of normal-sized worms burst forth from the cone-shaped protrusions and small pus-filled sacks about their parents' bodies. They burrowed beneath Melissa's skin.

And still Melissa screamed, somehow not yet dead as a horde of the grotesque creatures ate away at her body. Her screams stopped at last when the worm that had chewed up her hand bit off her head and swallowed it whole.

Still unable to move, no longer clinging to the hope that she was merely the victim of some twisted joke, Kit fought back panic and tears. Pedro covered his eyes, mumbling something over and over again about it not being real. Jordan remained seated on the floor where the worm had knocked him, his eyes fixed on empty space.

The worms, big and small, slowly retreated to their corners. Jordan gasped and crab-walked backward as the worm that had knocked him over slid by, a trail of blood and mucus left in its wake. Kit shuddered as it passed.

The creatures returned to the shadows, and the candelabra brightened. Kit slowly took in the room. It was empty, save for the three of them, Melissa's severely mangled remains, and streaks of blood and gore leading to each corner.

For a long while, the three survivors remained silent.

"Wh-Wh-What the fuck, Pedro!" Jordan's voice startled Kit from the safe space inside her to which she'd withdrawn.

"Me?" Pedro hugged himself closely. "I didn't do... *that*!" He pointed at the half-eaten corpse. "D-D-Do you think she's dead?"

"Her fucking head is gone!"

"Maybe it's some sort of trick. You know, special effects... trick photography..." Kit needed to believe it had to be. Her mind could think of no other way to make sense of what she had just seen. "Maybe she's doing this, getting a little payback for what you did to her in biology, Pedro."

"That was just a joke!" Pedro paced the room. As he ran his fingers through his hair, he knocked the mask he had perched on the top of his head to the ground. He didn't seem to notice he'd done it. "Those things are harmless to humans."

"Do they look like they're fucking harmless?" Jordan said, taking a step toward the body. "This is no trick photography, Kit." He ran his hands over his milky face. "They took her fucking head!"

Something about the boys' panic made Kit angry but surprisingly calmer. "Let's just think for a moment. We don't know—"

A door appeared on the wall opposite them. She spun around and saw that the door they'd passed through earlier was gone.

Four down to three
All wrapped up in sin
Have they figured out yet
The way out is in?
The mannequins dance
With each move you make
Yours to control
Whose life they will take.

"Who are you?" Kit circled the floor. "What do you want from us?"

The door opened. Kit peered into the darkness that awaited them.

"What do we do?" Pedro asked.

"How the hell should I know?" Jordan answered. He frowned then gasped. "Wait!" He patted himself down as if bugs were crawling all over him. At last, he pulled his phone from a back pocket. After staring at the screen and hitting a few buttons, he threw it against the wall.

"What?" Kit pulled her own phone from her pocket. The screen was black. She tried to power it on, certain she'd charged it before leaving the house. The phone remained dead. "What the hell?"

"Mine, too," Pedro said. "It's like this place just sucked the life right out of it."

Jordan took a deep breath. "Maybe we should just wait here. This room seems safe enough now."

"Safe?" Pedro threw up his arms in disgust. "What if those things come back? I don't know about you, but I'm not sticking around to get eaten." He started toward the door.

"Wait," Kit said, grabbing his arm. He shook it free, but she stepped in front of him. She raised her hands, palms out, showing him she meant no harm. "I think Jordan's right. Think about it. That voice we heard, those stupid rhymes…it's like we walked into some sicko's game. So far, we've only made it to the next room when one of us"— she swallowed—"left the group."

"I'd hardly say Melissa *left* the group." Pedro's nostrils flared, his eyes darting about the room. "In fact, parts of her are still with us."

"You know what I mean." Kit took a deep breath. "That creepy kid left the first room, and we moved on to the second. Melissa died in the second room, and whoever's doing this wants us to move on to the third. I say we stop playing his stupid game and just wait here for the police to come looking. I bet we only have to wait a few hours tops before my parents get worried and coerce Tabby into telling them where we went." She nodded, her chin quivering. "Tabby's no good at keeping secrets."

"Sounds right to me," Jordan said.

Pedro paced a moment longer then stopped. "Okay."

A rumble came from behind them. The back wall began to move.

Jordan ran to it, followed by Kit then Pedro. Together, they pressed their palms flat against it and pushed off their toes with all their might. The wall's progress never halted.

When the wall had cut the room in half, the three gave up. Jordan wiped his brow. "Looks like we don't have a choice." He looked at Kit. "Yeah?"

She nodded.

"This is so fucked up," Pedro said, turning toward the door.

Jordan took Kit's hand. Kit took Pedro's. Side by side, they squeezed into the next room.

A candelabra lit up the darkness. The room was noticeably smaller than the last, no bigger than the average hotel room. Seeing that it was empty, they walked to its center. Kit examined the corners. One second, she saw nothing. In the next, thin wooden mannequins appeared in three of the four corners. The corner matching that where Melissa had died remained empty.

The mannequins' arms ended in bayonets. Their faces, as bald and smooth as the rest of them, somehow seemed to be looking at them.

"Uh, guys…" Kit let go of the boys' hands and blocked their paths with her arms. "Don't move."

"Mannequins." Pedro's breath came short and fast. "Why did it have to be mannequins? It's like whoever's doing this knows our biggest fears."

"What do you mean?" Jordan asked.

"When I was little, I played hide-and-seek with my mom at a department store, except she didn't know I signed her up to play. I hid in the center of one of those circular racks and stayed real quiet. Eventually, I nodded off. My mom thought I'd been kidnapped." He sighed. "When I finally woke up, the place was empty. All the lights were off. I went up to the first person I saw to ask where my mom had gone, but the person had no face. I screamed and ran, only to bump into another faceless person. Mannequins, of course, but I was too young to know better. Really messed me up. I hid until an employee found me the next morning, crying in a break room cupboard. I've been scared to death of mannequins ever since. Just like Melissa was afraid of those worms."

"That's…" Jordan scratched his head. "That's impossible. How could they know that?"

"Is it? It's this house, man. It's always been messed up. *It* knows, man. This house knows everything."

"You're not making any sense. I bet that boy is doing this. That shitty poet's voice even kinda sounds like his. How could the house—"

"Shhh!" Kit had only been half listening. While the meatheads were talking, she had been studying the mannequins and their slight and sporadic movements. With a theory in mind, she swung her arm. The mannequin in the front-right corner lurched forward.

Pedro jumped. The mannequin in the back-left corner took a step toward Jordan. Jordan slowly backpedaled away, and the mannequin in the back-right corner charged at Kit.

"Nobody move! Nobody move!" To Kit's surprise, the boys actually listened. She let out a breath. "It's like the limerick said: when we move, they move. We're controlling who they kill."

"How do you know that?" Pedro asked.

"I was watching them from the start. If I'm right, when I move"— she gestured with her eyes toward the mannequin closest to Pedro— "that mannequin moves toward you." Gesturing again, she said, "When you move, that mannequin moves toward Jordan, and when Jordan moves, that one moves toward me."

"So, what do you think we should do?" Jordan asked.

"Stick to the original plan." She relaxed her arms. "Nobody move."

Pedro ran his fingers through his hair. One of the mannequins inched toward Jordan. "No, no. I don't like this." He began to pace.

"Stop moving!" Kit shouted. She took a step toward Pedro.

"Guys," Jordan said, his palms out at his sides. "We all need to calm down."

"Calm down?" Pedro scowled, still pacing. "Easy for you to say. What's to stop you two from teaming up on me, huh? First, that kid vanishes. Then, Melissa's head gets bitten off. I know I ain't doing this. And even if you're not behind it, I can see the looks you two give each other. You're planning something." He paced faster. "You're planning on making it to the next room without me!"

As he paced, the mannequins drew closer. Kit hadn't noticed just how close the one behind Jordan had gotten to him until the mannequin's arm drew back to strike.

She sprinted the four steps between her and Jordan and tackled her boyfriend to the ground. Two people screamed, and as she landed on top of her would-be boyfriend, she realized one of them had been her. Blood dripped from a gash along the back of her head, where both hair and skin had been snipped. What remained of her blond curls quickly darkened and matted.

She looked down at Jordan, who stared up past her, his eyes wide in terror. He didn't move and didn't make a sound. After a moment, through pursed lips, he whispered, "It's right above you."

Kit grabbed onto his jacket and rolled them both to the side. The mannequin's blade thumped into the ground where they'd lain. They got up and backed away from it, an easy task, as its movements were slow and stilted. Behind it, though, a second mannequin was moving much faster. Kit threw her arms around Jordan and held him still. The mannequin froze.

"Oh shit... Pedro," Jordan said. He could see over her shoulder, likely saw what she already knew to be true but didn't yet have the nerve to look. She buried her face in Jordan's jacket.

He started to pull away, but she held him tight. "Don't move. Not until they start to back off."

Jordan waited a second then pushed her off him. He ran to his friend's side.

Kit turned around just in time to see the point of the mannequin's blade retract from Pedro's chest and out his back. The mannequin returned to its corner, where it vanished into shadow.

Jordan checked for a pulse, crouching and putting two fingers to the side of Pedro's neck. His eyes filled with tears. "I don't really know how to do this."

Kit placed her hand on his shoulder and said softly, "He's dead, Jordan."

He slapped her hand away, stood, and reeled to face her. "And that's your fault, isn't it? The mannequin that killed him... It was tied to your movements, wasn't it?"

Kit stared at her feet and began to cry, but then the hurt, the betrayal, rose up inside her with maddening fury. "I killed him when I saved *your* life, you selfish asshole!"

The anger melted away from Jordan's face. His cheeks flushed red. "I-I-I'm sorry." He stepped toward her. "How's your head? Let me have a loo—"

From three to two
Our fun's nearly done
Now two of you
Soon only one.
Let's finish our game
How time really flies
The choice is all yours
Who lives and who dies?

A doorway appeared. Jordan roared, raising his fists at the ceiling. "One chance! Just one chance at you, you mother—"

Her body trembling, Kit pulled Jordan close and pressed her lips tightly against his. She closed her eyes and savored the moment. When she finally let go and opened her eyes, he stared back at her, stunned, his face redder than a sunburn. He tried to say something but only blubbered.

She smiled sheepishly through her tears. "If one of us is going to die tonight, I...I just wanted to make sure I did that first." She'd seen enough horrors that evening and was already feeling the weight of Pedro and Melissa's deaths on her shoulders. She wasn't sure she wanted to live with the guilt of knowing she'd survived at the expense of Jordan's death, too. No, she would enter that next room and ensure he survived.

She considered Pedro's theory: that the house was somehow playing off their worst fears. If so, it had done so in the order they'd chosen their numbers, but also in the order they'd died. *So, what will be next, the fear of the person who picked the third spot or the fear of the third person who will die?* She tried to think of her worst fear but only came up with being alone. *How can anyone die from simply being alone?*

Jordan scooped his arms under Pedro's and strained beneath the weight. "Help me lift him."

"What are you doing?"

"Maybe we can carry him into the next room. You know, like get double credit or something."

"That might be the stupidest thing—"

"It doesn't hurt to try! Maybe we can both get out of here alive tonight."

Kit considered this then bent down to help him with Pedro. Each draped an arm around their shoulders. For such a small boy, Pedro's dead weight was staggering. They limped toward the open doorway just as the wall behind them began to rumble.

As they passed through, Pedro's body vanished. Kit was happy Jordan couldn't see her fresh tears in the dark. She'd been foolish enough to allow herself to hope.

The room brightened in a sort of blue-white glow, though Kit could see no light source. It was small, barely eight feet all around. And unlike those before it, a table sat in the middle. An old-fashioned revolver sat on the table.

"Ha!" Jordan blurted. "The house doesn't know us. There's nothing supernatural going on here, just some sickos playing a sick game."

Kit frowned. "You don't really believe that. Not after all we've seen."

"I'm not afraid of guns. Are you?"

Kit shook her head. "So what, then? I suppose they want one of us to kill the other. I won't kill you, Jordan, and I won't let you kill yourself."

They stared at each other a moment then sprinted for the gun. Kit almost had her hand on it when Jordan swiped it right from under her. They stepped away from the table, Jordan with the gun out at his side. The chime of an old grandfather clock echoed through the room, followed by an unnerving *tick-tock, tick-tock.*

If time runs out
And no one's dead
Then twice as much
Blood will shed.

Jordan shook the revolver at the ceiling. "Fuck you!"

"Give me the gun." Kit held out her hand. "I'll make this easy for you. I don't want to live if it means having to kill you, anyway."

"No, you're going to live." He closed his eyes and put the gun under his chin, then to his temple. Tears streamed down his face. The revolver rattled in his shaking hand. "What's the best way to do this?"

Kit walked over to him. She took a deep breath, trying to hold herself together while her own tears fell as she grabbed his hand, held it in both of hers, and brought the barrel of the gun to her forehead.

Jordan pushed her away. "Stay back!" Again, he raised the gun to his temple. The clock began to tick faster. Jordan groaned and gritted his teeth. His shoulders heaved as his eyes squeezed shut. He held his breath.

Then, he released the air. His shoulders relaxed, and the gun swung at his side. A second later, it was back at his temple, Jordan again trying to summon the courage to do it. The clock ticking grew louder and faster. He roared. Every muscle of Jordan's body tensed as his finger danced on the trigger.

Again, he failed to shoot. His gun hand fell by his hip. "Oh, that fucking clock!" He shook his head. His eyes were wide, his gaze darting about erratically. Every part of him trembled. "I mean, how do we even know they'll kill us both? We could just not do anything."

"We have no reason to think they... it... this house won't do what it says." More softly, she said, "It's okay."

Jordan raised the gun one more time. He pointed it at Kit. "I'm sorry. It's just that I already have Ohio State and Michigan scouting me. I could get out of this town, be somebody huge. And you..."

Kit bit back her tears. She was thankful he hadn't finished that sentence. She was getting what she wanted, but that didn't make his words—that and the knowledge she'd been so wrong to care for him—hurt any less.

The gun clicked.

Kit opened her eyes.

Jordan stared at the revolver in wonder. "It's...it's empty." The cylinder dropped open. A wave of tiny red specks poured out from it. A second wave poured out through the hammer.

He howled and dropped the gun. It hit the ground and exploded into thousands more of those tiny red specks, which all seemed to flow directly toward Jordan's foot.

At first, Kit thought they were some kind of acid pellets, the way they ate away Jordan's hand so quickly. But on closer inspection, she saw that they were an army of tiny spiders unlike any she'd ever seen before; their abdomens were bulbs swelling with blood. But the spiders weren't just the blood-sucking type. They devoured skin, muscle, bone—everything they fell upon until nothing remained.

Jordan continued to scream as they made their way into his mouth and eyes. Kit watched, sniffling with her arms crossed, knowing she could do nothing for him and not sure if she wanted to.

When no trace of Jordan remained and the spiders had disappeared into the cracks in the walls and floor, Kit stepped around the table and waited for the door to appear. She didn't know what to expect, and she doubted there were any real winners to the vile game. Defeated and ready to accept whatever fate awaited her, she stepped into the next room as soon as the door opened.

Kit stood in a closet with no ceiling, but the walls climbed so high, she might as well have been in a chimney. She could see the moon shining above and feel the crisp cool air on her skin. But the walls were smooth and polished, flat and unscalable. She had no way out.

No way out but in. She stared at an oblong box erected against the far wall. She knew what it was and had a feeling who it was meant for.

Come into my world
And sleep 'til the night
When youth has the will
And their number is right.

"The house needs new blood."

Kit jumped. The strange boy they'd encountered at the house's entrance stepped past her and stood in front of the coffin.

"I'm sorry," he said, turning to face her. He fell back onto the coffin lid then through it, and he was gone.

The coffin lid swung open. Kit couldn't see what was inside. She approached. When she was a foot in front of it, she could see the withered husk of a corpse set against the back wall. The letterman's jacket it wore read Alderman across its right lapel. Under it, someone had embroidered a tiger rearing up on its hind legs, its teeth and claws bared.

Kit ran her finger over it. She had seen similar insignia in her school's trophy case. *We were the Tigers before the Yellow Jackets. But that was before I was born.*

The corpse pitched forward. Kit stepped out of the way. When it hit the ground, it vanished into dust. Not even the jacket remained.

Kit felt nothing: no sadness, no pain, and no fear. Only defeat. She stepped into the coffin. As the door closed behind her, she leaned back, closed her eyes, and drifted into sleep.

Halloween, ten years later.

Cole had made a point not to go out for Halloween ever since his sister and her friends had gone missing. He'd told his parents and the police where they'd gone, and Tabby had backed up his story. But the police had searched the old house in and out and had found nothing.

Not knowing had been the worst part. All those years went by without word or evidence of what might have happened to his sister, whom he'd loved above all others. But the house remained, a monolith to his loss. It had no right.

So when he convinced three of his new high-school friends that they should all go over to that creepy haunted house on Waterford Lane on Halloween and trash the shit out of it, he did so with the intent of finding some sort of closure. In truth, he planned to burn the place to the ground.

Seeing the house and yard all decked out in Halloween décor floored him. It excited his friends, but he wanted nothing to do with it.

Until he saw a girl standing on the porch.

Come one, come all
Into this house of fright
Will the brave step forward
And embrace the night.

The words were nonsense and seemed spoken directly into Cole's ear. And the voice… it sounded a lot like his sister's.

Sawmill Road
by Ronald Kelly

Three miles south of Pikesville, down the rutted, dirt stretch of Sawmill Road, Scott Anderson pulled his car to the shoulder and sat there for a minute, letting the engine idle. Finally, he cut the ignition and stepped out. It was late afternoon, but for mid-spring it was balmy, nearly humid; the way it usually was in Tennessee at that time of year.

He circled the front of the Chevy Impala and leaned against the opposite fender. It gave him an unobstructed view of the scattering of ancient, rundown structures directly across the road. Just looking at them made him anxious. He took a pack of Marlboros from his shirt pocket, tapped one out, then lit it.

Scott wasn't there five minutes before the sound of a vehicle came from the direction of town. It appeared over a rise; a white Dodge pickup hauling a zero-turn mower, a weed-eater, and a chainsaw on a flat-bed trailer. As it roared past, the man inside—beefy, bearded, and sporting an orange UT Volunteers ball cap—gave him a sideward glance. Immediately, the fellow's eyes widened in recognition. Scott noticed that the placard on the side of the truck door read HATCHER'S YARD SERVICE / GOD GROWS IT, WE MOW IT. He couldn't help but smile.

The truck ground to halt twenty yards further on, sending a cloud of clay dust in the air. Then, slowly, it backed up. The driver hopped out, looking eighty pounds heavier than the last time Scott had seen him. But that had been, what? Twenty…twenty-five years ago?

"Scott?" the big man called. A big grin blossomed in his salt-and-pepper beard. "Scott Anderson, is that you?"

"One and the same. How's it going, Chuck?"

Chuck Hatcher trotted the rest of the way—looking like a Clydesdale in overalls—and vigorously shook Scott's hand. "Fine, hoss! Just fine. What brings you back to Pikesville? Are you on furlough?"

"No, I'm retired," Scott told him, taking a long drag and expelling it through his nose. "Uncle Sam doesn't need an old dog like me in his army anymore. I left the service five or six years ago."

"Is that so?" Chuck followed his friend's gaze, across the dirt road, to the collection of old buildings. Thicket grew high and wild between them—milkweed, kudzu, pink-headed thistle. Just seeing it all seemed to have the same adverse effect on him. He fumbled in his hip pocket and brought out a can of Grizzly. Chuck popped the lid and planted a pinch of tobacco in the pouch of his right cheek. "How's your wife doing?"

"Terri? She's fine. A couple more years of school-teaching and she'll hang it up. Thought we might travel. You know, the RV thing. How's Alma and the kids?"

Chuck laughed. "The kids ain't kids anymore. Sue is a nurse practitioner and Billy; he's starting his second year of diesel mechanic school. Alma always wanted him to be a doctor or lawyer or such, but he's too much like his old man. Doesn't have the brains it takes to fire a spark plug twice."

Chuck joined his pal on the fender, causing the Chevy's shocks to drop a couple inches. "You know, Tony's still up north."

Scott nodded. Funny how that name had popped into their heads at the same time. Tony DePrusso, the displaced boy from New Jersey whose father had moved down south to work at the Ford glass plant. Tony was the third member of the Pikesville Trio, as they called themselves back in 1975. "Is he still with that pharmaceutical company in Cincinnati?"

"I reckon so. Hell, I haven't seen him in thirty years. It's probably been longer for you."

Scott nodded. Just stood there, smoking and staring across the road.

They remained like that for a few minutes more, immersed in their own thoughts, enduring a stretch of awkward silence they had never shared before. Then Chuck spoke.

"Do you remember that summer?"

"Yeah," Scott replied. He exhaled and stared at the old sawmill through a blue haze of cigarette smoke. "Yeah...it's hard not to."

Chuck shuffled his boots nervously in the clay dust, his eyes glued to the rusty chain-link fence that surrounded the property and a buckshot sign that read HALCOMB'S MILL—HARDWOOD, CEDAR, & PINE. "You're damn right about that," was all the big man could say.

They had been twelve that summer—Scott, Chuck, and Tony—and it had been a hot one. The temps had hovered in the upper-eighties and nineties, even at night. But it had been a fun summer...up until early August.

They'd ridden their bikes from one end of Mangrum County to the other; from the old railroad bridge that bordered Swanson County, clear to where the forest grew darker and wilder at the Fear County line. There, they would go no further and turn back. They practically slept in the old tree house out back of Chuck's double-wide, listening to Kiss, Peter Frampton, and K.C. and the Sunshine Band on the 8-track boom box that Tony had gotten for his birthday and flipping through old issues of Famous Monsters of Filmland magazine, as well a couple of Playboys that Scott had spirited away from his dad's underwear drawer without him knowing.

It was also the summer they had been obsessed with Sawmill Road. Or, rather, the *ghost* that supposedly haunted that lonesome stretch of Mangrum County backroad.

Most ghost stories spring from small town folklore and, over time, become the stuff of local legend. And, boy, that one had been a doozy. As they had heard it told, back in the fall of 1958, the owner of Pikesville's one and only sawmill, Chester Halcomb, had gotten into a hellacious fight with his wife one evening. Disgruntled, he had gotten sloppy-assed drunk at the local honky-tonk and, against his better judgment, decided to fire up the sawmill in the dead of night and start on an order of two-by-four pine planks he had scheduled for the following day. Chester had bought a pint of Jim Beam from the tavern and taken it with him, getting drunker and more unsteady with each swallow he took and each length of lumber he pushed against the big forty-eight-inch sawmill blade.

Finally, the alcohol had caught up with him…in a devastating way. He passed out as he split the last board to completion and, in the process, split himself as well. Chester Halcomb had fallen face first into the blade and the saw-teeth had grabbed hold of him, dragging him along the conveyor, cleaving him completely in two, from scalp to scrotum. If he had come to his senses long enough to scream, no one heard him. The sawmill was a far piece from town, and no one was privy to his gruesome fate until his workers arrived the following morning to find one half of him lying to the right of the cutting stand and the other to the left. Legend had it that the blade of the sawmill was still spinning when they got there, the gaps between its teeth caked with flesh, hair, and slivers of fine, white bone.

After that, the sawmill didn't stay open for very long. Chester's brother, Alfred, took over the running of it, but he didn't have a head for business and shared his sibling's appreciation of strong drink. But that wasn't what shut the place down. Before long, accidents began to happen. The saw would crank up at the most unexpected times, during repairs and such, and, a time or two, workers claimed that a ghostly hand had shoved them from behind as they fed the lumber into the blade. Fingers and hands were lost, and they all knew it was only a matter of time before one of them ended up in the same shape as Ol' Chester. By the spring of '59, no one would set foot through the front gate, including Alfred himself, who had lost his index finger and thumb on his right hand to the saw. The younger Halcomb claimed that his big brother had been the culprit of his misfortune; the sour stench of liquor and a familiar laugh coming from behind as he slipped—or was *pushed*—into the spinning blade.

They padlocked the gates after that, and no one would go near the place. Except for the Pikesville Trio. Hell, they had to go…just to find out for themselves.

It was the 3rd of August when they made their move. They told their parents that they were having a sleep-over at the treehouse, which was nothing out of the ordinary. They had eaten supper on the Hatcher's back deck. Chuck's dad had grilled hot dogs and they had them with Golden Flake potato chips—the brand with that freaky clown on the bag—and the homemade mustard that Chuck's grandmother made; a mustard so hot that it burned your mouth going in and turned your asshole into a flaming inferno on the way out.

They horsed around in the treehouse until ten-thirty or so, waiting until the house lights had been off for a while. Then they quickly prepared for their journey. They took an old Army backpack that Tony's dad had brought home from Nam and packed snacks they had bought from the 7-11 in town; two RC Colas, a Nehi Orange for Scott, Hostess Twinkies, three Slim Jims, and a pack of Pop Rocks, just for good measure.

"This is a major operation here," Chuck had insisted. "We need to keep our energy and strength at the max!" Scott and Tony both knew the abundance of snacks was mainly because Chuck liked to eat and had a colon like a bottomless pit.

It was a quarter past eleven when they jumped on their bikes and headed south for Sawmill Road. There was full moon in a clear sky that night and it lit the way when the street lights were left behind. They didn't reach their destination until a little before midnight, mostly because Scott and Tony had to slow down a time or two for their buddy to catch up. Chuck had been a little on the chubby side back then, plus he was riding a girl's bike that his dad had discovered at the local landfill. The boys had doctored its two-toned pink and purple frame with a can of Krylon electric blue, but there was absolutely nothing they could do about the missing bar between the handlebars and seat.

When they got there, they flipped the kickstands of their bikes and stood before the locked gate. The buildings that stood beyond the chain-link barrier were dark hulls and tall stacks of weathered lumber could be seen here and there; completely abandoned when the sawmill had closed sixteen years earlier.

A collective chill ran through them as a horned owl hooted nearby and a whippoorwill answered it somewhere in the distance. The night was sweltering, so any chill that they felt was due to a mixture of excitement and anticipation—and, yes, a generous helping of fear—and nothing more.

"So…are we going?" Tony asked. "Really?"

"Yeah, really!" Chuck sneered. "Are you going pussy on us or something?"

Tony glared at Chuck like he wanted to rip his head clean off; that Italian temper that he bragged about. "You're the turd pumping pedals on a *girl's* bike! You can break out the Barbies and Easy Bake Oven when you get back to your playhouse."

"Cut it out, Moe and Curly," Scott told them. "Come on. Let's go." Before anyone could protest any further, he jabbed his fingers into the gaps of the chain link fence and begin to scale it.

Soon, he was on the other side. Tony was right behind him, but it took a good twelve minutes for Chuck to do the up-and-over. "Get the lead outta your ass, fatso!" Tony yelled at him.

"I'm gonna whale the living tar outta you, piss-ant!" Chuck huffed as he straddled the top, caught his breath, and then began the trip down.

"Y'all hush, will you?" said Scott, lowering his voice.

"Why?" asked Tony. "There's nobody around to hear us."

When Chuck finally made it to the ground, they turned and stared at the long open building that housed the conveyor stand and the big saw at the end. They forgot their squabbling and slowly walked past tall stands of lumber in that direction.

"I heard that they had to bury Old Man Halcomb in *two* pine caskets," Chuck said. "And that Mrs. Halcomb had to buy an extra plot in the Pineville Cemetery to bury him in."

"Aw, that's a bunch of crap," Tony told him. "Why would they need two coffins? The undertaker could just, you know, sew the two halves together and put him in one box."

"Well, that's what I heard," Chuck said with a glare.

Scott shucked a flashlight from his hip pocket and snapped it on. The pale, yellow beam illuminated the lumber yard and its main structure. "Get your lights out. We'll split up."

"What do you mean...*split up?*"

Scott rolled his eyes. "Three guys going in three different directions."

"Yeah," said Chuck. "Do the math."

With their flashlights cutting pale pathways ahead of them, they parted. Scott headed toward the building with the buzz saw. Chuck went right. Tony went left.

They walked around and explored for fifteen minutes, before coming to the realization that the place wasn't half as spooky as their imaginations made it out to be.

"There ain't nothing worth seeing here," Chuck called out. "Just some ol' piles of lumber and some cedar logs that ain't ever gonna be cut."

"Big waste of a trip," added Tony from near an old logging truck with four flat tires.

"Just keep looking around," said Scott. "Might as well get the full tour."

Scott entered the main building, which was really no more than a long, pitched roof on eight sturdy wooden supports. Beneath was the cutting table. It consisted of two individual platforms with rubber conveyor bands that led to the big saw at the very end. He shone the beam of the flashlight on the circular blade. It was huge; a good four feet across. It was pitted and caked with rust, but the jagged teeth showed no sign of flesh and blood. He had to admit that he was disappointed it wasn't as gory as local legend made it out to be.

Suddenly, someone cried out in the darkness. It sounded like Chuck.

"Chuck! Are you okay?" he called. "Did you step on a snake or something?"

No answer. Just crickets chirping in the night.

Scott was about to leave the cutting table, when he saw a pale glow emerge around the corner of a high stack of old lumber. At first, he thought it was the beam of a flashlight, but it was much too bright and an eerie pale blue in color. *What the hell is that?* he thought to himself.

Then, abruptly, it came into full view.

Part of what he saw was Chuck. His friend's face was stricken with fright; his eyes wide and his mouth slack and open. The front of Chuck's shorts was dark where he had pissed himself in shock.

Chuck wasn't alone. Something had him by the back of the neck, holding him suspended in mid-air. Chuck's sneakers looked to be a good ten inches or so above the ground.

The thing that held Chuck was a man. Or, rather, *half* a man. He was tall and lanky, dressed in blood-splattered shirt and trousers. From his open chest beat half a heart; sluggish, torn, spurting luminescent blue blood. The man's head had been ripped in half by jagged steel teeth. It sat, lopsided, on his splintered neck-bone, misshapen, dark brains seeping from the open cranium. The trauma had dislodged the man's right eye ball. It hung from the open pit of its socket, dangling from the rubbery stalk of its optic nerve.

As the thing floated—not walked—toward the cutting shed, another glow emerged from the far side of the logging truck. Scott's heart hammered with terror as the second half of the apparition appeared. It was just as gruesome as the first; its physical structure cut open and torn apart from its moorings by merciless, spinning steel. Organs glistened from exposed wounds and the half-crescent of the ghost's lower jaw worked silently...as though attempting to say something. The arm of the man's left half extended outward and, from his work-calloused hand, dangled the suspended form of Tony. His friend's face was pale and trembling. His eyes had rolled up into his head until only the whites were showing.

Scott didn't know whether to rush to help his friends...or turn tail and run. He knew he couldn't abandon them, though. The code of the Pikesville Trio didn't work that way. They'd made that pack in private, laying the third blade of a Case pocket knife across their palms and sealing it with the ceremonious mingling of their blood.

The boy was starting toward the two halves of the floating apparition, when a godawful racket sounded behind him. He turned the beam of his flashlight upon the buzz saw. Gears and pulleys, fused together with rust years ago, suddenly came to life. The machinery hitched a couple of times, then sent the saw blade spinning in a mottled orange blur. The jagged, one-inch teeth were unseen as the blade picked up speed, but he knew they were there...hungry and horribly destructive.

As the dissected ghost approached the cutting table, carrying his captured friends in tow, Scott knew precisely what its intention was. *Oh God!* he thought. *Oh God...what am I gonna do?*

Then it came to him. An absurd notion that a grown man would have probably dismissed entirely...but one that seemed plausible to a boy of twelve.

Scott took off running, heading toward the front gate that lay beyond the two halves of the glowing entity. As he moved, the two portions moved toward him, shifting inward, as if intending to block his way. *Let me get past him,* his thoughts pleaded. *Please, let me get to the other side!*

Scott poured on the speed, injecting a little Flash into his low-top Converse sneakers. Soon he was leaping between the two halves. As he passed, he felt a coldness like none he had ever experienced, even in the snowy months of February. He knew his pals were feeling that frigid sensation even more so than he was.

Then he was beyond the two converging halves, sprinting across sawdust-laden earth. He skidded to halt and turned just in time to see the twin apparitions join and become one.

Instantly, Chuck and Tony were released. They dropped to their knees and remained there for a moment, attempting to regain their bearings. When they did, they rose to their feet and joined Scott.

They stood there, petrified, wanting to escape the lumber yard in the worst way…but also captivated by what took place next.

The rusty machinery grew quiet, the blade of the saw was motionless, and the thing that stood before them slowly turned around.

They had never seen a photo of Chester Halcomb, but they knew that was who it was. The ugly wounds, the flesh and bone that had been ripped asunder; all had been restored. The middle-aged gentleman stood there, unsteady, looking addled and confused. He stared down at his glowing hands, then up at the three boys.

"I…I'm dead," he said. It was a voice that was more in their heads, than in their ears.

Scott swallowed dryly and nodded. "Yeah."

"But…what happened?"

"You were drunk," Chuck explained. "Passed out…fell into…"

"The saw." The poor man looked completely lost. "How long ago?"

"1958. Going on seventeen years."

Grief threatened to overcome his narrow face. "My wife…"

"Works at the dollar store in town," Tony told him. His voice was strangely flat, as though he hadn't yet recovered from the shock of what had just happened.

"And my daughter?"

"She's a registered nurse," said Scott. "Works in a hospital in Dickson Springs. She's married…has two kids."

The lines of torment on Chester Halcomb's face slowly softened, as though he had come to terms with what had taken place, both then and now. He stared at the three boys for a long moment. "I'm sorry," was all he said. Then the glow faded, and he was gone.

And the Pikesville Trio left that awful place, never to return.

That was, until today.

"Scott?"

He pulled his eyes away from Halcomb's sawmill and looked over at his old friend. "Yeah?"

"Did it really happen? You know, we were just kids…"

The statement angered Scott for some reason; as though Chuck was trying to steal something away from him. Something horrible, yet precious.

"Do you have to ask that?" he snapped. "Of course, it did. Don't you remember how cold you were days after that? How you couldn't get rid of the goosebumps and it was nearly a hundred degrees in the sun? Don't you remember those finger marks on the back of your neck that didn't go away until October? Or how Tony changed? How he lost his swagger and wouldn't hang out with us. Hell, he wouldn't even talk to us. And his hair? You remember his hair."

Chuck nodded and spat, sending a spray of tobacco juice into the dirt. A white streak had appeared in Tony's jet-black hair almost overnight; one that went from his forehead, all the way to the nape of his neck. They remembered Tony's parents taking him to doctors, trying to figure out what had happened. But the Pikesville Trio knew. They knew good and well what had caused it.

The two stood there for a long moment, then Chuck turned and shook Scott's hand once again. "Well, partner, I've gotta run. I have two more yards to mow before I head home to supper."

"Take care, Chuck," Scott said. "I'm heading back to Chattanooga tonight. I probably won't be seeing you again for a while."

Chuck glanced back at the sawmill, then turned away. "No…at least not around *here*."

Scott nodded and finished his cigarette as Chuck fired up his pickup and headed on down the road. A moment later, he was out of sight...but far from out of mind.

He tossed the butt of the Marlboro into the dust of Sawmill Road and ground it beneath the sole of his shoe. As he walked around the front of the car to the driver's side, he heard something echo from across the road.

It was faint...but it almost sounded like the clank and grind of ancient machinery attempting to come to life.

Before the metallic whine of the buzz saw could reach his ears, Scott Anderson started his car, made a sharp turn in the roadway, and headed back toward town.

Bettor's Edge

by Tim Meyer

The living room reeked of water damage and old money, but Dylan McGraw hardly cared; he had the itch nothing could scratch, save for a briefcase stuffed with hundred-dollar bills.

The first thing he did upon entering the sizable luxury suite was check the bathroom, specifically the toilet to make sure it was operational. He flushed, and was relieved when the water circled the bowl and disappeared. Next, he turned on the shower head, stuck his hand in the stream to test the pressure and temperature. For the water to warm, it took longer than expected, but the pressure was fine.

Next, he moved into the bedroom and inspected the power. The lights came on, the lamp next to the bed blinked to life, and more importantly, the television started without delay. HBO was readily available, just as the placard on the nightstand declared.

"At least I'll have *Game of Thrones* to get me through this," he said, dropping himself on the king-sized mattress. Tucking his hands behind his head, Dylan closed his eyes, tried his best to shut off his brain, but his thoughts were running a thousand miles a minute, in all different directions, and he couldn't catch up.

"Dammit," he said, lifting himself up. He swung his feet off the bed, lowering them onto the plush carpet. He'd kicked off his shoes and removed his socks, leaving them at the front door—an old habit— and now enjoyed the way the fluffy threads felt against his bare feet. He curled his toes, allowing his nerves to experience every fiber, the sensation traveling to his arches, past his heels, and up his ankles. He could have done that for hours, but he wanted to explore more of the suite, gain a sense of what was to come.

If anything.

"This place doesn't look haunted," he said as he walked out of the bedroom, into the living area, and headed for the windows, floor-to-wall sheets of crystal-clear glass that overlooked Atlantic City, New Jersey. Outside was dark.

The hour past dusk had suffocated the sun, and the city stood weary, a lost, nearly-forgotten metropolis looking as if its last days were hiding just around the corner. A few neon signs promoting the names of other casinos were lit with a fuzzy brightness, but the rest of the strip looked dim and left for dead. Dylan remembered how alive the city had been in his youth, remembered when his parents and grandparents drove him down the shore to walk the boards and eat at fancy restaurants. Hell, even ten years ago, when he'd first turned twenty-one and had gotten the taste for the betting life, a flavor he'd developed an addiction to, the place had been lively and full of lights and sounds, and... well... *people.*

Yes, plenty of those.

But now, the streets and bars and strip joints—hell, the casinos—were pretty empty, even on weekends.

The city wasn't what it had been, but it still clung to its charm, at least through Dylan McGraw's eyes. From the window, he could pinpoint the location of every backdoor poker game being played, every underground prop betting ring front, every chicken and dogfight currently being held. Dylan kept away from the latter because animal abuse was bullshit, but any other type of bet he could get action on, well... Dylan didn't say "no" too often. Even when the odds were stacked against him.

And, surprisingly, he'd done all right. Survived the last ten years on prop betting alone, and never once had trouble paying the bill of whatever sleazy motel he was living out of, had never gone to sleep hungry.

Until recently, that is—until a spell of shit luck.

A few weeks of bad bets had put him in the hole, about twenty grand, which was all he had in savings. *Stupid shit luck,* he thought, thinking back to the local high school basketball game that only put ninety total points on the board, when the over (ninety-three) had been all but guaranteed. That was an anomaly, he thought, though that one anomaly had robbed him of six grand. Then there were the more *unconventional* bets. Sports betting was fun and all, made up the bulk of his winnings, but the stranger bets were what really cranked Dylan's engines, drove him deeper into the world of gambling degeneracy. This past week, he'd lost bets on how many inches of rainfall were reported during last Tuesday's storm, lost big when he took the under on how much Disney's latest movie would gross at the box office on opening weekend, and lost *bigger* when his favorite porn site failed to reach ninety-million views last Friday. It was a rough week made rougher when his buddy, Mitch Yates, told him about a peculiar bet he and his cohorts had assembled.

Mitch had pitched it like this: *"We found a one-legged stripper and bet her she couldn't climb to the top of the Ram's Head water tower in under thirty seconds."* It was one of those wagers that didn't come around often, but when it did, you didn't pass on it.

After meeting with the stripper and determining she was in no way fit enough to reach the top—*let alone in thirty seconds*—he'd placed five grand on her failing.

But the woman had scaled the thing in under twenty-seven, forcing Dylan to cough up every last penny he had to his name.

The soul-crushing replays of the past week dispersed when something moved behind him, flickering in the reflection of the suite's window.

He spun, his throat ratcheting down, making it hard to breathe.

There was no one behind him.

Nothing.

Jesus, he thought, *been here for five minutes and I'm already jumpy.*

He pressed his back against the window, placed his hands on his knees, and sucked in a deep breath. His heart pounded in his ears. When he realized he was being an idiot and that this was the easiest fifty-grand he'd ever make, he chortled.

Then the phone rang, which startled him a lot more than it should have.

"Stop being a jackass," he coached himself, making his way over to the nightstand in the bedroom. He took the phone off the cradle and said, "McGraw here. Make it snappy. I have premium cable television to watch."

"Mr. McGraw," spoke the familiar voice. "Glad to see you've settled into your room. Enjoying your stay thus far?"

The bettor.

The man who'd approached him two days ago with this crazy proposition. A man he'd never met before. A man who pulled up to him on the street while Dylan was in line at the local hot dog truck. He'd stepped out of the back of a nondescript black sedan with the windows tinted. Dylan had spotted him immediately, saw him approach, another man following close behind. At first, he'd thought the man was a detective or maybe a government official, and Dylan had begun to wonder what it was he'd done. Nothing he was aware of, he'd been sure of it.

Next thing he knew, he'd found himself in the back of the sedan, drinking a dirty martini and listening to the man's pitch.

One night in the haunted suite atop the Sugarstone Casino. Fifty grand.

"Enjoying it just fine," Dylan said, his eyes searching the room for more moving shadows. "A little dated, but cozier than I imagined."

"It's one of the finest suites in all of A.C."

"Just haunted, that's all. Right?"

There was a pause, and Dylan thought the call had dropped.

"You still there?" he asked, his eyes still bouncing between the room's dreary décor. Old peeling wallpaper, abstract paintings that inspired nothing, and lamps that wore an inch of dust on its exterior. It was clear no one rented this room. Ever.

"Yes, still here, Mr. McGraw. Still here."

Dylan chuckled. "I have to say, man. Fifty grand for one night seems like a poor bet on your part. I mean, we both know there's no such thing as ghosts. So, come on. Come clean. What's the catch? You a guy who gets off on this sort of thing? I'm half expecting you to show up in a gimp suit and a sex swing. I mean, I'm broke, but I ain't *that* broke, so if that's the gig, man—I'm out."

Another wave of silence. "I assure you, Mr. McGraw, this is nothing like that."

"You got cameras in here?" He looked to the corners of the room, where the ceilings met the walls. "You spying on me?" He didn't see anything, but that didn't mean they weren't there. Built into the walls. The television. Hell, they could have hidden a camera in the smoke detector or the Keurig. "You are, aren't you? You want to watch... whatever this is."

"You're mistaken." His voice was humorless. He sounded bored by Dylan's accusations, as if this were something he'd expected.

Or he's heard it before.

A shiver scattered across his network of nerves. "Then what is it? You have to admit, man—I agreed to this on some pretty shady details. I think now that I'm here and committed, you should give me a little more info. I mean, shit—I don't remember you telling me your name."

He swore he heard the man titter, but he wasn't positive. The man's voice, when he spoke, gave no inclination that he found any of this amusing. Even when they had spoken in person, the man gave no hints that this was simply a game to him.

"That's because I didn't, Mr. McGraw. You were so swept away by my offer that you never bothered to ask."

That sounded like an untruth to Dylan's ears—surely he wasn't *so* blinded by the offer that he didn't ask for the man's name or his credentials. He didn't know anything about the guy on the phone, not a single thing other than he had a brown paper bag with fifty grand stuffed in it and was willing to part with it in exchange for a night in a haunted casino suite. To McGraw's ears, that had sounded like easy money.

But now, he wasn't so sure.

"Who are you?" Dylan asked, feeling his heart rate spike. There was still time to back out. He could build back his bankroll some other way. He knew a few sharks with low rates. He could borrow ten, fifteen grand, double it within a week. Local basketball games or grinding it out in Texas Hold'em, it could be done.

He didn't need *this,* whatever *this* was.

"Does the name Miranda Hoskins mean anything to you?" the man asked, and the very mention of the girl's name drove an invisible stake through Dylan's heart.

He opened his mouth to reply, but the words wouldn't come; it was like someone closed their fist around his larynx.

"I'll take your silence as confirmation of the truth." The man didn't speak again, not right away.

"I didn't do anything," Dylan blurted out, almost involuntarily.

The bettor made an amused noise, the first time that night he'd deviated from his tough persona. *This was fun for him now.*

"Didn't you?" he asked.

Dylan glanced around the room nervously, waiting for the door to bust in, waiting for the trap to spring.

"I didn't do anything, man. This is a mistake. You've... you've got the wrong guy."

The bettor clicked his tongue. "No need to make excuses, Mr. McGraw. Own your past. Your mistakes. Your misguided decisions."

"I don't know who you are and what you think you know, but that girl... wasn't my fault. I didn't have anything to do with it."

"Hmm. That's weird. I don't believe you."

"Jesus Christ," he said, and then slammed the phone on the cradle.

Dylan marched across the bedroom, into the living room, and grabbed his jacket, throwing it over his shoulder. Next, he went straight for the door, charging like a bull down Pamplona. He cursed himself the whole way there, thinking how stupid he was, and how smart he'd been in the past when it came to placing bets with strangers. Being flat broke probably played a part in his foolishness, but still, that wasn't a good excuse. Being smart had kept his head above water all these years, kept him from needing to get a real job.

Kept him alive.

When he reached the door and turned the knob, he found it locked from the outside.

"What the fuck?"

He tried the knob again, turning harder, but the lock didn't budge.

"No. What? This..."

The phone rang again. Dylan turned, found himself staring at the far wall's window, the reflection it cast. In it, stood the shadow from earlier, only it wasn't a shadow anymore.

It was a girl.

Seventeen. Maybe eighteen. Her skin ashen, grayed from death's eternal touch. Dark rings circled her lifeless eyes. Her blouse was as dirty as the day she died, the printed flowery depictions stained with earthy strokes of mud and grime. A trickle of blood leaked from her nose. Rainwater soaked her head, her hair endlessly wet and curly. Her colorless lips moved, twitched like the wings of a butterfly in the throes of eventual death. A perpetual chill sliced through her, and her body trembled.

"Oh, fuck that," Dylan said and scrambled into the bedroom, slamming the door behind him.

The phone continued to ring. He waited for the girl's spirit to come knocking on the door, and then realized it was a ghost, and, to the best of his knowledge, ghosts didn't knock.

They enter at their own will.

He locked the door anyway. The phone never stopped ringing, and he figured it wouldn't unless he answered or ripped the power cord out of the wall.

"What the fuck is this?" was how he answered the call.

"It is what I said it was," the bettor replied, sounding fuller of himself now. Happier. *The fucker* is *enjoying this*. "One night. Fifty grand. *If* you survive."

"Survive?" He punched the wall, nearly breaking his fist. "You said nothing about surviving."

"Didn't I? I believe I did. I also believe you were so fixated on the fifty grand that you didn't understand what you signed up for."

"I didn't—I didn't think…"

"No, you didn't *think*. And I expected so much more from you, a man who's *survived* the last ten years on *thinking* alone."

"That girl, the one you mentioned?"

"Miranda Hoskins. You know her name. Don't act like you don't."

Dylan knew her, all right. He'd never forget her.

"Yes. *Her*. She's here."

"Of course she is."

"How? I mean…how is that possible?"

"I told you. The Sugarstone Casino is a special place."

"It's haunted? For real?"

"Not quite."

"Jesus, man. Just tell me."

"There are some places in this world that are…let's use the word *thin*." He clicked his tongue, and the sound carried like a shotgun blast directly into Dylan's ear. "Yes, *thin* is best. It's a thin place, a place where two worlds meet, merge, cross over—the land of the living and the land of the dead."

"Jesus fucking Christ."

"But it's a funny place, because, the spirits that wander those halls and the casino floor—they're not tethered there. Sugarstone's not a haunted place, per se. No, places are rarely haunted. Usually, people are."

"What are you saying? She… she followed me here?"

"Miranda Hoskins…" His voice stumbled a little when he spoke her name, a stutter that hadn't been there before. "…has been following you for a long time, Mr. McGraw. She haunts you. Because of what you did to her."

"I didn't…" He wiped sweat from his forehead. Perspiration dripped from every pore. "I didn't… fucking… kill her, man. I didn't. I swear to God. I didn't touch a hair on her head."

"No…" The bettor sniffled. "No, maybe not. But you didn't save her."

Dylan couldn't hold his emotions any longer. His mind broke, and tears sluiced down his cheeks. "How do you know these things?"

"Because… I've been in that very room, where you now stand. Because I've seen her with my own eyes. And I've listened to every…word…she had to say."

"Who—Who are you, man? Tell me."

A deep breath in Dylan's ear. A silent spell.

"My name is Morton Hoskins, and Miranda was my daughter, you sick son of a bitch."

Before Dylan could fathom a response, the lights cut out, sinking the suite into the deepest darkness he'd ever known.

"You never overplay Jacks, man. Everybody knows that."

Mitch Yates was a cocky prick but a hell of a card player, and Dylan respected him for both. He didn't exactly admire him, because, after all, Mitch wasn't the kind of guy you'd follow into battle. He walked on the wild side, made crazy bets when opportunities emerged, and treated women like total garbage. Dylan respected him, but he never wanted to grow up and become him.

Still, he acted like the big brother Dylan never had. Took him under his wing. Showed him the streets, how to play cards, where to find backroom games; every penny Dylan would eventually earn was all because of Mitch and his "blueprints," his self-proclaimed method of winning.

"Queens. Kings. Aces. Play the heck out of them. But you overplay Jacks, and you're gonna get burned. Not all the time, but enough to leave a couple scars. Especially in the casinos where you're playing against noobs who watch this shit on TV and think they're gonna be the next Worlds Series of Poker Champion. They'll over play

their Queen-Kings and the next thing you know, you're in a coin-flip for your entire bankroll."

They hustled down the street, trying to make the next game. It was six blocks over at a strip club Mitch frequented. They passed dark alleys Dylan was mostly scared to look down. This wasn't the best of neighborhoods, and sometimes, stopping to tie your shoe or taking a minute to examine spent hypodermic needles in the gutter tripled your chances of getting robbed. It was the kind of neighborhood where, if you heard a newspaper rustling as it scraped along the sidewalk behind you, you ran like hell.

But for some reason, Dylan did look down the next dark alleyway. Curiosity, maybe. Perhaps the universe was working its magic and the attraction to that particular alley was magnetic. Maybe he couldn't avoid the impending disaster, even if he tried.

The visible darkness allowed a semi-obscured view to the end of the alley where Dylan spotted a moving heap, a shadow that undulated from its position on the ground. It flopped around, almost gracefully, like a carefully-planned dance routine, the artsy kind, something interpretive, the kind Dylan could never understand. What he knew from dancing came from strip clubs and sleazy bar scenes.

He stopped following his mentor.

"What are you doing?" Mitch asked.

He didn't respond. Instead, he moved into the mouth of the alley, inspecting the shadow, its frolic with the dark. Something that felt like cold fingers brushed against his bones, but he ignored it, shifting his focus on the dim mess ahead.

"Dylan?"

Again, no response. He inched his way deeper into the alley, and it felt like floating.

The shadow faced him, and as it did, he realized it wasn't a shadow. It was a woman with pale skin and huge dark circles around her eyes. Her nose was bleeding. White foam bubbled on her lips, the corners of her mouth. She spotted Dylan approaching, began to crawl toward him like the dead girl at the end of The Ring, *the part where she climbed out of the goddamn television.*

"Holy shit," Dylan muttered, backing up once the dark lines in her face became visible. Her blouse was ripped and torn, revealing her bruised, dirty flesh beneath. Dylan's eyes didn't have to wander far to spot the reason she was out here—no more than a few feet from her, a spent syringe glimmered in the frail moonlight. The needle was dripping its last droplets of poison.

"Pleath," the woman rasped, as she reached for him. "Bad...drug...bad..."

A hand fell down on Dylan's shoulder. He almost screamed.

"What is this?" Mitch asked, amused. "Well, shit. Looks like we got ourselves a junky." His eyes drifted from the woman and over to the weapon she'd chosen to brutalize herself with. "Oh shit, looks like she's overdone it."

"We have to help her," Dylan said, reaching into his pocket for his phone. Before he could grip onto it, take it out, and flip it open, punch those three famous numbers, Mitch stopped him.

"Let's wait this out," he said with the devil in his eye.

"What?" Dylan shook his head. "Man, if we don't call 9-1-1 right now, she's gonna die."

"Wanna bet on it?"

He treated Mitch's words like a sucker punch and backed away.

"What the fuck are you talking about, man?"

"I'm talking about a bet, you idiot. You said she's gonna die, I say she's gonna soldier up and live this one through." He glanced over at the girl, smiled. "She's a fighter. I can tell."

"I'm... I'm not betting on..."

"A grand."

Dylan whipped his head back and forth. "No... That's...that's so fucked up."

"Two?" Mitch took one predatory step toward him. "Twenty-five hundred? I know you're good for it, Dill. We cleaned up pretty well these last few weeks. The poker gods have been kind."

"I'm saving that money."

"For what?"

"College?"

Mitch sneered. "Who needs college when you got the edge, man. When you play the odds, over a lifetime, you'll always win. Remember that."

Dylan thought about running, screaming for someone to help while he called the paramedics, but something kept him there, rooted to the dark alleyway.

"Five grand. That's my final offer. Take it or leave it, but you have to hurry up." He nodded at the crawling woman. Her pace had slowed. She was fading fast, either dying or heading into a coma from which she may never awake from.

Dylan cleared his throat, unable to speak the words his brain told him to. Finally, he squeaked out one, lonely word: "Okay."

They turned toward the woman. She glanced up at them, her eyes pleading, filling with tears. Her body didn't move. After a few moments, she closed her eyes and never opened them again.

Fifteen minutes later, Mitch felt her wrist for a pulse, and then turned to his protégé.

"Guess you're five grand richer, kid," he said as Dylan turned and purged what he'd eaten for dinner onto the sidewalk.

When the lights came back on, Dylan rushed into the living room, immediately arming himself with the lamp next to the door. He ripped the cord from the outlet and tied it around his arm, doubting the lamp would protect him from the woman's vengeful spirit. But it was better than nothing.

When he faced the living room, defending himself from an angry specter immediately fled his thoughts.

"M-Mitch?"

Mitch was in the center of the living room, hanging from the ornate chandelier, the rope that had been tied around it. The noose was pulled taut around his noticeably raw throat. His head hung awkwardly to the side, as if someone had buried an axe three-quarters of the way into his neck. An eerie stillness held his body hostage.

"Jesus Christ," Dylan said, stumbling into the center of the room. He landed on his knees a few feet from where his friend had hanged himself.

Or... *where someone had done it for him.*

Mitch's eyes suddenly flickered with life. His body began to contort and spasm. Strangled sounds emanated from his mouth as he continued to wriggle like a suffering worm. Dylan crab-walked away from the center of the room. After another few seconds of squirming, the rope tethering Mitch finally broke, sending him plummeting to the floor. Mitch landed feet first, but he had no strength to support himself and went sprawling to the ground.

"Holy shit!" Dylan shouted, immediately rushing to Mitch's side.

Mitch gasped for air, struggling against the noose. Dylan helped loosen the knot. Once free, Mitch sucked in wind.

"Are you...how...are you alive?" The angle of Mitch's neck didn't make much sense; his vertebrae was clearly broken, had snapped during the hanging. By all counts, Mitch shouldn't be breathing. Yet, here he was. Alive. *Very* alive.

"She's...she's...here."

No shit, Dylan thought, examining more of his friend's injuries. His pallid skin was deeply bruised, purple and yellow marks that ran down his arms and neck. It looked like he'd been beaten with a baseball bat, but not recently—maybe several days ago.

Then it clicked.

He's not real. He's...

Dylan blinked and his friend was gone. His own breath left him just as quickly. Spinning in a circle, he looked for any actual evidence that Mitch *had* been here, something he could use to disprove the notion that he was going crazy. The chandelier was no longer swaying, remained still as it had been when he first got there.

He looked so real.

But there was no evidence, not a single hint.

Then he looked to the window, the mirrored reflection, and saw *her.*

Miranda Hoskins.

She was nearing him. He whipped around and faced her, the woman he'd once watched die in an empty alleyway. She hadn't overdosed like Mitch had suspected. Dylan had read the story in the paper a week after it happened. Her dealer had given her poison, cut her fix with ricin. If he'd dialed 9-1-1 when he first arrived, they might have had a shot at saving her. Mitch always told him that there was nothing they could have done, that she would have died anyway, but Dylan never believed him.

And now she was here.

In the same room.

Dead. But not.

She approached him. His eyes fell to the open wound on her arm, where she'd injected the poison that killed her. The hole was about the size of a quarter, black with rot and ruin and unearthly decay. And there were...*things* sticking out of it. Little obsidian ribbons undulating from the fluid surface, looking like rippling blades of grass on a windy day. Stretching, the things seemed to get bigger with each step Miranda took.

Dylan found his back against the window, and he stole a glance at the streets of Atlantic City. It was a far drop, and he was worried— if the specter wished—she could shove him to his death.

If she can touch me.

By his estimation, she *was* a ghost, and traditionally, ghosts were transparent. Using his knowledge of the supernatural, which he had gathered through endless hours of phony ghost-hunting programs, he doubted she could hurt him. Of course, he knew nothing of the real thing. The truth of the beyond was a mystery to him.

Dylan pictured himself barreling through her, racing toward the door, down the hallway and into the elevator. But the second he went to put his plan into motion, those black *somethings* exploded forth from Miranda's arm. They reached out and stretched like taffy, three in total, grabbing him, lifting him off the soft, shaggy carpet. One went for his throat, corkscrewing around his flesh like the tentacle of some deep-sea monster around an unsuspecting galleon, and choked him. The two others gripped him underneath his arms. They pushed him against the window, held him there.

"Please!" he shouted, before the black vine tightened around his throat. The ghost's peculiar extension was as thick as an elevator cable, had swelled to three times its size since escaping her wound. "I wanted to save you!"

The apparition did not speak. Miranda only smiled, knowingly, her lips curling on one end. Her dark eyes stared as she paced back and forth, as if she were contemplating what to do with him.

Then, the vine released his throat. She continued to hold him in place as he pled for his life.

He followed the fluid motion of the black vine, watching it scoop an object off the ground, a tiny something that looked like a...

A needle.

Shit.

"No, please. I... I don't deserve this."

The ghost looked like it wanted to laugh but a wry smile fixed her lips instead. Before Dylan could protest once again, the needle was already entering the softest spot in the crook of his right arm, sinking the contents of the syringe into his veins, flooding his system with...

...poison.

He fought against it, squirmed, tried to wriggle his way to freedom, but it was no use. Every effort to break free failed. She picked up another needle and stuck him again. Then a third. He had no idea where they were coming from, but by the fifth stick, he felt lightheaded, woozy, and nauseous. By the seventh stick, his world had grayed near the edges. By the tenth, he was lost to a blurry veil from which he would never recover.

The last thing he saw before fading out was the crooked smile of the woman he could have saved, the woman who'd won him a cool five grand and pushed him down this path of moral decay.

If he wasn't so numb, he would have screamed.

"Sorry to bother you, Chief Hoskins," the young detective said, pacing the living room of the Sugarstone suite. "But since the room is under your name, thought you might be able to I.D. the kid. Paint us a better picture of what happened here."

Morton Hoskins walked over to the wall of windows and peered down at the corpse. The deceased's flesh had already taken on a dark hue, deep gray patches that resembled gathering storm clouds. Morton's eyes bounced from the dead kid to the dead girl in the window's reflection. She placed a gentle finger over her smiling lips. From her arm, the black extensions slithered and twisted, as if begging to be fed again.

Christ, Morton thought to himself. *I thought this would end it.*

He'd already delivered her the two fuckwads who'd watched her die, who'd placed bets on her survival. He thought that would make her go away, release her from this existence. But the way she looked at him, the way her eyes glimmered with the need to feed, the way the black tongues growing out of her arm licked the air with an eternal hunger; that told him his work wasn't done.

"Morton?" the detective said, snapping him out of it.

"Yes?"

"The kid? You recognize him?"

It took a moment to deliver the lie. "No, never seen him before."

"Hmm. Just another junkie that broke into your room, wrecked the place, and then overdosed?"

"Yes."

The detective eyed him as if he could smell the deceit. "Well, that would explain the broken door frame. And the...mess."

Morton nodded.

The detective closed his notepad. "I guess that's it then. Sorry for bringing you out here like this, but, you know, protocol and all. Wouldn't want to deviate from the rules just because you're the boss."

"I appreciate your due diligence."

The detective smiled. "At least that's another scumbag junkie off the streets."

Morton's face went rigid, lost some color.

The detective's smile immediately went missing. "Oh shit. Sorry, boss. I totally forgot about Miranda."

"It's...all right."

"I didn't mean it like that, I—"

"I said it's all right, detective."

"Miranda, man. She was...different."

Morton nodded. "Why don't you get out of here. I'll finish up."

"Are you sure?"

"Yeah."

"I'll stay if—"

"I'd like to tidy up a few things, alone, if you don't mind."

"Yeah..." The detective looked like he knew leaving him was wrong, especially with so much evidence that could be contaminated. Plus, the coroner hadn't even shown up yet. "I don't have to tell you not to trespass the yellow tape, do I?"

Morton laughed. "No. No, I'm not going to muck up a crime scene."

The detective laughed nervously as Morton showed him to the door, thanked him, and wished him goodnight.

Once he was gone, down the hall and into the elevator, Morton returned to the center of the room. Facing the window and the shadowy outline that stared back at him, he held his arms out in surrender.

"How many more?" he asked, almost out of breath. He felt like crying. In his eyes, tears were born. "How many?"

"Just one," a frail, raspy voice whispered in his ear.

Before he could react, defend himself in any way, a long black vine rose from the floor, possessing a syringe.

His final scream was cut short by the needle slamming into his voice box.

The Graveyard

by Lee Mountford

That place freaked me out.

I know it shouldn't. After all, I'm fifteen years old, and, despite what my mother says, that means I'm almost a man. And men shouldn't be scared of graveyards. They were just places where the dead went to rest.

That's what Dad always said. And they are as normal and safe as a convenience store or a park.

And yet, every night, I feel the need to look out my bedroom window; the one that overlooks an old graveyard, which is attached to the ancient-looking church. I do this just to check that everything is safe, and that there is nothing... unnatural...wandering around down there. Even now, as I look down at the gravestones—all of which are weathered to varying degrees, some even crumbling and threatening to topple over—I fully expect to see a shambling corpse come shuffling into view.

It doesn't, thankfully, and all remains quiet. But there are stories about that graveyard that circulate around school.

People in this town have gone missing over the years. More than is normal for a small community like ours, and many of those were last seen close to the church and graveyard. No one is buried there anymore, and the church is no longer in use, long since abandoned. There are tales of things living inside: inhuman things. Some say monsters, most say ghosts. Whatever they are, apparently their ghastly wails can be heard sometimes at night. I have to admit, on occasion, I have woken up in the dead of night, sure I'd heard something myself.

But Dad says it is all childish...what was the word? Superstition! That was it! Stories told by liars and spread by the gullible.

There were no such things as monsters or ghosts.

So, it should have been easy to meet Sean out there, as we had planned. But that was not the case, I was just too afraid. So I backed out.

The whole thing was his idea, and it had been planned today at school. Sean was always pushing people into doing things they didn't want to, and if he ever got the impression someone was unwilling or nervous about one of his ideas—as I guess he did with me when he came up with this brainwave—then that only made him push harder. Despite being a friend, I guess it was true that he could be a bit of a bully.

The screen of my mobile phone lit up again. It was another text from him.

Nearly there. I guess you can just watch me from your window then if you aren't turning up. Just keep watch up in the chicken seats! Real men are brave. Like me!

I decided to ignore it, as I had the previous message, where he told me he was going on his own after I'd backed out. It was pointless saying anything to him, because if I did, he would only get even more insistent that I jump to his command.

Eventually, even though I hoped the thought of going to that place alone would prove too creepy for him and he'd back out, I saw someone approaching the boundary wall. There was no doubt it was Sean, easily distinguishable from his shock of messy blond hair and his tall, gangly frame.

He paused at the stone wall—one that stood a full foot higher than him—and looked around.

Back out! Please, just let him back out so he won't tease me about this!

No such luck.

I saw him jump up and grip the head of the wall before scrambling up its rocky surface.

Sean may have been a bully, but he was brave, I had to give him that. And my cowardice now meant he wouldn't let me live this down for a while, and I had a few weeks of teasing to look forward to.

He was soon able to swing his legs over the top and adjusted himself to a sitting position. Sean then turned his head and looked back in my direction. Though he was too far away to see clearly, it was obvious he knew I was watching, and he actually waved, before dropping down out of sight.

What the hell was wrong with me? Dad was right, there was nothing down there to be scared of. But I just couldn't shake that creeping feeling that washed over me whenever I looked at the place. I even had to break into a sprint whenever I walked past at night. And even during the daytime, it was at least a fast walk.

I don't think I really believed the stories, and I certainly hadn't seen anything scary or out of the ordinary, but as soon as I had looked out there tonight, I knew I was going to back out, and saw the teasing and ribbing I was due as the better option.

Soon I saw Sean come back into view again as he moved farther away from the boundary wall he'd dropped down behind and deeper into the graveyard. He weaved between headstones, both small and tall, and ran over the graves, holding his arms out by his sides like the wings of an aeroplane clearly enjoying himself.

And then something happened. Something that caused me to gasp as I felt my heart freeze. All of that primal fear—or, what my Dad called "irrational nonsense"—I'd felt about that creepy old graveyard suddenly seemed justified.

Something stepped out from behind a tall gravestone close to Sean. It was hard to describe and not just because of the distance between us, but because my mind struggled to make sense of it. At first, I thought it was just a shadow, cast by something out of view, but as the horribly long arms of the thing reached out and seized Sean, I saw the shadow actually had a weight to it, a certain mass, and colours beyond just black, such as mottled greys and dull yellows.

The thing stood up to its full height, uncurling like a balled up insect, and was soon much taller than Sean. It then easily scooped him up in its grasp, quickly pulling him back behind the gravestone and out of sight. It all happened in an instant, and Sean didn't even have a chance to scream.

I sat and watched in shock and terror, my heart racing as the hairs on the back of my neck stood on end.

What the hell was that?

Panic surged through me at the idea that something had taken Sean. Something that should not have existed. Something my Dad had insisted was make-believe, made up by liars and spread by the gullible.

But I knew what I had just seen.

I continued watching for a few moments more, praying for Sean to re-emerge unharmed, but after ten minutes had passed, then fifteen, I knew I had to do something. So, I ran to my parent's room and burst in, screaming for their attention. They were sound asleep, and my sudden outburst startled them. My mother even let out a sharp yelp as they awoke in shock. I told them what I'd just seen, tripping over words that refused to leave my mouth fast enough.

At first, they looked worried, but when I reached the part about the shadow-thing taking Sean, I saw the expression on my Dad's face change.

It wasn't worry anymore. It turned to confusion. Then to disappointment.

"Are you sure it wasn't a nightmare?" he asked, not even trying to hide his annoyance and disappointment in me. I told him it wasn't a nightmare, that I knew what I had just seen.

But Dad didn't believe me. Neither did my mother. And, no matter how much I tried to persuade them otherwise, I was simply ignored. Eventually, my Dad raised his voice and ordered me back to bed.

I sloped off, back to my room, and again looked from the window and out over the graveyard, hoping to see Sean alive and well. But I watched for hours and saw nothing. No movement at all.

Was Dad right? Had I fallen asleep and become confused in a state halfway between dream and reality?

I could go down there and check for myself, of course. I could show some courage and help out a friend in need. But the thought of that filled me with dread, similar to what I'd felt when I'd seen that shadowy-thing take Sean.

My cowardice prevailed, and I did nothing, eventually falling asleep in the early hours of the morning.

At school the next day, my friends all noticed Sean's absence.

Where is he? Is he playing hooky again? Is he ill?

I was exhausted and a bundle of nerves all day, and deeply ashamed at my cowardice last night, so I didn't say anything. Sean skipping school was not uncommon, so no one was overly concerned. All except me.

Because I knew he was dead.

So, I was therefore more than a little surprised when, after cutting down a quiet street during my walk home from school, I bumped into none other than… Sean.

"Sean?! What the hell! Are you okay?"

He frowned. "Of course, why wouldn't I be?"

"Because of last night. In the graveyard."

"Oh, you saw me?" he asked with a grin. "I wasn't sure if you were watching, you chicken."

"But… I saw what happened."

"What do you mean?"

"That… *thing*! The thing that grabbed you!"

His expression was now one of bewilderment. "Dude, what the hell are you talking about?"

I took a breath, struggling to make sense of everything. I was certain of what I'd seen the previous night…*wasn't I?* But here Sean was, looking right as rain, and seemingly confused about what I was talking about. "So…nothing happened?" I asked.

"Well, I explored the place a little," he replied. "Spent maybe a half hour there, then hopped the wall again and left. But…" his face broke out into a conspiratorial grin and he lowered his voice, "I did find something there. Something really cool!"

"What?" I asked, almost whispering myself.

"Can't say," he replied with a chuckle. "But it's amazing. Seriously, you won't believe it until you see it."

"Tell me," I pressed, the need to know suddenly rising. I hated being deliberately kept out of the loop with things. It made me feel like an outsider.

"No way. If you hadn't been such a coward, you would have seen it yourself last night. But you stayed home in bed, like a little girl."

I should have expected that. In truth, I was surprised it had taken him even this long to call me out for bailing on him. I felt myself bristle with anger and shame.

Not only had I proven him right about my lack of bravery, but I'd also, apparently, completely imagined some kind of ghost or monster, as well. Something that obviously wasn't real.

Just like little kids did when they got scared.

"Tell you what," Sean said with a sneer. "We can try again tonight, if you want. We'll sneak out and go back to the graveyard. Then I can show you what I found. And, trust me, you're going to be amazed. Unless, of course, you don't have the balls for it," Sean said as he grabbed his own nut-sack and laughed.

I felt myself scowl. "I'm not a chicken!" I shouted. "You're on. We'll go there tonight."

Sean nodded his approval. "Cool. But you aren't gonna back out again, are you?"

"I won't back out." I stated and puffed out my chest.

"All right then," he replied. "Meet me outside the wall at ten tonight. And be ready to be amazed."

With that, Sean walked past me, bumping me with his shoulder as he did. I felt nervous about what I'd just agreed to, but I was equally angry at myself for thinking I'd seen something that had clearly been imagined. I was reminded of my Dad's disappointed face after I'd told him what I thought I'd seen last night.

So, come hell or high water, tonight I was going to prove I wasn't a coward. I was going to go to that creepy graveyard with Sean and see just what it was he thought was so cool.

"You ready?" Sean asked.

I wasn't sure of the answer. We stood before the old, stone wall that circled the perimeter of the graveyard. The wind was cool, but not cold, yet I still felt a shiver run down my spine. Night had set in a while ago, and it was well after midnight. My heart raced, but I was determined to prove my mettle to Sean.

"Let's go," I said.

He smiled. "Perhaps you aren't a coward after all." Sean then took a step back in order to give himself a short run-up. After a few long strides, he leapt, and his hands managed to grip the stone capping at the top of the tall wall. His toes instantly found purchase in the generous, mortared gaps between the stone blocks, and he quickly and effortlessly scrambled up and swung a leg over the top, straddling the wall, and looking proudly down on me. He then waited, saying nothing.

This, it seemed, was my invitation to join him.

Despite the trepidation I was feeling, I did just that. Every instinct was screaming at me to run, flee, and go home to safety, but I knew I had to ignore all of that. I needed to man-up. This was a tough world, and I couldn't be ruled by fear. It was more than just proving to Sean I wasn't a coward—it was proving it to myself, as well.

My climb up the wall wasn't as quick or as elegant as Sean's. After my initial leap, I almost lost my grip on the top, barely reaching it with my fingertips. And I also struggled to use the toe of my shoes to push myself up as he had, losing my footing more than once before I was finally able to heave myself to the top and join Sean.

I looked out over the graveyard before me and the chill I had been feeling only intensified.

Of course, I had seen the inside of this place before, but only from the safety of my bedroom window. This was different. It was closer. And it felt much more dangerous.

"Creepy, isn't it?" Sean asked with a snigger.

It was. A thick layer of mist had settled across the ground, and headstones poked through it like mountaintops through the clouds. The streetlights outside of the graveyard's boundary didn't penetrate very far inside, and, other than the moonlight, there wasn't a single light source inside, which ensured the darkness was deep and foreboding. Off in the distance, I could just make out the imposing structure of the adjoining church, with its old brickwork, high windows, and dilapidated roof.

The whole place was like a cliché, right out of a lame horror movie. But up-close and personal, it felt anything but lame. And making matters worse, the ground inside of the wall was much lower than that outside, with the stone barrier acting as a retaining structure against the level difference. It meant that, after the drop, getting back out would be much more difficult. In truth, I didn't know if I could leap high enough to make that climb.

But Sean had gotten out last night, I reasoned, and that meant there must be a way.

I still wanted to turn back, to just spin myself around and drop from this wall, safely outside the graveyard. But, as if sensing my anxiety, he quickly jumped down inside of it, his feet causing a dull thud as they penetrated the mist and hit the ground.

Sean looked back up to me, his grin still firmly in place. He knew I was wavering.

I took a breath, swung my leg over the top of the wall, and dropped…landing inside next to Sean. I stumbled as my feet made contact and fell, landing face first in the cold, wet grass. I expected to hear Sean's laughter at my clumsy dismount but was surprised to be met with only silence. I got quickly to my feet and turned to face him, braced for his teasing, ready to tell him to shut up.

But, instead, I felt my breath catch in my throat.

Sean was gone.

I looked around, frantic, sure I would see him running to hide behind a tree or headstone in an effort to scare me. But the nearest object was too far away for that to be possible. I'd only lost sight of him for a brief moment after falling on my face, but had been up again in an instant, only to see he had completely vanished. Surely, there hadn't been enough time for him to make it to any kind of hiding place in that time?

So where the hell was he?

"Sean!" I yelled.

I quickly shrunk back at the sound of my own voice echoing around me in the otherwise silent night air. It had been loud—too loud—and I feared it could draw the attention of something…unsavoury.

Stop being a coward! I admonished myself, trying to force rational thought over the fear that was building.

But it was no good. No amount of rational thinking could explain Sean's disappearance. I felt my heart-rate speed up. I had to get out of here.

Not caring that I may have been leaving Sean alone, I took a few quick steps back to the wall and leapt. But my fingertips fell agonisingly short. I jumped again, trying to scramble up the uneven surface, but simply slipped back down, scrapping my shin as I did. I even tried to grip the stone and slowly climb it but was unable to get a good enough hold.

The panic rose within. And, as it did, my efforts to scale the wall drew less and less success, and I quickly realised I was not going to get back out the way I'd gotten in.

Which meant only one thing.

I would have to venture deeper into the graveyard and find an alternate way out.

So I turned to look at the route ahead, my mind still reeling from Sean's inexplicable disappearance. My legs felt rooted to the ground, and the thought of heading deeper into this place, and walking between the headstones and markers of the dead, was almost enough to seize my heart. A sense of unknown danger seemed palatable, even if somewhere inside my rational mind was trying to get my attention and tell me there was nothing to be scared of.

Even Sean's sudden disappearance, my mind tried to argue, could be explained if I just forced myself to calm down and think.

I took a deep breath and exhaled slowly, willing myself to gain some form of composure.

Then I heard a noise to my right that caused my head to whip around quickly to meet it.

Had my ears been playing tricks? Or was that...a laugh? It had been so brief I couldn't be sure, but it was certainly my first thought. My breath caught in my throat and any notion of regaining a calm state suddenly evaporated.

"H...hello?" I stuttered.

The laugh sounded again, this time unmissable.

It was the laugh of a child.

A high-pitched giggle that came from behind an old and weathered headstone up ahead. It had an echoey quality to it.

My whole body shook, and I felt my bladder loosen, but peeing myself barely even seemed to register because I soon saw something peek out at me from behind the stone marker. Even from this distance, I recognised it was a face. Small and, were it not for the fact it was horribly decayed, child-like. Its eyes were a solid milky-white.

"*Helllllllloooo,*" the thing replied in a whisper that sounded hoarse and pained.

Instinct kicked in, thankfully overcoming the fear that had previously frozen me to the spot, and I ran. I knew I was running deeper into the graveyard, but I just needed to be away from...whatever the hell that thing was.

I weaved between headstones and my feet pounded atop the resting places of the deceased. Had I not been so terrified, it might have felt disrespectful. But the vision of that dead, child-like thing behind me pushed me on, and I ran until my lungs burned.

Eventually, I could run no more, and every breath felt like inhaling fire. I stopped and bent double, pulling searing air into my body. I felt dizzy and struggled to keep my knees from buckling. I could still see that rotten thing creeping out from behind the headstone.

"Helllllloooooo."

I looked back as I continued to pant, expecting to see the thing lumbering through the mist after me but saw nothing. Then I turned to examine my surroundings, knowing I had to formulate a plan to get out of this place as quickly as possible.

And that was when I saw him, sitting on the ground—legs covered by the layer of mist—and back propped up against a large, stone mausoleum. His head lolled to one side. His skin was pale and his open eyes were blank. He also looked a little gaunter than he had only minutes ago.

It was Sean. And he was obviously dead.

Had been for a while, I knew, looking at the condition of the body slumped against the tall mausoleum.

Which made no sense, as I had seen him only minutes ago.

I screamed and screamed as the level of terror I was already feeling suddenly spiked.

"Chicken!"

The voice came from the direction of the body, but from a space beyond it; behind the mausoleum. And it sounded different—like that child-like thing I had seen earlier. It was ethereal, somehow, and strained. But, at the same time, familiar.

A figure moved into view from behind the stone structure. Its movements were stilted, like a marionette learning to walk.

Sean.

"This can't be real," I said in a voice that was barely a whisper.

Sean laughed as he slowly moved closer. He looked similar to the body that lay on the ground, except his eyes were completely white, and the dark-purple tongue that slid from his mouth was impossibly long and fat.

"*It made me bring you here. It made me,*" he said. "*It wakes up every few decades to collect more of us. And it is feeding again now.*"

"Please," I said, my voice little more than a pathetic mewl. "Please, just let me go."

Sean continued to stalk toward me with those stunted movements. "*Nope. Sorry. The things here want you. You're already dead, your body just doesn't know it yet. And you'll live here forever with the rest of us. It hurts. Oh boy, does it hurt. All the time. Such sweet pain.*"

If my bladder had not emptied earlier, then it surely would have now. Again, I ran, thankful I was able to summon strength enough to force my body into action.

But I did not get far. I stopped in my tracks at the thing that stood before me, motionless in the dark. It was tall, towering well over seven foot, and covered with a dark cloak that hung down to its feet. A wide-rimmed hat covered its head, but its pale face was perfectly visible. It had unnaturally wide eyes that bulged horribly from their sockets. The nose was gone, replaced only by a fleshy hole where it should have been, and there was a skeletal, grinning mouth, devoid of any lips. The tall thing didn't move, but bore its horrible gaze down on me.

This can't be real. It can't be real. Can't be real.

As if reading my thoughts, I heard the monstrous watcher before me start to chuckle, and its teeth chattered together as it did.

Desperation clouded my senses. I had never felt such terror and danger before in my life. Perhaps this was just a dream and I would wake up soon, all safe and warm in my bed, with my parents standing over me.

I turned again, about to run, but saw that was not going to be possible. Suddenly, the graveyard was teaming with life, all of it horrifying.

The ungodly forms of the dead and the otherworldly started to emerge, crawling out from behind gravestones, trees, and even rising up out of the mist itself. The figures that moved toward me were human, or used to be, but had rotted and decomposed to various degrees. All had milky-white eyes and were twisted and misshapen in some way. An impossibly thin man dressed in dull rags pushed an old, Victorian wheelchair forward, with loud squeaks ringing out with every revolution of the large wheels. He was practically a skeleton, with loose strips of grey flesh hanging from his bones. Another was a woman, dressed in a high-necked black dress, hair up in a bun. Her eyes were wide, face horribly gaunt, and jaw completely missing so her black tongue dangled down to her neck.

And, amongst them all, one figure stood motionless, taller than the others. Its body was skinless, and the exposed flesh dripped with glistening blood. Where a face should have been, there was a large, pulsating hole, filled with sharp, needle-like teeth.

As I took in the sight of these things, my heart started to beat at a rate I had never known before, and a pain shot down my left arm. Breathing became difficult, and I was unable to carry on my desperate screams. Excited murmurs sounded out from the demonic horde that slowly closed in from all sides.

"Please," I managed to wheeze out, begging, and dropped to my knees as the world became blurry. I felt a cold hand on the back of my neck, and I turned my head. Through squinted eyes I was able to make out Sean standing above me, looking at me with those white, dead eyes.

"It's time," he said. My heart felt like it was on fire, and each horrible beat sent out another jolt of electric pain from the failing organ. The world spun and darkness claimed me...

...and then, I was being pulled along the ground. I opened my eyes again. I was still in the graveyard, it was still night-time, and these creatures were still all around me. But the pain from my chest was gone. I lifted my head and saw something that caused me to cry out in horror, my voice sounding different.

Somehow…echoey.

My body lay on the ground, face down and motionless. And I was being pulled away from it.

I turned to see what was dragging me, and what I saw—a terrifying and impossible, multi-eyed thing—should have shattered my mind. At once I knew that this…entity…was the thing behind all the madness here in this graveyard. This ungodly and eldritch nightmare that almost defied description. And it continued to pull me, with thin, writhing arms, toward its gaping mouth.

Sean walked beside me as I squirmed and fought.

"*It's going to feed on you now,*" he told me. "*And look over there.*" I followed his pointing hand, and could see my house way off in the distance. The light to my parents' room was on. "*Your father has just had a nightmare,*" he told me. "*So he's going to check on you. Won't find you, though. But you told them about this place, and soon your body will be found here, along with mine. They'll say we died of heart attacks. But, one night in the next few weeks, your dad is going to come down here with your mum. He won't be able to let go of what happened, you see. So he'll come, and your mum will follow. Everything has been laid out already, so there is no stopping it now. And then you will get to see them again, and they will live here with us forever.*"

I looked back at my house again. The light to my room came on. I knew my Dad would find it empty. And then he would come for me. I screamed and cried and wailed as the creature pulled me into its mouth and swallowed me whole.

Join My Club

by Somer Canon

Outside, the sky went up forever. The expanse held a peaceful quality, a serenity in its vastness. It was better out there. Inside, where the rooms were small and the noises were too loud, Mommy cried and yelled and Daddy hit him. Outside, there were butterflies and big, colorful spiders in the tiger lilies. Within the shade of the big pine tree, he could pretend he had his own house, a place where he made all the rules. In *his* house, there was no yelling, and he could have pretend-pancakes for dinner every night. Beyond the shadow of the great tree there were also noisy birds and colorful cars; lots of neat things to look at. Nobody told him to go away or hit his face in the safety of the outdoors.

That particular day, it was really bad inside. Mommy made watery scrambled eggs for breakfast, and Daddy got so mad that he pulled her back to their bedroom by her hair. She cried, and Daddy called her bad names. There were loud thumps and screams, but when the deeper, rhythmic slapping started, it scared him more than the sounds of Mommy being slammed around. He knew that that distinct slapping was specifically adult and hearing it mixed with Mommy's cries and Daddy's grunts sent him rushing out the front door, his favorite stuffed dinosaur clutched tightly to his chest.

He was sitting on the cinderblock stoop, petting the soft toy, hoping the stray cat would visit him. It was nice and rubbed its head on him, and he liked when it purred. Mommy always told him not to touch it, saying it was gross and dirty. She chased it off whenever she saw it, but he didn't mind that it wasn't smooth and pretty like the kitties on TV. It was nice having something that was happy to be around him.

Walking around to the side of the house, he hoped for something to grab his attention. Nothing did, but he stood still a moment, waiting for that special-interesting-something to keep him occupied until Mommy called him to come inside for dinner.

He jumped when he heard a metallic knocking. It was coming from the little metal closet where the lawnmower was kept. Mommy called it a lean-to. He didn't like it in there. It was small, with only enough room for the mower and the weed whacker. It smelled bad, and it was dark. In the back corners, the sunlight, no matter how bright a day it was, could never reach, leaving shadows that made him think there was something in there. Something hiding from the light.

The knock came again, and he started to get scared. His eyes darted towards the front of the house, but he'd get in big trouble if he bothered Mommy and Daddy when they were in their bedroom.

"Hello?" a voice called from within the lean-to. It was a child's voice. His fear lessened, and he reached a hand out and knocked on the side panel. There were three returning knocks from inside.

"What's your name?" the voice inside asked.

"Timmy," he answered, feeling a little shy. The voice inside giggled.

"Really? My name's Tommy. We almost have the same name."

Timmy laughed. It was looking as if the day's excitement was going to be better than the stray kitty. "How old are you?"

"Seven," Tommy answered, his voice having a tinny echo to it. "How old are you?"

"Five." Timmy worried that a bigger kid might not want to play with him, would see him as just some baby.

"I'm older than you."

"Yeah," Timmy said, expecting rejection.

"I used to live here, you know."

"You did?" Timmy asked, surprised.

"Uh huh. My parents didn't want to stay, though, so I guess that's why you live here now." Tommy sounded a little sad.

Timmy and his parents hadn't lived in the house for very long. Their place before only had one bedroom and he had to sleep on the couch. It was nice to have his own bedroom where he could go and be alone so he didn't bother his parents. They were always telling him he was too noisy, even when he was being as still and quiet as a picture on the wall.

"Which room did you sleep in? The one with the brown carpet or the pink carpet?" Timmy asked.

"The pink carpet. The one with the brown carpet has that door, and my parents didn't trust me to stay put at night." Tommy answered, still sounding a little sad.

"I sleep in the pink carpet room too! It's a real nice room, and the window is right over my new bed, so I can look and see the moon, if it's out. Did you sleep by the window?"

"No, my bed was up against the other wall. Do you have a lot of toys? I had a lot of cars and trucks and this really big teddy bear my grandpa got me."

"I don't have a lot of toys, but, my mommy says if I'm good, I might get a bike for my birthday. I'd go so fast on a bike."

"It was really nice riding around here on my bike," Tommy said.

"That's so cool!"

"You wanna join my club?"

Timmy perked up. "Really? Can I?"

"I asked you, didn't I?"

"Yes! I want in your club!"

"Awesome! Just slide open the door and come inside with me."

Timmy paused. "In there?"

"You scared?" Tommy asked.

Timmy was afraid of admitting his fear to an older kid. Tommy would laugh at him if he knew that Timmy was scared of the stupid little lean-to.

"It's not scary in here, Timmy. You know where I'm scared to go? In the house. The grownups are mean and angry, and your dad does bad, bad things."

Timmy lowered his eyes and hugged his stuffed dinosaur tight.

"My parents are like that too. I hide from them in here. It's not scary in here because they're not in here. It's just me, but maybe it could be just *you* and me." Tommy said.

"Why do you come all the way here to hide? Isn't there a place at your new house to hide?"

"This will always be where I live," Tommy said, that sad note back in his voice.

"Do your parents worry about you being gone? I'm not allowed out of the yard."

"But would your parents really notice if you weren't here? If they're like mine, they never even look out the windows to see if you're still here. Do they ever poke a head out the door to say hi to you or offer you snacks or drinks? I bet they don't, because they're happier when you're not around them, Timmy." Tommy's voice sounded shaky, like he was close to crying.

Timmy sniffled, hoping Tommy didn't hear. He wiped the tears from his cheeks and used the softness of his dinosaur friend to wipe his eyes.

"Come inside, Timmy, and we can play. No mean parents. Just us."

Timmy looked again towards the home's entrance. He wanted so badly to play with the boy, but there was a sick feeling in his tummy, and he wanted his mommy, to feel her hug him and tickle his cheeks and be wrapped in her sweet-smelling, soft warmth. He wanted to feel her love.

Another tear ran down his cheek. No. Mommy would yell at him if he went to her, and, if she didn't, Daddy would whip his butt. Tommy was right and that hurt his heart.

"Come join my club, and let's play." Tommy said.

Wiping his face on his dinosaur again, Timmy steeled himself. He had to jerk the metal door as it was bent and didn't stay on its tracks. When the door was finally open, he peered tentatively inside. The air was usually hot in the lean-to and smelled so bad he could taste it, but not this time. There was a chill in there, but it was somehow not refreshing on that hot day. It had a fetid nature to it, mixed with the stink of rot and gasoline. It made Timmy uneasy.

"Tommy?" he asked, trying to keep the fear from his voice.

"I'm back here," the voice whispered.

"I can't see you," Timmy said, shaking.

"But you can hear me, can't you? I'm right here. You just have to come in."

Timmy whimpered. He started to worry the older kid was playing a cruel trick on him. Maybe Tommy was behind the lean-to, and when Timmy stepped inside, he would run around and close the door, leaving Timmy in total, suffocating darkness.

"Can I see your face?" Timmy asked.

"Timmy, I'm right here," Tommy said, gently. "Look."

The lawnmower was pushed slightly, and it rolled towards Timmy, but it traveled only an inch or two. He smiled.

Excited at the prospect of a new playmate and his fear forgotten, Timmy stepped carefully inside, finding a place for his foot that wasn't occupied by the dirty, old lawn equipment.

His breath was taken away. He couldn't draw in air. His dinosaur fell to the ground and he tried to reach his hands up to his throat, but found they seemed to weigh a ton, too heavy for him to lift.

"Don't be scared, Timmy," he said. "It's not scary in here with me."

But Timmy was scared. He couldn't breathe or move. It felt like hours as he stood like a tree, stiff and still, unable to make a single noise. His chest was aching to expand with precious air, and his head was hurting awfully bad. It was getting hard to see. The metal handle of the lawnmower was glinting in the sunlight, but the colors were going dark, and his head was feeling funny.

He was jerked free of something. There was a feeling of being light, like a big, wet beach towel had just been lifted off of him. The terror of not being able to breathe forgotten, he went to Tommy, who he could clearly see sitting in the back corner, smiling at him.

"Welcome to the club," Tommy said. "Now we can play. And it's just us."

The Cemetery Man
by John Everson

If a girl ever tells you that she thinks it would be hot to have an intimate date with you in the cemetery, I'd recommend walking steadily away. I didn't.

I wish I would have.

Kendra Jenkins was a quiet girl. The sort of wallflower type that blends into crowds better than blue into gray. But she had this thing about her. Maybe it was the crease in the corner of her eyes. Maybe it was the slight tremor in her voice when she talked; not of fear, but of nervous excitement. Her voice wavered and dove as she'd softly talk about the things that really got her going. I remember meeting her at an adult education class I was taking on film noir appreciation. Her feet would twitch whenever the instructor played a clip of an old black and white movie. Especially at the parts where the film showed a pair of black shoes striking the pavement in an increasing rhythm, as the focal character realized that he or she was being pursued by something in the shadows.

After watching her calves tremble with excitement during one too many Hitchcock films, I had to ask her out one night after class. We had coffee at a little Bohemian place, and I knew she was having difficulty saying the things she wanted to say. Or maybe she just didn't know what to say. Her eyes blinked nervously whenever I looked directly at them. She looked away and played with her hands.

Finally, when the conversation got really awkward, I asked her if she wanted to take a walk. She nodded, and I paid the bill quickly. Minutes later, we were walking down a sheltered street, and passing a cemetery. It was an old one, the grounds well sheltered by a forest of trees. Kendra's feet slowed, and I could see the now-familiar signs of excitement in her body.

"Do you want to go in?" I asked.

I felt really weird about undoing a girl's bra while I had her bent over a gravestone. That said...weirdness didn't stop me. A guy has to have priorities. And tits beat propriety hands-down any day.

Kendra moaned as my fingers fumbled with the clasp across her spine, and when she decided I was taking too long, my hands were suddenly joined by her own fingers and the clasp snapped open. I don't know why they make those damn things so hard to open; it's like they're protecting gold or something...well, on second thought...

My hands slipped under the front of her bra, and, in seconds, she'd shrugged out of it so that two brown nubs begged me for kisses beneath the moonlight. How could I say no? Trust me, I didn't. And Kendra didn't either. For all her shyness and awkwardness earlier, once we were inside the wrought iron gates of the cemetery, she lost all inhibition.

"Did you ever see Jean Rollin's *The Iron Rose?*" she asked me as my lips suckled her ear.

"No," I whispered. "Is it a noir?"

"Not as such," she gasped. My fingers had slipped beneath the belt of her jeans. "Rollin was a French director who experimented in the '70s with a slew of movies mixing eroticism and horror. *The Iron Rose* was about a couple lost in a cemetery. At first, they're playing with the forbidden and making out in a tomb...but then, they get spooked, and they can't find their way out of the graves."

I looked up from sucking myself a good mark of new ownership on her neck and saw the pointed spears of the fence posts just a few rows of graves beyond us. "I don't think we'll have that problem," I suggested. "The gate is just over there."

"Yes," she said. "But what if it wouldn't open when we tried to get out?"

I trailed my tongue across her neck up to the underside of her jaw. "Then we'd climb the fence," I said.

She rolled her eyes. "You have no sense of futility."

"No," I agreed. "Because what I'm doin' right now is definitely not futile." With that I closed my teeth on her left nipple, and rolled it around on my tongue and teeth.

She moaned appreciation as my fingers fumbled with the clasp of her belt with just about as much success as I'd had with her bra.

The lights of a car flashed across the landscape of the cemetery, and we both pressed ourselves low to the stone until the dark came again. Kendra pushed herself off the flat surface of the broad cemetery stone and pulled me down to the grass before it. "Let's lie with the dead," she said, and then giggled self-consciously.

I couldn't believe this was the same girl who couldn't maintain a steady conversation at the coffee shop just an hour before. When we'd crossed the border into the cemetery at night, she'd seemingly switched personalities. Not that I was complaining.

"I love the dark," she said, as if reading my mind. "That's why I love the old movies so much. They're all about shadows. I'm not real comfortable in the daylight."

"I don't know why," I said, trailing my tongue down from her breasts to circle the thin dark pit of her navel. "You're beautiful."

She snorted. "Uh huh. While the lights are out."

My tongue slipped lower, and she stopped protesting. And then I heard a moan. Normally that would be something to make a man proud, when his tongue was making her talk...so to speak. But in this case, that moan wasn't coming from the throat just a couple feet above me.

I looked up, and her eyes flickered wide at the same time. "What was that?" I whispered.

She shook her head silently.

I twisted my neck, craning for a glimpse at what had made the noise. All I saw were tombstones. Gray-white stone silhouettes against the black of the sky as far as the eye could see. "I don't see anything,"

I whispered.

Her hands slipped first down my back, and then up along my spine. I shivered.

Then the moan came again.

I rolled off Kendra and into a crouch. With my shirt off and my pants half down my thighs, I must have looked like an ass. Like some guy crouched down about to take a shit. But I wasn't worried about how I looked. Someone was interrupting my enjoyment of tits, damn it. And it was not making me happy.

"Come on," I said, pointing at a stone crypt not too far away. "Let's get out of the open and away from the road."

Kendra nodded and held her shirt up against her bare chest with one hand as she held my fingers in the other while we sprinted together between the tombstones. When we arrived panting at the crypt, I read the name carved into the stone over the door. Tchichovesky, it said.

"I can't pronounce that," I said.

Kendra snorted. "I think it's Polish," she grinned.

"That doesn't help."

"Try the door," she suggested.

I laughed. "Right, like that's going to be left wide open." I reached out to test the iron grate that locked the Polish dead within this Chicago cemetery and oddly enough, it gave. Unlocked.

"After you," I suggested, when the heavy steel door to the inside of the crypt creaked open.

"Such a gentleman," Kendra said, but she also didn't wait for me. By the time I'd stepped all the way inside and turned, she'd dropped both her shirt and the rest of her clothes.

"Have you ever wanted to fuck in a tomb?" she asked, as her arms slipped around my waist.

"I gotta be honest…" I started to say. But then her tongue was in my mouth, and there really wasn't much point in trying to finish the thought. I quickly forgot about whatever noises I'd heard outside, because well…there was a naked woman underneath me. And her breasts were…do I really need to explain myself here?

At some point, she rolled me over, straddling me and rocking on my hips like I was some kind of decidedly non-puritanical carnival ride. Carnal ride, is what I was. In the dim light of the moon that lit the mausoleum we were in, I could still read the names of the tombs that were set in the wall behind her. The last name all read Tchichovesky. But there was one, closer to the floor, where the stone marker had been removed, and you could see the glint of a coffin just beyond.

I tried not to look, because seriously, coffins and erections? Guys—trust me on this, they don't generally mix. And I did not want to lose mine at that particular moment.

Nevertheless…when I heard the moan again from just outside the door of the tomb, I pulled out and away from Kendra.

"Something's out there," I whispered.

"So stick with me here," she said.

My eyes must have bugged out of my head at that, because she laughed. Out loud.

"What's the matter," she whispered. "Am I scaring you?"

I shook my head. "No, the fuckin' noise outside is creeping me out."

She laid back on the cold dusty stone of the crypt and looked up at me with clear intent. The spark from the darks of her eyes still shone in the shadows. She arched her back so that her tits stood up and demanded attention.

"Haven't you always wanted to fuck in a tomb?" she whispered again.

You know…in all honesty, I have to say that my answer to that was a big no. But at that particular moment, the mounds of her breast and the dark shadow of her pussy and the husk of her voice all pretty much cancelled out the fact that we were naked in middle of a house of bones. I found my erection again and briefly forgot the sounds from the graveyard outside.

Everything was great (if a little weird) until the screaming began.

This time when I pulled out, it was over.

"What the fuck was that?" I said. My cock withered wetly between my thighs like a limp weed.

Kendra sat up, hands suddenly eclipsing her chest. "I don't know," she whispered. The sex was out of her voice now. Her hand grasped for her shirt, and, in a flash, that amazing chest was covered in cotton.

Together, we trembled our way to standing and moved toward the door to the crypt. The noise from outside came again.

"Ohhhhowwwwwuhhhhhh!"

I forced myself to be the "man" and poked my head partway through the opening in the door. Just as I did, something cracked like a rifle shot outside.

The moaning stopped instantly.

That's when I saw him. A white face moving slow and deliberate amid the old stones. His eyes were black pocks in a head that seemed to glow on its own in the moonlight. Silver hair and skin so pale it hurt.

He moved across the graveyard like a wraith himself, but I knew in a heartbeat that he was real, not made of shadow and fear. A man walked amid the graves quiet and careful…but deliberate and steady. I knew in that moment this was the man to avoid. If you were in the graveyard and not dead…this was the man who would haunt you.

I did not want to be haunted.

"Get dressed," I hissed, and I could hear Kendra adjusting her clothes behind me as I watched the figure stalk the darkness between the stones. I buckled my own belt and pulled a shirt over my head.

"We need to go," I whispered. "Someone's out there."

Someone, was not really what I was thinking. More like…some *thing*. I held a finger to my lips and cautiously stepped out of the door of the crypt and back out and into the night. It's weird how you can "hear" the air move. While we'd been in the tomb, everything had been dead silent (no pun intended, honest). But as soon as we stepped outside, the world felt broader, and I could hear the thin movement of air across the rocks. From somewhere far down the row of headstones,

I heard that tortured moan. And then again came a sharp report. It probably sounded louder than it really was, given the lack of any other noise. I thought it was a gunshot.

I took Kendra's hand, and, together, we dashed between the headstones toward the exit. We both hunched halfway over, trying not to be seen by whatever lurked deeper in the grounds. I don't know if it really helped us to be unobtrusive, but it did slow us down. Have you ever tried running and crouching at the same time?

Nevertheless, we skulked our way stone to stone until the exit gate was in sight. I was just starting to breathe a little freer and straighten my running posture a bit, when my foot struck something soft and I stumbled.

Kendra's hand abruptly left mine, and I heard her stifle a shriek.

"What's wrong?" My whisper came out more like a strangled yell. Kendra wasn't looking at me though. Her eyes were locked on the thing that lay on the ground between us.

The thing I'd stumbled over in my stagger to the gate.

The thing whose mouth gaped open beneath a pair of empty black eyes that stared sightless toward the moon.

"Holy shit," I whispered, and knelt on the ground next to her. "I think he's dead."

"Yeah," Kendra said. Her voice was low and soft...but completely lacking in fear.

"That guy must've shot him," I said. I could hear the panic edging into my own voice. "We've gotta get outta here!"

"I don't think so," she said.

"What do you mean, you don't think so? There's a guy walking around here shooting a gun, and there's a dead guy right in front of you. I can put two and two together, and I don't think we should be here right now."

"I meant, I don't think that other guy is what killed him," Kendra said. "Look at his face. Closely."

I leaned closer and shifted to stop my shadow from blotting out the moonlight. The guy looked...old. His face was dirty white and covered with creases and scars. His hair was greasy and unkempt; at a quick glance, he appeared (and smelled) like a street bum who'd been lying here for the day. Or the week.

But Kendra was right. It was more than that. His skin wasn't just dirty and creased...it was discolored. The skin appeared to be flaking off like dandruff. His teeth were yellowed and cracked. The closer I looked, the less human the dead man appeared.

"Look at his hands." She nodded at the arm closest to me.

I followed her gaze and saw fingers gnarled like claws, blackened nails grown long enough to warp and twist. Tufts of hair curled out from below his knuckles. All I could think of was an article I'd read once that debunked the myth that when you're dead, your nails and hair keep growing, feeding off your rotting flesh...

"OK," I agreed, "He looks creepy as hell. But I still think the guy with the gun killed him."

I pointed at the blackened hole in the corpse's chest. You could see bone beneath the ragged opening in his tattered shirt.

"See any blood?" Kendra asked simply. I opened my mouth to argue—maybe to suggest the lack of splatter was due to cauterization?—but from somewhere not too far behind us, I heard another moan.

"Let's go," I demanded, grabbing her hand. "Now."

I pulled her to her feet, and, together, we ran the last few yards to the cemetery gate. We rounded the corner of the gate, and, when I looked back, I swear I saw the pearly white head of the guy I'd seen from the door of the tomb stalking toward the gravesite we'd just vacated. Was he coming back to get rid of the evidence, or was he coming for us? I didn't want to stick around to find out. I forced Kendra to run for the next five blocks until the cemetery was completely out of site.

"Are you scared of a dead body?" she asked when we finally came to a halt, and I leaned down to clutch my knees as I gasped for breath. Kendra, interestingly enough, barely seemed to have broken a sweat. I made a silent vow to start working out again. Clearly I was in piss-poor shape.

"No," I wheezed. "I'm scared of *becoming* a dead body. And sticking around the cemetery when some guy's walking around shooting people seems like a good way to become one."

"I'm not sure I want a guy who's that easily freaked to walk me home," she said. I turned to look at her in surprise and saw her eyes staring hard at me, unblinking. She was hungry for something and completely unshaken by what had just happened.

"Oh, am I walking you home?" I asked.

She shrugged nonchalantly and began to walk ahead of me. Gunfire, a stalking killer, dead rotting corpses...they all disappeared from importance as I remembered the feel of her breast in my hand.

"Which way do you live?" I asked, as I hurried to walk by her side.

Kendra lived just a few blocks from the cemetery, in an old brick apartment building that had not seen a facelift since the '70s. The hallway inside was paved in tight weave orange and gold carpet, and the stairway rails were painted utility green. But the feel of the building instantly changed when we stepped through the door of Kendra's apartment.

"Welcome to squalor," she said, as she flipped on the living room light.

It was hardly that. It was more like a museum of light and dark. Kendra had covered most of the apartment's bland beige carpeting with long black and gray carpet overlays. The passionless walls were nearly obscured by the array of poster-sized frames. Her apartment was a mosaic of black and white photography. Some of it was instantly recognizable. She had displayed movie stills from classic noir films like the haunting *Laura*, and the gleefully twisted gaze of Robert Walker as he outlines a murder in *Strangers on a Train*. There were several Hitchcock stills actually, including one provocatively deadly image from Janet Leigh's fateful shower in *Psycho*. And even without any actor's faces in the frame, I instantly recognized the opening running feet and trench coat from *Kiss Me Deadly*.

She saw me eyeing the art and smiled. "I like noir," she said. "A lot."

I nodded. "I see that. Gives the place color," I joked.

She raised an eyebrow, but didn't laugh.

"Do you want a drink?" she asked.

"Bourbon on the rocks," I said. "Hold the rocks."

She grinned. "Now you're just fuckin' with me. Although, I have to point out, you forgot to wear your private dick hat. But you know what, I can do that. Are you okay with Knob Creek?"

"It's not my favorite," I said. "But it'll do in a pinch. Just don't call me a dick again."

"Then don't be one."

She disappeared into a galley kitchen and left me alone to explore the two gray couches and four black and white walls of the living room. The place was small but definitely comfortable. Especially if you loved old movies. I sat down on one of the couches and stared up at the wall, trying to name all of the different films the photos and posters came from. They didn't all announce themselves. Her tastes ran deep. As glass clinked on the counter in the kitchen, it occurred to me that Kendra was a ringer in our film class. I'd guess from the look at her walls that she knew more about noir film than our professor.

I don't know when she slipped into her bedroom, but when she came back with my glass of amber "bad judgement" she was wearing a black silk robe. From what its silky thin material revealed, she wasn't wearing anything beneath it.

"Can I buy you a drink?" she asked, feigning a noir bad girl throaty husk.

"I think you already did." I took the glass and tilted it back, enjoying the burn of bourbon in my throat. The faint scent of lavender caught my nose, and I grinned as the liquor threatened to make me cough.

"Drink fast," she advised, plopping down on the couch next to me. I could see the pale curve of her calf as she rubbed it suggestively against my own.

"Why?"

"Because we got naked a little while ago in a cemetery," she said. Her voice was a rough whisper. "And that just makes me hotter than hell."

"You don't care that we also saw a dead guy?" I asked.

She took my left hand in her own and slipped it beneath her robe to a place both prickly and warmly wet.

"Clearly not," I answered my own question.

It was the first time I ever fucked someone beneath the leers of both Janet Leigh and Lana Turner, I have to say that. And probably the most energetic exercise I've ever had as well.

Let's just say when I woke up the next morning, things hurt that I didn't know I had. And that's probably enough said about that.

I watched the local paper the next couple days, looking for news of a corpse discovered in the cemetery. Which, as I write this, sounds like a stupid thing. What else would you find in a cemetery but a corpse?

Still, usually the stiffs are buried behind those iron gates, not lying around on the grass.

No "murder in the graveyard" stories appeared.

Kendra didn't seem interested in talking about the dead guy, but she lit up every time I mentioned the cemetery. It seemed to be about the only thing though that could get her to talk. She turned out to be something of a cemetery buff and had pictures from all sorts of famous cemeteries around the country. Green-Wood Cemetery in New York. Resurrection Cemetery in Chicago. St. Louis Cemetery in New Orleans and a hundred less famous places in between…Wherever she travelled, she said she always found the local burial grounds. She was one of those people who took gravestone etchings, so it made a lot more sense to me how hot making out on a gravestone had been for her.

We went out a few times over the next couple weeks, but none of our dates were quite like the first. That shy girl came back for long uncomfortable stretches. Frequently, she'd look distracted and stare over my shoulder when we were having a conversation. Or, more like, I was having a conversation. She really wasn't saying much.

I was starting to think that maybe this wasn't going to go anywhere. We hadn't gone back to bed since that first, bizarre date. Maybe that had been "heat of the moment" for her and she really wasn't that interested in me. I wasn't sure what to make of it.

Then one week in class, we watched the classic 1949 noir film *The Third Man*. I was sitting behind her since I got to class late. When the nighttime gravedigging scene began, her calves started rocking. She was wearing a summer skirt, and I grinned as I watched the hem shifting and shivering back and forth around her anxious legs. I swear I think she wanted to take one of the shovels and dig up a coffin herself.

After class, I asked if she wanted to go out for a drink.

She shrugged. "Maybe?" she said. "I've got some stuff I need to get done tonight, though."

I don't know what made me say it…probably her reaction to the graveyard scenes in the film. Grabbing for something to bring her attention back, I blurted, "We could stop at the cemetery afterwards?"

She paused. Her lower lip trembled; not much, just enough to show her thoughts were turning.

"It's a date," she said. "Pick me up in an hour? I need to change."

"Don't go changing…" I said, but she shook her head.

"Don't make me change my mind."

"Got it," I said. "See you at nine-thirty."

When I pressed the button to ring her apartment, Kendra didn't buzz me in and invite me up. Instead, her voice came over the tiny intercom speaker. "I'll be right down."

A moment later, I could see the elevator open just beyond the foyer. Kendra appeared, wearing a slinky off-the-shoulder black dress with fringe trailing across the top of her knees. She also wore black fishnet stockings and leather ankle boots. She'd pulled back her hair tight and wore red lipstick. She could have walked out of the movie we'd just watched earlier tonight. I felt like a bum in jeans and a brewery t-shirt.

When she stepped outside, I whistled.

"I believe I'm underdressed," I said.

She smiled but shook her head. "You promised me a cemetery," she said softly. "I just wanted to be ready this time."

I took her to The Penultimate Stop, a late-night bar on the edge of downtown that featured some fine mixology, but also had an impressive couple dozen taps. She ordered a Negroni, while I tried an obscure IPA. We talked a little about *The Third Man*—she was a big Orson Welles fan, but admitted it was the cinematography, not the actor, that really made the film.

When the bartender refilled our drinks, she made a point of saying "that's the last for me." She didn't talk much after that as we drank; her eyes roved the room, "people watching." The Negroni disappeared quickly.

"Care for a walk through the tombstones?" I asked when I noticed there were only cubes of ice left in her glass, and her gaze had stagnated to stare out of the bar window to the dark empty street beyond. Her eyes quickly met mine for the first time in several minutes.

"I thought you'd never ask," she said.

The cemetery was just around the block from The Penultimate Stop. I sometimes wondered if the place had gotten its name because of the graveyard. One last drink before you die? Kendra's step quickened the closer we got to the entrance.

The night was quiet; a faint breeze rippled the hair on the back of my neck as we slipped past the black wrought iron gates and down the main path through the cemetery. Stars pierced the blanket of night above like faint Christmas lights. The moon was only just beginning to rise.

Kendra's hands clenched my arm.

"I'm so glad you're here with me," she said.

I realized it didn't matter that it was *me*—she just needed someone who would humor her gravestone fetish. But still, I was glad to be the guy. Part of me knew she was damp already, just from walking into the place after dark. I intended to make her sopping wet before the night was through.

Her hand moved up and down my arm as we walked down the asphalt path that twisted and wound around the gravestones. At one point, I felt her massage the curve of my butt, and I began to look for a place that we could duck off the path to do what we'd come here for.

"Want to sit down?" I asked, pointing beyond a few rows of grave markers to a small clearing near a tree. There were bushes that hid part of the area from the path, which seemed ideal for what I had in mind.

But Kendra had other thoughts.

"Can we find that crypt we were in last time?"

She gave me one of those looks—you know, the pouty mouth, big dark eyes, "If you really love your baby doll, you'll do this thing for me" look.

"It's over this way," I said, and we began walking toward the older section of the cemetery, where there were larger stones. And eventually, full-fledged small stone houses.

I led her across the grass, winding between the granite stones toward the old gray tomb. There were several in this area, but I recognized the one we'd been in last time. A guy doesn't forget when he makes out in a mausoleum.

Somewhere behind us a night bird shrieked. At least, I hoped it was a night bird.

"You don't think that guy is wandering around tonight, do you?"

I shook my head instinctively. But then, of course, began to wonder if he was out there somewhere nearby. Maybe shooting someone. Causing distant shrieks that weren't birds at all.

"Let's get out of sight anyway," I said and pulled her to the door.

It opened like the last time, and we stepped into the heavy smell of must. I hated to think of the reason. There were small doors where I knew the coffins of this family lay in state. I turned my back to them and took her in my arms. Kendra's eyes sparkled with excitement. Her tongue moved with urgent excitement against mine. As her hands roamed my back, my own slid down to move up and under her dress. I could feel the silk of her hose and the garters that held them. And I was about to pull her down to the ground when she broke our wet kiss with words I didn't want to hear.

"Can you open one of the crypts so we can see the coffin?"

She was breathing heavy and her eyes looked desperate. I wanted to, but I couldn't say no.

"I'll try," I whispered.

There were six doors in the wall behind me, and I reached down to the lower middle and turned the silver handle.

The small door creaked open.

"Let me see," she whispered. She pushed around my shoulder to peer into the dark opening.

"Can you pull it out?" she asked.

"I don't think that's a good idea," I said.

She rubbed against me, shifting her thighs to scissor my leg. "Please?"

I reached into the darkness until my hands found the cold surface of hard wood.

Going against all of my instincts, I grabbed hold of the thing with both hands and pulled. The coffin shifted and moved easily out of the hole. Part of me was disappointed at that; I'd hoped it would stay put.

Kendra gasped audibly when the surface of the coffin came into view. A moment later, her tongue was in my mouth.

Seconds after that, and I was stripping the dress from her shoulders.

As the call of the night birds echoed eerily from outside, I laid Kendra down on the cold marble ground and uncinched her bra.

She didn't wait for me to work on the rest. In seconds, I was shirtless myself and sucking on her chest as her black stockinged feet wrapped around my waist.

I tried to slow us down, but this was going to go fast no matter what. Her wetness coated my skin as I moved from her mouth to her nipples and back again. I slid inside her without a thought.

Something creaked nearby, but I couldn't take my mouth from hers to look. I honestly didn't care at that moment. She was hotter than ever before, her fingers clawing my back, her legs dragging me, locking me deeper.

Without warning, she shifted her weight and rolled, pressing me down to the ground. She was grinning as she began to ride me cowgirl style, black garters easing up and sinuously down against and above my hips.

"Don't pinch," she complained, and I barely heard her.

"I said stop it," she said again.

"I'm not doing anything," I gasped.

Kendra's eyes opened. They stared at me, then at the position of my arms—which made it impossible for me to be the one pinching her.

She looked down at the blackened nail kneading at her soft white skin.

That's when I saw the face *behind* Kendra.

It was a ghastly, pasty face. A mask of frozen skin and blue veins. And a mummified hand reached around her ribs to rub and pinch a nipple.

Outside, something shrieked. This time the sound seemed much closer.

"I don't think we should have opened the coffin," I whispered.

Her eyes grew very wide. To her credit, she didn't scream. Instead, she moved her own hands until they encircled her breasts, and the blackened things that massaged them. And then slowly, carefully, she eased the hands back and away from her.

Then she turned to face the dead man who had taken advantage of her. I thought she'd finally let loose and scream when she took in the hideous visage that had crept out of the coffin to feel her up.

"Not so hard," she said instead.

I couldn't see the corpse's reaction; her body blocked his face from my view. But I could see his gray arms reach around her back, and those dark, wrinkled fingers dig into the skin near the slope of her ass and drag their nails upward.

I heard her moan in excitement instead of fear, and I finally found the courage to sit up.

"Kendra?" I whispered.

I leaned to the side and saw something I hope that someday I'll be able to forget. Though I doubt it.

Kendra had her lips on the pale dark lips of the corpse. And as I realized this, I saw her arms reach around his shriveled back and pull his crypt-cold skin close to hers.

The dead guy made a sound like gravel in a grinder, and suddenly he stood up, and yanked Kendra with him. She squealed with surprise, but didn't escape his grasp as he pulled her into the coffin he'd vacated. Kendra struggled then, a flash of white skin on gray, black garters on purpled veins, their bodies sliding against each other and the silken cushioned sides of the inside of the coffin. And then the dead man reached up and pulled the lid of the coffin shut with a loud slam.

It sounded final.

I leapt up from the floor and grabbed at the lid of the coffin, scrambling to pull it back open so I could get Kendra out.

The lid wouldn't budge.

I strained against it, my fingernails bending with the force, but nothing happened.

"Kendra!" I yelled. I thought there was a thump from inside. But she didn't answer.

"Kendra!"

Shrieks and high-pitched cries came from just outside the crypt now. A minute ago, I would have cowered and stayed inside. But I couldn't anymore. I had to find something or someone to help me open the coffin.

I pushed open the creaking metal door and stepped out into the graveyard. Night covered the ground in a cloak of dark shadow, but the stars gave enough light for the tops of the gravestones to reflect in a blue-white gleam against the night.

Something moved to my right. A flash of white against the shadow. I turned and saw a woman's face heading right toward me. Her mouth was open in a silent scream. Her arms were raised, reaching out to me as if begging for help.

Behind her, a man gave chase. His arms raised in the air behind her. I saw the barrel of a gun silhouetted for one second against the stars.

"Stop," I cried, and moved to intervene. In a heartbeat, they had passed me by, her feet pounding fast between the stones.

Then there was a sharp pop, I assumed from the gun, and she gave one sharp, pitiful screech, and fell to the ground. The man followed her down, disappearing between the stones.

Without thinking, I ran to where they'd disappeared. But when I arrived, the man was already raising himself up from the ground. The woman—an older, wrinkled thing with a pallid complexion—lay still on the earth. For a moment, I thought she looked like an image from one of Kendra's noir films. Bleached of all color, her cheek a stark contrast to the black ground.

"Why did you have to kill her?" I gasped.

The man shook his head.

I realized in that moment I had seen him before. This was the same man who had stalked the cemetery on the first night Kendra and I had come here. He had deep-set eyes, silver hair, and a hawk nose. We'd dubbed him, The Cemetery Man.

The man shook his head and slid his gun into a holster on his belt.

"I did not kill her," he said simply. "She was already dead."

My confusion must have shown visibly on my face, because he smiled and reached out a hand to touch my shoulder.

I flinched, stepping back.

"I won't hurt you," he said. "I *can't* hurt you."

"You did a pretty good job on her. And I saw one of your other victims here a couple weeks ago."

"I don't hurt anyone," he said. "I'm just the guardian. I put those who should be slumbering back to sleep."

"You killed her," I insisted.

He shook his head and pulled the gun from his belt. Aimed it at me.

"No," I cried, putting my hands out in surrender.

That didn't stop him. The gun exploded at short range and a cold finger drove through my chest.

I knew I was done. He'd fired at close range, and this had to be the last few seconds before my brain registered the fatal hit...

...but I didn't fall over.

"I told you, I can't hurt you," he said. "Because you're alive."

"I don't understand."

The Cemetery Man pointed to the woman on the ground. "She died months ago. But sometimes the dead are restless." He gestured with one hand around the graveyard. "It's my job to send them back to sleep."

I put a hand to my chest, where the bullet from his gun should have lodged. There was no blood.

"This gun is for the already dead," he explained.

I couldn't quite process the fact that this man wandered the night with a gun that "killed" the dead. And so I moved on. The reason I was out here by myself flashed before my eyes, and I forgot about the dead woman before us.

"I need your help," I said. "I know of someone your bullets can hurt. And I need you to use them. My girlfriend is in danger."

The words *grave danger* actually ran through my head in that second.

"I must put this one back where she belongs," he said.

"There's no time. I need your help now," I insisted.

I could see a spark in the depths of those black eyes, and then he nodded.

"This way," I said, and began to retrace my steps to the crypt. The Cemetery Man made no sound behind me, but when I looked over my shoulder, I confirmed that he followed.

I led the way through the stones and into the small house of death where I'd last seen Kendra. The dark outline of the Cemetery Man waited silent in the doorway, as I reached down to pull open the lid to the coffin that now held Kendra as well as a dead man.

Like before, I couldn't raise the lid.

After watching me struggle for a minute, the Cemetery Man stepped forward and pointed for me to move out of the way. And then, with sure hands, he reached down and grabbed at the lips of the wooden box.

The lid creaked open.

Inside, the mummified remains of a man lay erotically entangled with my girlfriend.

They didn't appear to be moving.

"It's time to return to sleep," the Cemetery Man pronounced.

At his voice, the ashen head of the corpse turned slowly, until its teeth gaped at both of us standing above.

I swear it shook its head in denial before it began to extricate its decaying limbs from the creamy legs of Kendra.

Wasting no time, the Cemetery Man drew the gun from his holster, and with the flick of his finger, fired off a spectral shot.

The dead man's eyes widened, and then he lay back down abruptly, his dirty tangled hair draped across Kendra's naked shoulder.

I reached down and grabbed her by the arm, pulling her away from the corpse.

But she was dead weight.

"Kendra," I whispered, as her head lolled. I had raised her shoulders above the top of the coffin, but she didn't move.

I slipped my arm under hers and propped her up as I pressed my head to her chest, listening for a heartbeat.

There was none.

"She made her choice," the Cemetery Man said. "And now she sleeps with the dead."

"No," I said. "That thing took her...please, you have to do something. Help me. Help *her*."

The Cemetery Man gazed at me, dark hooded eyes like entryways to the place beyond where the gravestones led. The place where Kendra had gone. I felt the truth beaming from them in the dark.

"I can do nothing for her but help her remain asleep," he said. "I must go now and finish my work of the night. I'd suggest you put the coffin back as you found it and leave her and this place. This is no place for the living."

With that, he disappeared back through the door and into the night.

I was left holding the lifeless body of my girlfriend, her legs still in the coffin tangled with the desiccated legs of a dead man.

What did I do? Drag her out and tell the police that a ghoul had killed her? I could just imagine how that interrogation would go.

After some consideration, I kissed her cheek and laid her back down in the box. It's where she had wanted to go, I realized, after all. I reached behind me and grabbed her boots and dress from the floor, draping them over her naked body.

She looked peaceful and happy there, with her lips facing the wrinkled gray lips of the original occupant. It occurred to me that I'd been cuckolded by a corpse.

I let the lid slam shut and pushed the box back into the chamber.

Then I grabbed the silver handle and secured the door.

When I was sure I'd left nothing else around to give evidence of our liaison here, I stepped out into the night and shut the mausoleum door behind me. I walked back to where I'd seen the Cemetery Man kill (okay, put back to sleep) the old woman, but her body was gone. Somewhere in the distance, a night bird cried, and I peered into the shadows, struggling to catch a glimpse of a ghostly white man skulking amid the stones.

"Here I am," a voice said from behind me. I must have jumped a foot in the air.

"You scared me to death," I gasped.

He shook his head. "I don't think so."

"Will she wake up?" I asked.

He shrugged. "It's impossible to say. None of them should wake up, but lately, my nights are busy more and more."

"How long have you been here?"

He shrugged again. "A year? A decade? A century? The nights bleed into one, and every dawn it all slips away. All I know is that I'll be back again tomorrow to keep them asleep."

"I can't believe she's gone," I whispered. The finality of it all had hit me.

The Cemetery Man nodded. "Life is fleeting. A fickle gust of air that comes and goes without warning."

There was nothing I could say to that.

"Thanks for your help," I said, and extended my hand.

He reached out to take it, and his fingers passed right through mine like a chill breeze.

"Enjoy it while you can," he said.

And like the end of a film reel, his face suddenly dimmed and melted away, leaving behind the background of the starry night sky.

New Blood, Old Skin

by Glenn Rolfe

Dallas remembered his son, Bentley, telling him about the noises in the night. Chomping sounds, Bentley had said. The nightmare reminded Dallas of something, but he could never put his finger on what exactly. Maybe a scene from one of his old books? Sarah said it was a phase. Monsters under the bed, boogeyman in the closet. After a series of 2:00 a.m. wake ups courtesy of Bentley's bloodcurdling screams and finding their boy curled up in the corner of his bedroom, sweating and crying, things seemed to calm down. By the end of that summer, Bentley was sleeping through the night again, and thankfully, so were they.

Now, with his son off to college in Gorham, and the house to himself with Sarah on the road with her band, Dallas was ready to turn his boy's room into his writing space. Sarah convinced him to start a new novel. He'd been out of that realm for more than two decades. While his last paperback release, a horror tale of a lizard man preying upon a small Maine lakeside community, hit the shelves pre-eBook, pre-Amazon, he was ready for the challenges of today's publishing world. Sarah questioned his insistence on not writing another horror story. And honestly, he wasn't sure he could write anything else, but he wanted to try. He wanted to be taken seriously this time around.

After removing the bed and placing most of the leftover belongings into the closet, he walked to the oak dresser by the window, the perfect space for his new desk, and began removing the drawers. A paper slipped free and fluttered to the floor.

Bending down to pick it up, he put the drawer down and lifted the lined piece of notebook paper. It was a crude drawing of a monster with four arms and horns on its head. Scrawled at the top of the page in blue crayon was: Mister Beasty.

Two red circles for eyes and a mouth full of jagged teeth made the creation terrifying to look at. The crude drawing gave Dallas the creeps. Even now, he felt goose bumps break across the backs of his arms. He crumpled the paper and tossed it into the trash can.

The unease struck him funny.

When he and Sarah had first purchased the house, he'd written and sold several books, all of them paperback horror, in this very room. He sat in this spot writing outrageous stories about satanic cults and backwoods swamp creatures. Fueled by a bottle of whiskey and a pack of cigarillos, he wrote through the nights and slept the days away while Sarah was rehearsing or at a gig with her band.

It all changed when Bentley was born. Sarah left the group and entered nursing school. Dallas took to the basement to smoke and drink and write his pulp horror while they turned this room into Bentley's nursery.

Unable to make his late-night drinking and writing fests work with taking care of a newborn, Dallas joined his wife in setting his artistic career on hold to take care of the baby. He took a 9-5 job at Gilson Press in Portland where he became a copyeditor for romance novels. Dallas thought he'd miss the adventure of creating his own novels, but honestly, he'd been half drunk or exhausted too many of those nights to remember what he'd scribbled. In the end, he didn't miss the hangovers or the stress of deadlines.

Just under eighteen years later, and he was ready to revisit the creative side of his mind.

He managed to get the heavy dresser out of the room to the garage with the rest of Bentley's old bedroom furniture.

His brother-in-law showed up promptly at 1:00 p.m. with the new desk he'd made to Dallas's specifications.

"Clive," Dallas said, walking out to greet him.

"Dallas," Clive nodded. "Got her all prettied up and ready for you."

Together, the two men eased the desk out of the truck bed and through the front door. It was a tight fit, but they managed.

"Going in Bentley's old room?" Clive asked.

"Yep."

They got it down the hallway and found the door to the room was closed. He didn't remember shutting it on his way out. They set the desk down. As Dallas reached for the knob, he heard a wispy scratching noise coming from within the room.

"You hear that?" he asked Clive.

"I don't hear anything."

Dallas placed his ear to the door. He could almost make out words.

He tried the knob and nothing. It wouldn't turn.

"Something wrong?" Clive asked.

"The knob's frozen. It won't turn."

"Oh, I get it," Clive said. "Is this some practice for your next book?"

"What? No."

"Oh, Sarah mentioned you were getting back into writing. You do write horror books, right?"

"Not this time," he said. "And this thing really won't budge."

"May I?"

Dallas stepped aside. It opened for Clive without issue.

"Huh?" Dallas said.

They got the desk set before the open window.

Did I open that?

They talked about Sarah's band getting back together and going on the road. Her group, The Scratch, weren't huge back in the nineties, but they had a decent and loyal following here in the Northeast, and both Dallas and Clive were happy to see her making the most of her talent again. She'd always been a great songwriter and guitar player. The conversation briefly went back to Dallas's return to writing before ending on Clive and Shirley's successful venture into the handcrafted furniture business.

They made plans to get together after Sarah got back next week, and he saw Clive out.

Dallas grabbed the brand-new laptop Sarah had gotten him for his birthday three weeks ago and made his way to his new writing room.

Sitting on the new desk was the drawing of Bentley's monster.

Mister Beasty.

The window slammed shut, causing Dallas to drop the laptop. He caught it before it hit the ground but was startled again when the door banged shut behind him.

Crouched in the middle of the room with the computer clutched in his arms, Dallas's gaze darted back and forth from door to window.

As he tried to wrap his head around what was happening, the doorknob to the closet began rattling as if someone was desperately trying to open it.

"Who's there?" he cried.

The rattling stopped.

Despite the fact there was no longer a breeze in the room, the drawing of Mr. Beasty drifted from the desktop and floated to the floor.

Dallas got up and hurried for the door. He was fearful the knob would be stuck again, but he faced no resistance. He made his way down to the kitchen, set the laptop on the counter, and tried to stop his hands from shaking by tucking them under his arms and pacing the floor.

This doesn't fucking happen in real life, just in bad fiction.

Entity. Ghost. Monster.

They were outrageous concepts.

You used to write that crap.

Used to.

And will again.

No, I'm done being a hack. I'm going to write a suspense novel.

Yeah, sure you are.

He was ready to argue with himself when a loud crash came from down the hall.

The door to Bentley's old room began to open and close. Slamming shut again and again like something out of *Poltergeist*.

He looked around for a weapon, anything solid he could swing. His options were the broom or the Swiffer jet mop. He chose the latter and made his way toward the slamming door.

Chomping sounds. He heard Bentley's tiny voice echo in his head.

The sound of the door opening and closing had him picturing a set of giant chompers clamping down over and over, trying to eat him whole.

As he stood before the swinging door, he felt two feet tall and ready to be swallowed.

"What do you want?" he yelled, his voice cracking.

The door stopped instantly, remaining closed for a short breath before creaking open again, inviting him in.

Armed with the cleaning instrument, he stepped across the threshold and held his breath waiting to see what happened next.

His brand-new desk lay on its face.

Sticking out from beneath it was the damn white lined paper.

Tentatively, Dallas crouched and snatched the drawing from the floor.

He glanced at the drawing and did a double take. It had changed. Mr. Beasty now held a large knife, red crayon pooled beneath it where a new figure appeared lying prone at Mr. Beasty's feet with a blue t-shirt and brown shorts, just like the ones Dallas was wearing now. Two x's for eyes told him all he needed to know.

The door slammed shut behind him.

Dallas spun, dropping the paper, went for the doorknob, but it refused to budge.

"No, no!"

Taking a step back, he hauled the Swiffer over his shoulder and proceeded to attack the door, hacking away at it like a lumber jack in full swing. The cheap plastic cleaning device splintered into pieces within the first three strikes, leaving him with a purple rubber handle and the metal pole it was attached to.

Breathing heavy, sweaty and shaky, Dallas dropped the Swiffer's remains, closed his eyes and clenched his fists.

This can't be happening.

Now you sound like a man stuck in one of those bad stories.

Shut up.

The voice in his head gave way to a scraping sound, like someone dragging the base of a snow globe back and forth across a tabletop. He turned to see a blackness swiping across the glass of the window, as if someone were rolling black paint across it. The sunlight of the outside world slipped away more and more with each swipe until the only light remaining came from the crack below the door.

That too disappeared as the floor on the other side of the barrier creaked and a shadow appeared.

In the room, the light of day bled dry and left Dallas in the dark.

Blindly, he rushed toward the window and knocked his shins against the fallen desk. He sucked in a breath as he tumbled forward, smacking his face on the corner of the desk as he rolled to the floor. Moaning, he lifted his head and felt blood rolling down his cheek. Hot pain lit from the gash he found just below his left eye.

A door in the room opened.

He couldn't see it, but the sound came from his left.

The closet.

Even in the dark, he could make out a large shape emerging from the corner of the room.

No, you're imagining this.

Wrong. It's me.

Who?

You know who.

Dallas crab-walked backwards until his back was firmly against the wall.

Scratchy footsteps, like a child scuffing the feet of their footie pajamas across the floor, started in his direction.

"Please," he whimpered. "Please, just leave me alone."

Closer and closer, the entity in the darkened room approached.

"Please," he whispered, crying now.

Terrified, he smelled something awful, like the scent of putrefied potatoes. A light wind, a breath, touched his bleeding cheek.

He closed his eyes and screamed.

"Help me!"

The door to the bedroom opened.

"Dallas?"

Clive.

When he opened his eyes, Clive was coming across the room, reaching for him.

Dallas sat on the floor, the new desk back in its place below the clear sunlit window.

"My goodness, Dallas," Clive said as he took Dallas by the hand and drew him to his feet. "What in the world happened? Are you okay?"

Dallas put a bloody hand on Clive's shoulder and craned his neck so he could see behind him.

Clive turned, following his gaze.

"What is it? How did this happen?"

Dallas took a step back and noticed the blood print he'd left on the shoulder of Clive's white t-shirt.

"Come on, man," Clive said. "I think you're going to need stitches. Let's get you to the hospital."

Dallas touched the wound.

From when I fell.

After that thing painted the window black.

Before it came out of the closet for me.

What came out of the closet for me?

Oh, you know.

His new laptop sat open atop the desk. He pushed past Clive and saw a bold title centered in the fresh document. The cursor blinking idly beside the words:

MISTER BEASTY.

He stumbled away from the device and discovered he was alone in the room.

Where's Clive?

He was never here.

But I saw him.

Like you saw the thing in the closet?

His laptop had vanished, too.

The new desk sat naked as it had been when he and Clive placed it there earlier.

Dallas felt dizzy. He walked out of the room, down the hall, and found his laptop still sitting on the kitchen counter where he'd left it.

"I need a drink."

He went to the cupboard above the toaster oven and pulled the half empty bottle of Knob Creek from the top shelf and a glass tumbler from the shelf below. He filled the glass halfway and tossed the auburn liquid down his throat. Wiping his lips, the fiery brew blazing its way down to his stomach, he poured a second, and tucked the bottle under his arm. He carried them with him as he slipped the laptop under his other arm and made his way back to his new writing room.

Peeking around the corner prepared for any anomalies, he saw the room remained as he'd left it. He set the bourbon and the tumbler down, and then set his laptop beside them. It was a start, but there was plenty missing.

He hurried to the garage and fetched the box with all his old writing space shit in it and dumped the dusty cardboard into his leather chair. Wheeling his things into the house and down to his new/old space, a title came to him.

Mister Beasty?

No. Hell no.

What then?

This Room is Alive

Yes, indeed.

He entered the room, set the box next to the desk, and downed the tumbler before refilling it.

The warm devil felt nice.

Hello, old friend.

Welcome back.

Why, thank you.

Dallas placed his set of Universal Monsters figurines along the back of the desk. An old Freddy Krueger action figure stood beside an almost impossible to find set of Graboids and an action figure of Valentine he'd purchased shortly after *Tremors* came out. Next to them, he placed his old Camel ashtray and a snow globe featuring a skull at the center of a wintery graveyard (he could almost hear it being slid back and forth across the desktop). At the bottom of the box was the old word processor he'd forgotten about. He left it there and set the box aside. He'd need to get a cool mousepad (he still preferred using a mouse to the touch pad). For the final touch, Dallas pinned Bentley's drawing of Mister Beasty to the wall next to the window.

He sat down, pulled his chair up to the desk, sipped from the tumbler, opened a new word document, and typed:

This Room is Alive

This room is alive. I know, because it's been trying to communicate with me.

The words came fast and easy after that opening line. The bourbon filled his gut and numbed his apprehension and fears. He was shocked at how easily he slipped into his old skin.

I thought you were going to write something serious.

What can I say? I was convinced to do something scarier.

He pulled up his Amazon Music Player on his laptop and pulled up Genesis's *Invisible Touch* album and skipped to track 3. Lyrics about a thousand dreams and a million screams brought a smile to his face.

Before he knew it, Dallas was drunk and finishing up chapter eight of his new horror novel.

It was dark in the room, and his eyes were blurry and burning from a healthy amount of booze and the light from the computer screen. He wanted one of his old cigarillos but settled for a joint he'd been holding onto for a special occasion.

Saving his work, he adjourned to the front porch.

Stars gleamed and twinkled in the clear night sky above as he planted his rump on the steps, and sparked the joint. He took notice of the paint flaking off the rail next to his head. The porch could certainly use a fresh coat of paint, he'd have to try and remember that this week. It was one of a handful of things Sarah had asked him to work on in her absence.

Relaxed and in a world he'd stayed away from for far too long, Dallas rose and walked down the driveway.

The cicadas were out tonight. Summer was winding down. Behind him, he heard a tapping that steadily grew to a chomping sound. Glancing up at the window to the writing room, he could swear he saw a shadow moving in the light of the computer screen.

You know who I am?

I guess I've always known.

Good. We have work to do.

We certainly do.

Dallas squeezed the tip of the joint and tucked it away for later. Walking into the house and toward his writing space, the chomping sounds ceased as he turned into the room.

The drawing above his laptop showed Bentley's monster beside a man with x's for eyes working at a crudely drawn desk.

"Mister Beasty," Dallas said. "Let's get back to work."

I knew you'd come around.

And Mister Beasty was right. Like new blood pumping through old skin, Dallas felt alive, reignited, as he wrote about spirits in the night, pulp or otherwise, it just felt *right*. He typed his way through the wee hours of the morning and straight to dawn.

The Glimmer Girls

by Kenneth McKinley

Hattie Winklemeyer thought she was hearing things. So much so, that she shook her head with a quick twitch, as if a mosquito was buzzing her ear. She couldn't have heard Mr. Girard right. Did he really say they'd all be earning $10.00 a week for painting the dials on watches? That couldn't be. She was only making $6.00 a week at the garment factory across town. She tried to not let her nervousness show as she raised her hand.

Mr. Girard peered down at her from the raised platform he was standing on as he was addressing the group of new recruits, his bushy, gray eyebrows bobbing up and down over the top of his horn-rimmed glasses. "Yes? Ms… Winklemeyer, is it?"

"Umm… Yes, sir. I'm sorry. What was it you just said? I'm afraid I didn't hear you correctly. Umm… Could you repeat that last part, please?"

She could feel the other applicants staring at her in disbelief, as if even daring to ask him to repeat the wage information would cause it to disappear in a puff of smoke.

His brow furrowed at having to repeat himself. "I said, 'You girls will sit at these stations here.' "

He pointed to a long bench divided into individual work stations forming a makeshift assembly line.

"Each of you will apply our UltraGlow luminescent paint to the various watches and clocks that come down the line. When you've completed your assigned batch, you will put the timepieces here in this cart on the end. Is that clear?"

The women nodded in unison. Mr. Girard continued.

"You will arrive and be ready to work at your station at 7:00 a.m., Monday through Friday. I will not tolerate tardiness."

He stared directly at Hattie while saying the last part causing her to gulp.

"Lunch is at noon and lasts half an hour. Quitting time is at 5:00 p.m. The whistle will sound for each of these. I will require you to work mandatory overtime, as needed. The salary is $10.00 per week. You'll pick your checks up over there at the payroll window during your lunch break on Fridays. Are there any other questions?"

The women were all smiles as they shook their heads. You could feel the excitement in the air as he led the new hires to fill out paperwork.

Monday morning arrived and Hattie had a good case of nervous butterflies dancing in her belly as she sipped her morning coffee. Something felt strange on her wrist as she raised her cup. She looked down and smiled. Smiling back was the illuminated face of the wristwatch she'd painted during her training session, now securely fastened on her arm by a leather strap. It would take some getting used to, but Mr. Girard was adamant about all his employees wearing one of United Radium Corporation's new timepieces. Her latest accessory showed it was 6:10 a.m. in an eerie green glow. Time to get moving before she missed her trolley and was late to her first day of work.

United Radium Corporation was a booming business after the war and had expanded its production line to accommodate the increasing demand for its radioactive products. Radium was a huge hit. Pocket watches were yesterday's news. Wrist watches were all the cat's meow now. United Radium Corporation touted in its advertising that the green glow on the soldier's wrist watches helped win the war and people were buying them left and right. Stores couldn't keep them on the shelves, and Hattie and her coworkers couldn't be more pleased at the opportunity to restock them with the fruits of their labor.

The city was bustling. Buildings were going up everywhere, and the automobile was taking over the streets. Hattie pulled in a deep breath as she hung onto the overhead rail of the trolley. Yes, she could smell progress and prosperity in the air and none too soon. She was living in a cramped apartment on 62nd Street. This new job of hers would help build a nest egg and finally allow her to get out of tenement housing.

United Radium's facility was on the east side down by the train terminal, a thirty five-minute trolley ride for Hattie. As she stepped off at her stop, the butterflies in her stomach made their return. She took a deep breath and followed a girl she recognized from her hiring class inside.

She hung up her coat in the employee's closet and made her way to the workstation. Hattie rounded a corner and ran smack dab into a towering monstrosity. She gave a startled gasp as the figure stood a foot taller than her. Dressed head to toe in white, it wore heavy black gloves and an apron, and looked through bug-eyed lenses. It was carrying a glass vial of some unknown liquid with metal tongs.

"Look out, Miss. You almost made me spill this batch," a muffled baritone voice rumbled out from under the garb.

Hattie blinked in confusion as the figure lumbered past her and headed toward her work area. She approached warily as the factory whistle blew, signaling it was time to start. Mr. Girard shooed the women toward their stations with an impatient clap of the hands.

"Come, come, girls. Let's get started. No time to dillydally. Time is money, you know," he said, his eyebrows still bobbing up and down.

She took her seat. They furnished the work area with fine-tipped camelhair paint brushes of various sizes, neatly folded cloths, a magnifying glass, and a tray of glass beakers filled with the company's patented UltraGlow paint. They positioned a cart of watches waiting to receive their radioactive treatment alongside each chair. The strange-looking figure with the bug eyes set the beaker of paint he was carrying in the tray of the station next to hers. After the job was complete, he removed his glasses and white hood revealing disheveled sandy brown hair and a nervous smile. Hattie chuckled at how he transformed from a frightening behemoth to a tall, but unassuming man with a simple unmasking.

"Kinda spooky looking when he's all done up in that outfit, huh?" asked the red-headed girl with freckles on her nose sitting to her left.

Hattie nodded, and watched the man disappear around the corner on his way back toward wherever he worked in the factory.

"Hi. I'm Beatrice. Beatrice Reynolds. You're one of the new girls, aren't you?"

By this time, Hattie had regained her composure. She accepted Beatrice's outstretched hand and shook it, admiring the matching wristwatch she was wearing.

"Pleased to make your acquaintance, Beatrice. My name is Hattie. Hattie Winklemeyer, and yes, today is my first day."

Beatrice returned Hattie's smile.

"Pleased to meet you, Miss Winklemeyer." Her smile slowly fell off her face, as her eyes scanned Hattie's workspace. "I was wondering if Clara was coming back. I guess not."

Hattie felt the sudden, melancholy change in her demeanor.

"Excuse me? Who is Clara?"

The red-head nodded toward where Hattie was sitting.

"She was the girl you're replacing. Got real sick. Doctor's weren't sure what it was."

She looked over Hattie's shoulder and then turned to the left and to the right, making sure no one could hear their conversation. "Rumor has it she had the Great Pox."

When Hattie shook her head in confusion, Beatrice added, "You know? Syphilis?"

Hattie's eyes got big and she felt her cheeks turn bright red. This wasn't a topic of conversation she was used to having.

"I don't believe it what they say," her co-worker continued. "Clara is a good girl. Her Johnny is still over in Europe cleaning up the mess the Kaiser left. She's been patiently waiting for him to return home for almost two years. She didn't do anything. I don't care what they say."

Hattie took this all in. She could relate. Her Walter was killed over in the trenches of Belgium while she was waiting back home. It wasn't like she didn't have offers. That scoundrel, Thomas Stanton, was making unwanted advances on her as soon as Walter's ship left the harbor. She had held her honor and didn't succumb to his foolery, but she had to endure the rumors, anyway.

The morning went by quickly. She was having trouble getting all the numbers covered with UltraGlow until Beatrice gave her a pointer.

"You have to put the tip of the brush in your mouth and keep the point as sharp as you can."

Beatrice demonstrated by inserting the end of the brush between her lips. When she pulled it out, the point had a nice, tight cone-shaped edge.

"See. Like that," she said, as she dipped the end in the paint and flawlessly covered the watch numbers and hands without dribbling color on its face. Beatrice was all proud of herself, but Hattie wasn't convinced.

"Don't you get paint in your mouth? Isn't that bad for you?"

Beatrice chuckled.

"No, silly. Oh, it's not the greatest tasting. It's a little gritty, but you get used to it. Mr. Girard assured us that UltraGlow is perfectly safe. In fact, one of our other factories makes Radium Water."

Hattie's face lit up with recognition.

"Oh wait! I've heard of that. I saw it in the newspaper. That's supposed to be really good for you. It says that it prevents cancer and everything!"

Beatrice nodded knowingly and added, "Mmm hmm. I even paint my nails with it."

Hattie looked down at her coworker's fingers. They gave off a dull glow from the shadows under the work table.

"Well, I'll be," Hattie exclaimed. "They really do glow!"

"You think that's something. You should see them at night."

Beatrice looked around to make sure no one was in earshot before leaning in toward Hattie to divulge one more juicy nugget.

"Besides, the men down at the Cotton Club just love them. They can't get over how beautiful they look," she whispered.

Hattie's eyes bugged out. "You get into the Cotton Club?" she asked, incredulously.

"Mmm hmm," she said and looked down at Hattie's empty left hand. "You're not married?"

Instinctively, Hattie clutched her hand to her chest before shaking her head. "I was, but Walter was killed over in the trenches"

Beatrice nodded, knowingly.

"It's okay, Hattie. When you're ready, I'll get you into the Cotton Club and introduce you to some very nice men."

Hattie blushed and said, "Oh…I don't know."

Beatrice leaned back in her chair, so she could get a good look at her coworker and said, "Listen, Hattie. You're too good lookin' of a girl to become an old spinster. Now that Walter is gone, you need to do what's right for you."

Miss Winklemeyer hesitated as she chewed on this last comment. She slowly began to nod. "Maybe you're right."

And with that, a friendship bloomed.

By Friday, Hattie had settled into a groove. She was getting faster at her job which kept Mr. Girard's outbursts temporarily at bay. That didn't stop him from silently patrolling the floor like a shark waiting to attack his next unsuspecting victim. Beatrice had introduced her to the other women during their lunch break, who were starting to accept Hattie into their group.

Lizzie was a tall, vivacious blonde bearcat with blue eyes and had a penchant for talking really fast, like she was auctioning off farm implements. Dorothy was a petite brunette with big, doe-like brown eyes and a warm smile that set Hattie at ease immediately. Betty and Bonnie were twin sisters Hattie couldn't tell apart, if it wasn't for the mole on Bonnie's chin. They both had fair, freckled skin and auburn hair pulled up into tight buns.

The six ladies had just picked up their checks and were strolling down the street to eat their lunch in the park. As the sun was shining on their excited faces, Lizzie led the charge, her mouth going a mile a minute talking about their plans to visit the Cotton Club that evening.

"Oh, I can't wait! I'm going right over to Gimbels and purchase that dress I saw in their window this morning. You just wait and see, girls. It's simply the bee's knees!"

The women tittered, as Lizzie's excitement had a way of being infectious.

"How about you, Beatrice?" Lizzie asked. "What are you going to wear tonight?"

Beatrice flashed her Cheshire Cat smile.

"Oh, I'm sure I might be able to find *something* to wear," she said.

This brought on another bout of giggles. It was common knowledge Beatrice had more dresses than the whole ladies section at Gimbels.

"Whatever I decide to wear, you can bet I'll simply be...RADIANT!" she added, holding up her fingers and flashing a bright smile.

Dorothy inspected her co-worker. "Did you UltraGlow your teeth, too?" she asked, incredulously.

"I most certainly did!"

Another round of giggles from the group.

Dorothy nodded approvingly.

"That's a good idea. I like it. I think I'm going to do that before I leave today."

A chorus of "me toos" erupted from the group.

Lizzie glanced over at Hattie. "How about it, Hattie. Have you decided whether or not you're going tonight?"

Hattie's eyes shifted nervously, as the group's attention was now centered on her decision.

"Oh, I don't know."

"C'mon, Hattie," Lizzie, Beatrice, Dorothy, and Betty chided in unison.

"Yes, Hattie," Lizzie continued. "You know you're going to have so much fun and *everyone* will be there!"

"Not everyone," came a reply from the side of the group. It was Bonnie and she wasn't looking so good. Her skin gave off a shiny paleness, her normally green eyes were wet and rheumy.

"You okay, Bonnie?" asked Beatrice, resting a concerned hand on her friend's shoulder.

"Yes. No. I don't know." She shook her head trying to decide the status of her condition. "It's this toothache. I can't stand it!" Bonnie groaned. "I've been taking this for it, but it's not helping."

She pulled a brown glass bottle out of her bag and removed the cork taking a long pull. When she put the cork back in the decanter, she handed it over to Beatrice to examine. Beatrice read the name printed on the label—Laudanum.

Bonnie rubbed her protruding jaw. "I'm sorry, girls. Maybe next week," she slurred.

A round of sympathetic clucking and well wishes were bestowed upon their friend.

Riding the trolley home, Hattie tried to decide what to do about the invitation to the Cotton Club. The prospect of a fun night out on the town was tempting. She couldn't remember exactly when the last time she cut a rug, but it had to be before Walter went to basic training. That was what? Four years ago, now? Hattie shook her head at the thought of how much time had gone by. It seemed like only yesterday she was embracing Walter on the docks before he went up the gangplank. She could still taste his last kiss goodbye, and if she concentrated really hard, the faint aroma of Brilliantine.

No, no, no. This was no good. She couldn't keep pining for someone who was never coming back. Her Walter was buried in the soil of some foreign country she would never visit. It was all right to remember him, but she needed to move on with her life. Her new job at United Radium Corporation as the first step. Maybe a night out with the girls would be the second.

"Excuse me, Miss."

The sound of the masculine voice startled her out of the depths of her thoughts. A hand touched her shoulder. Hattie whipped her head around and came face to face with the owner. The passenger was a handsome man, close to her own age, his deeply tanned face with a square jaw and piercing blue eyes was only inches from her own. Instinctively, she clutched her chest and took a couple of wobbly steps back. The man recognized the fear and attempted to disarm her with a dashing but genuine smile.

"I'm sorry if I frightened you, but you dropped your sweater."

Hattie could only blink repeatedly, not understanding what he was trying to say.

"Your sweater?" He held up the garment. "You dropped it."

Recollection finally took hold, and her expression shifted from confusion to embarrassment.

"Th... Thank you," she stammered.

As she reached out to collect the article of clothing, the trolley passed through the shadows brought on by the afternoon sun setting behind the Mercantile Bank. Even in the gloom, Hattie saw the man's eyes widen as something captured his attention. She followed his line of sight to her bare arm.

What in the world? she thought.

Her exposed forearm was glowing and reminded Hattie of the color of the tarnished copper dome on the capital building.

"Why that's absolutely stunning," the gentleman said.

Hattie searched the man's face for any traces of mockery. Finding none, only wonderment, she gave a sheepish smile in return.

"How do you do it?" he asked.

"I... I don't know. I've never seen it like that," she said, admiring the pleasing glow.

The trolley slowed down, and the man looked up at the street signs coming into view.

Well. This is my stop. It was very nice to meet you...err..."

"Hattie. My name is Hattie Winklemeyer."

His face brightened, and he nodded his approval.

"Very nice to meet you, Hattie. My name is Charles Lawson, but most people call me Charlie."

"It's very nice to meet you...Charlie."

Was this really happening? Hattie felt like she was having an out-of-body experience. Was she really standing here introducing herself to this handsome stranger? And just like that, the man hopped off the trolley and disappeared around the corner. Hattie felt like she had turned a corner, too.

Hattie couldn't believe she had summoned up the courage to go through with it, but here she was meeting Beatrice and the rest of the girls a couple of blocks away from the club. Beatrice had connections to get into the swanky establishment, and all of her co-workers were dressed to the nines. Hattie adjusted her dress trying to get used to her newly purchased ensemble.

"Stop fidgeting, dear. That dress is the oyster's earrings on you," Lizzie said.

Hattie flashed a nervous smile as she made one last modification before flipping her feather boa over her shoulder. "Do you really think so?"

"I don't think. I know so. It's simply the berries, dear," Lizzie assured her, as the rest of the groups heads were bobbing in agreement.

Hattie giggled. This was all so new to her, so exciting. It wasn't only her dress that she was going to have to get used to.

A line was wrapped around the block with hopeful patrons looking to be allowed into the club. The rhythmic cadence of the house band permeated through the closed entrance that was guarded by a doorman who Hattie thought looked uncannily like a robust version of Douglas Fairbanks.

Hattie placed a hand on Beatrice's exposed shoulder.

"How are we ever going to get inside? They're not letting anyone in."

Beatrice smirked and gave her a wink.

"Leave it to me," she said.

She went up to the doorman and whispered something in his ear. He began to nod and shifted his bulk off of the stool positioned next to the door. Beatrice waved them over as the bouncer opened the door. The volume of the music spilled out and overpowered the angry protests of the crowd as they realized the girls were being let in before they were.

Inside, the Cotton Club was jumping as Fletcher Henderson was leading the band in a lively set of tunes. The maître d' led the women over to a table near the left side of the stage. Hattie's head felt like it was filled helium as she tried to take in all the sights. She simply couldn't get over that she was in the legendary Cotton Club.

"Hattie. If you keep spinning your head around like that, it's going to fall off," Lizzie teased.

"I can't help it! I've never seen anything like this. Beatrice, whatever did you tell that man at the door that made him let us in?" she asked.

"Oh, Clark? He's a good egg. Don't you worry your pretty head none about him," she said. She turned to Lizzie and held out her hand. "Butt me."

Lizzie was already reaching into her purse before Beatrice got out the last of the sentence. She pulled out a silver cigarette case as the rest of the girls were instinctively pulling out their black holders and affixed their "butts." The ladies passed around the lit candle on the table to light their cigarettes.

Hattie was in awe at how cool and collected they all were, while she sat there in star struck wonder. The band finished its number and the club erupted in applause. Fletcher Henderson announced they'd be taking a short set break and would be back on in five.

The girls chatted excitedly amongst themselves and admired the handsome men that would walk by nodding. From time to time, some would stop and exchange pleasantries. Beatrice seemed to know everyone, for she called them all by their first names and introduced various ones to Hattie, not that she would remember a single one by the end of the night. Everything was an excited blur. All she knew was that there were a lot of elegant handshakes and kisses on the cheek. They all complimented the girls' UltraGlow smiles and the pale green luster of their nails and skin.

Lizzie announced she had to go take a powder and asked if anyone else wanted to go too. Hattie accepted the invitation and followed the blonde toward the back of the crowded club. As she was still taking everything in as she walked, she bumped into a tall body that was coming around the corner.

Embarrassed, she said, "Oh, I'm so sorry. Please excuse me."

"Hattie? Hattie Winklemeyer?"

Startled someone would know her name, Hattie looked up into a familiar face. Looking back was the man from the trolley.

"Charlie?"

"The one and the same. Fancy meeting you here"

"Yes. Well, this is my first time. I'm here with some girls from work," she said, as she pointed to her group sitting on the other side of the club.

"That's great. I'm here with a few of my friends, as well," he replied and pointed over to his group. "Perhaps you'd like to dance later?"

Her face brightened, partially from blushing and partially from excitement. After a moment, she began to nod.

"Yes. I think I'd like that."

Charlie grinned with his perfect smile. "Great! I'll bring my friends over and introduce them to all of you, if that's all right."

Lizzie popped her head over her friend's shoulder and startled Hattie. She was so lost in conversation with Charlie that she had forgotten all about her. Lizzie piped up.

"That would be perfectly fine. Now, if dear Hattie here would be so kind to introduce me to her friend," she chided.

Hattie quickly regained her composure. "Oh! I'm so sorry. Lizzie, this is Charlie. Charlie, this is my friend, Lizzie."

Pleasantries were exchanged and the two groups intermingled the rest of the evening. Charlie, as promised, asked Hattie to dance and the two quickly became inseparable as the night wore on. Hattie couldn't wipe the smile off her face if she tried.

Monday morning came and young Miss Winklemeyer was still sporting a three-mile smile for all to see. She couldn't help it. It felt like it had been a very long time since she was this happy. Hattie had a new job, a great group of new friends, and Charlie promised to call on her later this week. She practically floated to her work station.

"Good morning, Beatrice!" she said and began setting up her brushes, barely able to contain her giddiness.

"Huh? Oh… good morning, Hattie," her coworker croaked.

Hattie looked over and her smile faltered. Beatrice didn't look like her usual perky self. Her skin had taken on a shiny, grayish pallor and perspiration beaded at her hairline.

"You okay, Bea?" she asked.

"Ugh. I think came down with something. I don't feel so good and I ache all over, especially my jaw and neck," she said, while rubbing the area with her palm.

"Yeah. You don't look well," Hattie said.

"I think there's something going around. A few of the other girls are missing today, too."

Hattie looked around and noticed a few empty stations. "Bonnie's not here?"

Beatrice looked up and surveyed the scene.

"Oh. No, she's not. I heard she got much worse over the weekend."

"That poor dear. I'll have to stop by after work and see if she needs anything."

Beatrice straightened up as she saw Mr. Girard making his way over. "Uh oh. Here comes Ol' Square Britches. Best not let him see us talking."

With that, the girls hurried to get their stations set up before their boss came over and had something to complain about. Mr. Girard was like many of the other bosses Hattie had come in contact with in her few short years of being employed. Not very well liked. Never had anything nice to say and only cared about the *bottom line*.

She heard his voice boom a few stations away as he scolded a petite girl with hair as black as pitch.

"What seems to be the problem, Miss Mayweather? Why are you not ready to go? Did you not hear the factory whistle blow? Because, I assure you that it most certainly did! Do you not want your job here at United Radium Corporation, Miss Mayweather? Because, if you don't, I'm more than positive we can find someone to replace you!" Mr. Girard's voice thundered.

Miss Mayweather took the tongue-lashing without so much as a peep in response, but Hattie could see her lower lip quivering. She hoped the poor girl didn't break down in front of Mr. Girard. She didn't want him to get the satisfaction of knowing he'd made her crumble.

By lunch time, Beatrice had Hattie worried. Her condition was worsening to the point where her coworker could hardly sit in her chair without being slumped over. An hour before quitting time, Beatrice had begun to moan with every breath. Hattie nervously watched her through her peripheral vision. She'd asked numerous times throughout the day if there was anything she could do, to the point where she was afraid she was annoying Beatrice.

"What in tarnation is going on here, Miss Reynolds?" a voice thundered behind them, almost causing Hattie to fly out of her seat. Beatrice barely had the energy to turn her head and look at her boss.

"Why you haven't even finished half of your allotment today, Miss Reynolds!"

"She's really not feeling well today, Mr. Girard," Hattie said, trying to defend her coworker.

"I don't remember asking you a damn thing!" Mr. Girard shook his finger at her. "Look around, Miss Winklemeyer. Look at all these empty chairs here today. How am I supposed to keep production going when I have workers missing and people like Miss Reynolds here who are too busy lollygagging because they have the sniffles?"

Hattie slinked back, wishing she was a mouse that could crawl in a hole and hide. Mr. Girard turned his attention back to Beatrice.

"I suggest, Miss Reynolds, that you go home tonight and take a tonic. Because, come tomorrow, I expect not only all of tomorrow's allotment finished, but these here, as well."

With that, he stomped off. The room fell deathly quiet, and the only sound was Beatrice's low moaning with each breath.

The next morning, Hattie arrived at work to find Beatrice wasn't at her station. Her friend was always at work before Hattie and with the way she looked yesterday, she was worried for her well-being. She had tried to call her on the telephone, but Beatrice didn't pick up. Looking around United Radium Corporation, there were more empty stations than the day before.

This illness must really be something.

She hoped it wasn't anything serious and that, if she went over there to check on her, she'd have better luck than when she stopped over at Bonnie's flat yesterday after work. Hattie had knocked on the door several times, but no one answered. The curtains were pulled and she couldn't hear any noise from the inside. She would've tried calling once she got home, but Bonnie didn't have a telephone.

Not only was Bonnie and Beatrice's station empty, but so was Betty's. Mr. Girard was making his way across the floor, and Hattie hurried to get started working. With all of these girls missing today, he wasn't going to be in a good mood. She didn't want to give him a reason to focus his frustrations on her.

After work, Hattie took the trolley over to Grand Avenue near Beatrice's apartment. She knocked repeatedly on her door and listened for any movement inside. The curtains were pulled on her window, too, and there was no light emanating through the edges.

Hattie was about to give up when she heard a thump from inside. Placing her ear up to the door, she knocked again.

"Beatrice? Are you in there? It's me, Hattie."

She listened and didn't hear anything.

"Bea? It's me. I came over to see how you were. Are you in there?"

She put her ear up to the door again and was about to pull it away in defeat when she heard what sounded like a moan followed by a dragging noise.

"Bea? Is that you? Are you okay?"

The dragging noise came closer. Finally, she heard the lock on the door click and it opened a crack. The smell that wafted through the opening made Hattie's stomach flip. All she saw was a sliver of darkness between the door and the jam.

"Beatrice?"

The door slowly creaked open another few inches. A dragging sound came from behind the door. Hattie craned her neck toward the opening, trying to get a look to see who was on the other side. The stench was overpowering, like fly-blown meat.

"Bea? Is that you?"

A groan followed, and a head slowly emerged from behind the door. Hattie barely recognized her friend. She looked like she had aged thirty years overnight. Her skin was the color of clouds on an overcast day and shined dully from the layer of perspiration coating it. Her lips were chapped and cracked like an old boot that been left out in the weather for too long. To say Beatrice's eyes were rheumy was a gross understatement. Thick globs of mucus-like substance leaked out and ran down her cheekbones. Her once lustrous garnet fire hair was now patchy clumps, exposing open sores. Hattie's friend looked like a walking corpse, and smelled like one too.

"Dear Lord, Mary and Joseph! Beatrice, what happened?"

Beatrice Reynolds let out a groan Hattie would not soon forget. It sounded like a wounded animal on the precipice of death. The odor emanating from her as she talked smelled horrific, carrion rottenness. She clung to the door handle to stay upright. Hattie reached out to keep her from falling over, and she wished she hadn't. Beatrice's skin felt like hot grease that had splattered on the stove. Heat was radiating off her. Hattie didn't know what kind of fever it was, but it wasn't good. Her friend needed medical attention now.

"Come, Bea. We have to get you to the doctor."

"I… I probably shouldn't…"

"Shouldn't nothing. You're going and that's all there is to it,"

Hattie lowered her coworker to sit in the doorway then went and hailed a cab to take them to the nearest hospital.

It was a late night for Hattie. She spent the evening telling the staff everything she knew about Beatrice's condition and work environment. Dragging herself out of bed was a real chore, but she knew there was no way she could miss work and chance losing her job. She had spent most of the night alongside Beatrice's hospital bed. Her friend was in and out of consciousness moaning deliriously about turning out the lights, until the doctor came in and gave her a sedative. They didn't have any conclusive answers about Beatrice. They were just as baffled as Hattie. How could her friend go from simply not feeling well to this condition in 24 hours?

When they turned out the lights in Bea's room, an eerie pale-green glow lit up the room. At first, Hattie thought it must be some streetlight outside the window. Then, she saw the glow was coming from Beatrice's bed. She even saw a representative from United Radium Corporation talking to the doctors as she left. Hattie hoped Beatrice wouldn't lose her job.

As she was riding the trolley to work the next morning, Hattie noticed her body was beginning to feel stiff and sore. It had to be from sitting in the uncomfortable hospital chair all night long. By the time she got to work, her body was really starting to ache.

Not only was Beatrice's work station empty, but so was every other one in her row besides Hattie's and Lizzie's. Mr. Girard was chomping on his cigar over in the corner while talking to a man who looked like the one from the hospital. Whatever the man was saying to Mr. Girard, he wasn't liking it one bit.

"No, no, no, Stillwell! That simply won't do. We need to get one of our doctors over there immediately, before the press gets wind…" Mr. Girard looked around the shop. "Come with me into my office," he ordered, and set off to his glass partitioned office and shut the door behind them. From the looks of Girard's animated gestures and muffled growls, the man named Stillwell was definitely getting an earful.

By the time the work day was over, Hattie's condition had worsened. Her teeth and jaw ached like she had been kicked by a mule. All of her limbs and joints felt like they were molten lava. On her way out, she stopped into the ladies room to splash some cold water on her face. Afterwards, she looked into the mirror and could only shake her head.

Her jaw was swollen and a hard lump was beginning to protrude from her right cheek. The color of her skin had gone battleship gray and a greasy sheen of perspiration covered her face. Yellow strings of mucus built up in the corners of her eyes and her breath—it smelled like roadkill fermenting in the summer sun. She couldn't stand the sight any longer, so she grabbed her purse and hurried out of the bathroom.

All the lights were off in this section of the factory except for Girard's office. The door was open a crack, and he was talking into the telephone.

"God damn it, Stevens. I don't care what you have to do, you keep the press out of there. As for that doctor, he needs to take a long vacation. What? I don't care how you do it. No, there's a site over on 36th and Griffith where they're pouring cement tomorrow. Yeah, that would be a good place. The Reynolds woman? Have them put in the report she had syphilis. I don't give a tinker's damn what he thinks. It's our ass that'll be on the line, not his. I'm not shutting the UltraGlow line down. No, Bailey is working on a new formula that's not as toxic. By the time anyone starts sniffing around here, he'll have us up to speed with the new formula, and we'll say that's what we've been using all along... Hold on a second. Who's out there?" Girard bellowed.

Hattie looked down and saw that her skin was glowing its dull green radiance which was giving her away here in the dark. She took off running around the corner and headed for the door before Girard could see who it was.

Hattie didn't stop running until she got to the trolley. As the trolley took off, she tried to catch her breath and make sense of what she had heard.

Was everyone's illness caused by the UltraGlow paint? And they knew about it! They knew what it could do! That's why they all wore those heavy aprons anytime they were near it. And then that bastard, Girard. Not only did he know, but he was paying off the doctors to falsify the poor girl's medical reports, saying they had syphilis! Oh, poor Beatrice!

She had to get to the hospital to check on Beatrice before those scoundrels got away with their lies. The trolley hit a bump and caused Hattie to click her teeth. Immediately, she felt something wasn't right. She placed a finger and thumb into her mouth and pulled out a hard object.

My tooth!

She examined the object in her palm. The once white enamel was now a sickly greenish color, and it smelled to high heaven. A whirlwind of thought overtook her. She couldn't believe this was happening. First, the girls and now her.

A hand touched her shoulder.

"Hattie? Is that you?" asked a familiar voice.

She turned to face Charlie. His eyes and perfect smile quickly turned to a look of terror.

"Uh… Hattie. Uh… hi, how are you? It's uh… good to see you. Well, I need to be going. Take care."

And just like that, he leaped from the trolley, as if he couldn't get away fast enough. Hattie looked around and noticed all the passengers were staying clear of her. She reached into her purse, pulled out a mirror and gave a startled gasp. Hattie could not believe what was looking back at her.

Hattie ran up her steps as fast as she could on her wobbly legs, opened the door, and hurried to lock it behind her. She leaned her back against the closed door and sobbed. Hattie was so scared and didn't know where to turn. She didn't have any family within 500 miles. Her Walter was long dead, and Charlie had looked at her like he'd seen a leper.

Hattie ran her fingers through her hair and something didn't feel right. She looked at her hand and a big wad of hair was stuck between her fingers. The end had a clump of diseased looking flesh attached that smelled like old fish guts.

She shook it out of her hand as if she had touched a hot stove and ran toward the bathroom. The reflection looking back made her let out a scream and she quickly covered her mouth. Where the patch of hair came out was an open sore that oozed yellow pus. Her sobbing only made her jaw ache that much more. Her body was falling apart before her very eyes. She opened her mouth and reached inside with a finger to probe around. Two more teeth fell out of their sockets simply from touching them. They clinked into the porcelain sink like two diseased marbles. Hattie reached back into her mouth. She couldn't stop herself, now. She was past the point of no return and had to see what other sideshow atrocities awaited her examination.

Clink. There went another tooth. Clink. And another one. She poked around the empty sockets that used to house good, healthy teeth. The gums oozed a fetid yellow slime that tried to slide down her throat. Quickly, she opened the medicine cabinet and grabbed a brown bottle of tonic. She took a quick swig and swished it around in her mouth. The liquid burned like hellfire. Hattie spat out a mouthful of brownish-yellow sludge into the sink.

Mesmerized, she reached into her mouth to inspect what effect the tonic had, if any. She felt something odd at the back of her mouth. She couldn't quite get her fingers back there. She opened a little wider. Still nothing. Wider still. Almost there. As wide as she could.

SNAP!

Hattie's whole bottom jaw snapped off, coming to rest on the top of her chest, dangling by a rancid strand of flesh. Her blackened tongue danced back and forth in midair trying to form words.

In his office, Mr. Girard puffed away on his cigar. He had just got off the telephone with Stevens. Everything was going as planned. With a little luck, this fiasco wouldn't cost him near what he'd been afraid it would cost. It was amazing how little you had to spend to cover up a shit show when you had dirt on some of the key players.

He looked down at his wrist watch. The UltraGlow dial illuminated back that it was almost midnight. He took the watch off and put it in the top drawer. He would wait until the new batch of watches with the improved formula of UltraGlow came out. No sense taking any chances. He snickered to himself.

Rising from his chair, he stretched the kinks out of his back. It had been a long day. He barely had enough girls show up today to warrant opening the doors. But tomorrow was a new day. There was a new batch of recruits coming in the morning. He needed to get home and get some sleep.

Sliding his chair in, he thought he heard a noise. Girard looked out the windows into the inky black of the factory. Nothing. He shook his head while grabbing his coat and chuckled again.

Screech.

There it was again. Looking out, he thought he saw a faint glow coming from the hallway that led to the work-stations. He rubbed his tired eyes and looked again. The glimmer was getting brighter, as if someone was carrying a pale green lantern toward him.

"Who's there?" he bellowed.

Screeeeech.

His arms broke out into gooseflesh at the sound. He heard something else that sounded like a moan. The source of the light was getting closer. When it turned the corner, Girard's cigar dropped out of his mouth as he let out a scream. He ran back into his office, and hurriedly shut and locked the door, but it wouldn't keep out that god forsaken moaning. The door began to shake on its hinges. When it burst open, Girard's bladder let loose all over the floor.

"No! It can't be!"

"Yes, you Ol' Square Britches. It can!"

Reaching out and grasping his shirt, with pale green fingers, was Beatrice, Lizzie, Bonnie, Betty, Dorothy, and Hattie. They held him down while he screamed and screamed. Hattie brought up her illuminated hand that held a container with enough UltraGlow to paint a whole week's worth of watches, and Mr. Girard gagged as they poured it down his screaming throat.

Haunted World

by Robert McCammon

Well, I knew it was the end of the world for sure when I walked into my den and found William Shakespeare sittin' in my Barcalounger.

At least I think it was him. Anyways, it was one of them fellas wore starched collars and a velvet suit and said a lot of "thees" and "thous" like they used to do every year at the high school senior play down the road. I called Vera in. I said, "Vera, come in here and take a look at this right quick!" and she came runnin'. Of course, we'd seen ghosts before, just like everybody else in the world had by then, but Will Shakespeare sittin' in your den watchin' *Cross-Wits* on the TV is a damn peculiar sight.

Every so often he'd speak, as if he were tryin' to answer the *Cross-Wits* questions. Then he'd rest his head back, and I saw him close his eyes and heard him say, "Woe is me," clear as a church bell. By then Ben Junior had come in, and he pressed in between his momma and me, and we all three watched the ghost tryin' to talk to the man on TV. Ol' Will was the same as the other spirits: He wasn't all there. Oh, you could make him out all right, and even see the color of his hair and skin and suit, but he was kinda smoky too, and you could see the chair right through him. He reached out toward the lamp beside him, but his hand was misty and couldn't touch it. "Woe is me," he said again, and then he looked at us standin' in the doorway. His eyes were sad. They were the eyes of a man who was lost on a long trip and couldn't find the right road again.

Vera said, "Would you like me to change the channel?" She was always mannerly to house guests. Even uninvited ones. Ol' Will started to fade away then, bit by bit. Didn't surprise us none, 'cause we'd seen the others do it too. In another minute just his face was left, floatin' in the air like a pale moon. Then nothin' but his eyes. They blinked a couple of times, then those were gone too. But we all knew ol' Will hadn't vanished for good, and he hadn't gone too far away neither. He was like all the other ones roamin' around the haunted world. Hell of a mess, that's for sure.

Wasn't too long before Ben Junior said, "Dad?" and he motioned me and his momma over to the big picture window in the front room, the one that has such a pretty view over the meadow. It was October, and the world was turnin' deep red and purple. The sky was that greenish-gray it gets just before it happens. Vera said a while back that the sky reminds her of a lizard's skin, and I guess that about hits the nail on the head. Ben Junior pointed, and he said in a quiet voice, "There's another one."

Vera and I looked, and of course we saw it. Have to be blind as a bat in a Bundt cake not to see one of those things, once they get started.

The tornadoes are always that peculiar lizard-skin color. One of 'em whipped right across Pennsylvania Avenue in Washington, D.C., the other day. I saw it on the five o'clock news. Anyway, there was a tornado whippin' and whirlin' down the hillside into our meadow not two hundred yards away. Things started poppin' and creakin' in our house like the whole place was fixin' to come unjointed. A light bulb blew out and right after that the power went. "Lord," Vera whispered, standin' beside me in the lizard-green light. "Lord have mercy."

You could see 'em in the tornado, goin' around and around and tumblin' over each other from the bottom of the cone to the top of the spout. How many were there it was hard to say. Hundreds, I reckon. Some of 'em were smoky, but others looked just as solid as you and me. The tornado was spittin' 'em out hither and yonder, and they were fallin' to earth like autumn leaves. They drifted into the treetops and onto the grass, and they fell over the fence and onto the road that leads to Concordia. Some of 'em were tattered to pieces, like old rags caught in the blades of a lawn mower, but others stood up and staggered around like Saturday night drunks. The tornado took a turn away from our house and marched up the hillside again toward the south, spittin' out ghosts with every whirl, and then Vera reached out and pulled the curtains shut, and we all stood in the twilight listenin' to the trees moan as the tornado went on.

"Well," I said, because there wasn't much else to say. Deep subject, I know. Cold, too. Vera walked over to the wall switch and flicked it up and down with a vengeance, but the power wasn't goin' to come back on for quite a while. "There goes a hot dinner," she said, and she sounded like she was about to cry. I put my hand on her shoulder, and then she kinda folded up against me and hung on. Ben Junior sneaked a peek through the curtain, but what he saw he didn't care for, because he let the curtain drop back real quick.

Someone—somethin'—called from outside. "Mary?" It was a man's voice, and it was terribly lonely. "Mary? Are you in there?"

I started to go to the door, but Vera held me tight. We both knew I had to go. I pulled away from her, and I went to the door and opened it.

On our front porch stood a frail-lookin' man with dark hair slicked back and parted in the middle. He wore a dark suit—black or brown, I couldn't really tell. His face was pale and kinda yellow, like spoiled milk. He took a step back when he saw me, and he was wearin' old high-top shoes. He was shiverin', and he looked around himself. If he saw all the others staggerin' about in the meadow, nothin' registered on his face but pure puzzlement. Then he looked at me again, and when his mouth opened, his voice was like the chilly wind. You felt it more than heard it. "Mary? Is Mary waiting for me?"

"Mary's not here," I told him.

"Mary?" he asked again. "Is she waiting for me?"

"No," I said. "Not here."

He stopped speakin', but his mouth stayed open. His eyes looked wet, like those of a dog that had just gotten kicked in the ribs. "I don't think you know anybody here," I told him, because he seemed to be waitin' for somethin' else. And then his mouth closed, and he turned away from my door and started across the meadow in his high-topped shoes. "Mary?" I heard him call. "Mary?" He started fadin' away as he passed a Roman soldier sittin' sprawled in the grass, and he was almost gone when a little boy in knickers ran right through him. The man who was searchin' for Mary faded away like a Polaroid left in the noonday sun too long, but the Roman soldier stayed where he was, and the little boy ran into the woods. There were maybe forty or fifty others out in the meadow, wanderin' around like strangers at a weird garden party. Or a Halloween party, it bein' October and all. Out on the edge of the meadow there was what looked like somebody from Revolutionary times, a skinny man wearin' a powdered wig and a three-cornered hat. Near him was a cowboy in a yellow duster. Over there on the other side was a black-haired woman in a long blue gown that trailed on the grass, and not far from her stood a man in a suit, lookin' around as if he was waitin' for the next bus. The blue mist of ghosts trailed from the trees like cobwebs and drifted over the meadow in an ankle-deep haze. Ghosts were all in the woods, and you hear 'em babblin' and calling' in a bedlam of accents and languages. "Dan!" I heard one American-speakin' woman—ghost, I mean—shout from over on the edge of the woods. "Damn it, Dan, where's my robe?" she hollered, as she walked buck naked across the grass. Not walked, actually. Kinda wobbled is more like it. The wind hit her and tattered her to pieces so we didn't have to look at her big, old flabby butt anymore. Ben Junior was peekin' out beside me, and I shoved him back inside and shut the door.

Vera and I just stared at each other, there in the gloom, as the ghosts hollered and chattered outside. We heard an Indian war-whoopin', and somebody screamin' that she'd lost her cat, and somebody else raisin' a ruckus in what sounded like Greek to me. They were all searchin' for their own world, the one they used to be part of. But of course they couldn't get back there. They couldn't find anybody or anythin' that was familiar, because this wasn't their world anymore. It was our world. And that's the hell of it. See?

I remember what Burt Truman said. I remember, because it seemed so right. Burt looked at me, his eyes huge behind those bottle-bottom glasses he wears, and he said, "You know why this is happenin', Ben? Well, I'll tell you my opinion. You take the air and the water nowadays. Both so polluted you can't take a safe breath or a decent sip. And what happened on them beaches last summer, all that garbage and crap washin' up 'cause the ocean can't take no more. He lifted up his glasses and scratched his nose. "Seems to me Heaven—or Hell—can't take no more either. And all the dead folks are gettin' cast back up on shore. Whatever that place is that kept the dead, it's full to overflowin'. The dead folks are washin' back up into our world, and that's God's truth or I ain't sittin' here in Clyde's barbershop."

"Bullshit," Clyde said as he clipped Burt's side burns. Clyde has a voice like a steam shovel with stripped gears. "Damn ghosts are comin' through the ozone hole. That's what they said on Dan Rather yesterday."

"God's shut with us," Phil Laney offered. He's a deacon at the Baptist church, and he was gloomin'-and-doomin' long before all this started. "Only way for us to fix this is to get down on our knees and pray like we've never prayed before. I mean, serious prayin'. We've got to get right with God before this thing'll be fixed."

"Hell, this thing's done broke to pieces," Luke McGuire said. Ol' Luke's a big fella, stands about six foot three and wears raggedy overalls, but he's got the best farmland in south Alabama. "Just like a machine," he said as he rolled himself another cigarette. "You bust a cylinder on your tractor, ain't prayin' that gets it fixed. You bend a blade on a tiller, you don't get on your knees and kiss the ground until it's straight again. Hell, no. The world's a machine. Thing's done broke to pieces, and the repair shop's shut down."

This was the sort of conversation that could fill most of a Saturday afternoon and evenin' and still leave you goin' in circles. But I mostly thought of what Burt said, about the dead overflowin' and washin' back up into our world. The tornadoes brought 'em back, of course, but I knew what he meant. Heaven and Hell were like busted pipes, and the ghosts were spillin' out.

And right about then, as Luke and Phil were arguin' hammer and tongs, a knight in tarnished armor walked past the window of Clyde Butler's barbershop. Walked right out in the street, he did, and Mrs. Beacham in her green Oldsmobile swerved the wheel and crashed into the front of Sammy Kane's Stag Shop for Men. Clothes dummies flew all over the place, broken arms and legs lyin' on the pavement. That knight just kept on goin', fine as you please, and he took a few more rusty steps before he vanished into the unknown. But he didn't go far. We all knew that. He couldn't go far, see. He was still stuck in the haunted world, like all the other dead folks.

After all that commotion had died down, Luke McGuire picked his teeth with a splintered match and brought up the question: "How come the ghosts are wearin' clothes?"

Not all of 'em were, of course, but most of 'em did. We thought about that for a little while, and then Luke went on in that thick drawl of his that always makes me think of mud simmerin' in the bottom of a ditch. "Clothes," he said. "Ghosts of people are one thing. But are they wearin' ghosts of *clothes?*"

We drifted into talkin' about what ghosts were, and that was a tangled thicket. Then Clyde brought up the next skull knocker. "Thank God they're ghosts, that's all I can say." He brushed hairs off Burt's shoulders. "Not solid, I mean." He glanced around at everybody, to see if we'd gotten the point. We hadn't. "You can drive cars through ghosts. You can put your hand through 'em. They don't need food or water, and they can't touch you neither. Take that fella in armor just walked past here. Think you'd like to feel him slap you upside the head? I looked out my window this mornin' and saw the woods full of damn ghosts, blowin' in the breeze like old newspapers. One of 'em had a long black beard and carried a sword 'bout as big as ol' Luke. Think you'd like to get stabbed a few times with somethin' like that?"

"Wasn't a real sword," Luke observed sagely. "Was a ghost of a sword."

"Yeah, and thank God for that," Clyde steam-shoveled on. "What do you think would happen if everybody who ever died in the whole world came back?"

"We might find out," I said. "Seems like that's happenin' right now." I knew, like we all did, that this thing was happenin' not just in

Concordia, Alabama, but in Georgia and North Carolina and New York and Illinois and Wyoming and California and everywhere else under the sun. Ghosts were roamin' the streets of London and Paris, and stompin' through Red Square. Even the Australians were seein' ghosts, so when I say haunted world that's exactly what I mean.

"Thank God, they're ghosts and not real," Clyde said, as he finished up on Burt. "There you go." He handed Burt a mirror. "Slicker'n owl shit."

Luke switched on the barbershop's TV to catch the midday news. There was a report from Washington, D.C. It showed somethin' that looked like Thomas Jefferson, sittin' on the steps of the Capitol and cryin' his eyes out.

It hit me then, as I was standin' in the gloom starin' at Vera and the ghosts were catterwaulin' outside. The power was out. How were we gonna see the TV show tonight? They'd been advertisin' it for a week. Tonight Tom Edison was supposed to be a guest on the Johnny Carson show. I'm talkin' about the Tom Edison who invented the light bulb, the genuine article. Seems Edison—his spirit, I mean—had been talked into appearin' on TV. Tonight was the night. Shirley MacLaine was supposed to be a guest too, but she wasn't even dead yet, so what did she know? Anyway, the power was off!

I went to the phone and called Clyde. "They got the juice back on over here," Clyde said, speakin' from eight miles away. The phone was hissin' with static, but I could hear him good enough. "I just got a call from Phil, too," Clyde told me. "His TV's out. I reckon mine is at home too. You want to watch that show, come on over to the barbershop tonight. Hell, I'll get us some beers and we'll have a time of it."

I said that was a fine idea. Ben Junior was tuggin' at my sleeve, and Vera was starin' out the window again. I hung up the phone and walked over to see what had been roused up this time.

More Roman soldiers were out in the meadow. I guess they were Roman, but I'm not sure. There were about a hundred of 'em, and they had shields and swords. Ghost shields and swords, I mean. And there were about a hundred or so Chinese-lookin' fellas too, half-naked and with long braids in their hair. Well, the Romans and the Chinese had taken to fightin'. Maybe they were tryin' to finish up an old battle, or maybe all they knew was fightin' and that was their job. The Romans were swingin' their ghost swords, and the Chinese were kickin' with their ghost legs, and nothin' but mist was bein' hit. From out of the woods swarmed other ghosts: cowboys, musketeers, guys with bowl-shaped haircuts and long robes, women in lacy dresses, and black Africans with animal-skin shields and spears like in that English movie Ben Junior and me watched one Saturday. All the ghosts swirled around each other like they were part of a big churnin' whirlpool, and I'm tellin' you that the noise they made-hollerin' and screamin' at each other was somethin' fearsome. No doubt about it: Even when people were dead, they still couldn't get along. Then a few dogs were even runnin' around out among the ghosts—ghost dogs, snappin' at ghost ankles. Maybe there was a horse or two out there, but I'm not sure. Anyway, it looked like Animal Heaven had started overflowin' too. "Lord save us!" Vera said, but Ben Junior said, "Neat!" and I saw he was grinnin'. Boy's got a strange sense of humor. Takes after me, I reckon, because I was kinda fascinated at the sight of all those ghosts tanglin' and whirlin'.

Vera turned away from the window, and that was when she screamed.

I looked. I think Ben Junior let out a strangled squawk. It might've been my voice.

Standin' in front of us, right in our pine-paneled livin' room, was a red-bearded man with a double bladed battle-ax. That sumbitch stood at least six foot six, taller even than Luke McGuire, and he had on some kind of ragged animal skin and a metal skullcup with bull horns sticking out on either side of it. His face looked like a lump of meat wrapped up in wrinkled leather. He had green eyes under red brows as big as scrub brushes, and he let out a holler that shook the room as he lifted that battle-ax up over his head.

What would you have done? I knew he was a ghost and all, but at a time like that you don't think exactly calm. I shoved Vera out of the way of that battle-ax, and I picked up the first thing that came to hand: a lamp table beside the couch. The lamp flew off of it, and I thrust that little wooden table up like a Vikin' shield, my shoulders tensin' for the shock.

It didn't come. The battle-ax, a misty thing, went right through the table. I swear I saw a glint of metal, though, and old blood on the edge. I could smell that sumbitch, sure enough; he smelled like a dead cow. He took another step forward, crowdin' me, and he flailed back and forth with that battle-ax like he really thought he was gonna hit somethin'. His face was splotched with red. Ever heard the expression, "mad as a ghost"? I just made it up, 'cause he was mad as hellfire sure enough. He chopped the ax back and forth a dozen times, and the rage on his face would've been terrible if he'd been flesh and blood instead of colored mist. I laughed, and that made him madder still. The ax kept whippin' back and forth, through the table. I said, "Fella, why don't you put that toy away and get the hell out of my house?"

He stopped choppin', his big chest heavin' up and down. He glared at me for a minute, and I could tell he hated me. Maybe for bein' alive—I don't know. Then he gave a growl and started to fade away. His beard was the last thing to go. It hung in the air for a few seconds, workin' as if it still had a mouth under it, and then it went.

"Is it gone? Is it gone? Ben, tell me it's gone!" Vera had scrunched herself up into a corner, her arms hugging herself and her eyes wide and starey. I didn't like the looks of them. Ben Junior was kinda dazed. He stood where the Vikin' had been, feelin' around in the air.

"It's gone, hon," I said to Vera. "Wasn't ever here, really. You okay?"

"I've never...I've never...seen anything...like that." She could hardly get a breath, and I set the table down and put my arms around her while she trembled.

"They're not real," I told her. "None of them are. They're just...pictures in the air. They hang there for a while, and then they go away. But they're not real. Okay?"

She nodded. "Okay," she said, but she sounded choked.

"Dad?"

"Just a minute. You want me to go get you an aspirin? You want to lie down awhile?" I kept my arms around Vera, for fear her knees might give way.

"Dad?" Ben Junior's voice was a little higher. "Look at this."

"I'm all right," Vera said. She had a strong constitution. Livin' on a farm for over twenty years makes you that way. "See what Ben Junior wants."

I looked over at the boy. He was standin' there, starin' at the table I'd just set down. "Dad?" he repeated. "I...don't think this was here before."

"What wasn't there before?" I walked over beside him, and I saw what he was talkin' about.

On the table's surface was a single diagonal scratch. It wasn't much. The tip of a nail might've done it. Only Ben Junior was right, and I knew that at once. The scratch hadn't been there before. I touched it to make sure it was real, and ran my finger along its length. The lamp's base had green backing on it, to keep it from scratchin' anythin'. I looked at Ben Junior. He was a smart boy, and I knew he knew. And he knew I knew, too.

"Vera?" I tried to sound calm, but I don't think I did. "Let's drive on into town and get some dinner. How does that suit you?"

"Fine." She took my hand and wouldn't let go of it, and I walked with her to the closet to get her sweater. Ben Junior went back through the hallway at a cautious pace, stirrin' the air before him with his hands to make sure nothin' was there, and a minute later he returned with a jacket from his room. I got my wallet and the keys to the pickup, and we went outside into the gray-green twilight. The driveway was full of fightin' ghosts: Chinese, Romans, an Indian or two, and a husky fella wearin' a kilt. I backed the truck right through 'em, and none of 'em seemed to mind.

On the drive to Concordia I turned on the radio, but all the stations were screwed up with the most god-awful static you ever heard. I switched it off real quick, because the noise sounded to me like the whole world was screamin'. Vera touched my arm and pointed off toward the right. Another tornado was movin' across the hills, blowin' red leaves before it and leavin' ghosts in its wake. The sky was green and low, shot through with pearly streaks. Half-formed, misty figures swept past the truck. I turned on the windshield wipers.

We passed Bobby Glover's pasture. There were so many ghosts wanderin' and staggerin' around that field it looked like a spirit convention. Things that looked like pieces of filmy cloth were hangin' in Bobby's barbed-wire fence, and they were growin' arms, legs, and heads. An old woman dressed like a Pilgrim was walkin' in the middle of the road, and she saw us comin' and made a noise like a cat gettin' skinned as the truck went through her. I looked back in the rearview mirror and saw blue mist floatin' in the air where the Pilgrim lady had been a second before. Somethin' occurred to me real strange just about then: Somewhere in the world my own father and mother were wanderin'. Vera's mother, too; her father was in a rest home in Montgomery. Somewhere all our ancestors were out in the haunted world, and the ancestors of everybody who'd ever drawn a breath. I hadn't seen any ghosts of babies yet. I hoped I wouldn't, but you never knew. Peculiar thoughts whirled through my brain, like those red leaves thrown by the tornado: My father had died six years ago, and my mother had gone on a year later. They could be roamin' the jungles of Brazil or the streets of Dallas for all I knew. I hoped my father didn't come back in Tokyo. He'd fought the Japanese in World War II, and that would be pure hell for him.

About three miles from Concordia, we came upon a station wagon that had gone into a ditch. Both the front doors were open, but nobody was around. I stopped the truck and was gonna get out to take a look, hut I heard what sounded like Indian war whoops off in the woods somewhere. I thought about that scratch on the table, and I swallowed hard and drove on.

I took the next curve pretty fast. Anyway, we were on him before we knew it. Vera screamed and her foot plunged to the floorboard, but of course the brake pedal was on my side, and I sure as hell wasn't gonna hit it.

He looked more ape than human, really. He was monstrous, and he wore a tattered lion's skin that still had the lion's head on it. He bellowed and charged the pickup, his fangy teeth showin'. I tried to swerve, but there wasn't much use, and I sure didn't want to go into a ditch. The caveman lifted a club that had sharp rocks embedded in it, and he swung that thing like it weighed a feather.

The club turned to mist an instant before it would've hit the fender. I heard the caveman bellow again—right up next to my head, it seemed like—and I gave the truck all the gas she could handle. We sped on down the road, the engine poppin' and snarlin'. I guess that caveman—ghost of a caveman, I mean—must've thought we were somethin' good to eat. I looked in the rearview mirror, but he was gone.

"It wasn't real, was it?" Vera said in a quiet voice. Her gaze was fixed straight ahead. "It was just a picture that hung in the air, wasn't it?"

"Yeah, that's right," I answered. I thought about the scratched table. My fingers were clenched real hard around the steerin' wheel. That table hadn't been scratched before the Vikin' sumbitch had swung his ax at me. My mind was wanderin' in dangerous country. The Vikin' was a ghost, with the ghost of a battle-ax. Just a picture, hangin' in the air. So how come the table was scratched, as if the slightest edge of metal had grazed it?

I didn't care to think about that anymore. Such thoughts made the hair prickle on the back of your neck.

Concordia was a small town, hardly much to look at, but it had never been prettier. The sun was goin' down fast, into a lizard-skin horizon, and Concordia's street lights were glowin' in the murk. We went straight to the Concordia Cafe. It was crowded, I guess because a lot of folks had the same idea as us. Bein' with real people was a comfort, though the food was as bad as usual. You can be sure that ghosts were the prime topic of conversation, and every so often somebody would holler for everybody else to look out the windows and you could see spirits on Main Street. The sky flashed and flickered, blue lightnin' jumpin' from horizon to horizon, and we all sat in the Concordia Cafe and watched the parade of ghosts. Here came a fella dressed up in a tuxedo, his hair gleamin' with pomade, and spats on his shoes, and he was callin' for somebody named Lily in a broken voice, ghost tears runnin' down his cheeks. Then a Nazi soldier ran past, carryin' a ghost rifle. A little girl in a nightgown, her hair red and curly, staggered along the street callin' in a language I couldn't understand. Some of the women wanted to go out and help her, but the men blocked the door. It was a ghost little girl, and the hell if we wanted her in here among the livin'.

A whole bunch of 'em wandered past the cafe: half-naked Egyptians brown as berries, women in gaudy dance-hall duds, a pair of fellas in those tall caps with fur on 'em, and ghosts in rags. And then the ghost of a boy about twelve, Ben Junior's age, came over and peered in the cafe's window, and he was joined by the ghost of a woman with long white hair and no teeth. A man in a striped prison suit looked in another window, and peerin' in over his shoulder was the ghost of a tall, skinny fella in clown makeup. In a few minutes more they were all around the cafe, starin' in through the windows at us, and Lord knows our appetites fled. Fifty or sixty ghosts were out there, lookin' in and maybe longin' to join us. Grace Tarpley, the head waitress, started closin' all the blinds, then Mitch Brenner and Tommy Shawcross got up from their tables and helped her. But as soon as all the blinds were down and the windows sealed up, the ghosts outside took to moanin' and catterwaulin' and that was the end of our dinner. Some folks—live folks, I mean—started cryin' and wailin' too, specially some of the children. Hell, I even saw a couple of men break down and start bawlin'. This wasn't no fun, that's for sure.

Anyway, the noise comin' out of the Concordia Cafe must've scared the ghosts off, because their voices started gettin' fainter and fainter until finally it was just the live people moanin'. Then Gracie let out a scream that almost lifted the roof, because the old farmer sittin' by himself at a booth in the back, an untouched cup of coffee on the table before him, suddenly stood up and faded away. Nobody had known him, but I guess we all figured he was from the next county. It was gettin' so you couldn't tell the livin' from the dead anymore.

The night moved on. It seemed like nobody wanted to go home to their haunted houses. Jack and Sarah Kelton came by our table for a few minutes and said the power was still out their way and they'd heard the lines were all fouled up. Which didn't sound so good, since the Keltons lived about two miles closer to town than us. The lights flickered off and on a few times in the cafe, which made everybody scream to high heaven, but Gracie said the men were workin' on the wires down the road and not to worry because there were plenty of flashlights and candles. As Jack talked on about seein' a ghost he swore was Abraham Lincoln strollin' along Highway 211, I looked out the blinds and watched the blue lightnin' cracklin' across the sky. It was a bad night here. Hell, it was a bad night everywhere.

I don't know how many cups of coffee Vera and I had. Ben Junior got stuffed on potato chips, and gettin' his belly full is a true miracle. Anyway, the crowd started thinnin' out, folks decidin' to go home to sleep—if they could sleep, that is. It was almost time for the Johnny Carson show, and I paid the bill and took Vera and Ben Junior to Clyde's barbershop down the street.

The regulars were there, and the cast-iron stove was stoked up warm and ruddy. The TV was on, the show about ten minutes away from startin'. We found chairs and sat down next to Phil and Gloria Laney. Luke McGuire was there with his wife Missy and their two kids, the Trumans were there and so was Sammy and Beth Kane. Clyde had a few sixpacks of Bud ready, but none of us felt like a beer.

The show started, Johnny Carson came out—all serious this time, didn't even crack a funny—and he showed a few old pictures of

Thomas Edison. The first guest was a fella who'd written a biography of Edison, then Mickey Rooney came on because he played Young Edison in a movie a long time ago. The next guest was a man who talked about the ghosts appearin' all over the world, and he said ghosts had been seen from the Sahara Desert to the South Pole. He was an expert, I guess, but exactly what at I don't know. While the talkin' was goin' on, buildin' up to Edison appearin', I was thinkin' about the scratched table. What had made that mark? The edge of that Vikin's battle-ax? No, that couldn't be! The ghosts were just pictures hangin' in the air. They weren't real. But I thought about that station wagon we'd seen in the ditch on the way to town, and the sound of Indians war-whoopin' in the woods.

I remembered Clyde saying, "What do you think would happen if everybody who ever died in the whole world came back?"

Ghosts of everybody who'd ever died was one thing. But what if— I liked to choke thinkin' about this…what if everybody who'd ever died in the whole world *did* come back? Maybe as ghosts first, yes, but…maybe they weren't always gonna stay ghosts. Maybe death had reversed itself. Maybe some of 'em were already turnin' solid, a little piece at a time. As solid as the sharp edge of an ax blade. As solid as Indians, who'd pulled somebody out of their station wagon and—

I shook those thoughts out of my head. Ghosts were ghosts. Weren't they?

Shirley MacLaine came on next, carryin' a crystal ball. She said Thomas Edison was a good friend of hers.

And then it was time.

They lowered the lights in the studio, I guess so Edison wouldn't get spooked. Then all the guests started callin' his name and Johnny Carson asked the audience to be real quiet. They guests kept on callin' Thomas Edison's name and askin' him to join them, but the seat next to Johnny's desk stayed empty. It went on awhile, and pretty soon Johnny got that look on his face like when he has a talkin' dog on the show and it won't pip a squeak. I mean, the whole thing was almost ridiculous.

"I need a beer," Luke said, and he reached for one.

His hand never got there. Because suddenly we all gasped. There was a shape just beginnin' to take form in that empty chair next to Johnny's desk. Some of the audience started talkin', but Johnny hushed them up. The shape was becomin' the body of a man: a white-haired, sad-faced man, dressed in a wrinkled white suit that looked as if it had been slept in for quite some time. The figure got clearer and clearer, and damned if it wasn't the man who was in those old yellowed photographs.

"Got on clothes," Luke rasped. "How can a ghost wear clothes?"

"Shush!" Phil told him, and he leaned closer to the TV.

Clyde turned up the volume. Thomas Edison his own self was sittin' in that chair on the Carson show, and even though the lights were dim he blinked as he looked around as if they stung his eyes. He was tremblin'. So was Johnny, and 'most everybody else. Thomas Edison looked like somebody's frail, scared old grandpap.

"Hello, Mr. Edison," Johnny finally said. He sounded like he had a chicken bone caught in his throat. "Can I...call you Tom?"

Edison didn't answer. He just shook and gasped, plain terrified. "Stage fright," Burt said. "Happened to me once when I gave a speech to the Civitan Club."

"Tom?" Johnny Carson went on. "Do you know who I am?"

Edison shook his head, his eyes wet and glassy.

"Mr. Edison," Shirley said, "we're all your friends here."

Edison gave a soft moan, and Shirley recoiled from him a little bit. "Tom?" Johnny tried again. "Where did you come from?"

"I...don't..." Edison started to speak, but his voice was wispy. "I...don't..." He looked around, gasping for words. "I...don't...belong here." He squinted at the audience. "I don't...like this place."

"We all love you," Shirley told him. "Tell us about your journey, and what you've seen on the other si—"

If ever hell broke loose on earth, it was the next instant.

Somebody in the audience took a picture. You could see the quick pop and glare of the flashbulb, right in Tom Edison's eyeballs.

Another flash went off, and a third. Johnny Carson jumped up and shouted, "No pictures! I said no pictures! Somebody get those cameras!" The studio lights came on, real sudden. Tom Edison almost jumped out of his chair. People in the audience were rushin' the stage, and Johnny Carson was yellin' for everybody to stay back, but you could hardly hear him over the noise. More flashbulbs were poppin', and I guess somehow the reporters had gotten into the studio when they weren't supposed to be there. Lights flashed in Tom Edison's face, and all of a sudden he reached out and plucked that crystal ball off Shirley's lap, and he threw it straight into the TV camera that was trained on him. The camera smashed, zigzag lines goin' all over the screen. Another TV camera trained on Edison and caught him as he stood up, screamed at the top of his lungs, and vanished in a whirl of blue mist. "Everybody sit down!" Johnny was shoutin'. People were still tryin' to get closer, and now you could see folks grapplin' with each other like a backwoods wrestlin' match. "Everybody please sit—"

The screen went dark. "Somebody stepped on a cord," Burt said. Static jumped and jittered across the screen, and then a message came on: NETWORK DIFFICULTY. PLEASE STAND BY.

We stood by, but the Carson show didn't come back on. "He picked it up," Luke said quietly. "Did you see that? He picked it up."

"Picked what up?" Clyde asked. "What're you babblin' about?"

"Thomas Edison picked up the crystal ball and flung it," Luke told him, and looked around at the rest of us. "A ghost picked up somethin' solid. How can a ghost pick up somethin' solid?"

Nobody answered. I almost did, but I kept my mouth shut. I didn't want what I was thinkin' to be true. Maybe I should have said somethin', but the time slipped past.

Lightnin' flared and crackled over Concordia. About three seconds later, the barbershop's lights flickered once, twice, and went out. All of Concordia lay in darkness. Vera grasped my hand so hard I thought my knuckles were about to bust.

"Well, that's that," Clyde said. He stood up in the dark, and Luke lit a match. In its pale glow we all looked like ghosts. Clyde turned off the dead TV. "I don't know about everybody else," he said, "but I'm goin' home and get a good night's sleep, ghosts or not."

The group started breakin' up, and Clyde locked the doors. "We ought to go to the Holiday Inn over near Grangeville," I told Vera and Ben Junior as we were walkin' back to the pickup. "Maybe they'll have the power on over there. All right?"

Vera wouldn't let go of my hand. "No," she said. "I can't sleep in a strange bed. Lord knows all I want to do is get in my bed and pull the covers over my head and hope I wake up from this nightmare in the mornin'.

"Holiday Inn might be safer," I said. Instantly I regretted it, because Vera stiffened up. "Safer?" she asked. "Safer? What's that mean?"

If I told her what I was thinkin', that would be all she wrote. You'd have to peel Vera off a wall. Ben Junior was listenin' too, and I knew he knew, but still and all, home was where we belonged. "All right, hon," I said, and put my arm around her. "We'll sleep in our own bed tonight." Vera relaxed, and I was mighty glad I hadn't steered her into dark, deep water.

We started off. The pickup's headlights were a comfort. Maybe we should sleep in the truck tonight, I thought. No, we'd all have cricked backs in the mornin'. Best to get on home and pull the covers over our heads just like Vera wanted to. I found myself thinkin' about the rifle down in the basement. I ought to get that out and loaded. Wouldn't hurt to have it beside the bed if I needed—

"Look out, Ben!" Vera shouted, and I went for the brake, but too late.

The caveman was standin' in the road. He snarled and lifted that club studded with sharp-edged rocks, and as he swung it I could see the muscles ripple in his ape-like shoulders.

I expected the club to turn to mist. I wanted it to. I prayed for it in that long instant as it came at the fender in a powerful blur. Oh, God, I prayed for it.

The club smashed into the front of our pickup truck with a shock that lifted us all off the seat. Vera screamed and so did Ben Junior, and I think Ben Senior let out a scream too. One of the headlights shattered and went out. I felt and heard somethin' boom and clatter in the engine, behind the crushed radiator. The truck lurched, and steam bellowed out around the crumpled hood. The caveman jumped back as the truck passed him, but I think he was scared just as witless as we were. I looked into the rearview mirror and saw him standin' there in the glare of the red taillights. Lightnin' flared behind him, over dark Concordia. I think he was grinnin'. He swung his club, and he started lumberin' along the road in the direction we were goin'.

The truck was laborin'. "Come on, come on!" I said, and I kept my foot to the gas. Vera's scream had broken; she was a shakin' moan, pressed up against my ribs. "He hit us, Dad!" Ben Junior said. "That sumbitch hit us!"

"Yeah," I told him. Wheezed it, really. "Yeah, I know he did."

The truck kept goin'. Chevy builds 'em strong. But I watched the gauges and I listened to the engine racketin', and I knew the eight miles home was askin' way too much.

Finally, with a groan and a shudder, the engine quit. I let the truck coast as far as she'd go, and I prayed again, this time for a slope to take us home, but I knew the road was flat as a flounder all the way to our front porch. We rolled to a stop, and we sat there.

"We've stopped, Dad," Ben Junior said.

I nodded. One part of me wanted to wring his neck. One part of me wanted to wring my own neck. Vera was sobbin', and I put my arm around her tight. "Don't cry," I said. "We're all right. We're gonna be fine. Don't cry, now." She kept cryin'. Words were cheap.

We sat for a while longer. Out in the night we could hear the freight-train roar of a tornado movin' through the hills. "Dad?" Ben Junior said at last, "I don't think we ought to stay here all night." I hadn't raised a dummy, that was for sure; I was the dumb one, for not insistin' we go to the Holiday Inn.

I hesitated at openin' the door. Vera was clingin' to me, and I'm not sure whose heart was poundin' harder. I was thinkin' about the caveman, with his club that must've weighed seventy or eighty pounds. He was between us and Concordia, and every second we wasted brought him closer. I got out of the truck real quick, pulled Vera out, and Ben Junior scrambled out the other side. Lightnin' crackled overhead, and you could hear tornadoes moanin' in the night.

"We've got to get home," I said, maybe just to steady up my own nerves. Once I had my hands on that rifle and we were shut up in our bedroom with our backs to the wall, we'd be just fine. "Sooner we start, the sooner we'll get there."

"It's dark," Vera whispered, her voice shakin'. "Oh, Lord, it's so dark."

I knew she was talkin' about the road that lay ahead. I knew every curve and bump in it, but tonight it was a road that led through the haunted world. Out in the woods were Indians, Roman soldiers, Nazis, Chinese karate kickers, at least one Vikin' with a battle-ax, and God only knew what else. And behind us, maybe stalkin' somethin' good to eat, was a caveman with an eighty-pound club.

And all of 'em, all the ghosts, maybe gettin' more solid by the hour. What was gonna happen, I wondered, when all the billions and billions of people who'd ever died in the world were back on earth again, hungry and thirsty, some of 'em peaceful folks for sure, but others ready to chop your head off or bust your skull with a club? One rifle suddenly seemed an awful puny thing. I had a thought: If we got killed, we wouldn't stay dead very long, would we?

The tornadoes sounded closer, whirlin' more ghosts into the woods. I said, "Come on," in the calmest voice I could manage, and I pulled Vera along with me. Ben Junior walked close to me on the other side, his hands clenched into fists. We had a long way to go. Maybe a car would come along. Maybe. This wasn't a night fit for travelin'.

The road ahead was dark, so very dark. We had no choice but to walk it.

Ghost Blood

by Kelli Owen

As the crate marked TOP SECRET was pushed into the stacks of the warehouse and the credits begin to roll on the drive-in's forty-foot screen, Neil tossed the butter-soaked towel at the laundry tub near the door. He shrugged when he missed, knowing he'd pick it up later. Instead, he leaned against the concession counter to watch the headlights come on one-by-one.

It was the ninth time he'd seen *Raiders of the Lost Ark* since it had come out over two years ago—eight of those were this fall, when it hit the drive-in market—but he didn't mind. It was much better than the *Porky's* run at the beginning of summer. A record number of kids in trunks and fake IDs had flooded the field for most of June and July because of the rated R hormonally charged comedy. Neil didn't care— *let them watch it*. But the local police disagreed, and Neil had to deal with uniforms at the gate, as well as wandering the lot during the film, for two whole months. Oddly, it was never the same officer, which only convinced Neil they were simply taking turns watching the movie for free.

Being the second Sunday of September meant there were only a handful of cars in the lot, as expected. The Stardust Theatre drive-in was quieting down for the season since it was getting too cold to keep windows open for the clip-on speaker. Of course, it was also Sunday, which was a single feature night. Since the movies shown at the drive-in were all in at least their second run, people didn't always want to pay to watch an older movie, even at a discount, and especially with many of them popping up in the video stores. But mostly it was quiet because teens heavily dictated the drive-in business. And with school back in session, Sundays had returned to being a night of curfews for those who cared about their grade point average or had strict parents.

Neil watched as the moviegoers half-heartedly tossed their garbage toward the fifty-five-gallon drums used as trashcans at the end of each row, missing their targets almost as often as they hit.

Leaving their wrappers and paper cups wherever they landed, the cars followed the reflector posts single-file to the exit and slowly pulled out of the field and onto Tower Avenue.

People are slobs. Neil shook his head at the garbage in the lot and sighed. Working double duty as both concession and lot attendant, he found himself not just resigned but ultimately glad to clean up after them. Because while $3.00 an hour was less than any of the stores in the mall were paying, there was a much better chance the only blood at the drive-in would be on the forty-foot screen. And Neil avoided blood, whenever possible.

Neil had spent the first three years of his life believing everyone saw the world through the wash of bloodstains. Whether it had been casually wiped clean or scrubbed with industrial chemicals, if blood had once been there, he still saw it.

Everywhere.

When his mother cut herself preparing dinner and he had referred to it as *new blood*, it had taken her almost an hour to understand what her toddler was trying to explain. They spent the next several years talking to doctors and getting both his eyes and mind examined and re-examined countless times. He was called special, scary, and even a freak on one occasion, by medical professionals, priests, and social workers, all refusing to believe what he was telling them. Neil could see *old blood*, or as he began to call it, *ghost blood*.

Thankfully, before he got to kindergarten, his parents accepted him for what he was, and they moved to a new town to give him a clean slate. No one outside his immediate family knew what he saw, and no one looked at him as anything other than a kid who seemed overly empathetic for his age.

As a child, Neil *hated* going to friends' homes, preferring visits—especially the sleepovers—happened at his house instead. After explaining how much he dreaded bathrooms and kitchens, his parents not only allowed their home to be the hub of his youth, but his father worked a second job for a time to afford another move—into a new development where no one had ever lived, *or bled.*

Things other students saw as *normal* often took Neil a moment to adjust to. Ghost blood and new blood were quite similar, and it was often hard to tell the difference without actually touching it. He'd held his breath countless times, slowly reaching for a blood-speckled sink only to come away with nothing on his fingers and release a heavy exaggerated sigh. It wasn't clean to him, not if anyone had ever had a shaving accident or a bloody nose. Something as simple as an animal shelter or hospital would give him nightmares for weeks. But Halloween and horror movies were great—even Indy's Nazis, with their melting faces, were better than the nurse's office at school. He much preferred *fake* blood to both old and new. It was easily spotted and a completely different shade of red to him, though his parents swore it looked the same to them.

But tonight included blood in the real world rather than on the movie screen. And he'd likely never forget what Tracy had looked like earlier, when she left in the middle of their shift.

His co-worker had endured her own horror, with the unexpected arrival of her monthly cycle. She had chosen the wrong night to wear the cute white pants with the cuffs rolled up—the ones that made her ass cheeks look like perfect little pillows.

Less than an hour into the movie, Tracy had rushed to the bathroom and returned with horrified embarrassment on her face. As she sheepishly explained the situation, he glanced down. He didn't mean to. He didn't want to. And he immediately regretted his errant gaze, as he tried not to show his disgust and told her to just go home, urgently pushing her out the door. She was grateful, but he knew full well his abrupt encouragement for her to leave was less about being a good guy and more about not wanting to see it.

But he did. He saw it. Because that was his life.

Those white jeans were forever ruined for him now, even if she bleached them. He would still see the blood, as if it were never cleaned. The splotch on her pants combined with the red socks pushed low and equally red scrunchie holding her hair up high, almost appeared as part of her outfit, but he knew better.

Scrambling out the door, she promised she would cover for him on Friday to make up for leaving mid-shift. This was wonderful news and almost made up for what he'd seen. At least now he wouldn't miss the first annual MTV Music Video Awards he had been looking forward to all summer.

As part of becoming the hub house for all his friends, his parents had gotten cable several years earlier, as well as an Atari 5200 game system. The MTV channel had been around for three years, but this was the first year they were doing awards. Neil had been disappointed to find his name on the work schedule for that night but was now overjoyed he wouldn't miss the show after all. Though he was on no level thrilled about Tracy's absence, which meant he would have to clean the girl's bathroom tonight.

Neil left the door hanging open as he exited the concession stand with the speaker tote in hand. He walked through the lot, covering each stand with a waterproof sleeve and picking up garbage as he went. Seeing what he thought was an empty JuJube box, he bent to grab it and instead found a discarded Van Halen *1984* cassette tape with the ribbon pulled free. His first thought was a pencil and a few seconds of winding to fix it and have some free Eddie Van Halen, but then he noticed the shiny brown tape was actually stretched and torn—someone had fought to get this unstuck from their tape player and lost the battle.

"Oh well," he spoke to the empty field around him. "For all the hype, there's only three good songs on it, anyway. Of course, I'm sure at least *one* of them is up for an award."

He rolled his eyes and kicked the cassette toward the nearest garbage can, the tape flapped like a kite ribbon during its brief flight. He picked up his pace cleaning the field, racing the credits above him on the screen. The last speaker covered and the field cleaned of debris, Neil returned to the concession stand with the empty bin. Behind him, the film ran out, and the screen went white. He didn't notice. His eyes were fixed on the end of the building. There was only one task he needed to finish to close up for the night, and Neil swallowed the lump forming in his throat.

Neil turned off the projector and retrieved the cleaning cart—complete with mop and ringer, rags, and various chemicals. He pushed it along the short sidewalk to the bathrooms on the backside of the building. Neil glanced at the boys' room, but figured he'd better do the worst first. Swallowing hard, he looked at the door of the girls' room as if it were alive.

He did *not* want to go into that bathroom. Tracy wasn't the *only* girl to have ever bled in there, on purpose or by accident, and the idea of seeing a girls' only public bathroom made his stomach flip. It was something he never thought he'd face, and now here he was, staring at the doorway like his life would change beyond it. For a hot moment, he thought of just *not* cleaning it and hoping Mr. Lowenstein wouldn't notice. He sighed. He knew better.

Best to get it over with.

Neil took a deep breath and pulled the door open, holding it wide so he could wheel the cart in before him like a shield. A sickly yellow from the bug lights bounced off the whitewashed cement floor and walls and gave the room a strange glow. The slight buzzing of the bulbs seemed louder than usual as his cautious gaze turned to dismay.

He may have been expecting *some* blood, but what he saw made bile rise to the back of his throat. Worse than the nurse's office. More concentrated than any hospital room he'd seen. The stains he could see were so absolutely horrific, he even imagined he could smell them—the thick copper scent as strong as if his nose were smeared with it rather than the floor.

He closed his eyes and took several deep breaths, convincing himself he could not actually *smell* it, only *see* it. Grabbing the cleaner bottle and a rag, Neil stepped over the stain and moved to the sinks. He sprayed the porcelain and glass with the ammonia mixture and wiped them down as quickly as possible, staring at the floor behind him in the mirror the entire time.

The wide swath of bloodstain on the floor made no sense to him. He knew a small amount of blood could spread a long way, but this seemed to be more than that, and he wondered if the location had *always* been a concession stand. *Was it an old slaughterhouse? Had there been a farm here, and the building had been repurposed?* The streak of blood started near the first stall and moved across the floor to the last—the extra wide stall recently upgraded for handicap accessibility.

It was Sunday. It was a slow day. Heck, he didn't even remember anyone walking past concessions to use the bathrooms. And whether or not Mr. Lowenstein noticed, Neil couldn't stomach the idea of cleaning the stalls. Considering the stains in the rest of the bathroom, he could only imagine the horrors waiting for him behind the stall doors. Neil wiped the sinks down and he would do the floor, but there was no way he was opening those doors and seeing the blood-spattered toilets, handprints, and whatever other nightmares his mind could conjure up.

He shook his head, decision made, and sidestepped the thick stain on the floor. Neil dropped the rag and spray bottle into the tray, and pulled the mop from the water to squeeze it in the metal ringer. He slapped it onto the floor and moved it with a quick flick back and forth under the sinks. Knowing he was skipping the stalls, he walked to the far wall with the intention of mopping himself backward to the door and out of the nightmare room. As the mop moved through the wide stain on the floor, the blood unexpectedly swirled and smeared in the thick cloth threads.

Neil froze.

He stared at what he had believed was a stain. A *large* stain. But this was fresh. This was *new* blood.

He looked around the bathroom, knowing now it wasn't all ghost blood and trying to discern where the difference began and ended.

Jesus, did someone hurt themselves? Was the floor wet? Slippery? Is this somehow my fault?

The rest of the bathroom was spattered, like bathrooms tended to be, from bloody noses and small injuries cleaned and bandaged at sinks. The new blood seemed to be only the wide swath which moved in front of the three stalls, from the first to the last.

Is the person still in there bleeding?

The thought terrified Neil, and he gasped loudly as he turned to face the handicap stall. He reached for the door, acknowledging the blood he had only *thought* he could smell was instead all too real and filling his nostrils. It flavored his fear and sped up his breathing.

The door burst open, and Neil stumbled backward to avoid it, as he came face-to-face with not just the girl who was bleeding, but the person who had made her bleed. The man, his eyes wild with panic, rushed at Neil. Reflexively, Neil swung the mop still in his hand. The man caught the handle with his hand mid-arc and held it and Neil's arm above them both for a beat. Behind the man, Neil couldn't see the girl's face, only a pair of dirty Reeboks, pushed down red socks, and rolled up cuffs of once-white jeans.

Tracy!

Neil needed to get away. He needed to get help. He needed to *react*. His internal voice screamed through a thousand commands, but he heard only one of them.

Run!

Neil let go of the broom and spun to race for the bathroom door. He pushed it open and exited into the night air without slowing down. He heard the heavy footsteps pounding behind him, and he headed left.

Hell no, he thought, as he passed the boys' room, knowing it had no other doors and he'd be trapped inside.

A hand came from behind and swiped down the back of him, finding purchase on the fabric of his shirt at the shoulder. Neil pulled free as he reached the end of the building and turned on a dime—an ability he'd gained due to all the *shuttle runs in gym class*.

The concession door still hung open, and he mentally spurred himself to get there. To get to the phone inside.

Swinging the door behind him as he entered, he caught a glimpse of the butter-soaked rag he'd missed when tossing it at the laundry bin earlier. Neil kicked it out into the path of the assailant and sprinted to the counter where the phone hung on the wall like a beacon of hope. He lifted the receiver, thankful for push buttons rather than rotary, and pounded out his own number. He heard his dad answer just as the door swung open hard enough to slam against the wall.

The man entered.

"Dad, send help! Come now!" He dropped the phone and let it hang from the long curly cord, bouncing lightly inches above the floor.

Neil looked around for a weapon. The utensils were all washed and put away for the night. The pizza tray was too far away. The push broom seemed to be his best chance, and he grabbed it and held it like a baseball bat.

Behind him, he could hear his mother yelling in the dangling receiver. In front of him, he locked eyes with the intruder.

The man sneered and took several quick steps toward Neil, holding his gaze the entire time. The man didn't see the greasy butter-soaked rag in his path. His foot rose up toward the ceiling and his head went backward in an exaggerated arch. Neil watched the man lose his footing and go down hard, his head slamming into the tile-covered concrete floor.

Cautiously stepping forward, broom still raised high, Neil saw a small puddle of new blood spread out from the man's head. He gasped, as the man blinked several times and pushed himself up to a sitting position.

"No, no, no..." Neil's eyes widened as the man stood.

The man's expression was full of renewed anger and determination. His eyes seemed to darken as they narrowed at Neil.

Neil turned around and headed for the door near his end of the concession stand, desperately running through his options. The drive-in was in the middle of nowhere. Tower Avenue didn't have any homes or businesses for almost a mile to the north, and to the south, nothing but the graveyard and the empty highway beyond it. The sparse woods surrounding the lot were his only chance, and he planned on sprinting into the darkness of the trees. Neil would find cover and wait. He didn't have to wait forever, he told himself, just until help arrived.

Neil pulled the door open and immediately scrambled to back out of the way, dodging Tracy as she rushed past him into the room.

A primal scream came from Tracy, her eyes crazed, her face speckled in her own blood. She ran straight for the man, both hands gripping a tire iron held over her head. The noise that came from her as she swung the metal bar at the man's head was inhuman. The sound the iron made as it connected with bone reverberated and told Neil the man wouldn't be getting up this time.

Tracy followed the man to the floor and knelt above him. She continued swinging, connecting, and destroying the intruder's skull. Neil watched in horror, almost as afraid of her as he had been of the man.

"Tracy!" Neil yelled her name, but she didn't seem to notice, and she swung the iron yet again.

Neil cautiously approached her, as Tracy raised the weapon high above her. He grabbed it firmly to prevent its downward motion. His hand slipped through the blood and gore covering it.

"Tracy," he screamed with urgency rather than fear this time, his voice deeper and more commanding.

She turned to meet his gaze, her expression pure adrenaline. Pure survival.

"Tracy..." He lowered his voice and saw her eyes swim into focus on his face. "He's dead. Okay? You can let go."

She turned back and cocked her head slightly, considering the remains of the man on the floor for a long moment. Neil didn't know if she was examining him for signs of life or accepting what she'd just done. She finally released the tire iron into Neil's grip and fell to her bottom, scrambling backward until she bumped into the cabinet below the counter. She pulled her knees up to her chest and wrapped her arms around them. Like a frightened child, she turned and looked up at him.

"Neil?"

He bent down, setting the tire iron on the floor, and put a hand on her shoulder. "It's over, Tracy. You're okay, now."

She grabbed his hand and pulled it close to her. Neil could feel her pulse in her grip. He slid down to sit beside her, pulling his hand free and wrapping his arm around her instead. She leaned into him, sobbing quietly, as he looked around waiting for help to arrive.

The blood from her injuries covered most of her exposed flesh, and was smeared across the cabinet door and the floor near her. Neil couldn't tell what was injured on her but knew the medics would figure that out.

Neil heard the sirens in the distance grow steadily louder. It was over. They were safe. He sighed with relief and looked at the concession stand around him.

The dead man's wounds oozed, the blood pooling underneath his still form, as it spread outward, stretching across the floor toward Neil like a crimson shadow. He pulled his knees up, moving his feet away from the encroaching fluid. Pieces of brain and bone were splashed across the cabinets, with bits stuck to the ceiling from Tracy swinging the tire iron up and down. Bloody handprints decorated both doors *and* the counter. Neil stomach turned as he cringed, realizing no amount of bleach would ever truly fix the chaos around him.

Last Call at the Sudden Death Saloon

by Allan Leverone

WELCOME TO SPRINGVALE, the sign read.

There were a million similar signs welcoming travelers into a million little towns all across the United States. But most towns were content to stop at the welcome.

Not Springvale. Below the welcome message, stamped onto the sign in a squiggly font apparently meant to be creepy, read the words THE MOST HAUNTED TOWN IN AMERICA. The signpost was listing maybe thirty degrees off the square, and it looked as though, at some point, someone may have blasted the thing with a shotgun, as a series of tiny holes peppered its surface.

Seth Milton slowed his ancient Datsun 210 to snap a picture of the sign with his cell phone on the way by. It was never a good idea to come off the accelerator once he'd gotten the damned shitbox up to cruising speed because he couldn't be too sure the car wouldn't just give up the ghost and creak to a stop on the side of the road, never to run again.

Give up the ghost, Seth thought. *That's a good one, considering where I'm going.*

The risk of getting stranded on the side of the road was worthwhile in this case. A photo of the sign would make a great accompaniment to his story, particularly if an online magazine were to buy it. Seth could see the layout in his mind before he'd even activated the camera app on his phone.

He snapped the pic and eased down on the gas and held his breath for a moment, wondering if this would be the time his thirty-five-year-old rust bucket quit on him for good. The Datsun kicked a couple of times and then reluctantly picked up speed, signaling its displeasure by spewing a toxic cloud of black smoke out its tailpipe.

Seth breathed a sigh of relief and watched through his rear view as the welcome sign disappeared around a bend in the road. At some point in the not-too-distant future he was going to have to buy another car, and when that time came, he didn't know what he was going to do, because he sure as hell didn't have the money.

Freelance journalism didn't exactly equate to a steady paycheck, and driving around the country writing about "Haunted America" was probably not the way to achieve that steady paycheck, either. Real-life supernatural stories were a niche market. The people who were into them were *really* into them, but the rest of society couldn't give a shit.

Seth sighed.

All it takes is one viral story, he thought with the optimism of the terminally deluded. *Maybe this is the piece that will finally propel me on my way.*

The motel was straight out of the 1960s, long and low-slung, with a gravel roundabout driveway and a crumbling concrete walkway running the length of the structure. Seth thought it could have come from the set of the old movie, *Psycho,* the one where Anthony Perkins murders Janet Leigh and then shocks the audience by wearing a dress.

Given his perpetual state of poverty, Seth knew he couldn't afford anything nicer, but in any event it was a moot point. The Cracked Headstone was the only game in town as far as lodgings were concerned.

Seth parked the Datsun in front of the motel office and sat quietly after killing the engine. He'd driven sixteen hours straight to get here, stopping only for coffee and burgers and gas, and he wanted to take a moment to relish not having to concentrate on keeping the car on the road.

He closed his eyes, picturing the WELCOME TO SPRINGVALE sign leaning to port like a drunk in the process of falling to the floor. A vine had worked its way up the metal signpost and begun wrapping itself around the sign itself, and something about that visual was bothering Seth.

It was obvious the town's elders were trying to portray Springvale in a certain light; why else would they brag about being the "most haunted town in America"?

And Seth could understand their reasoning, given Springvale's…sketchy history. If dozens of people had gone missing in *your* town over the last few years, all disappearing without a trace, and your police department couldn't seem to do a damned thing to stop it, you might feel your only option for survival as a community would be to play up the disappearances, to draw tourists to your miserable little shithole by advertising what may or may not be supernatural occurrences.

It made sense in a weird, twisted kind of way.

But the vine.

And the tilting signpost.

Those things weren't part of the calculus. Those things were real, and legitimately creepy. It was as if the weight of the town's history was pulling the sign down, slowly but surely, and the vine covering the sign was Step One in a process that would end with the forest retaking the whole goddamned place.

Maybe, given Springvale's gruesome history, that would be for the best.

Or maybe Seth was just overtired.

He opened his door, shoving it hard with his shoulder because the 210 had suffered frame damage in a long-ago accident and none of its pieces quite fit together properly anymore. A loud screech accompanied the action. He hoped he never had to sneak up on anyone, because it sure wasn't going to happen if he was driving.

A flimsy screen door opened into the motel office, and it screeched almost as loudly as had the Datsun's door as Seth pushed his way inside. The door slammed behind him but didn't latch, remaining maybe an inch ajar.

Guess I won't need to ring the bell to rouse the clerk.

By the time he made his way to the desk, a tired-looking middle-aged woman had appeared from somewhere in the back, a smile on her face that couldn't quite convince her eyes to play along. A nametag pinned to her blouse informed Seth her name was Deb.

"Welcome to Springvale," Deb said. "The most—"

"I know," Seth interrupted. "The most haunted town in America. I've seen the sign."

"It's our claim to fame. Probably not the ideal thing to be known for, but you don't get to pick your fate, I suppose."

"It's exactly why I'm here."

"It's why most people show up here," the clerk said. "And why my husband insisted on such an…unconventional name for this place when we bought it. He thought calling it 'The Cracked Headstone' would fit Springvale's sinister vibe."

She lowered her voice conspiratorially. "This place used to be a Motel 6."

Seth laughed. "Sinister is exactly what I'm after. I'm a journalist and I'm writing a story on Springvale's unsolved disappearances. The story focuses on the events not as crimes but as manifestations of the town's supernatural history."

Deb nodded. "Well, I've lived here all my life, and I can testify to the town being haunted. I've seen things you wouldn't believe."

"Care to go on the record?"

She smiled. "Sure, if you can see fit to work our little motel into your story."

"I think I can manage that," Seth said.

"Then just let me know when you want to talk. In the meantime, I can tell you exactly where to start your research."

"Is that right?"

"Oh yes. It's the epicenter of all supernatural activity in Springvale."

"And where would that be?"

"The Sudden Death Saloon."

Seth raised his eyebrows. "The Sudden Death Saloon? Do all the business owners in town embrace the ghost thing?"

She smiled. "You gotta do what you gotta do. But in the case of the bar, the name is especially apt."

"How so?"

"It's located inside a portion of what used to be known as the Springvale Sanitarium."

"A health resort?"

The woman smiled. "Not exactly. You want the plain English version?"

"Please."

"It was an insane asylum. And it was enormous. The better part of six states all across the Midwest sent their most dangerous mentally ill patients to the Springvale Sanitarium when they couldn't figure out what the hell else to do with them."

"That's a pleasant thought," Seth said.

"No kidding. And the conditions." She wrinkled her nose. "Well, let's just say they were…primitive."

"People were sent there to die."

She nodded. "And it wasn't like those poor souls just passed on to whatever comes after this life. Supposedly, the sanitarium staff experimented on many of the worst-off patients. Brutal, bloody limb transplants and other surgeries were—again, allegedly—conducted under conditions that were practically medieval."

"I researched the town before coming here," Seth said. "Why did none of this stuff show up online?"

"Self-preservation. By the nineteen-sixties the sanitarium had shut its doors for good. When that happened, the town fathers wasted no time whitewashing the ugly history of the facility in the name of salvaging what little was left of Springvale's reputation." She shrugged. "I guess they did their job pretty well."

Seth wished he'd turned on his recorder for this. It was gold, and he knew immediately the clerk's words would play a prominent role in his story, provided he could corroborate them.

He knew also he would be able to.

"Anyway," Deb continued, "the spirits of those sanitarium victims continue to haunt Springvale. There were hundreds of them, and I suppose they'll be stuck here forever, just like the rest of us."

Seth stared at the woman. It crossed his mind that maybe he should let *her* write the damned piece; she was thoughtful and well spoken and her story was spellbinding.

"Why would anyone put a bar in a place like that?" he said. "Given its bloody history, why wasn't the building demolished after the sanitarium closed its doors?"

The clerk's laugh was short and bitter. "Good question," she said. "I think this town is just so wedded to its horrific history that we're like motorists driving past a particularly bloody car crash. You know you shouldn't look, that nothing good will come from it if you do, but you just can't stop yourself."

"Wow," he said. As a guy who made a living—more or less—using words, he knew he should be able to come up with something better, but that one syllable was truly all he could manage at the moment.

"One last little tidbit before I let you go." The clerk had lowered her voice again. "Rumor has it that Jeffrey Halston bought the sanitarium property lock, stock and barrel several years ago."

"Jeffrey Halston the billionaire tech mogul?"

"One and the same."

"What the hell would a forty-something year old rich guy want with a place like that?"

"You got me. I don't know if he's ever even been to Springvale, but that's the rumor. And around here, rumors tend to be true."

As soon as the Cracked Headstone's desk clerk told him the terrible history of the Springvale Sanitarium, Seth had known the Sudden

Death Saloon would be his next stop. The potential Jeffrey Halston connection was just icing on what was becoming a particularly delicious journalistic cake.

He tossed his stuff on the bed and took a quick shower and after a quick meal at a diner down the road, turned his attention—and his ancient car—toward the "epicenter of all supernatural activity in Springvale."

The former sanitarium had been built high on a hill, a stone torture-chamber/fortress looming over the town like a fifteenth-century European landowner's castle.

At some point in the distant past, the town had hacked a small "scenic pulloff" into the forest adjacent to the road a couple of miles from the structure, offering curious motorists a spectacular photo opportunity of Springvale's only tourist attraction. Seth pulled to the side of the road and snapped a few pictures before slipping back into his Datsun to finish his drive to the Sudden Death Saloon.

He turned the key and nothing happened.

A second try was no more successful.

"Dammit." Seth sighed and popped the hood. Climbed out of the car and peered into the engine, without the slightest notion what he was looking at or what he was looking for.

He scratched his head and considered his options. There weren't many. Cell service in Springvale was virtually nonexistent, an appropriate situation for a town that seemed stuck in a long-ago age, but a serious drag when it came to dealing with a thirty-five-year-old piece of shit car that may suddenly have quit running for good.

And the sun had set while he was eating dinner.

Not only that, he was roughly halfway between "civilization," in the form of a town of maybe four thousand people, and a business that constituted the entire reason he'd come to Springvale in the first place.

The decision was an easy one. It would be a long walk down a dark, deserted road in either direction, so he might just as well get some work done. He grabbed the backpack containing his computer, digital recorder, and pens and notebooks, and then began trudging up the long incline toward the Sudden Death Saloon. He would worry about his car later.

The motel clerk was right. Springvale was one haunted place.

Maybe the disturbing stories he'd heard back at the Cracked Headstone were bothering him more than he realized, but Seth had no sooner left his disabled car behind than he began to experience things he could only describe as...inexplicable.

Within a hundred yards of starting his walk he could swear he began to hear the gibbering of tortured spirits. They cackled and threatened, not in any understandable language but on a more elemental level.

Seth had read once that the producers of the movie, *The Exorcist*, had inserted audio of pigs being slaughtered into the sound track at a volume too low to be consciously perceived but loud enough to cause unreasoning terror in the moviegoer's brain. This felt like the same thing.

From off to his right came a vaguely human moaning, the sound a restrained and gagged man might make as caretakers performed hideous experiments on him. Seth did his best to push the image from his brain and walked on.

A scream pierced the night from the woods to Seth's left and he jumped, literally leaving his feet for a moment before coming back down and stumbling on the uneven pavement. The sound was so close he thought if he extended his arm, he might be able to reach out and touch...something. What that something might be he didn't know and doubted he wanted to find out.

His heart was pounding and his breath coming in tortured gasps as he continued, praying for a car to come along and pass him, just to remind him he wasn't alone in this town that was turning out to be a tiny slice of hell on earth.

Nobody came.

He tried to tell himself he was out of breath because he was an out-of-shape man hiking up a steep hill with a moderately heavy pack strapped to his back, but he couldn't quite pull it off. While all of that was undoubtedly true, the real source of his distress was the fact that he couldn't stop picturing screaming mental patients strapped onto rusty tables, covered with disease-infested blankets, while their masters cut them and slashed them and drove them to premature, agony-filled deaths.

And those ill-fated victims were still here.

They were *really* still here.

Writing tales of true-life supernatural events had always been kind of a lark for Seth Milton, a tongue-in-cheek way to make a living while smirking inside at the suckers that actually believed the stuff he wrote.

Now he believed.

It was an epiphany, a realization over the course of a thirty-minute stroll along a pitch-black deserted road that there really were things the human mind could not comprehend, even the mind of a smug, self-assured young man who had received a Syracuse University journalism degree following a four year academic full ride.

The horrors continued as Seth marched resolutely forward, propelled not by bravery or even the desire to do his job, but by a white-knuckle terror that worsened with every sibilant hiss and undefined groan, whimper and wail coming out of that—literally—damned forest.

Just when he thought he could take no more, that his heart would simply explode in his chest and leave him clawing at his rib cage as he died along an empty road in the middle of nowhere, the lights of the Sudden Death Saloon shimmered into view up the hill in the distance.

And Seth Milton knew at that moment everything would be okay.

The Sudden Death Saloon was located in what at one time had been the reception area of the old Springvale Sanitarium.

And it was massive. The lobby's polished marble floors gleamed dully in the dim lighting provided by wrought iron chandeliers suspended at least thirty feet over Seth's head. Scarred wooden tables had been placed in a seemingly random pattern in front of a long walnut bar that ran the length of the rear wall. Dusty liquor bottles were lined up along a series of shelves behind the bar, none of which appeared to have been moved since the day the place opened.

To Seth's disappointment, the Sudden Death Saloon was virtually deserted. A lone patron sat apparently passed out at the bar, his forehead pressed to its surface, ice cubes melting inside the watery remains of a drink next to him. It was impossible to estimate the man's age, but given his current state of unconsciousness, Seth decided it didn't matter much.

He wouldn't be answering any questions tonight.

It appeared only one bartender was on duty, and that man was currently occupied with desultorily wiping down the end of the bar farthest from Seth, paying not the slightest attention to his new customer.

Seth tried to choke back his frustration. He had risked dying of a heart attack for *this?* A dark, dingy bar inside a former mental institution patronized by one passed-out drunk and presided over by the most uninterested bartender in the history of the service industry?

He circled around behind the unconscious man and positioned himself directly in front of the bartender, finally getting results—sort of—when the man looked up from his work and said, "Help you?"

Seth recoiled.

He couldn't help it.

The man's eyes. They were as black as coal.

He swallowed heavily and glanced back toward the door, a reflex action designed to reassure his panicked brain escape might still be possible if he had to flee. By the time he returned his attention to the bartender, the man's eyes looked normal. Dark and hooded, yes, but at least they weren't glowing obsidian orbs.

"Well? You want a drink or not?"

"Uh, yeah. Yeah, of course."

"And…"

"Oh. Um, gin and tonic." Seth's heart was a jackhammer in his chest and he knew he had to get himself under control, or not only would he fail to get anything for his story tonight, he might not survive. He was that shaken.

The black-eyed bartender brought his drink, and Seth dropped a ten on the bar and walked away. He would start mining the man for information in a little bit, after he'd finished his first drink and hopefully felt more like himself. The liquid sloshed over the rim of his glass as he walked, his hand shaking uncontrollably.

He dropped into a seat at one of the tables situated roughly halfway between the front entrance and the bar running along the rear wall. Rubbed his eyes and sipped his drink. Told himself to get a grip. Everything that had happened to him since his car shit the bed could be explained.

The gibbering moans of mental patients were nothing more than the wind whispering in the trees. The sharp screams of the suffering dead were just owls hooting, or wolves howling, or loons crying in the distance. The bartender's strange black eyes were nothing more than a weird reflection of the dim light coming from those Victorian-era chandeliers.

Nothing supernatural or terrifying or even the least bit weird. It was all—

"I can't believe I missed seeing you come in!"

Seth jerked in his chair and looked up to see a young woman standing next to his table. She was maybe mid-twenties, pale and slim and ethereal-looking, dressed in a white silk blouse and long, flowing teal skirt. The woman offered him a smile and he returned it despite the fact his pulse had once again spiked from the interruption after almost returning to normal.

"I'm Seth." He stuck out his hand. "And you are?"

"Your waitress," she answered, and he immediately withdrew his hand, feeling like the world's biggest idiot.

"You're a waitress? Dressed like that?"

She laughed, the sound girlish, and reached across the table and took his hand. Seth looked into her eyes and found them warm and moist and welcoming, the complete opposite of the bartender's.

"My name is Monica," she said. Seth realized he was still holding onto her hand, like a drowning man who'd grabbed onto a life preserver, and he sheepishly released his grip.

"What brings you to Springvale?" she asked, as though what had just transpired was perfectly normal and not awkward and strange.

He went through his "freelance journalist traveling the country writing about real-life unexplained events" song and dance, and by the time he finished speaking, he realized two things simultaneously: one, he'd finished his drink, and two, Monica seemed fascinated.

She had taken a seat next to him at the table while he was talking, and she stared into his eyes like he was the guy from the beer commercials who was supposedly the most interesting man in the world. He'd never had a woman look at him that way, and he decided he kind of liked it.

"I want to hear more," she said. "And as my way of bribing you, your next drink is on me." The waitress leapt to her feet and was halfway to the bar before Seth could answer, returning in seconds and placing his drink on the table. Then she took his hand again.

"What you do is so exciting," she said. "How do you decide where to go next when you've finished a story?"

Seth sipped his drink. Monica must have an in with the bartender, he thought, because it was delicious. "I look for places with a documented history of supernatural activity. Then I drive there and interview the locals."

"Like me," she said with a smile.

"Yes, exactly. Like you." Another sip. "When I feel I have enough information, I wr-write my piece and submit it to different perod...peridic...periodicals. Then I move on and do it again."

"So you take turns driving with your partner?"

"Partner? I don't have a partner, it's just me."

"But you must have to tell your editor where you're going."

Seth chuckled. Took another drink and said, "I work flee...fl...freelance, so my material is edited by the staff at whatever newspaper, maz...magazine or website buys my story."

"Ohhh." Monica was staring at Seth with a burning intensity, and Seth realized he was having trouble focusing on her, which was strange because he was only on his second drink. He almost never started slurring his words before last call. And even with the long walk here, last call should still be hours from now.

"But your girlfriend must know where you're going, right?"

Seth sipped his drink and tried to concentrate. Something was bothering him about Monica's line of questioning, but he couldn't quite put his finger on what it was. He just felt so *fuzzy*.

He realized he'd forgotten what the waitress had just asked him, and that was rude as hell. "I'm sorry, what did you want to know?"

"I said, surely your girlfriend knows you're here." She was speaking slowly now, enunciating carefully. It was thoughtful of her and super helpful.

"Nope. No girlfriend," he said. "No wife, no partner. Nobody knows I'm here, actually."

"Come with me," she said suddenly, rising to her feet with the grace of a dancer. She tugged insistently on his hand.

"Where are we going?" Seth stood quickly and stumbled, and Monica steadied him as he worked to control his swaying.

"You want to know all the secrets of Springvale, don't you? Isn't that why you came here?"

"Well...yes," Seth said.

"Then follow me." She started across the room in the direction of the bar, Seth trailing behind. He clung to her hand and tried to focus on it as it swam in and out of his blurred vision while they walked.

"Come with me and you'll learn everything," she said, and her words somehow made perfect sense to Seth. He looked up and saw the bartender watching closely as they disappeared into the back room. Seth was unsurprised to see that the man's eyes seemed to be blacker than ever.

They crossed a hallway and began descending a set of steep stone stairs into the bowels of the old Springvale Sanitarium.

They walked for a long time, or maybe it just felt like a long time. Seth couldn't tell. Their footsteps echoed along the darkened corridors, bouncing off damp stone walls as they weaved through the facility that had once housed madmen as prisoners and other madmen as their captors.

Within seconds, Seth was hopelessly lost. Retracing his steps and escaping through the bar would be impossible. He gripped his guide's hand and tried to remain upright.

"Where are we going?" he whispered but Monica had fallen suddenly silent.

More twists and turns led them to a closed metal door. A frosted glass window prevented Seth from seeing what lay on the other side of the door, and he was suddenly certain he wanted no part of it, whatever it was.

Monica rapped her knuckles sharply on the glass, and a moment later the door swung open to reveal what resembled a hospital room. A stainless steel operating table sat in the middle of the room, fitted with arm and leg restraints.

And gutters running along both sides, like might be found on an autopsy table.

Seth swallowed heavily. He had little choice but to follow Monica into the room. "What the hell is th—"

The words caught in his throat as he spotted a bed placed in the far corner of the big room. Lying unmoving on the bed, covered by a thin blanket, lay a gaunt, frail man. Thin wisps of brown hair sprouted from his head in odd directions, and the blanket covering his body rose and fell with the rhythm of his breathing.

He was awake and alert and his gaze locked onto Seth with eyes that were somehow…greedy.

Hungry.

Ravenous.

But Seth barely noticed the man's eyes, because the skin on his face…it was unlike anything Seth had ever seen. It hung slack from the man's cheeks and jawbones, weeping with sores, pus draining slowly from suppurating wounds. It was as though the skin was in the process of…dripping off his frame like melting ice cream.

Seth clapped his hand to his mouth, suddenly sure he was going to be sick. Acidy bile filled his mouth, and he swallowed it back.

"What the hell *is* that?" he ventured.

"Seth Milton," Monica said. "Meet my father, Jeffrey Halston."

Even through his fog of fear and confusion and disorientation, Seth recognized the name immediately. "Jeffrey Halston the billionaire?"

"So you've heard the name."

"What…what's wrong with him?"

"What do you know about flesh eating diseases?"

Seth shrugged. "Nothing, really." He couldn't take his eyes off the skeletal figure still staring him down from the hospital bed across the room. Halston was supposed to be in his late forties but this man looked double that age. Triple.

"Well," she continued, "Daddy was vacationing in the Amazon a few years ago and contracted a rare form of the disease. It's slow moving but inexorable, and results in death. It is incurable."

The room was spinning and Seth realized he'd clapped his hand to his mouth again. As if sensing he was about to fall to the floor, Monica slid a chair behind him and he dropped into it.

"He's in the final stages," Seth whispered.

"Yes."

"It's taken years to get to this point?"

"Oh, no. Progression of the disease is slow, but this stage is reached in about eight months. Give or take."

"But you said…"

"I know what I said."

"I…I don't understand," Seth said, although he thought he might be starting to.

"Every eight months or so, we are able to extend Daddy's life."

"And how do you do that?"

"Via what you might call…extraordinary measures."

The bile was back in Seth's mouth and he didn't think there was any getting rid of it now. "What kind of measures?"

"Having billions of dollars at your disposal allows one to take advantage of opportunities not available to the average citizen," Monica said. "Opportunities like experimental treatments for rare diseases."

"Experimental treatments?"

"Yes. You see, the disease that consumes Daddy's flesh cannot be removed from his system. It is inside him forever. But the skin, that's a different story. Transplants are possible. Daddy's own recent history proves that point beyond a shadow of a doubt. Following a transplant, he is able to maintain a relatively normal lifestyle for several months before the inevitable occurs, and the search for another donor must begin. And that's where you come in."

"Me?" And just like that, everything became clear. The unexplained disappearances in Springvale. The rumors of Halston's purchase of the old Springvale Sanitarium. Monica's relentless curiosity about whether anyone knew he had traveled here.

Everything.

The eccentric billionaire relocates to the "most haunted town in America," pays a surgeon a king's ransom to do his dirty work every few months, and every now and then an unsuspecting tourist drawn to the town by its gruesome history disappears without a trace.

It was perfect and horrifying and foolproof, and Seth knew the reason for his dizziness and confusion was that Jeffrey Halston's daughter had spiked his drink.

He knew also if he didn't escape now, he never would. He leapt from his chair and staggered across the room and somehow avoided falling on his face.

But the door was locked.

"There's nowhere to go," Monica said calmly. "And besides, I summoned the surgeon the moment I spotted you. I knew you were the one."

"No," Seth said.

"Yes. And he's just about ready to begin."

"No," Seth said again. He was talking to himself as much as to Monica.

She smiled. This really was one beautiful woman, "Oh, yes. Now, why don't you do us all a favor and climb up onto the table? You understand that you have no choice, correct? There is no escaping the property and nowhere to go even if you could."

And Seth knew she was right.

The Ring of Truth

by Thomas F. Monteleone

"I even shot a pregnant woman once," Reitmann said.

His voice was hard and crisp and totally without emotion, but there was a scary smile forming at the edges of his mouth.

I sat on the floor, listening to his story while rock music filled in the dead spots. My three roommates and I were all half-drunk, but the wine did nothing to dispel the palpable sense of dread, the stench of a triumphant evil which pervaded the room.

The lights from our Christmas tree colored each of our faces in various hues of horror and revulsion, but nobody told Reitmann to stop—especially after he told us about the "Ring of Truth."

Denny Reitmann was one of those guys you meet in college and you just *know* he isn't going to be around for the commencement exercises. At least *I* knew it.

Ex-high school jock—but not the quarterback or shortstop type—Denny was your basic offensive guard, or maybe a catcher. In high school, he was the guy who could never get the experiments to come out right in chem lab, who was always clowning that he'd cut off his fingers in metal shop. He was the one who could eat fifteen hot dogs at the Spring Fever Fair, and cut the loudest farts during P.E.

And when a guy like Denny Reitmann went to college, it was only because there was nothing better to do at the time.

Then, it seemed like all of a sudden there was a shitty little "military action" going on in Central America, but most people didn't care about places like El Salvador or Honduras or Nicaragua. The stock market was fluctuating as usual, interest rates were rising, and the import-wars were getting pretty fierce. A lot of the second-level nations like Mexico and Brazil had stopped paying even the interest on their billions-plus loans to the U.S., and a nasty recession was getting ready to take a bite out of the country's hind-parts. As a result, the poor minorities were being ground up in society's gears pretty good.

But if you were twenty years old, white, and going to a monstrous diploma-factory like the University of Maryland, everything seemed to be just fine.

Denny Reitmann roomed in my dormitory on the College Park campus, and although you couldn't say that he was my friend, or that I hung around with the guy, I guess I knew him as well as anybody did. He didn't seem to have any real close buddies. Oh sure, everybody laughed at his crude jokes, and we all shook our heads when he would proudly announce his abysmal grades, but none of us was really "tight" with him.

It was like all the guys could sense Denny's true "essence"—kind of bleakness. A void where his feelings should have been, is probably the best way to describe it. I mean, you could look into Reitmann's eyes and not be completely sure there was anything behind them.

It was right after Christmas vacation in my sophomore year, and everybody was piling back into their rooms to start boning up for the end-of-the-semester grind—the Finals.

Everybody, that is, except for Reitmann. He came back with the rest of us, but only to clean out his dresser drawers, desk, and closet. "I'm packin' it in, you guys," he told anyone who would listen. "I figured it out, and even if I ace all my finals, I'm still gonna flunk-out, so what the fuck, huh?"

I guess a few of us tried to talk him out of it in a half-assed kind of way, and some of the other guys took him down to the Rendezvous for a farewell bender, but the overall reaction to Denny Reitmann's departure from academe's fair grove was a big ho-hum. Besides, there wasn't really much time to mourn the dead; those Finals were always a bitch, right?

I made out all right with all of them, even Organic Chemistry — the only one that really had me sweating. I knew that without decent numbers in Organic, not even that semi-bogus med school in Grenada would let me through the door. Thus triumphant, when Semester Break finally arrived, I went off with my roommate, Bob, to ski in western Massachusetts at this great slope called Brody Mountain.

When we came back to the dorm to begin the Spring Semester, there was the usual joking and back-slapping and glad-handing. Everybody seemed keyed-up for the start of the long haul into summer. So it wasn't until a bunch of us were getting ready to take the hike to the dining hall that somebody noticed the postcard tacked to the bulletin board by the door to the lounge.

Postmarked at Fort Benning, Georgia, the card bore a short, typed note which read:

> Hey Guys,
> I was getting board, so I joined the Marines. They shore do make things rough on us down here, but I think its going to be O.K. I like the rough stuff. Study hard and (smile) don't be like me.
>
> Denny Reitmann

"Jeez," someone said. "The asshole joined the Marines, can you believe it?"

"With Reitmann, I'd believe anything…" I said.

"I guess that's what happens when you get B-O-A-R-D," said my roommate, pulling the card off the corkboard and tossing it in the trash can.

Everybody had a quick a laugh, and we piled out the door, on our way to get some overcooked vegetables and the day's Mystery-Meat Special. By the time we entered the dining hall, the conversation had become fixated upon the perfectly shaped ass of a blonde girl standing several places ahead of us in the line. I don't think anybody gave Denny Reitmann another thought until he came back from a place everybody started calling "the 'Dor"…

...right before Christmas a year later. I was almost mid-way through my junior year. Bob and I had taken an apartment with two other guys from the dorm, and we were having a great time playing the sophisticated-young-man game.

A lot can happen in a year. I had discovered Mahler and Beethoven, French wines like Poulligny and Cabernet, the irrefutable logic of Bertrand Russell, the lyrical essays of Loren Eiseley, and—well, I think you've gotten the point. I was becoming enlightened and enriched and all that shit.

I was also becoming terrified of the El Salvador war.

They say that everything that goes around, comes around, and goddamn if this wasn't the whole Vietnam mess all over again. The radio was daily talking about Sandinista body-counts versus GI casualties—as if we were talking about sporting events instead of people killing each other. The network and cable evening news looked like an old Sam Peckinpah film, and I kept thinking about how close we all were to being part of the horror show.

The horror show crept a little closer the day the apartment phone rang five or six times before anybody bothered to answer it.

"Hello..." I said.

"Jack, is that you?"

"Yeah, who's this?"

"It's Reitmann! It's me, Jack. How ya doin', man?"

I did a mental double-take, realizing at last with whom I was speaking.

Reitmann, for God's sake! Talk about the last guy I'd expect to hear from...

"Yeah, right...well, how are you, Denny? Where are you? What've you been doing?" I found myself saying the semi-automatic greetings, asking questions I didn't really care to have answered.

"I'm back on leave...from the 'Dor, man. They were lettin' us finish up our hitch a little early 'cause-a Christmas—you know how that goes..."

"Yeah, right," I said, at a total loss as to what to say next. What the hell did he want, calling me? How did he find the number? And most importantly, why *me*?

"Listen, I'm at my mom's place, and it's gettin' kinda beat around here, and I was wonderin' if I could stop over for little while, huh?"

"Jeez, Denny, I don't know...we're all getting ready to study for some exams."

"Your mom gave me the address," he said as though not hearing me. "And guess what? Your apartment's pretty close to my mom's, so it's no hassle, man. I'll see you around eight, okay?"

Before I could say anything, he'd hung up. I told Bob and Mike and Jay we were going to have company, and received a mixture of reactions. Of which, Mike's was the best: "Well, at least he can tell us some war stories..."

And he certainly did.

"A *pregnant* woman..." said Jay. "Christ, Denny...why?"

"Because she was a fuckin' 'beaner,' that's why!" Reitmann's eyes were like tiny steel balls, like a rat's or maybe a raven's. "They all carry grenades and shit, man...they all want to kill themselves an American. And besides, it was my job...I was a Sniper."

"What do you mean?" I asked. Mike passed me the chianti bottle and I poured another glass. I was already blitzed pretty good, and this last one was just icing. I had been amazed at how the Marines had changed Reitmann in such a short time. His playful, kind of dumb, but almost likable, mannerisms had been sawed-off along all the edges, filed down until there was only a crude undercarriage left. And on that raw frame, the jarheads had constructed their killing machine—a guy full of hate and poison and a belief that everybody in the world was ultimately out to get you. Reitmann looked at me as I exhaled.

"A sniper, man! Don't you know what a sniper is?" His voice had turned suddenly acidic, condescending.

"Yeah, I guess, but maybe you should clarify any misconceptions we might have."

Reitmann explained that Snipers were specially trained "gyrenes" who spent upwards of thirty days at a clip out in the jungle, alone, playing a crazy survivalist game, eating whatever they could find, and shooting whatever moved. After a month or so like that, they would report back to their Base for a few days R & R, and then back into the 'bush' for more grub-eating and beaner-popping.

Denny smiled that half-crazy smile as he nodded. "Yeah. You see, we were special, my squad. You had to be special to be picked for the 'Black Aces' platoon…that's what they called the Snipers—the Black Aces."

"Why?" asked Bob.

Reitmann shrugged. "Don't know. They just did. My sergeant had these special decks of cards. Don't know where he got 'em, but it was a deck of nothin' but aces of spades, you know? And when we first got to Usulután, he passed out a deck to each of us Snipers."

"What for?" asked Jay.

Reitmann smiled, chuckled a bit. "That was the neat part, man. See, each time we zapped a beaner, we were supposed to leave one of them Aces on 'em. It was like a sign that all the Sandies new about— they all knew the snipers were real bad-asses, you know?"

"Kind of like a calling card," said Jay.

"Yeah, I guess." Reitmann was looking far off, as though reliving moments in the past. Again, that weird smile was starting to format the corners of his mouth. "I used to use their own knives or bayonets, and stick my Aces to their chests—ain't no way they'd miss it that way."

"I guess not," I said.

"Hey, they were scared shitless of the guys in my squad! Especially after my sergeant started the 'Ring of Truth'."

Denny Reitmann smiled and nodded to himself. There was a cold shine in his eyes that gave me a chill.

"The 'ring of truth'?" asked Jay. "What was that?"

"Check this out," said Denny, as he jumped limberly to his feet. His hand lifted his bulky sweater above his waist to reveal a brass ring attached to a leather harness. The harness slipped over his wide belt.

"Here it is," said Reitmann. The ring was perhaps four inches in diameter. It looked awkward and uncomfortable.

"I don't get it," I said. "What're you talking about?"

"We used 'em to carry our ears, man," said Denny. "That's how we earned early leave on our hitches."

"Your *ears?*" Bob started giggling. He was pretty drunk.

Reitmann looked at him with cold, black eyes. "Yeah, man. You see, every time we sniped somebody, we'd cut off their right ear and put it on our ring. When we'd come back to Base every thirty days or so, we'd turn in our ears and get credits towards an early 'out'."

"Kinda like savings-coupons," said Mike. "Or green stamps..." He looked as repulsed as the rest of us and had not been trying to be funny.

Reitmann grinned, then chuckled. "Yeah! Yeah, I never thought of it like that! Coupons...I like that." He paused, his ball-bearing eyes turreting about the room. "You see, with them ears, there wasn't any bullshit about how many beaners you plinked. Great system, huh?"

"Yeah, just great," I said, perhaps a little too sarcastically. Some things never changed, and I wasn't really surprised to hear the Marines were still using such incentive programs.

Reitmann's expression shifted as he glared at me. Teeth bared like fangs, jaw muscles taut, the flesh about his eyes all pinched inward.

"You don't like that, Jack?" he said tauntingly. "A little too strong for you, huh?"

Jay cleared his throat. "Let's face it, Denny...it's a little strong for anybody, don't you think?"

"Christ," said Mike. "How'd you keep them from rotting? Didn't they start to stink after a while?"

"Yeah, they stunk a little, but it wasn't as bad you might think. After you been out in the bush for a couple weeks, everything smells like it's dead." Denny chuckled at this small jest.

"But most of us used to carry a mess-canister of formaldehyde. I'd stick 'em in there for a couple days, then dry 'em out on a flat rock in the sun. After that, they'd usually hold up 'til you got back to base anyway."

The conversation deteriorated from that point onward, and as the effects of the wine wore off, everybody had about enough of Denny Reitmann. I think it was right when he told us that he planned to carry a .45 caliber automatic on his person for the rest of his life (so that he could "waste anybody who fucked with him"), that I announced I had to get up for an eight o'clock class.

Everybody else picked up the suggestion and suddenly Reitmann was being escorted to the door. He paused and looked at us for a moment, then he smiled.

"You buncha pussies think you got it good, don't you? Well, I'm tellin' you...your turn's gonna come. You'll see what it's like to finally be a man."

Mike grinned. "I don't think so, Denny. I told the Board I was a fag."

We all laughed, and Denny appeared insulted, perhaps a bit angered. I didn't think it was a good idea to intimidate this poor asshole.

"You can laugh all you want, but just remember that it's men like me that's protectin' all the wimpies like you guys. That's why I'm goin' back..."

"What?" I said. I couldn't help myself. "Why?"

Denny's grapeshot eyes gleamed. "Cuz I got a score to settle with a couple more wet-backs...for the guys in my squad that didn't make it?"

"Jeez, Denny, that's nuts," said Bob.

"Do you know what the Sandies do when they catch a Sniper?"

Before any of us could answer, he continued: "They always cut his dick off and stuff it in his mouth."

Reitmann grinned crazily. "Yeah. That's the way I found two of my buddies..."

Nobody spoke for a moment, and the silence grew quickly awkward, painful.

"Good night, Denny," I said. "Be careful. When you go back..."

He grinned that crazy grin for the last time that night and slapped my arm extremely hard. "You too, Jack...all of you. And who knows, when you guys get down there, I might be the guy waitin' to greet you when you get outta the chopper!"

"I wouldn't be surprised," said Jay.

And then we shut him out into the night, into the void where our thoughts never ventured. I can remember a great sense of relief passing over me, as though I'd been told a great plague had finally ended.

"That sucker's stone crazy," said Mike.

"I feel sorry for him," said Jay. "They've turned him into a monster."

"He's a fucking psychopath," I said. "I don't ever want to see the son-of-bitch again. He gives me the creeps. Did you ever try looking into his eyes?"

"Can you believe he's going back?" asked Bob.

"I hope he stays there," I said. "Him and his 'Ring of Truth'."

Five years later, people were still dying in Central America, and the newest President (God, how I loathed the man!) was trying to get the country out of the whole mess "honorably." It was a joke, but nobody was laughing.

Especially me.

The year I finished medical school, the Draft Lottery pulled my birthday up as Number Nine. Very, very bad. But I had already started my first year of Residency at Johns Hopkins, specializing in laser micro-surgery on the nerves and capillaries. Since this was a fairly new field, the Army decided that I could be very useful in saving severed, or partially severed, limbs.

And so even though I was drafted, they gave me a commission, and after boot camp, shipped me off to a V.A. hospital in Philadelphia for some experience before getting a free ticket to the San Salvador Base Hospital and a chance to save a few GI's extremities.

We had a ward in Philly for 'Dor vets who came back in such bad shape, they'd never been able to leave. Para- and quadriplegics; the Johnny-Got-His-Gun basket cases; men with half their skulls and brains and faces blown away; guys with so many organs missing, they had to stay forever hooked up to series of artificial support machines; and the Section Eights, the Funny Farmers.

Of course, that's where I saw Denny Reitmann again.

It's funny, but I had almost been expecting it on an unconscious level. I had tried to forget about the night he showed us the brass ring on his belt, but I knew it would shamble through the back-corridors of my memory forever.

Denny Reitmann and his "Ring of Truth."

I knew, even back then, that both of them would be part of that psychic baggage I would always carry with me. And when I first entered the part of the hospital known as the "Permanent" Ward, walking down the rows of beds which contained every horror and abomination committed to human bodies you could ever imagine, I had an odd feeling pass through me. It was like those times when you can sense someone watching you, usually in a crowded, public place, and you turn around and bang, there he or she is—caught, staring right at you. I experienced a kind of psychic, preemptive strike as I accompanied Dr. Barahmi on his rounds. In an instant, I *knew* that I would see Reitmann in one of the beds up ahead. It was an unshakable certainty, an absolute knowledge, and it caused my knees to go weak for just a moment.

Catching myself on the rail of the nearest bed, I paused and shook my head, as if to clear it. Please, I thought. Not Reitmann. Anybody but him.

But I found myself walking past the beds, scanning the faces of the doomed souls within them, actually searching for the familiar features I knew I was going to see.

"Jack!" Reitmann's voice was raspy. "Jack Marchetti!"

Turning to the right, I saw him waving his arms frantically. His complexion was pallid under the fluorescent light, his eyes like single spheres of birdshot, were sunk into his skull. There was no impish grin about to appear in the corners of his mouth, there was no pinched sneer. His face was a design for panic and fear and despair. Reitmann looked hideous to me—a specter from a past I wanted to forget.

"Hello, Denny," I said softly, my voice shattering.

I reached out and shook his hand.

"You know this man?" asked Dr. Barahmi.

I nodded, fighting a lump in my throat. I thought I might actually faint, or maybe heave my guts out. Denny appeared anxious, as if there was a terrible fear inside, just waiting to break free. He wouldn't let go of my hand. "You a doctor now, Jack? You come to get me out of here?"

I could only nod, then shake my head, confused.

Denny burst into tears as he tried to speak. "All you guys tried to forget about me...everybody wanted to forget about me...everybody but you, Jack. I knew you were different from the rest of them..."

I swallowed with difficulty. "I'm...I'm no different, Denny. *I'm probably worse*, I thought.

Dr. Barahmi patted my shoulder, and backed away to give us a private moment. It was at that point that I noticed the absence under Denny's sheets. Picking up the covers, I could see that he had lost both limbs just below the knee. Denny suddenly stopped his crying.

"Mine," he said in a terrible, raspy whisper, "got me on my third day back, the motherfucker..."

"You shouldn't have gone back. You'd made it, you were safe."

He shook his head. "None of us are ever safe, Marchetti. Not even guys like you."

There was something about the way Reitmann intoned that last sentence which made me recall his calling us "pussies" for dodging the draft any way we could. Ducking the pain and the horror had been a double-edged sword. A part of me was of course glad I hadn't been maimed or crippled, but there was another part of me which carried a shapeless guilt for not taking my chances like all the poor bastards in the ward which surrounded me. This was not a subject I liked to dwell upon, or even think about, but there was something about Reitmann which was bringing it to the surface.

"You've been here since the last time I saw you?" I covered up the stumps of his legs, tried to look into his spooky eyes.

"That's the ticket, man. Right after New Year's my legs bought the farm, and they skied me outta there. Been here ever since."

"Why? You look like you could have prosthetics with no problems. A little therapy and you could be walking all over the place."

He chuckled inappropriately. "Even with new legs, I couldn't get away from them..."

"What? Away from *who?*"

"So I figure: why bother?"

"Denny, what're you talking about?"

He looked up at me and started laughing. "Didn't they tell you, Jack?" His throat filled with a hyena-like cackling and he threw his head back against his pillow. "I'm as crazy as a shithouse rat!"

Dr. Barahmi appeared soundlessly by my side and tapped my shoulder. "I am sorry. You could not have possibly known. Come. Perhaps we should leave now."

Numb, I must have nodded my head, and allowed the Chief Surgeon to guide me to the exit from the ward, and out into the antiseptic nothingness of the central corridor. But even out there, I could hear the lunatic laughter of Denny Reitmann. As we entered the elevators, the cackling seemed to change into a wind-swept wailing, a preternatural banshee's scream. The sound echoed in my skull even as the doors closed and we began our descent. It was at that moment that I knew I must try to help Denny Reitmann.

Spending a few hours in the Medical Records Library told me all there was to know about him. After stepping on the mine, he lost a lot of blood before the medics could get to him. After suffering from severe shock, he lapsed into a coma for almost a month. When he woke up on the hospital ship to find his legs gone, whatever was left of his mind—whatever part the Marine Corps had not already ravaged—caved in. For the better part of the next three years, Denny exhibited all the symptoms of catatonia. Gradually he began to respond mimetically to the most routine stimuli, and, after a visit from a member of his Sniper squad, he finally started showing signs of a possible recovery.

He made an effort to locate the others in his squad, and this desire for contact was very helpful in Denny regaining his verbal abilities. For the next two years, the entries in his file were the expected kinds of progress-notes on a recovering schizophrenic. His chemotherapy, originally high doses of Prolixin, had been tempered over time to include the usual spectrum of anti-hallucinogenics like Haldol, Mellaril, and finally settling on the old stand-by: Thorazine. He responded well in both group and individual therapy, and the notes on that period of his treatment were encouraging. Denny's prognosis changed from "guarded" to outright optimistic until…

…until he learned that the other members of his squad were dying off, one at a time, but quickly and inexorably.

When Denny learned that the last cohort from his "Black Aces" squad had died, his condition deteriorated rapidly. His file noted increases in chlorpromazine-therapy, his repeated mentions of "visions, voices, and sounds in the night." His hallucinations increased, and he became extremely paranoid and fearful of each coming night.

It all sounded rather typical to me, but not having had any psychiatric work since the survey-stuff at med school, I figured the best thing to do would be to check with Denny's therapist, Dr. Michelle Jordan.

Her face was vaguely familiar to me when we met in her office. I guess I'd seen her walking in the halls or in the elevators but, prior to finding Reitmann, I wouldn't have had much reason to talk to her. Dr. Jordan looked very good for a woman in her early forties, and she seemed pleased to see me take an interest in her patient. Which was fine with me. I mean, some of the more insecure types feel very threatened when another doc tries to study one of their guinea pigs.

"To be honest with you," I said softly, "in my thoroughly unprofessional opinion, Denny didn't seem very crazy to me."

Jordan fired up a Winston. On her desk lay a huge ceramic ash tray from the Occupational Therapy Shop (I recognized the mold) overflowing with butts. "No, he doesn't show any symptoms unless you get him on the subject of his squad."

"Are they all dead but him?"

She nodded, took a deep drag.

"How the hell did he find out?"

"Denny became a prolific letter-hack. He had managed to keep in touch with each one—there were only eight of them, actually."

"And they're all dead. Seems pretty weird, don't you think?"

Jordan shrugged, dragged.

"You know how they all died?"

She nodded. "A variety of things. A couple from diseases. The rest were accidental."

That struck me as very weird, very strange. "Foul play suspected in any of them?"

Dr. Jordan smiled. "'Foul play,' Doctor? Do you read a lot of English mystery novels?"

I smiled, maybe blushed a little. "What I meant was: Do you think any of them might have been killed? You know—murder?"

"You know, I've never really given it any thought. Why do you ask?"

I shrugged. "I don't know, really. What's he afraid of at night?"

"He won't tell me," said Dr. Jordan. "If I could find out, I could maybe help him work past it."

"Maybe he'll tell me," I said, getting up. The room was so rank from the cigarette smoke, I had to make tracks.

"They want this," said Denny as he reached into the drawer of his bed-stand, fumbling around for something.

I had visited him just before nightfall and had closed off the bed's privacy curtains to suggest we were more alone than we were. I hoped he might open up to me.

"Who's 'they,' Denny?"

Ignoring my question, he kept rooting around in the drawerful of junk until he found the object he was looking for. He held it up for me to see.

"This is it. You remember what it is, don't you, Jack?"

Even in the dim light, the brass ring seemed to glow with an eerie warmth, a power. It was a talisman of evil, a magnet which could draw the darkness to it. I felt a tightening in my throat as I looked at the ring. My eyes felt as if they might start watering.

"Yes," I croaked. "I remember it."

Denny laughed, his eyes beading down like Timken bearings and staring off into space. "It ain't really the ring they want, Jack…it's these…"

Denny gestured along the ring, and I knew immediately that he was seeing things I could not see. And I knew now who 'they' must certainly be…

It was funny, but it was right at that moment that I realized how wrong I had been about poor Reitmann. I thought back over how I had consigned him to humanity's trash heap, how I'd condemned him for being such a soulless bastard, for letting the jarheads turn him into a fucking monster. But now, as I sat there watching him twitch and leer and squirm in his bed, I knew that the guilt was writhing and twisting through him like a swarm of maggots feasting on a fresh kill. It was eating him alive like a cancer, a leprosy of the soul.

Looking at Denny was like looking into a mirror. That's the way it is whenever we really take the time to look at anybody else, I guess.

"I'm the only one left," said Denny. "They got everybody but me."

"Why would they leave you 'til last?" I said almost in a whisper.

He chuckled, pointed at the flat sheets below his knees. "Because I'm the easiest...I'm not going anywhere."

It seemed as good answer as any, and I nodded, but said nothing. I couldn't think of anything to say. How do you tell a guy with grooves of terror etched permanently into his face there's no such thing as the boogeyman? How do you explain that the embodiment of guilt can assume many shapes and guises? That we all create prisons of our own devise?

No. That's all bullshit to somebody who's been standing on the edge of the Pit, who's been hearing the demon-cries, and the flap of the leathery wings of madness.

"Help me, Jack..."

"What can I do?" I looked at him and, for an instant, he appeared to be a little boy, propped up on a fluffy pillow, waiting for a bedtime story. There was a simple pleading in his features, and for the first time, a sadness in his eyes.

"Stay with me...when they come, if you're here, maybe it will help."

I looked out beyond the privacy curtain to nearest window—a black rectangle where night tapped upon its pane. A tomb-like quiet pervaded the ward, as though it waited collectively, expectant like a crowd at a public execution.

"Will you, Jack?"

"What?" I looked back and the little boy was gone. Denny was again the steel-eyed, twisted wretch. He was just a piece of litter tossed out the window while we all careened down Hell's highway. My mind was wandering. I hoped I didn't appear to be ignoring him.

"I said, will you stay with me, Jack?"

The thought of sitting by his bedside until he fell asleep should not have freaked me the way it did. My gut reaction was to say no and simply slip away into the night. Denny Reitmann was waiting for something, and I didn't want to hang around to find out what it was.

But I tapped his shoulder reassuringly and forced a smile to my face. "Sure, Denny. I'll stay."

Some of the anxiety seemed to go out of him after that. He smiled, closed his eyes, and nodded his head. I thought about giving him a shot to put him out for the night, and getting me off the hook, but I just couldn't do it to the guy.

In addition, there was a part of me that wanted to know what he was so damned afraid of. If he thought his victims were coming back to reclaim their ears, I wanted to be there to help him get through the trauma.

I owed him that, at least.

Crazy or twisted or whatever—Denny Reitmann had sacrificed his legs. I'd never even given up anything for Lent.

And so I sat there in the darkness watching him lay on his back, eyes closed, chest rising and falling. Starlight and the albedo of a half-moon spilled through the nearby window, giving everything a whitish-blue cast. The air was tinged with medicinal smells such as ether and iodine, punctuated by the night-rattles of labored breathing, of troubled sleepers coughing and rasping through their dreams.

I don't know how long I sat there, listening to night-sounds, but at some point I must have slipped into a half-sleep, because my neck jerked up, snapping back to reluctant consciousness. For a moment, I didn't remember where I was, and the disorientation startled me. Responding to some atavistic stimulus, my heart began hammering and I was instantly awake. I looked at my patient, who slept calmly.

Then, suddenly, he opened his eyes, wide awake. It was weird the way he just came awake like that.

"What is it, Jack?" Reitmann's voice reached out in the darkness. I looked at him, just as a draft of cold air passed over us.

"What do you mean, Denny?"

"Did you feel it, just then?"

I couldn't bullshit him. "The cold...? Yeah, I felt it."

"They're comin', man. It's tonight. I can feel it."

His face had become drawn and pale, his eyes jittering around, blinking furiously.

"Take it easy, Denny. Why would they wait until now, after all this time? Why would they...do it...when I'm here? Don't you think that would be too much of a coincidence?" I tried to smile casually.

"Maybe they've been waitin' for you too, Jack...maybe you owe them too?"

Reitmann's voice had a fragile edge on it, but his words still cut me. What the hell was he talking about?

"Listen...!" Reitmann half-whispered.

"I'm sorry, Denny, but I don't—"

I stopped in mid-sentence. I *did* hear something: footsteps, bare feet, slapping on the cold tile of the outer corridor, growing louder, getting closer. There was no rhythm, no pattern, to the sounds. A soft cacophony of uneven slaps and drags and shuffles.

"Aw, jeeziz...! It's *them*, Jack! I know it is!" Denny screamed and his voice seemed to resonate through the ward, as though we were inside a vast cavern.

The sounds of advancing feet grew louder, thicker. Whoever it was shambling up the hall, they made up quite a crowd.

Standing up, I started away from the bed, and Reitmann reached out to grab my arm. His palm was cool, but slippery with sweat. "No, don't go!"

"Denny, I just—"

Looking out into the ward, I blinked my eyes, lost my voice.

The ward was gone.

A low, living, ground fog was boiling up like dry-ice on a stage. All around us, the fog rolled in like waves on a beach. The double row of beds had vanished. The walls, windows, bedtables, everything…was *gone*.

"What the —?" There was a piece of me that desperately wanted to believe that this was one hell of a nightmare, that I'd better make myself wake up now because things were getting out of hand.

But there was no waking up from this one.

Denny must have seen them before I did because he started screaming, pulling himself out of the bed with his hands.

There was movement in the fog. Shapes coalesced slowly, like the ghosted images on a snowy television screen. The uneven cadence of their approach grew more distinct, and I could see the point men, the van, homing in on us.

Some of them were stick-figures, bone and tendon animated by the whirling, karmic forces which turn the gears of Eternity. Others, lean and brown-skinned, were more whole, but on the right sides of their heads, *none* of them had any ears.

Reitmann had pulled himself up against the headboard of his bed, teetering on his stumps. The drawer to the bedtable rattled open and he thrashed around the contents frantically.

"I got it! I got it right here! I got it!" He repeated the words over and over like a litany, and without turning around, I knew what Reitmann was looking for.

There was no way to tell how many of them were there, but I saw women and children among the ranks of soldiers. Some of them were so far gone, you couldn't tell male from female, though.

Oddly enough, the initial jolt of panic left me when I realized I couldn't run, that there was no place to hide. I accepted this and waited for whatever was to come.

The first wave of them reached the end of the bed, splitting their formation and swarming around both sides of it. I could smell their foulness, the corruption which steamed off them in acrid sheets. The air was thick with the sting of their hate, and I began suffocating. They surged all around me, pressing me into the soft decay of their flesh.

Reitmann had descended into babbling madness. A pitiful wailing escaped him as they surrounded him, absorbing him into their mass like a cancer would devour a healthy cell. He threw the ring at them, and it disappeared in their midst. Reitmann continued to scream, but I could no longer see him. I was overcome by a paralysis which also had a calming effect on my mind. I watched everything with the detachment of an only mildly interested spectator.

Abruptly, the screaming stopped, as though choked off. There was a finality about the silence which enveloped me as totally as the crush of putrid bodies. I could see their heads all turning, heads with new, right ears. Slowly, silently, they turreted about until the eyed and eyeless alike were all looking at me...

...Orderlies found me the next morning, sagged in my bedside chair. Reitmann had died during the night, leaving us with a bug-eyed, lip-peeled expression engraved onto his waxy face. One of the orderlies said Denny looked like he'd opened the cellar-door to Hell, and I wanted to tell him how close to the truth he might have been.

But I remained silent, waiting for them to gurney his legless corpse off the ward. My memories of what had happened were painfully crisp, having none of the ragged edges of a nightmare. But I also had the feeling there was a segment of the whole experience still missing. Something else had taken place last night, I was certain, but I didn't remember until much later in the day, when evening crept up to windowsills on stalking-cat feet.

I was in the hospital cafeteria standing in line. Ahead of me were several medics—part of a class receiving emergency field surgical training—and as I stared at their uniforms, a vision passed through me like a wide, cold blade.

An epiphany of sorts. I had a flash of memory which filled in the dead space. I suddenly knew what I had so obviously repressed.

"Are you all right, Doctor?" asked a nurse who had been standing behind me. Looking down, I saw the contents of my tray littering the floor. I felt as though emerging from a time-fugue.

"I don't know…" I said, and staggered from the line feeling the stares of others in the room as I turned in slow circles. I wanted to escape, but there was no place to run.

Then, remembering:

They had taken me to their battlefield. A vast, featureless plain where time melted and ran like lava, where light and shadow danced eternally at the limits of your peripheral vision. The ground was thick with their bodies. Stacked and jammed like endless cords of kindling wood, the arrangement of battle-corpses stretched off to the dim horizon in all directions. But there lay some who still lived, who still twitched and shook in the depths of the charnel-field, and it was for them that I had been brought. Down all the hours of the tunneled night, I pushed back entrails into ruptured bellies; pulled shrapnel from slivered torsos; sutured severed legs and arms…and ears. I washed myself in the equitable blood of revenge. There was no end to the carnage, no end to the tuneless song of their pain.

But it was not this knowledge which had so stunned me, as much as the certainty they would be coming back for me—*tonight* and every other night.

For as long as the hate burned like the heart of a star…
Forever.

The Gravedigger's Story
by Kathryn Meyer Griffith

Gazing through the frosted window as he stood inside, Bernard Stumpf thought he spied something thinly vaporous flit from behind a tree to a grave, one guarded over by an impressive stone angel with a sword in its hands, and then on to another grave. Hard to tell exactly what the mysterious shadow was because the wind viciously churned the night snow, and, if he squinted his eyes hard enough, he could see all sorts of strange shapes in it. It was often like that. So perhaps the figure might have been his imagination, might have been nothing; might have been a ghost.

Sometimes the shadows were and sometimes they weren't. Ghosts. He'd met many a spirit in St. Catherine's cemetery over the years. Some of them had been harmless echoes, barely visible, scarcely recognizable as what they'd been in life, and some of them had been evil remnants who were more than capable of hurting, if they were inclined to, the living. He made sure to stay far away from those varieties.

It was his curse to see the dead and, on occasion, being able to talk to them. Oh, he'd become used to the ghosts, and sometimes he would have thoughtful conversations with them. Not often, though. Ghosts could be quite pesky once they realized a living person could see and, even worse, hear them. Some could be mercurial, many selfish, and a few could be especially childish.

Bernard, built square and low to the ground like a compact tank, with weary eyes of blue ice, and silver hair trimmed close to his skull, lingered at the window and sighed. Once he'd been young, with muscled arms, strong limbs; a quick brain and a clever tongue; he'd had a family…a mother, a father, brothers and sisters, a loving wife, a spirited son, and a granddaughter who somehow had all met their deaths before him. Now, bent and used up, and except for the transient shades and his silent friends beneath the cemetery's earth, he was alone in the world. Everyone else human in his life was long gone—except for a finicky fat feline he called Casper, who let Bernard live with him. The cat, his best friend always at his side, slept with him and would traipse along behind him when he was out digging the graves. Casper would climb a nearby tree and peer down at him or would lay on the top of a tombstone watching as Bernard worked. Lucky cat. It didn't have to dig. He loved the creature, though, and the cat provided him with welcome companionship, so the partnership worked.

He continued to stare through the glass into the cemetery he'd cared for and worked at for over fifty years. Snow, a curtain of ivory, came down heavier now, and the ground beyond the window was covered in a deep, muffling blanket that hid most of the headstones or turned them into strange pale lumps dotting the grounds. Branches of the skeleton trees scattered among the tombstones were encrusted in glittering white and chattered in their tree language amongst themselves as the air tossed them about. So far, winter had proved to be a brutal one. The snow would not stop. It made it difficult to dig the graves with frozen earth. He should know. A gravedigger in a time when manual gravediggers, the men who dug the graves by hand with shovels, were becoming few and far between. Bernard one of the last of them. Time had moved on and more and more backhoes were now digging the graves for man, making these deep dark holes in the ground lickety-split. The frozen earth was no problem for the excavating machines. Who needed human gravediggers anymore?

St. Catherine's Cemetery had only kept a human gravedigger on their payroll as long as they had because the church and the cemetery hadn't had the money to buy a backhoe and a new dump truck. St. Catherine's being a small church in a rural town. The church's meager assets had changed last year when one of their congregation, Myrtle Johnston, had passed away and left her whole life's savings to the church. It had been a fortune and had enabled the church to do a total remodel, add solar panels to the roof and purchase a new dump truck, a shiny new backhoe, and hire a younger man to operate them.

They were putting him out to pasture. Simple as that. It hadn't come as a complete surprise. The church's cemetery, in the middle of a town ironically named Heaven, didn't have to beg for customers. There were a lot of old people in the church, and they died pretty regularly. Bernard had had to dig sixty graves the year before; this year, with the congregation steadily aging, there could be more. Digging that many graves was a load of work for an old man, because even with the church's increasing death rate, Heaven was booming. The Walmart Supercenter and the new car plant, where they made SUVs, had brought in a flood of new people to the town. Inevitably, eventually, that would mean more customers for the graveyard, which would mean more work for the gravedigger.

Pastor Tomas had informed him the week before that by the end of February he would be retired and the machine would take over. Bernard had been upset at first, then, after thinking on it, he realized, perhaps it was time. Long past retirement age, his body ached all the time and his memory failed him often. The church was going to give him a modest pension and let him remain living in the caretaker's house until he died, which was not a bad deal. He'd begun digging graves by hand, spadeful by spadeful, when he'd been just a boy of eleven, helping his father, who'd been caretaker before him, sixty years ago. On a freezing night like this one, the thought of retirement sounded heavenly. He smiled at the play on words.

His eyes traveled from the window to his wrinkled and gnarled hands. An old man's hands. When had that happened? When had he grown so old? Ah, he thought, remembering...it had happened when Ellie, his granddaughter, had disappeared ten years ago now. He had aged the winter she'd went missing along with the other two young women from town. They'd just vanished.

Ellie. He fought back the rage that had been with him since he'd lost her. She'd been a thoughtful girl with soft blond hair and laughing olive eyes; barely twenty years old. Her mother and father, his son Jared, had died in a freak avalanche during a skiing vacation when Ellie had only been ten years old. Both of them had died at once. Bernard lowered his head. The memory still stung after all these years. Losing them had been hard, but he'd had little Ellie to save his sad heart. After her parents died, she'd come to live with him, the only family she'd had left, in his house snuggled up against the cemetery. She'd brightened his life more than he could have hoped for. It hadn't been easy. Already an old man, he raised her for the next decade, and she'd quickly become his heart and happiness—until that fateful winter when his heart had shattered forever.

Ellie had gone missing on the fifth of December, first of the girls who would later be taken over the next couple of years, and the evil taunting letters to the local newspapers from the man who called himself The Butcher began the following week. The first letter claimed he'd taken Ellie. Then it went on in malevolent gory detail describing what he'd done to her—strangling her and then hacking her body into bloody pieces—before he'd killed and buried her in a place no one, he boasted, would ever find her. A place where he'd bury the others as well. The police had arrested a suspect for the women's disappearances right away. He'd been a loner named Hector Cummings who lived in a ramshackle house not more than five miles away from the cemetery. The police hadn't had enough evidence to keep Hector in jail, so they released him. Bernard had waylaid the suspect leaving the court house, grabbing him and staring into his eyes, searching for the truth.

"Did you kill those girls, Hector?" he had demanded of the man. "Did you kill my Ellie?"

"Let me go. Get away from me, you crazy old man," Hector had ranted beneath his breath as he'd roughly shoved Bernard to the ground. Then he'd leaned down over him and whispered, "What if I did? They didn't have enough evidence to charge me, so I'm a free man." The killer's laugh sounded practically demonic.

"*Did you kill my Ellie?*"

"Maybe I did and maybe I didn't." Hector had smirked at him, spun on his heels and walked away as the media with their clicking cameras and microphones trailed after him like manic groupies.

But Bernard had seen it in the man's eyes. They'd been eyes as flat as a spider's, soulless and cruel. They'd been the eyes of a murderer.

He'd butchered his Ellie for sure. He'd slaughtered those other girls all right, too. Besides being able to commune with ghosts, Bernard could look into a person's eyes and sometimes sense if they were telling the truth or not. Hector Cummings' eyes reflected nothing but guilt.

Bernard's obsession to make the monster pay, one way or another, for what he'd done to Ellie and the other girls had begun. Man's justice wouldn't do for him. Bernard would not rest, would not let himself die, until that monster lay six feet under.

Bernard moved away from the window, stiff legged from the arthritis that had become his very own demon, and stoked the fire. Standing there, he rubbed his hands above the flames to warm them. Exceptionally cold that night, it was supposed to be even colder in the morning.

No matter how inclement the weather would be, he had a grave to dig when the sun returned.

Releasing a groan, the old man left the warmth of the fire. The clock on the wall read almost ten, and he knew he'd need a full night's sleep to have the energy for what he had to do the next day. The temperature had been hovering around twenty-five degrees the last week and the following morning it would be nearer to twenty. The ground would be unforgiving. He'd been prepared for that, though. Earlier that day he'd spread out sixty-five pounds of charcoal, the cheap stuff he'd bought from Walmart, on the potential gravesite. Then he'd mixed in old issues of newspaper for kindling, squirted on a quart of lighter fluid and had set the site ablaze. As the coals had begun to spark, he'd covered the future grave with a metal hood he'd hand-fashioned years ago and often used, then laid on a blanket of insulation. It would cook the ground overnight, melting the inches of frost and snow and would allow him to dig the next morning in plenty of time for the afternoon burial.

The continuing snow, though, made it extra tricky. Bernard has seen snow as deep as forty inches in his time and had once filled in a grave at five below zero. He cringed remembering that day. That had been a miserable job. That dig. He'd had ice coming out of his nose, freezing above his upper lip. That had been the coldest day he'd ever had. Before he had finished, he'd feared his hands had frozen solid and would break off if anything knocked against them. He prayed tomorrow wouldn't be that bad. Even digging a grave in hundred degree weather was better than digging one in a blizzard. He should know. Yet, regardless of the weather, a family rarely canceled a funeral. Maybe a massive flood or an earthquake would cancel it, but nothing less.

He stoked the fire a final time before he called it a night. When he headed for bed, Casper rose on four paws and stretched, butt up in the air, and with a yawning meow padded into the bedroom to stake his claim on the bed. He'd found Casper, a bedraggled kitten, drenched and with his tiny bones sticking out like a porcupine's quills, on his porch one January dawn eighteen years ago. It'd been a frosty day, rainy, and he'd felt sorry for the kitten; made the mistake of feeding him, and the cat had attached himself to Bernard like a cocklebur ever since. He was a good cat, though. Casper always went outside to do his business and never tore anything up with his claws.

Right before Bernard climbed into bed, he glanced out the frosted window into the cemetery. Darn! A strange wispy shadow floated among the tombstones in the graveyard again. The snow, on the ground and still falling, made the night look like day. If there was some wraith out there waiting for him, they'd have to wait until morning. No way he was going out there in the freezing dark to talk to some ghost.

"See you tomorrow, who-ever-you-are. It's bedtime. Leave me alone," Bernard grumbled, as he pulled the dusty blinds down, then got into bed. Casper sprawled across it, belly and legs raised toward the ceiling; snoring lightly. That cat could fall asleep faster than any cat he'd ever had and he'd had his share of them.

"Move over, bed hog." Bernard shoved the feline over so he could crawl beneath the covers. His old bones were clicking together from the cold.

Something persistently tapped at the window, but he ignored it. Long ago, he'd had Pastor Thomas bless his little house so the ghosts couldn't get in. Otherwise, they'd never leave him alone. In minutes, he was snoring right along with his cat.

Bernard woke up to Casper's warm tongue slurping across his face. The cat was hungry or had to go out. Either way, 7:00 a.m., and Bernard had to get out of the warm bed. The grave he had to dig that day would take at least four hours of work. The burial ceremony was to be at three o'clock. He fed the fire then the cat. He'd eat later, after his work.

A glance at the calendar on the wall revealed what he already knew. December fifth. A shiver crept up through his veins, and he shook his head. He didn't want to think about any of that. He had work to do.

A blizzard still raged outside, and he felt sorry for the family of the dearly departed and their friends who would be attending the burial in the afternoon. It was a miserable day for a funeral. The graveyard beyond his windows resembled an elaborate ice sculpture, and he prayed the bed of burning charcoal had done its job and loosened the earth. Otherwise, his digging would be a heck of a lot harder. His muscles ached just thinking about it.

When dressed in long underwear, jeans, two layers of work shirts, thick socks, a black knit cap, warm gloves and his coat, he hobbled outside and, collecting the thin-bladed, steel-shank shovel he'd use to dig the grave, he trudged on through the deep snow.

The weather so horrible, Casper hadn't followed him out. That cat was no dummy. He knew if he went out in the storm, he'd be frozen for sure.

The ice pellets cut at the gravedigger's face as he made his way behind the house, climbed in and drove the old dump truck into the graveyard; parking it as near to the bed of charcoal, the new grave, as he could get. It wasn't easy. The plots in the cemetery were packed in tightly and someone's gravestone would end up in pieces beneath the truck's wheels if he miscalculated. It was a tricky thing to maneuver the weather-beaten vehicle; one he'd had since he'd purchased it brand new in 1985 and fiddled with year after year so it would keep running. Not an easy task but he'd been doing it for so long he knew what he was doing. Well, most of the time. There had been this one unlucky incident about two years ago when he'd backed the truck into someone's mausoleum and smashed up the front of the tomb. Bernard didn't like to think about that, either. Good thing the inhabitant had been past caring. Bernard chuckled. Pastor Thomas had not been happy, though. Just another reason, he supposed, he should retire, with his eyesight not so good anymore.

The minute he began digging, he figured on some kind of a problem. The bed of coals hadn't thawed the ground all the way down. He'd been digging, shaving the sides of the grave so they were straight, placing the wooden cribbing in one level after another as he had so many times before. Until the last foot or so, and then the ground proved nearly impossible to shovel out. His arms began to shake and yet he kept at it. What choice did he have? The grave had to be ready, waiting for the ceremony, the expensive casket and the artificial grass rug that would cover the gaping hole. Bernard had never not had a gravesite ready on time, and he wasn't about to start now. As the snow continued to fall around him, he dug harder, so hard the leg that pushed down the shovel began to hurt.

The grave was almost done when he glanced up and saw her...a white translucent figure wavering, fading in and out among the snow flakes, at the end of the open hole. She stared at him. At first his mind refused to accept the identity of the apparition. He dropped the shovel. His mouth fell open.

Hello, Grandpa, the spirit's voice, a soft whisper, somehow rose above the howling wind of the snowstorm. Then he realized the ghost's voice was in his mind and not only in the air between them.

Her arms lifted to him and her white face attempted a smile. It almost made it.

"Ellie?" He couldn't believe it. Her spirit had decided to visit him after all these years. He'd prayed for it, but it had never happened until now. Then he remembered…Ellie had been missing ten years to the day. An unusual happiness warmed him as he returned her smile, his frozen lips forming a stiff curve. "What do you want, child?" He didn't have to yell for her to hear him. She heard him well enough.

The ghost levitated over to him. *I missed you so, Grandpa.*

"I missed you, too, granddaughter." He felt tears rim his eyes and wiped them away. "Why are you here? Are you here because it's the anniversary of your abduction?"

No, I am here because he has died.

"Who has died?"

Hector Cummings…the man who murdered me and the other two women.

Bernard felt a sense of vindication. He'd been right. Cummings had taken and butchered those girls. Ellie, too. Now the monster was dead. In one way he experienced relief, but it didn't help his guilt, the rage or sorrow he still felt. Her ghost proved Ellie must truly be dead. All these years he'd had the tiniest of hopes she might still be alive somewhere, imprisoned or her memory lost, but still alive–since her ghost had never come to him…before. Now, he had to accept she resided in the land of the dead, and his grief was final.

"How did Cummings die?" he asked, curious.

Ellie's ghost did not answer.

After a long pause, realizing there would be no answer, he spoke again. "What do you want of me?" He stuck his gloved hands into his pockets. Covered or not, they were icicles like the rest of his skinny body.

I need a favor. Her see-through hands reached out in supplication. She looked as she had in life: young, pretty, her long fair hair flowing in the air and its strands merging with the snowflakes. She wore the clothes he'd last seen her in. Jeans and her favorite T-shirt with the cat face on the front. But she and her clothes were washed-out, all a pasty transparent gray. Her once beautiful jade-colored eyes were dull and haunted. It broke his heart to see her like that.

"Anything, sweetheart. Just tell me what you need."

You need to follow me. I have something to show you and something to tell you. Something to ask of you. The phantom's expression appeared solemn.

"You want me to go somewhere with you?" he echoed like a frozen parrot. "Now?"

Now.

His eyes looked at the grave he'd just dug, his eyebrows lifting a little in uncertainty. Good thing he'd finished it. All he had to do was cover the hole with the fake grass carpet. "Can you give me a minute or two to finish this burial site? Move the truck back to its garage? Funeral's in an hour."

The ghost bobbed her head.

As Bernard laid the fake grass carpet over the grave, fighting the wind to place it and laying rocks on the edges to keep it on, he questioned the wraith, "Where are we going? Can you tell me that? And why?"

Not far from here...through the woods...you will see when we get there. Bring your shovel.

"Can I take the truck?"

No. It is not far from here. We go through the woods. Park the truck where it belongs.

Okay, he fretted. He had to trust her. He climbed into the vehicle, drove it to the rear of the house and left it. Whenever he glanced behind him, he saw Ellie's specter tracking him through the snowfall, hovering above the ground, pale and patient.

He hated leaving the protection of the truck but got out and began to follow the ghost. The storm had strengthened as the day had aged, and he plodded through the deepening snow into the woods behind the cemetery squeezing between the close-set trees. So afraid he'd lose her, but he didn't.

They traveled for what seemed to Bernard like a long while. Perhaps the journey felt endless because he was shivering, tired, hungry, and lugged a heavy shovel. He had dug a grave and had missed lunch. Just when he thought he'd collapse from exhaustion, they arrived at their destination.

He recognized Hector's ramshackle hovel with the abandoned trash, rusted cars, chipped kitchen sinks, a tattered couch and broken chairs, around it the minute Ellie's ghost led him to it. He'd been there many times in the last decade, spying on Cummings hoping to catch him doing something, anything criminal. He'd never caught him doing much of anything but hiding in his wreck of a home.

They were behind the house when he turned to the ghost. "Why am I here?"

As I said, Hector Cummings died yesterday, his body is at the morgue and since there is no family or anyone who cares about him, he will be buried in a few days in a pauper's grave in St. Catherine's.

There's something here I need to show you. The ghost led him a distance into the woods far behind Cummings house, into a natural basin and stopped. Her dead eyes looked down and she pointed at something before her.

Bernard noticed the uneven ground under the snow right off and feared what it meant, what it might hide. A grave.

"Is this a grave, Ellie?"

It is my grave, our grave. All three of us. The ones Cummings tortured and killed. He buried our dissected bodies here in a mass grave with no prayers said over us. Our spirits have been uneasy ever since, but we were tied here to this place as long as our murderer lived. Waiting.

"Oh no," Bernard moaned and dropped to his knees into the white stuff, his gloved fingers reverently touching the snow above the mound. "What do you want me to do?"

Nothing now, yet mark this place because soon they will have to retrieve our bones and relocate them.

"Relocate them where?"

The specter met his gaze. *I want to come home, Grandpa. I, and my other sister victims here*—she waved her hand at the ground before them—*deserve to be buried in their, our cemetery, in consecrated ground; buried by their families who have searched, grieved, long enough.*

"You want me to dig up and rebury all of you?"

No, I want you to send the police here to dig us up; prove Cummings killed us. Send a letter to them from another town. Don't give your name. I do not want you connected in any way with the crimes. Once you tell them about this grave, they will release the remains, and the families will put them all to rest in St. Catherine's Cemetery. When you bury them, I with them, bury us together in that spot by the angel with the sword.

For now, when it comes, bury Hector Cummings' body beneath that same angel statue.

"Why would you want your killer buried in the same place as you and those others?"

I, we, have our reasons. Just do as I ask. Please? The ghost's eyes were shining. Her face stern.

He nodded. "All right. I'll send the police here. I'll bury Cummings where you ask. I'll bury you and the other girls there, too. But will you eventually tell me–"

Ellie's ghost evaporated, leaving him alone in the woods in the snow by an unmarked grave.

His return trek to his house proved to be a long hard one with his heavy heart and his confusion. Why would Ellie want her murderer buried beside her and the other victims for eternity and in sanctified ground? It made no sense. Ellie's ghost had left so he couldn't get that answer from her.

He drug his tired body home, got in his truck, scribbled a short note for the police about the buried bodies on Cummings property and stuffed it into a stamped envelope, careful not to leave fingerprints anywhere on it. He drove two towns over to drop it into an outside mailbox, cap pulled low as a disguise he tried not to let anyone see him.

When he returned to his house, the funeral was being performed in the cemetery, so he skirted around the grieving people and entered by his rear door. He didn't bother to eat or clean himself up. Instead, he yanked off his gloves, coat, hat, and in only his longjohns he collapsed on the bed. He tugged the covers over him and, Casper snuggling in beside him, he fell asleep. Later, after the funeral participants had all left the cemetery, he'd go out and finish burying the deceased, but he needed to rest first.

His last week as the cemetery's caretaker and gravedigger turned out to be a busy one, wrapping loose ends up and preparing for the new man to take over. That day the authorities were bringing the last of the three girls to be buried. The final funeral of the three. The examinations of the remains and the investigations had all been wrapped up and the other victims, including Ellie, had been buried over the last few weeks where Ellie had requested they be interred.

Nothing had been proved, so far, but everyone in town knew it had been Hector Cummings who'd killed those girls, who'd been The Butcher serial killer. They'd found other graves, other bodies, so far over twenty, surrounding his house. The man had truly been evil. It grieved Bernard to no end that the evil man would never face judgment for all his unspeakable crimes. His death, a heart attack, had been too easy a demise for him.

Ellie's funeral fourteen days before had been hard. Bernard had cried, though he'd tried so hard not to, over the coffin at the funeral home and later as it rested beside the open grave. He'd sent her a blanket of yellow roses, her favorites, and it caressed her coffin. The church had helped him buy the best arrangement he could find.

Ellie's service, as everyone in Heaven had loved her, had been beautiful, with so many flowers and donations. He still missed her as much as he ever had, but now she was finally home. Her image, as she'd been alive and as a ghost, haunted him every day. Ellie's spirit had not returned after she'd led him to the girls' grave, though he'd called her often.

After the last girl's funeral, he retired to his house, made a simple supper of soup and fell asleep before the fire, Casper curled in his lap. Crying had wrung everything out of him.

It must have been near midnight when he heard tapping on the window. A frigid night but, thank goodness, no snow. The big snow had melted weeks ago.

"What the–" Bernard grumbled, pulling himself up, the cat sliding to the floor with a startled meow before he scurried off to hide beneath the bed. The feline had seen something at the window. Ellie's ghost had returned.

The spirit beckoned him from the other side of the glass. *Grandpa, get warmly dressed*, the voice in his head said. *Follow me out into the cemetery. You will want to see this. Tonight you–we–will finally have our vengeance and our justice.*

Bernard put on his clothes, his coat, and scurried out into the night after his dead granddaughter. He wondered what the ghost wanted but he didn't have a chance to worry about it.

The cemetery was bathed in an eerie glow from a three-quarter moon in a sky filled with swift scudding clouds. The faint radiance lit up the bare-branched trees, the tombstones, the mausoleums, the whole graveyard as if it were twilight.

Shivering from both the cold and whatever awaited him outside, Bernard hurried between the tombstones trying to keep up with Ellie. The spirit stopped before the stone angel holding the sword. There hovering above Hector Cummings' final resting place were the other two dead girls, his victims in life. They were staring at Hector's grave, and they were smiling. Ellie had joined them.

Bernard started to ask what they were doing when he looked down to see something rising from Hector's grave. A slimy, dark ghoul of a manifestation. It extended to its full height and turned coal-like malevolent holes, or what had to be eyes, on the women encircling it. The manifestation was Hector, or what death had made of him; breathtakingly hideous, grossly misshapen from the human being he had been.

The female ghosts grasped each other's hands and glared at the entity.

What do you want of me, you whores? Hector demanded. The spectral ghoul laughed. *I had my way with you, killed you all, sliced you to pieces and enjoyed every moment of it. You screamed and screamed.* He rubbed his skeletal hands together gleefully.

We come to claim the retribution life never gave us, Hector. We come, Ellie announced in her ghost voice with an anticipatory grin, *to give out that justice. In death. We come for you.*

There's no way, you bitch, you can hurt me anymore now. None of you. I'm dead. You can't touch me. His laughter contained a hint of the demonic.

Not only can we touch you, we can and will send you to Hell for your crimes. Have you not wondered why you are still here, tied to your earthly grave, instead of having moved on?

By the look on his face she'd hit a nerve. For the first time his countenance reflected the beginning of fear. A growing touch of panic. He shrugged. *I imagined I would soon be going on to the next place. I've only been here a few moments, after all.*

You have been in your grave, Butcher, for months, Ellie told him with a sly smile. *Waiting for us.*

Months? Waiting for you? Why? Hector's remnant at last seemed to hesitate, be unsure. *Maybe,* it peered around at the graveyard, *I have been forgotten? I am sure I will soon move on to my next life. Soon. I cannot wait to find more young girls and continue what I started here.*

He had spied Bernard half hidden behind a tombstone, and Hector's ghost grinned chillingly and waved tauntingly at him. *Hi there, my old accuser…ha, could never catch me, you old fool. I was smarter than you. I killed your pretty little granddaughter, and many more, and there was nothing you or anyone else could do about it. I won! I won! Ha, ha, ha!*

Bernard would have run at the hateful creature and torn his dead throat out. But why…Hector was already dead. The living couldn't hurt him any longer.

But we *can hurt you,* Ellie's ghost spoke softly, as the dead women tightened the circle around Hector. *And we are…we are going to give you the justice the world never gave you. We are sending you to Hell where you will burn and suffer the same torment over and over that you forced all of us endure. Punishment for your crimes. For eternity. We, your victims, have waited a long time for this.*

Nah, you bitches don't scare me. I'm leaving. The specter tried to move, frozen where he stood, he found he couldn't. When he realized this, that they had him trapped, helpless, and for once he had no power, the monster lifted his ugly head, bared his decayed teeth, and howled.

And as Bernard watched with wide eyes, the three women's ghosts advanced on Hector's revenant and, with knives that had seemingly materialized from moonlight, they slashed and sliced at him until he was a mass of bleeding cuts, one leg nearly severed and an arm chopped off. They drug him down, screaming as only a dead thing could scream, back into his grave and all four of them vanished into the earth.

Hector Cummings' flat grave marker then burst into flames, morphing into a square of fiery charcoal, and crumbled into ash the wind gobbled up. Hector Cummings and his corpse, his casket, no longer remained in the sanctified ground of St. Catherine's Cemetery.

Ellie's ghost rose alone from the ground and came to float before Bernard, her smiling face at last reflecting peace. A luminosity brightened and expanded around her whole being. *I'm leaving now, Grandpa. Thank you.*

Then, because of a nagging suspicion, Bernard had to ask what he'd been dying to ask since Ellie had first appeared to him. *"How did Cummings die? Was it a natural death?"*

His granddaughter's ghost smiled. *No, it wasn't. I...we...helped him along. We could not leave his property, but we learned we could visit him...so we haunted and tormented him until his heart exploded in his chest.*

Bernard felt stunned. "Why now? You've been dead almost ten years. The other girls, nearly as long."

Ellie's oval of a face hovered in the air before him and her smile dissolved. *Because he was ready to do it again. Take three more girls and do to them what he'd done to us. Capture, imprison, and butcher them. I, we, couldn't let that happen. Not again. So we dealt with him. Now he will never hurt another innocent girl.*

Goodbye Grandpa. I love you. Don't forget me.

"I won't, Ellie," he promised her, sadness reclaiming him because he knew he'd never see her again, in this life anyway.

His Ellie melted into the night earth and silence took back the winter night.

Bernard stood there a long time by the angel tombstone, leaning against it now, his body shaking with the cold until he heard Ellie's sweet voice as if from far away, another world, say, *Goodbye Grandpa. Go home and be happy. Stop mourning me. I am finally at peace now. Happy. I love you....*

"I love you, as well, child. See you soon," he whispered.

He turned and slowly walked back to his house on the cemetery's edge. It looked inviting, safe, warm. Casper sat inside the window and made cat faces at him. Letting himself in, the old gravedigger smiled; also finally at peace with the world.

The Putpocket

by Alan M. Clark

The first time the mystery of the putpocket touched my life, I were a boy. The stories of people finding lost items in their pockets hadn't yet become common, so I didn't see the happening for what it were.

The second time, Papa had come home with a feast, said he'd traded for the food a fine silk handkerchief he'd found in his pocket, one lost years earlier. "Could be someone put it there," he'd said.

This small mystery grew much larger over the years, touched the lives of many others, yet only two people would ever find answers to the puzzle. I'm one of them.

I am Edward Fell, sixteen years old, born of a lowly station in 1850. A bad leg and a weak frame further limit my prospects. I've spent my life in the St. Giles District of London. My mum, Felicity Shepley, died when I were five. I don't remember her. Papa, Andrew Fell, died when I were twelve.

The other person with answers to the mystery is Hyacinth Shepley, my mum's sister.

For most of my life, Aunt Hyacinth has been nothing but unpleasant. Tall and thin, she were a slice of darkness. Her smile showed only in her eyes. She kept her dark hair oiled, held down with pins and combs. When very young, I had a troubling notion that she had an unseen companion, a ghostly sadness as followed her.

Though she got drunk enough to take men to her bed, she had no true companions, and lived only for her shop. Being an aproneer were merely for appearances. Truly, she earned as a userer.

When about town, she carried an oaken staff with a heavy iron pommel to use against children what came too close. "Nippers are dippers," she'd say. "Let them come for my purse and suffer my blows." She is rumored to have struck one boy in the head and killed him eight years ago. It's said he got away but died from his wound. The police made little effort to look into it.

Rarely have I seen Aunt Hyacinth treat anyone with kindness, save Papa. I'd got the idea maybe she fancied him.

When she looked at me, I felt small, like a bug she wanted to crush. I thought that were because of my gammy left leg what makes me walk with a limp.

Even so, she *wanted* me. We found her outside our lodgings one day when I were little. She grabbed me roughly by the collar, said to Papa, "Give him to me. You can barely keep him."

True enough—Papa and I were often one step away from entering the workhouse.

"I'll feed him, work him hard," she said, "make a man of him."

Though we rarely ate our fill, her words were anything but tempting. Quaking in my ratty shoes, I watched her cruel eyes in terror, felt small and helpless in her grip.

Papa removed her hand from my collar, gave our goodbyes. Once inside, he said, "She thinks she'd make your life easier."

"Please, no, Papa, I don't want it easier."

He nodded. We said no more about it that night. Ever after, if Papa spoke of our hardship, I thought of her with dread.

I'd like to say something good about Aunt Hyacinth, but can't until I've given more of my tale.

Papa did his best. We never shared a room with another family. Avoiding that may have grown his debt.

When I reached seven years, I began earning, working sweatshops. In dank chambers of houses and tenements, condemned as dwellings but allowed to hold small factories, I gathered with women and children to work for sweaters that were stern and often heartless. I made boxes and other paper products, trimmed or stitched leather goods, finished readymade dunnage, and more. The returns were small, yet Papa and I needed the funds.

One day, a sweater named Beatrice Fort, a true terror, come into her shop with sweets in a bag, a delicious drop for each of her five laborers, all of us children. Handing them out, she had a most anguished look. Were unexpected from the likes of her. Stranger still, were her words.

"Stole these some years ago from a girl what died here while in my employ. The sweets went missing from my pocket that day. But somehow they're back, bringing my regrets with them. I must close this shop. I'm so sorry to have mistreated you all." Wringing her hands and weeping, she left.

I were not sorry to see her go, just baffled...and upset to have to look elsewhere for work.

That were the first I knew of the putpocket, though I hadn't yet heard that word or name.

Our district were a miserable, overcrowded rookery, where most everyone looked for advantage over others, a place of wretched hovels broke up into one-room dwellings, sweat shops, and dens of iniquity. Poverty breeds cruelty. I were easy pickings for the bully boys. Spent much of my young life being afraid.

I didn't feel much safer in our lodgings. They were all one room affairs. Some had windows, some not. Some had walled up doors that used to go to other rooms. While I tried to sleep at night, the sounds from the streets coming through the thin walls—angry shouts, arguments, drunken laughter, cries of pain or woe—fed my fancy a dreadful fare.

"You have every right to be timid," Papa said to me. "But if you allow, I'll teach you to set aside fear, and show you how to fight back against the bullies."

I weren't much good at what he taught about fighting, but given the chance, I could land a blow what smarted. Did that a time or two—got a bloody do down in return. Each time, though, the bullying let up some after.

I found comfort in Papa's arms at night. A bricklayer, he were strong and had an easy manner. He got up before dawn each day to walk to job sites. He worked the daylight hours, arriving back home past dusk, bringing something to eat.

Though weary after a long day, he'd tell me stories while we sat enjoying supper by lamp light before bedtime. At first, he told tales with few harrowing parts. With time, his adventures became more hair-raising.

Papa found amusement in what unsettled folks; the indecent, the foul, the dangers of the world. Though he took care and never wanted to see another suffer, he liked gruesome stories of crimes and accidents. He chuckled at illness and death. I couldn't help but laugh at the worst things, the way he told them. More useful than lessons on fighting, he taught me to laugh at my fears.

He turned the blundering adventures of criminals into lighthearted tales. My favorite were about a bodysnatcher and his wife. She'd become upset to find out how her husband earned.

"'The lord knows what you're up to,'" Papa said, trying to sound like a woman. "'Take care or he'll send you to hell.'

"The bodysnatcher beat her, told her to mind her own business. And she did turn a blind eye to him. So much so that when he came home with organs meant for the medical men, she mistook them for fresh sweetbreads from the butcher. She served them up for supper!"

Papa's eyes twinkled with mischief in the lamp light. "Now, there's a right proper poke in his eye."

"Got what he deserved," I said.

"He didn't think so. When he discovered the truth, he cried, 'Bad enough I should sell the dead, but you've gone and made me a cannibal! What must the Lord think of me now?'"

How we laughed! Nearly lost my supper. And I sure didn't want to—that were the night he traded the silk handkerchief he'd found in his pocket for a feast. He'd brought home sprats, slices of pineapple, and treacle tart.

"Were the oddest thing," he'd said when he come home, "found a silk billy in my pocket lost years ago. It went missing on my way to give it to your mum, taken by a dipper for all I knew. Now, I know that coat pocket like I do the inside o' my mouth. How'd it happen? Maybe someone put it there. Well, never you mind, I says to myself, a pretty thing is all it is. We have no use for that handkerchief now. I made a trade in the market for all this here."

Papa became quiet and thoughtful for a moment. "Hmmm...my new assistant, young Carhill, said a year ago his father found a small purse in his pocket he'd lost long ago while at Covent Garden Market. I didn't think much of it when he told me. Now I see its likeness to what happened today."

"We have a mystery," I said.

"Indeed! I'll ask around, see if I can find out more."

Papa didn't bring home further tales of the mystery for a long while.

The lodgings I remember best were a room we had on an upper floor, had an uneven stain of red on the walls what caught the late setting sun through the sooty window, and lit up like the inside of a firebox. Even a cold day with no coal, it warmed me just to see it.

One hot summer day, Papa and Aunt Hyacinth stood talking in Great Wild Street below that window, people and traffic going around them. Aunt Hyacinth saw me watching and pointed. Papa turned to look up.

The window open, I heard her. Speaking above the street noise, she repeated her demand from years earlier. "*Give* him to me."

Papa shook his head, and she scowled.

I thought of the boy folks said she'd killed. Rumors of that happening had come that year.

When Papa came up to our room, I said again, "Please don't give me to Aunt Hyacinth."

"You are *my* boy," he said, setting me on his knee. "She sees me struggle to earn. She knows I failed to pay the nethers. Been meaning to tell you, we'll have to find new lodgings."

"Oh, Papa..."

He hugged and calmed my fears. I were eight at the time.

The next room had no window.

Papa gathered his frightful stories from where ever he could. He'd read to me or merely tell me a tale of suffering he'd heard; stories of accidents in the mills, cruel mayhem, or murder. Then he'd ask, "How likely that should happen to you too? You can't help imagining it—that's the point of stories. But think on that—how likely is it?"

I'd see what he meant. Got so, were I scared of something, I'd dare to imagine the worst. In fancy, I've had every disease and crippling there is, suffered missing limbs, died a thousand ways. If I imagined it "first and worst," as Papa put it, how likely was it that I'd suffer those things in my life? Had he not laughed so much in the telling, I might have got more of a chill from his words. But his humor were a contagion of sorts.

One evening, Papa said, "Today, Cheese Pete had a fright, *and* a delight. He'd left the job site for a bite and a dram. Come back white as a sheet, yet a foolish smile on his face. 'I were coming out of the Cross Keys in Endell Street' says he, 'when I felt a hand reach in my pocket. A dipper, I thought, whipping around. No one there! Yet these—' He held out a pair of spectacles. '—lost years ago, were in my pocket.'

"The close work had been getting too hard, and he couldn't afford new spectacles. He feared he'd lose his carpenter position. 'Were a ghost,' says he. 'I know it. Must be the putpocket I've been hearing about.'

"He said it's like a pickpocket, only backwards. Could be how I got the handkerchief back."

Papa must've seen I were shying away from his words. He let the matter go.

I didn't sleep well that night, thinking about a ghost reaching into my clothes.

"First and worst" worked with things I could know and see, but the unknown were different. Thoughts of unquiet spirits gave me the worst chills. Remembering the notion I'd had that something followed Aunt Hyacinth, I fancied ghosts were the unhappiness someone left behind. Should one find me, I feared the sorrow might rub off and make me as miserable as my aunt.

Papa had the cure for those frights too—he brought me stories about the wonderful things the putpocket had given people. In daylight hours, he told how some had found coin in their pockets, one a hefty purse. Others discovered long lost handkerchiefs or jewellery. "Just yesterday," Papa said, "saw a fellow on the crowded footway hold a watch over his head and cry out it had been returned to him. The joy on his face were something to see."

Only later, once I'd become at ease with them, did he add stories of spirits to our nighttime tales.

"Our township has more ghosts than anywhere else. 'Tis our history!" He spoke as if the spirits were prize-winning hogs at a country fair. "Disease and pestilence from long ago, poverty and crime, then and now, have bred the sort of cruelty and madness what keeps the dead among us. Telling such stories with friends when a child are among my fondest memories. You can be afeared of the ghosts, or, like I do, cock a snook at them." He grinned wickedly, thumbed his nose while wiggling his fingers.

As we laughed, I knew his delighted mood had brushed aside my fears yet again.

"Those who suffered terrible illness," he said, "lepers from the Middle Ages and the dead from the plague in the 1600s, make sport of spreading old diseases from the ancient marsh leading down to the Thames. Much of that foul bog is drained and paved over long ago. Yet, in our parish, the wetness remains. Unheard, the dead wheeze, choke, and cough out the sickening miasma." He made pitiful long faces, pretended agony and woe with such looks that I could but laugh.

Even so, that one had raised my shorts hairs. Papa must've seen I were spooked because he poked and tickled me. "They have no interest in little boys like you. What have you got they might want? Why, not a thing." He placed a warm hand on my cheek. "They go for the hail and hardy." He chuckled. "That's why I smoke—to give me a cough. Just that much and the ghosts turn away, taking their mischief elsewhere. And you…you've got your gammy leg." He chuckled again. "It ain't good for nothing."

I didn't believe he believed that, but loved him all the more for giving my defect purpose.

Our time together in the evenings, we spoke of many sorts of ghosts. By the time he doused the glim each night, and I lay beside him awaiting sleep, the darkness had become just shadows again, the sounds from outside merely senseless murmur.

Around that time, I asked myself if I believed in ghosts. Papa had indeed taught me how to set aside some of my fear. With his help, I'd lost much of my timid nature. More useful, I lost my timid manner. That helped with the bullies.

In my twelfth year, instead of trying to take me, Aunt Hyacinth asked Papa to send me to work daily in her chandler's shop. "She wants someone to run errands, make deliveries, and such like. Treats it a given you ought work for her. Said you'd do it should I tell you to, and that's what fathers did with lads. Told her it were your choice, and I'd ask. She says you need protection from hardship, from the hazards of the street."

St. Giles is a place thick with lurkers, macers, and mughunters, a great danger to life, limb, and purse for anyone seen as having anything of worth. Papa and I didn't have that look. The dangers to us were the open sewers, bad water, disease, and debt.

Aunt Hyacinth didn't care about my safety. She wanted a slavey and I were almost as good. Not wanting to show disrespect, I didn't tell Papa that. Yet I had the worrisome feeling he wanted me to work for her, perhaps because of the way he said his next words.

"'And how would you protect him, while he runs your errands and makes your deliveries?' I asks her. 'I pay protection,' says she, 'what puts constables and a magistrate in my pocket. Not too deeply, mind you, but well enough. Nobody will harm him while he's in my employ.'"

"Why would the police help her?" I asked.

"They don't. They help those she pays. Your aunt is in with criminals, family people."

He frowned to see my confused look, but shrugged. "I'm not so concerned about that as what she'd be cold-hearted."

I were relieved to hear Papa admit she were a hard woman.

"I don't like her," I said without looking at him. "The way she looks at me... She hates me."

"She's your mother's sister. What could she have against you?"

"Don't know, Papa. I'm afraid of her."

"She *would* be a taskmistress, that is a certainty, but surely no worse than the sweaters what hires you now?"

"Wouldn't she?"

We sat ill-at-ease for a time, an uncommon thing between us. Then he said, "I owe her money. She said she'd give good terms on your work counting against the debt. We shan't do better with the sweaters."

I frowned, chewed my lip, troubled with thoughts of her dark gaze.

Papa tried to hide his displeasure, wiping his face with his hands.

He worked too hard. While he enjoyed his tobacco, he denied himself drink, and no telling what else, to better provide for me.

"I need the help son," he said straight out, as if man to man.

I could not go against his wishes. "I've become so weary of sweat shop toil, I suppose Shepley's Chandlery would be welcomed change," I lied.

"Thank you, Edward," he said.

For a moment, I felt like a grown man.

Aunt Hyacinth maltreated me from the start, but not so any mark might show. On my first day, I were too slow retrieving a box of two penny candles for a customer. She struck me on the back of the head with her staff. She'd perhaps been careful not to break the skin. The lump and bruise hid beneath my hair. That were only the beginning.

I didn't have the heart to tell Papa.

I'd been working for her five months when an unfinished wall at a job site collapsed, killing him.

Losing Papa felt like my heart had been torn from my chest, the best part of me taken away.

Had little time to mourn proper. Aunt Hyacinth took me in like I belonged to her, but not in the way of family, more like property. She lives in the rooms over Shepley's Chandlery. Gave me a thin pallet on the floor of the storage under the stairs for my bed.

When asked about any funds Papa left behind, she said, "he owed much more than he had. 'Tis up to you to assume his debt to me. You shall work here at least until that's paid."

"How much? How long?"

"I'll have to consult the ledgers in storage to know the true amount."

I didn't like her answer. "May I help you find them?"

"Not now. We have much work to do."

Perhaps she saw the doubt on my face. Her hard eyes hot with anger, she growled, "No one would dare suggest I'd play the crooked cross."

I didn't believe her, yet I shut my mouth and turned away.

I then wished upon Aunt Hyacinth a curse Papa had told about. "Those who died in the wretched squalor of St. Giles," he'd said, "such is their envy, they want financial ruin for the prosperous, though it gets them nothing. Should that sort of ghost touch a man, he'll see his grip on his affairs loosen, his investments come to disaster, and the demands of debt become impossible to meet."

Yes, though I would be hurt should she be so cursed, I wished that upon her.

It were no real threat. I couldn't find it in me to stand up for myself, as it seemed my source of courage had gone with Papa. My life were in her hands and she did as she pleased with it.

Aunt Hyacinth had begun Shepley's Chandlery humbly enough, selling candles, oil, and sundries through a single room's window onto New Oxford Street. Now, she owned the building and had forgot her humble beginnings. She extended credit to all what'd have it and milked poor families for gain. The high interest on the loans were a cruelty, yet those what couldn't find credit elsewhere came to her. Those late in paying got visits from men she paid, a demander called Billy the Biter, and his fat-fisted bludger, Mr Paldough. Billy spent the night with Aunt Hyacinth on occasion. When he did, if I didn't keep to myself and his pale eyes found me, his mouth would take on a cruel twist and he'd make sport of belittling me to entertain my aunt.

Running Aunt Hyacinth's errands and making deliveries, I came to know many people. Most did not hold my aunt's deeds against me. Making deliveries to homes and businesses, I learned my way around the township's filthy, ill-paved ways; the routes around the worst of the open sewers, the high ground to avoid the tide of night soil that rose in standing water when the heavy rains came, and the secret passages that provided shortcuts to and through the gin shops, the gambling dens, and the brothels.

Just like Papa, my ears were eager for the tales folks told of the district and its history. And, like him, I heard of others who had found things in their pockets lost years earlier. Though I'd never lost anything of worth, I dared to dream of finding gold and silver in my pockets, so I could make my own way in the world.

I were too afraid to ask Aunt Hyacinth what she held against me, let alone try to reason with her. Often, I imagined telling her what I thought of her and leaving.

For all that, St. Giles were familiar to me. Though a slum, it were the world I knew. If I feared anything more than Aunt Hyacinth, it were change, for I had no expectations.

I toiled for her three years with no earnings.

One October day in my fifteenth year, she had me clearing out a damp storage room toward the back of the shop while she were out. "When the dustman comes, help him load his cart," she'd said. "Should customers arrive, tell them to return tomorrow. Should you fail to remove all this rot before my return, you'll have no supper."

The roof over the room had leaked for some time. Smelling of rot and mold, all within had been ruined. The dustman took three loads in his cart. Waiting for his return for the third, I rummaged in a small wooden cabinet at the back of the room. The lower compartment opened to reveal aught but dank air. The little drawer above were swollen fast. I got a hammer and beat on it. The cabinet came apart and I got the drawer free.

It held posts—the top one from Papa to Aunt Hyacinth. Though faded and smudged from the damp and mildew, I could make out his writing on the envelope. The ink had smeared on the leaf inside, the words hard to make out. I took the letters to my pallet under the stairs, hid them amidst the straw of the mattress.

Why would Papa write Aunt Hyacinth?

She had often spoken to him with more kindness than she gave others. I'd seen her gaze turn tender when looking at him. Whatever the feelings, I didn't think Papa shared them. Indeed, I thought he wanted to hate Aunt Hyacinth but couldn't.

"She weren't always like she is now," he'd said once. "Couple of years before you were born, she went to stay with an aunt in Lambeth. The aunt died, and our Hyacinth ended up in the Lambeth Workhouse with an ailment, were there for nearly a year. We didn't know or we would have helped. When she come out, she'd changed. Vowed never to be poor again. Of course she can't rise above her station—found that out quick—so she walks on the rest of us to make her way."

I knew the workhouse broke many who spent much time there. At the time, I didn't know what he meant by how she made her way. I'd thought she but had a disagreeable manner.

That night, after Aunt Hyacinth went up to bed, I got the letters out.

I set the one on top from Papa aside while looking at the remaining twenty or more pages. They seemed to be letters from Aunt Hyacinth to Papa. "Lambeth Workhouse" were printed at the top of each page. She must have written them while there. They weren't folded or sealed, had perhaps never been posted. Written with poor quality ink in her hasty script, I made little sense of them.

I picked up the letter from Papa. Holding the paper just so in the light, I made out the words.

Dearest Hyacinth,

You had your time with me, and now that's done. Don't make it worse with further demands. I shall have no more of it. You must accept that, whatever happens. You would but crush your sister should you persist. I believe you love her too much for that.

Warmest regards,
Andrew

I heard Aunt Hyacinth weeping in her chamber above, as she sometimes did. I had always thought she wept from well-deserved loneliness. Yet now, her pitiful sobs seemed to color the meaning of Papa's letter.

Had my aunt and Papa been lovers before he married Mum? Had he spurned Aunt Hyacinth in favor of my mother?

Then a notion I didn't like—that they had been lovers after he'd become wed. I pushed the idea away yet remained troubled.

Reading his words again, I changed the way I thought about them. Papa had merely carried out a task for her from a sense of duty. He had been good to Aunt Hyacinth, she wanted more, perhaps to be closer to him, to draw him away from Mum, and he'd put his foot down. Whatever she'd wanted, Aunt Hyacinth must have relented. She'd still held him in high regard years later, and that accounted for the looks I'd seen her give him.

Not long after, in late October, while I prepared to make a delivery, Mr. Rasher, a friend of Papa's, come in Shepley's Chandlery. He asked for lamp oil. I set down the parcel I meant to deliver and fetched his order. About to complete the sale, he looked me up and down. "Young Master Fell," he said, "you are the spitting image of your father as a young man."

Aunt Hyacinth, writing in the sales book, paused and looked up at me, eyes narrowed as if considering my likeness to Papa for the first time. Then another look—her features softened and that tender gaze she'd given Papa appeared for a moment. Perish the thought that a tender look should frighten. Yet it did frighten me, more so than her usual, scornful glare. I were old enough to know something of what passed between men and women, even if I had no experience. In that moment, I feared she'd demand I attend her needs in bed. Gave me a chill.

"On the account, then," Mr. Rasher said. "Good day to you."

His words had broken the spell of her gaze. She turned to go about her business.

I took up the package and hurried out. Walking through a light rain, I delivered the parcel to a tobacconist's in James Street.

Most of the tales of the putpocket came from the crowded streets near Covent Garden market, so while there, I asked a few people if they'd heard any new stories. A friend of mine, Bertie, all of seventeen years old, had a fruit barrow in Long Acre, near the market. He once gave me a badly bruised apple what looked like something had chewed on it, so I always stopped at his barrow with the hope of another.

No such luck that day, but when asked about the putpocket, he did have something for me. "I know a man found a pipe in his pocket lost four years ago, still had his choice of tobacco in it, fresh as the day it went missing. I've the oddest feeling I might recover a clasp knife I lost a time back." He laughed at his own words.

"I've rarely lost anything worth the trouble of looking for it," I told him.

He looked at me with a damnable pity but gave me a slice of apple.

"Some say it's a repentant pickpocket," he said, "putting what's stolen back."

"Thanks for the slice," I said, doffing my cap. "I have to hurry back to Aunt Hyacinth or she'll take her staff to me."

"Good luck to you, Edward," he called as I hurried away, "May the putpocket make a mistake and bless you with someone else's coin."

Passing through the Seven Dials on my way back, my hands chilled, I were about to stuff them in the pockets of my ragged jacket when I wondered if I might find something. I'd never thought of myself as fortunate, so I wasn't disappointed to find them still empty.

Of course there were nothing in them—until…suddenly, my right hand found something hard and cold. I pulled it out to have a look.

A jade comb for a woman's hair, it's decoration in the shape of a fan.

"The putpocket," I said, casting about to see who might have placed it. I saw no one near enough.

'Tis *a spirit, then*, I thought with a shiver.

I remembered Papa saying, "Beyond their sway over the fortunes of health and purse, the dead have little power here. They cannot easily make themselves known, nor exert much force in the world. Each, according to abilities held in life, might work a bit of mischief. One who'd been a smithy might wield a hammer for a moment. An artist could summon an image on a frosted pane or dust-strewn surface. A musician will possibly coax a chord from an idle instrument."

A repentant pickpocket seemed reasonable, then. But I'd never lost such a comb before.

I took a last look at it, now wet from fresh rain drops, and hid it in my pocket. Should Aunt Hyacinth see I had a thing of value, she'd claim it against what were owed.

To my surprise, when I got back to Shepley's Chandlery, I were holding the comb in my hand again. Aunt Hyacinth saw it right off, as though her gaze were directed to it by another—were the strangest thing.

"Where did you get that?" she cried. As she came for me, her eyes bulged, and her hands became claws.

Frightened, I stumbled back, dropped the comb. It shattered upon the floor.

She reached for her staff.

"The putpocket!" I said, turning back for the door to retreat outside.

She thrust the staff into the small of my back. I struck the door and rolled to the left. The pommel flew against my cheek.

"You'd use a tall tale to lie to me?" she howled.

Aunt Hyacinth struck me in the gut with her staff, then brought it up into my groin.

I fell to the floor, weeping and holding myself.

"Near Seven Dials," I sobbed. "It appeared in my pocket."

"How did I not recognize you that day?" she said, her face a rage of red and black.

She moved to the center of the room, opened the trap door to the cellar.

Knowing what were coming, I meant to flee, but the pain in my gut and lower down were too much.

She returned to me. "They said that boy died, but it were *you* all along."

Aunt Hyacinth dragged me by my jacket to the opening in the floor. She held me by the collar, put her face near mine. Her cruel eyes bore down on me while I cringed. "You *stole* my favorite comb, and now you've *broken* it."

I didn't understand. How could she think that?

Aunt Hyacinth shoved me. I tumbled through the opening, striking an elbow against a rung of the ladder. A deep muddy puddle, ten feet down, broke my fall. I cried out in pain. The trap door slammed down. Darkness swallowed me. I heard her move furniture to cover the trap door. There would be no getting out that way.

Cold and wet, coated in a sour smelling filth that might in part be night soil from the building's overflowing cesspit, I held myself in a blanket of self pity long enough for the pain to ebb. Dusk had fallen on my way back from Covent Garden, but I looked for light. I knew the foundation of the building were stone with wooden grates to allow air through. I might pry one loose. Sounds from without came to me before I saw light. I crawled toward noises from the street. Struggling against the slick, heavy mud, I pulled myself from the puddle at the center of the cellar. Weary, I rested.

Should I fail to get out on my own, how long would she keep me there? Rain had fallen on and off for days—I had to wonder how fast it made its way in. I'd heard tales of landlords letting cellars to families when the overcrowding of the parish were at its worst. They must have started dry enough. No one would choose to sleep in mud. Yet, families had lost members in some of those cellars, drowned when the hard rains came.

Then harder questions.

Did Aunt Hyacinth somehow mistake me for the boy she killed? Yes, that seemed so.

Why? Had she got a good look at him. Had he looked like me?

She believed he'd stolen the comb.

What did she know of the putpocket? She seemed to know there were tales. I shouldn't have been surprised. Just because Aunt Hyacinth had no friends didn't mean people didn't speak to her. Tales were passed around freely. For those of us unable to afford even the penny gaff, such stories were our entertainment.

Should the notion of the putpocket as ghost be right, might it be the spirit of the boy she killed? If Bertie's notion were right—the putpocket as repentant pickpocket putting things back, putting things right again—shouldn't it have given Aunt Hyacinth the comb?

I'd been surprised to find the comb in my hands upon entering the shop earlier. Then Aunt Hyacinth's eyes had gone straight to it, as if someone had whispered in her ear, "Look at what he holds!"

Papa had told me that those condemned to death had always been allowed to stop in St. Giles for a last dram on their way to the gallows at Tyburn. "Once topped," he'd said, "their ghosts seek more of our hospitality, returning to tempt others to commit terrible crimes. Some believe that one's mind, weakened with drink, might take up their villainous desires. 'Tis not uncommon to find that those who murder in the parish while the worse for drink are unable to explain the passions what drove them."

Aunt Hyacinth often had strong drink. Had the putpocket placed the comb in my hands when I entered the shop to goad Aunt Hyacinth into attacking me?

At that moment, I got a deep chill feeling—nay, a certainty—that the putpocket crouched beside me, there in the mud, no telling what sort of mischief on its mind.

Yet I sensed no threat. I became still, quieted my breathing, listened.

For all that I had to fear, I felt myself becoming drowsy. My body had warmed the mud beneath me. Once felt, the urge for sleep would not be denied. I dozed, dreaming I were a different boy.

"My comb!" the woman shouts.

She has a staff.

A blow to my head.

Addled!

Must keep my feet, get away.

The frightening woman, fast with her staff, not with her feet. She would avoid the worst of the mud. I have no care in my dash to get away.

Blood in my eyes. Growing ache in my head. Must find a place to hide and rest, before I keel over and go down.

A glance back. Faces turned to me. Concern, suspicion, anger. Not her face. She's lost sight of me, and I her.

The passage to Clark's Mews. Plenty of privies to hide in.

No—don't want to become trapped!

Under the iron mongers shop, a crawl with openings onto High Street and Clark's passage. Oh, bending down—the pain in my head...

Must crawl in as far as I can—she will look for me. Thick with mud here, something to discourage her.

Weak.

Pounding head.

Still have the woman's jade comb. It's worth the trouble. Meets my quota for the day, perhaps the week. The Master will be pleased.

My hot face feels better against the cold clay.

The dimming light fails.

I tossed and turned, feeling the wet clay under the chandler's shop, trying to rise from sleep. I didn't want to return to the place under the iron monger's, to become again that other boy, so like me. We could be twins, both of us struck with the same staff, both lying in the mud beneath a shop.

I rest until they come for me. I hear them. They complain of the smell. A man approaches, crawling. Fastens rope around my feet, crawls out. I cannot move as I'm hauled out from under the iron mongers.

People of the neighborhood. A constable!

He takes little interest.

Thankfully the woman with the staff isn't here.

I understand little of what is said. My head a muddle. So stiff. Cannot move.

I'm taken to a room, placed on a hard counter, left alone in the cold. The stiffness passes, but my limbs still refuse to move. The stiffness comes again. People come and go, as does the darkness.

I rest in a barrow among the dead! An old woman, and a man with half a face and missing an arm!

No voice to scream!

Squeaking wheels bumping over rough ground.

Am I...?

An open field.

I am lifted, placed in raw dirt beside the others.

I am...

My limbs arranged.

A vicar.

I am dead....in a pauper's grave.

Dirt falls upon me.

Unable to cry aloud, I cry within, "I am not done!"

Soil covers my eyes, falls into my mouth.

Time, endless and alone.

Settling, I suffer countless tiny mouths, seep into the earth like melting ice.

I am mingled with those who lie beside me. Briefly, I know the accident in the rail yard as took the man's life, the fever what released the old woman from her melancholy days.

I know little but solitude afterward.

I suffer this loneliness because of what I've done.

I would put it all back if I could.

...would put it all back if I could.

...put it all back if I could.

...it all back if I could.

...all back if I could.

...back if I could.

...if I could.

...I could!

Yes, with willingness, I might.

And I am untethered from my remains with but one goal.

I awakened with renewed willingness to crawl toward the light, an urgent need to get away from what had just happened in sleep; in what had to have been more than mere dream. I didn't want to end up like that other boy, my *twin*.

The closest grate caught the light from a gas lamp on the street. Reaching it, I heard a distant wailing outside as of someone in pain. I turned around and kicked at the grate. With each strike, the pained sound from without came louder. The grate split in two. I worked the pieces loose and crawled out to stand unsteadily in the lane.

Those walking by showed little interest in me or the wailing. Sounds of suffering common in the neighborhood, no alarm would be raised.

Now I could hear that it were weeping, coming through an open window of Aunt Hyacinth's bed chamber.

Good, let her suffer, I thought.

Yet her voice became more pained, turning to a wail of agony.

I didn't want to help her but couldn't turn away should she be in trouble. I moved to the shop front and pounded on the door. Awaiting answer, the wailing came louder still.

I moved around back of the building, where I knew of a cracked window pane. She'd have me for it later, but I broke the glass, released the lock, and crawled in.

No telling what she'd do to me if my help were not needed. I tried to put down such notions as I mounted the stairs to her chambers.

"Aunt Hyacinth," I called. "I'm coming to help."

No answer.

Reaching her door, I knocked lightly. Deciding she could not hear over her own wailing, I knocked louder.

"Help me," she cried, her voice cracking.

I turned the doorknob, fearing she stood on the other side, her staff ready.

The scene I discovered in the half-dark chamber frightened me all the more because it didn't make sense. Aunt Hyacinth lay upon her back in bed, the bedclothes beneath her soaked with blood that appeared black in the gloom. The linen over her bulged around her belly.

"I didn't know I were knapped," she moaned. Her face were slick with sweat. "Damn that Billy. I knew his sheath were too old."

Aunt Hyacinth let out a deep moan, followed by a strangled cry. "The child *comes. Help me!*"

Though I wanted to flee, I couldn't. How, I wondered, should I help? I couldn't ask, even as I approached.

"I cannot rise, cannot reach it," she said.

"I-I don't."

"You *must—*"

The cries that followed spurred me. I lifted the linen from the foot of the bed. Blessedly full of shadow, I saw little beneath. But the smell were one I knew from the grave—I'd dreamt it not an hour earlier!

"*Now*, before it's too late." The agony in her voice! Then, a cry that spoke of regret more than of pain, of sorrow more than fear. Aunt Hyacinth ripped the linen off. She bucked against her mattress, then lay still, spent. Perhaps she slept.

What I saw made me feel the fool. She lay in her night shirt, belly flat, no blood to be seen, her legs spread but a little. Again, shadow saved me. On the mattress between her knees lay a small brass ring catching the scant light.

I moved to pick it up, Aunt Hyacinth's eyes upon me.

"What?" she asked sharply.

"A ring."

"Give it to me."

I did, then lifted a blanket from the floor to cover her.

Her voice an urgent whisper—"Light the lamp,"

Once I'd done so, I found her sitting. She looked at the bedclothes, her face a mask of wonderment. "A nightmare, surely."

I feared she'd turn on me any moment.

Instead, she held the ring up to look closely. "Bring the lamp."

Shaking, I approached.

Yes, a brass ring. No setting, but a flat for a monogram. Half worn away, I made out only the last initial, a curling "S."

"Shepley," came from me unbidden.

"Yes," she said quietly, with a troubled look.

She grew pale, seemed to collapse, such sadness on her face.

I didn't know what to do, but as happened, nothing were needed. Aunt Hyacinth had closed her eyes.

She didn't awaken the next day. Allowing her sleep, I tended her shop best I could. Those who came to pay on debts, I told to come back the following week. They seemed grateful.

The next day, I worked up my courage, and awakened Aunt Hyacinth, brought her hot broth. I must admit, I were ready to throw it at her should she come at me.

She didn't. A calm had come over her. No anger in her eyes.

She sipped her broth, looked at me squarely. "Had a dream about a boy," she said. "I placed a ring on a cord round his neck when he were but an infant, just before giving him up at the Lambeth Workhouse. That is not dream but did indeed happen, long ago. Now, he's given the ring back—the brass one you found."

I thought about the boy in my dream but kept my silence.

"In the dream, he were the putpocket," she said, as if she'd heard my thoughts. "the one who brought back my comb. Forgive me, please, for accusing you of being the thief."

If she knew the ghost brought both objects, she knew she'd killed her own son. We didn't speak of it.

And at last, I'll say something good about Aunt Hyacinth: She has a pleasant smile. Though it were sad that day, she gave me one, the first I'd had from her. "Your brother, he were. I named him Andrew, after your father. Now I owe it to him to take care of you."

Again, I faced thoughts of Papa and Aunt Hyacinth together. I could accept them now.

In the days that followed, life got better. I helped with all undertakings at Shepley's Chandlery. Aunt Hyacinth welcomed my ideas. When word got around that she were forgiving debts, the shop began to prosper as never before.

Before I understood the ways of my fellow man, perhaps like most children, my greatest fears were of the unseen terrors of the night. Now, I'd learned a thing, and were a ghostly spirit done the teaching. Henceforward, I shall put as much stock in the hearts of ghosts as I do in those of living souls. Not all the dead are up to no good. My brother Andrew, the putpocket, had remained to set things right.

Swamp Vengeance
by Brian Moreland

As morning sun glowed on the tall sawgrass of Florida's Everglades, Merle Pritchett drove his airboat through the maze of water channels. The giant propeller whirred behind him. Warm wind whipped at his bearded face. He glided past swimming turtles, alligators, and water snakes. Above, an osprey circled in the clear sky. To his right, a flock of egrets flapped their wings over the reeds. Merle howled in delight. There was no place he felt more at home than in the wetlands.

He admired the pair of dead gators on his boat. The smaller one, a female, was a six-footer; the big daddy stretched nine feet from snout to tail. He put up a good chase, but Merle eventually tracked him. *A damn good hunting trip,* he thought. He had stayed at an old shack deep in the Glades, where the high-grass marsh merged with Big Cypress Swamp, an isolated spot where a man could poach gators far away from the eyes of the law.

When he reached a compound of tin sheds near U.S. Route 41, he pulled up to a dock behind Bubba's Swamp Meats. The butchers helped unload the gators and weigh them.

Bubba whistled. "Lordy, that's a good haul."

"Got more for you." Merle handed him containers full of live frogs and three dead rattlesnakes.

"Don't know how you do it, Merle, hunting out there by your lonesome. But keep 'em coming. Got a big demand for gator meat."

"As long as you're buyin', I'll keep supplyin'," Merle said.

Bubba slapped several green bills into Merle's hand. "I hope you don't go spending it all at the casino."

"Not today. I plan to surprise Darleen with a weekend getaway. Saturday's our ten-year anniversary."

"Thought you two split up. Last time you were talking divorce."

Merle scratched his beard. "Well, we're back on the rollercoaster. I'll tell you about it sometime over beers."

"That'd be fine," Bubba said. "Enjoy your weekend with the wife."

Liking the way the cash felt in his pocket, Merle tied his boat to his own private dock, then got in his beat-up Ford truck. It had a camper, where he often slept when Darleen was going through one of her moods.

As he reached the T-section of Route 41, he felt a familiar temptress pulling at his heart. He should have headed west, toward his home in Everglades City. Instead, he drove east and pulled into the parking lot of the Miccosukee casino. The temptress whispered in his ear about how much fun it would be to play slots and three-card poker all day and night; drink Jack and Cokes until he was happily loaded and passed out in his camper. He could certainly get away with it. Darleen wasn't expecting him back until tomorrow.

Merle gripped the steering wheel, aware this was one of those moments where the wrong decision could throw his life off course. Wrestling gators was easier than fighting off the seductions of Lady Luck. But last time, she took all his money and he'd returned home broke to a very unhappy wife.

With a deep, regretful sigh, Merle ignored the temptress and drove west to Everglades City, a small Gulf Coast town south of Naples. Route 41, the Tamiami Trail, cut straight through the marshlands. It wasn't uncommon to see alligators swimming in the adjacent canals. He drove around a large gator sunning in the road and dodged a jaw-snap at his tires.

On the radio, Jimmy Buffet sang about drinking margaritas. Merle thought about taking Darleen down to their favorite beach motel in Key Largo for a weekend of drinking, fishing, and wearing out the mattress. She had been irritable lately, complaining he spent too much time away from home, so he wanted to make it up to her. Their little getaways usually put their drifting marriage back on course.

When he arrived at his house, another man's truck was parked in his driveway. The red Chevy with the Confederate flag decal across the back window belonged to Billy Ray Radford, a bartender at the tavern up the road.

A stabbing pain of betrayal knifed Merle's chest. He grabbed his .30-30 rifle and snuck into his house. Muffled voices came from the master bedroom. Merle crept down the hall. Through a crack in the partly open door he saw his wife and Billy Ray in bed together.

Merle stopped outside the door when he heard his name.

"Will you do it, baby?" Darleen asked Billy Ray. "Will you kill him for me?"

"I don't know. What's in it for me?"

"You can have *me* all to yourself."

"I enjoy screwing you, Darleen, but that ain't incentive enough to kill a man."

She slapped his arm. "That's all I've been to you these past few months, a screw?"

"Maybe more than that," Billy Ray admitted, "but I won't risk going back to jail."

Darleen was quiet a moment. "Merle's got life insurance worth a hundred grand. He made me sole benefactor. I'll split the money with you, Billy Ray. Fifty grand to off my husband."

Red-hot fury burned in Merle's chest. He kept listening.

"How would we kill him without getting caught?" her lover asked.

"I've done thought all that out," Darleen said proudly. "I'll get Merle to take me fishing where Rumrunner Road dead ends into the Glades. Know the place?"

"Where drug boats do their drop-offs."

"That's mostly after dark. Merle likes to go fishing during the day when nobody's there. You'll hide in the sawgrass next to the road. While I distract Merle, you sneak up and shoot the damn fool. We'll dump his body in the marsh. Leave him to the gators."

Billy Ray chuckled. "Damn, Darleen, didn't know you could be so cold-hearted."

"All I care about is you, baby, and getting rid of Merle for good."

Merle shoved the bedroom door open and aimed his rifle at the two cheaters.

Billy Ray sat up against the headboard, holding the sheet against his bare chest.

Darleen screamed. "Merle! What are you—?"

"You dare cheat on me in *my* house? Conspire to kill me!" It took all his will not to put a bullet in their heads.

Billy Ray held up his arms. "Don't shoot, don't shoot. Please man, I didn't mean—"

"Shut up before I blow your balls off!"

The man shielded his crotch with both hands. He had several tattoos, including a Confederate flag that marked his right forearm.

Sobbing and rambling incoherently, Darleen stood, letting the sheet slip away. His wife's smokin' body never failed to rile up Merle's primal urges, and she knew how to use it to get what she wanted. She held out her arms like she wanted a hug. It felt wrong seeing her naked with another man in the room.

"Lord sakes, Darleen, cover yourself." Merle grabbed a T-shirt off the floor and threw it to her.

She pulled on the other man's shirt. It came to her mid-thighs. She kept blubbering and trying to embrace Merle. "It's all a big misunderstanding, baby—"

He pointed the gun at her. "Not another step, Darleen. Get back on the bed with your scumbag boyfriend."

"You can't blame me for cheating," she said. "I've been unhappy for years. Hell, you're more married to that damned swamp than to me." To Billy Ray, she said, "Don't worry, he's not gonna shoot us. Merle's not prone to violence. He'd rather run off and drink himself stupid."

"Shut up, woman. Let me think." Merle rubbed the rifle's trigger. He recalled several 'Florida Man' articles in the news: Florida Man shoots adulterous wife over sex tape... Blood found in Florida Man's bedroom... Florida Man charged with double murder...

I'm not ending up in prison over these two. Merle prided himself on having more self-control than the average Florida Man. His rock-steady thinking served him when hunting and whenever Darleen pushed him to the brink. He'd never laid a hand on her. When her incessant henpecking made him hot-headed, he'd storm out and leave for days.

But Darleen and Billy Ray had crossed a line that was unforgivable. Merle couldn't simply walk away this time, nor could he ever trust that he'd be safe. If Darleen was going to screw around and plot to kill him once, no doubt she would do it again.

Billy Ray slinked out of bed and grabbed his boxers. "I'm just gonna be on my way."

Merle fired a shot above the man's head. "You're not going anywhere, asshole. Back on the bed or the next shot's through your head."

Darleen's mouth dropped, and she looked, oddly, impressed with her husband. "Merle, I've never seen this side of you. If I'd known you cared this much…"

As he chewed on his anger like a lump of chaw, a plan began to form. Holding the two at gunpoint, Merle ushered them to the garage. He made Darleen wrap duct tape around Billy Ray's wrists behind his back, then his ankles, and a strip across his mouth.

Darleen jabbered the whole time, "All right, enough, Merle. You're taking this jealous husband act too far. Let the poor man go. You and I can work things out over margaritas. I'll even whip up a batch of nachos."

Her overconfident tone changed when Merle began to bind *her* wrists and ankles.

"Hey, easy with the tape," she griped.

Billy Ray suddenly tried to hop away. He was headed toward the back door which led to the yard. Merle grabbed a hammer off his work bench and flung it. The metal end struck Billy Ray's head. He fell against a pile of boxes and slumped. A patch of blood stained his hair, but the unconscious man was still breathing. Merle dragged Billy Ray like a roll of carpet to the truck and loaded him in the back camper.

When he came for Darleen, she was quivering. "Shit, what are you going to do to us?"

He placed tape over her kisser. "We're all going for a ride."

By the time Merle drove his truck back to his dock, storm clouds had formed over the Everglades, blotting out the afternoon sun. It took some effort, but he managed to get his bound-and-gagged captives onto his airboat, lying side by side in sticky puddles of gator blood.

Darleen glared up at her husband and kicked her bare feet at him. Billy Ray, conscious again, squirmed and screamed through his mouth-tape.

Merle put on his ear muffs and climbed into the elevated driver's seat. He fired up the big propeller, then drove the flat-bottomed boat over waterways and paths of flattened sawgrass. A startled heron took flight. A long alligator dove off a mud bed, splashing beneath the water. Merle's boat vibrated as he pushed the throttle to propel faster than normal. A flash of lightning snaked across the dark gray sky. Roiling clouds began to drop rain. At the bow, his cargo shivered as the cold drizzle soaked their bare skin. The anger in Darleen's eyes had been replaced by mortal terror.

Merle looked away from her, kept his focus on winding through the Glades. His logical internal voice questioned what the hell he was doing. Did Darleen really deserve to be punished in this way? Then he pictured his wife naked in bed with Billy Ray, and the primal anger took over again. Merle drove his boat for miles and miles, far beyond the boundaries of the airboat tours. The high-grass marshes began to merge with a forest of tall cypress trees. He coasted past his rickety hunting shack which stood on stilts a few feet above the water.

Another quarter mile through the swampy woods, he slowed down and cruised between mud islands. Here and there among thick vegetation jutted the wooden ruins of huts. Remnants of an abandoned Seminole village. There were many myths to explain why the whole tribe up and disappeared. Some superstitious locals believed the swamp Indians were frightened off by an evil trickster spirit.

Bubba, who told Seminole folklore, claimed the tribe had contracted smallpox after being visited by white settlers. The children and elderly died first, as did their medicine man. Recognizing their doom, the survivors carried off their dead and marched single file into the water until their heads were completely submerged.

"Every man and woman of that village offered their spirits to the swamp," Bubba claimed. "They became the animals and birds that live there. Look in a gator's eye and that could be a Seminole ghost staring back at ya."

Most people avoided these bog-woods on account of boaters disappearing and reports of strange sightings. Bubba had sworn on his mother's grave he once saw a corpse wading through the water. "Some bad mojo around that haunted village. I steer clear of it and you should too."

Merle didn't give a flying flip about Indian myths or ghost stories. He came here because the waters around the village islands were his best hunting spots.

He shut off the propeller and let the boat drift. Four gators floated nearby. A few more splashed near the banks of one of the islands.

Darleen and Billy Ray were sitting up now, huddled shoulder to shoulder. The gators' blood stained their skin, hair, her T-shirt, and Billy Ray's boxers. They smelled as ripe as chum bait. The cheaters tried to beg for mercy with frantic head shakes.

Merle grabbed a harpoon. With the sharp end, he sliced the silver tape to free Billy Ray's ankles.

"On your feet," Merle barked.

Billy Ray mumbled through the tape as he rose awkwardly. He turned his back and offered his bound wrists to be cut loose.

"Uh-uh, those stay bound." Merle eyed the man. "You ever been cheated on, Billy Ray? Ever come home to find a strange man in your bed with the woman you loved?"

Billy Ray shook his head nervously.

Merle said, "Way I see it, screwing another man's wife is one of the worst violations. Almost as bad as breaking vows."

Darleen turned her head in shame.

Merle glared at the other man and nodded to the water. "Get your ass off my boat."

Billy Ray looked around at all the gators and shook his head violently. Merle poked the man's chest with the harpoon, drawing blood. Darleen's lover stumbled back and fell into the water. He came up thrashing. It was only chest deep. He tried to make it to an island, but two gators struck quickly. Their jaws launched out of the water and bit down on Billy Ray's head and shoulders. Then he went under as the gators spun him around and around, their tails and pale undersides rolling over the surface. Once blood spread, more gators joined the frenzy. Each would claim a part of Billy Ray's body and store it under a log to be softened for eating later.

A few latecomers swam to the edge of the boat, hoping to be fed.

Darleen unleashed animal cries through her taped mouth, scooted to the center of the boat. She stared up at her husband, a trembling, tear-eyed basket case.

"See what you made me do," Merle said coldly. "I may not have been the best husband, but I've always been faithful. Wish you hadn't betrayed me, Darleen. But what's done is done."

He got back in the driver's seat and drove at a slow speed between the islands as he contemplated what to do with Darleen. Perhaps watching her lover being eaten alive was lesson enough. But Merle couldn't shake the anger, jealousy, and hurt he felt. Darleen secretly having sex with Billy Ray for months wounded Merle's pride and broke his heart. Plotting to kill him for insurance money cut much deeper. How could he ever forgive her?

The swamp was an unforgiving place. And most days, he felt more akin to that nature than the human kind.

He banked the boat's bow at a small island—a mud mound barely twenty feet wide. A thicket of briars surrounded it. Beside a broken, rotted cypress loomed a totem pole with carved animal faces. The paint had long since faded off the weathered gray wood. Atop its peak, a thunderbird perched with spread wings, staring down at them like a watchful god. This mud isle had always felt like a place of reverence to Merle, but not because of the ancient Seminole statue.

It was because of all the snakes.

This island was a breeding ground for deadly vipers. Dozens of black and banded cottonmouths were knotted together in a mating ball. More nested in the mud and climbed through the briar branches. A 'Red-and-Yella-Killa-Fella' coral snake slithered across a mossy log. Near the base of the totem pole a massive diamondback rattlesnake coiled. One curious water snake swam along the edge of the boat.

Darleen recoiled and started begging through the duct tape again. The desperate, mournful sound made it hard for Merle to think.

Using the harpoon, he sliced the tape binding her ankles and wrists. His wife peeled the tape off her mouth. "Merle, baby..." She stood and tried to hug him—a desperate surrender she performed to win his sympathy, usually after she'd lost a fight.

He held her back with the sharp end of his pole. "Don't come near me."

"Please, Merle, I'm really, really sorry..." she said through a gush of tears. "I've learned my lesson. I'll never cheat again."

Merle took no thrill in seeing her terrified. All he felt was the pain of her betrayal. The sad realization that the woman he'd married was not the person he thought she was. "It's too late for trying to yip-yap your way out. This 'damn fool' now sees what a cold-blooded snake you are. You deserve to be among your kind. Now get!"

She sobbed hysterically as he jabbed the harpoon to force her off his boat. Her feet squished in mud near the knot of water moccasins. One snakehead snapped at her ankle and missed, as Darleen jumped backward. She stumbled to the center of the island.

Merle pushed the boat away from the bank.

His wife shouted, "No, don't go! Don't leave me, baby!"

In a moment of weakness, or perhaps mercy, he thought Darleen deserved a fighting chance. So he threw the harpoon like a spear. It stuck in the mud a few feet from the totem pole. Above it, lightning crackled, illuminating the wood-carved thunderbird. The ground around it came alive with squirming snakes. The mating ball unknotted.

Hard rain poured down. Darleen's soaked T-shirt clung to her body. Her blond hair matted to her head. She attempted to grab the harpoon, but the rattler wouldn't let her near it. Every direction she moved, the water moccasins coiled in defense, their white mouths opening wide.

"Come back, Merle! Please, come get me!"

He put on the ear muffs to drown out his wife's screams. Unable to watch her struggle, he turned the boat around and propelled away.

At his one-room hunting shack, he drank straight from a bottle of Jack whiskey. Constant rain battered the roof. Beyond the front window was nothing but wet darkness and the creatures that thrived in it. He couldn't get Darleen out of his head. What she'd done. What he'd done in cold revenge. He felt no remorse for Billy Ray. Bastard got what he deserved. But Darleen and Merle had a history, many good times together. He'd proposed to her right here in this cabin. They'd danced to Van Morrison by lantern light and made love on sleeping bags spread out on the floor.

Tacked to the wall above his pillow was a photo of Merle and Darleen on their honeymoon in Key Largo. A couple of love-struck fools who thought they had entered wedded bliss. Over the next decade, they'd suffered a love-hate marriage that pulled them together and pushed them apart. Try as he might, he couldn't please her. Nothing ever seemed to make Darleen happy. Merle brought out the worst in her, and she brought out the worst in him.

Through all the shouting matches, shattered plates, and her crying in his arms, never once did Merle stop loving Darleen. They'd broken up too many times to count, but always kissed, tore off each other's clothes, and rocked their bed with make-up sex.

It suddenly hit him like a punch to the chest that his wife was gone for good. "Christ, I left her out there for dead."

Tears brimmed his eyes. He began to see the cruelty of how he'd punished her. Guilt gnawed at his heart. It had only been a couple hours. Maybe she was still alive.

Merle drove his boat as fast as he could through the cypress swamp. He shined a spotlight to carve a path through the night. Cold rain sluiced down his face. He shivered in his green slicker. If the vipers didn't bite Darleen, she could die of hyperthermia.

His spotlight found the totem pole. The snake island was completely underwater.

"Darleen!" He panned his light across the briars. Heart racing, he searched the shallow water and the dark swamp-woods beyond. There was no sign of her anywhere. The snakes were gone too. The harpoon stood where he'd thrown it. He pulled it out of the water.

Once again, lightning crackled in the night sky above the totem pole. All the teeth-baring animal gods leered at Merle with a force that felt like wrath. It made him shudder from more than just the rainwater streaming down his spine.

As his boat navigated between the trees and dripping dark ruins of the Seminole huts, he turned his searchlight. All the islands of the ghost village were submerged. He probed the beam up in the trees, hoping to find Darleen sitting on a branch but only found a damp screech owl.

Merle combed the cypress swamp for hours, calling out his wife's name. The storm clouds finally moved on to let silvery moonlight filter through the tree branches. The bog became noisy from a chorus of barking tree frogs. Even though the rain had stopped, it was looking hopeless. No one, especially a barefoot woman, could survive trying to walk through the swamp.

Filled with regret, he returned to the open area where he'd fed Billy Ray to the gators. God help Darleen if she attempted to swim across these muddy waters. Merle killed the engine and searched for any trace of her. He drifted close to a brush-covered island that was still above water. From a branch, he plucked a torn piece of T-shirt.

Feeling a sudden rush of hope, he yelled, "Darleen, you out there?"

What answered back raised his neck hairs. Wailing voices. As he studied the dark huts, he felt eyes watching him. The storm flashed. For a split second, he glimpsed shadow-shapes standing among the ruins. Then darkness shrouded the island.

What the hell? Merle rubbed his eyes. When lightning brightened the village again, there was no one there. He exhaled. *Just the storm playing tricks.*

Out of the corner of his eye, a large white spider crawled across a nearby log. He shined his beam on it. Not a spider—a pale severed hand. It was still attached to a hairy forearm that ended in a ravaged stump. A Confederate flag tattoo marked the riddled skin. The half-arm was raised up from the crawling hand like a scorpion's tail.

Merle was too in shock to figure how an uneaten piece of Billy Ray wasn't fully dead.

The resurrected hand turned, wagged its fingers at Merle. He imagined the dead man's head lodged under a log, somehow laughing from his watery grave.

The severed arm spider-jumped onto the boat, scuttled across the deck. Merle tried to club the damned thing with the harpoon. The hand crabbed left and right. When he missed again, it leapt and clamped around his throat. Choking, Merle gripped the stumpy arm. Billy Ray's strong fingers dug their nails into Merle's neck.

He wrenched the hand loose, flung it across the deck. It rolled, righted itself on spidery legs, and charged again, fingernails clicking across the metal deck. Merle stabbed the harpoon through the flag tattoo. He raised the impaled arm. The twitchy hand clawed the air. As he held the thing at bay, a gator launched out of the water. Its jaws clamped down on the arm with a bone-crunch and snatched it off the hook. The large gator then landed back in the water with a geyser splash.

Merle fell back in the passenger seat. His heart throttled up so fast he feared it might burst. Where the fingernails had raked his skin, his neck burned. As he collected his breath, several gator heads surfaced around his boat. They eyed him ravenously, intent on making him their next meal. Merle leapt into the driver's seat and powered up the propeller. The hull skidded over gators as he tore the hell out of there.

He was so shit-scared, he pushed the throttle dangerously close to tipping speed.

"Whoa! Whoa!" he yelled at himself and decelerated as the boat ran over patches of tall sawgrass. This stirred up another form of the swamp's strange nature. Heaps of frogs began leaping onto his boat. One landed on the passenger seat below Merle. It flicked its long tongue, latched onto Merle's forearm. The frog bounced like a yo-yo as he tried to shake it off. The deck became a slimy, undulating mass as an amphibious army hopped toward Merle. More tongues wrapped around his ankles.

He grabbed the frog dangling from his arm and threw it over his shoulder through the fan cage, where it splattered in the propeller. His boot squished the tongue-flickers attached to his ankle and kicked hoppers as they leapt. Another wave of frogs spilled from the reeds. Their vocal sacs bubbled as they croaked.

Merle grabbed an oar. Swinging the paddle like a broom, he swept frogs off the deck. He batted others that clung to the surrounding sawgrass. When the live ones were mostly off his deck, he gunned the engine, propelled so fast the remaining frogs flew off the edges.

He wanted to believe he was hallucinating, but his neck still ached from the chokehold of Billy Ray's bodiless hand. And the squished frog soldiers were proof that Merle hadn't lost his mind.

The engine started sputtering. He checked the fuel gauge. Nearly empty.

"Damn it!" He'd been so desperate to find Darleen that he hadn't paid attention to how much gas he was burning.

His cabin was just up ahead.

"Come on, you can make it," he urged the boat.

The engine coughed then died. The boat skidded across the water but stopped thirty yards short of the shack.

Merle cursed at himself. "What now, shit for brains?" It was after midnight and he damned sure didn't want to spend the night out here.

He called the one friend who would help. Bubba's recorded voice said to leave a message.

"Hey buddy, it's Merle. Got myself in bit of a jam. Ran plum out of gas and I'm stranded at my cabin. I need you to bring me some fuel soon as you can."

When he ended the call, the tree frogs croaked louder. Then stopped all at once.

A shriek cut through the stillness.

He angled his spotlight across the cypress woods. Other voices joined the first. Dozens of Seminole men and women stood between the trees, floating partly out of the water. Moss dangled from their rotted faces and bodies. Many held drooping, slime-covered things that might have been dead children. An old man with half a skull pointed a bony arm at Merle. The ghost tribe wailed louder, a mournful, hostile chant that gave Merle the shakes.

Then, together, all the dead sank into the water until their heads completely submerged.

Jabbing the oar into the water, Merle paddled for his cabin. Vegetation dragged against the boat's bottom. The bow kept turning in the wrong direction. He struggled to paddle on one side, then the other.

"Come on, damn it!"

Something splashed off to his right. His light shone on a frenzy that disturbed the water's surface. A massive nest of water moccasins rolled over one another, exposing black serpentine backs and pale bellies.

Merle paddled harder but was moving too slow. He abandoned the oar, picked up the long harpoon, and began poling his boat. Glancing back at the splashes, he yelped.

An island piled with snakes drifted toward the boat. As it drew closer, he discovered the island to be his wife's corpse. She floated facedown. Her body, punctured with bites, was bloated and misshapen from so much venom. She was drifting too fast across the still water. Merle caught sight of a long flapping tail behind her. A gator was pushing Darleen's corpse toward him.

"Crikes!" He poled faster, digging the harpoon into the mud. It was just a few more feet to his dock.

The drifting mound of snakes drew closer. His wife's head bumped against the hull. A large cottonmouth slithered over her wet hair and onto the deck. Whip-fast, the viper slinked toward Merle's foot. He swung the pole and knocked the snake into the water. More serpents invaded the boat.

As the hull knocked against the dock, he fell backwards onto the slatted boards. He threw the harpoon at the closest snakes as they tried to bite his boot. Then he grabbed his .30-30 rifle, shot the writhing mass coming off his wife's back. Snakeheads rose above the water as more moccasins swam toward the boat. Too many to fight off. They covered the boat's deck.

Merle stumbled-ran up the dock steps to his porch, into his cabin. Last thing he saw before shutting the door made him cry out. *No, impossible*. He swore his dead wife reached out of the water and grabbed the edge of the boat, raised her head.

He latched the door, fled as far back as he could in the small room. Gasping, he aimed his rifle at the entrance.

Hissing came from outside the cabin walls.

Slow footsteps *clumped* across the porch. A hand pounded at the door.

"Stay away from me!" Merle shot it full of holes until his gun clicked empty.

Shafts of moonlight spilled in through the checkered door. A shadow moved past the holes. He heard the scrape of nails down wood. Then the harpoon broke through the door. As each thrust of the hook chipped away splinters, Merle felt his sanity slipping away.

A bloated hand reached through a large breach, undid the latch.

The door creaked open.

Merle flattened against the back wall, shaking his head. His wife's bloated silhouette stood in the doorway. Snakes slithered around her muddy arms and legs. They nested in her hair. She entered the cabin, arms raised as if wanting to hug him. The snakes came in with her, a swarm of cottonmouths and venom.

The next morning, Bubba drove his fanboat to the gator hunter's shack. Merle's boat was twenty yards away in the reeds. The cabin's door hung open.

Bubba climbed up to the porch, peered inside, and gasped. On the sleeping bag, beneath a blanket of water snakes, Merle and Darleen's corpses lay tangled in each other's arms.

Merle's snake-bit face had frozen in an expression of pure terror. But it was Darleen's wide grin that disturbed Bubba more. Oddly, Merle's wife never looked happier.

Portrait

by Kealan Patrick Burke

"I found I could say things with color and shapes that I couldn't say any other way—things I had no words for."

- Georgia O'Keeffe

It was the winter of her eighth year. The girl stood facing the window in the living room, using her index finger to draw birds in the condensation. So far there were seven of them, each one a small M with rounded shoulders, like seagulls seen from a distance. Breath pluming in the cold, she had scratched one half of the eighth M in a small patch of ice that had formed near the edge of one of the panes when something smacked into the glass on the other side. She did not scream, though the thought was there. She had gone through too much in recent months to be so affected by unanticipated events. Instead she backed away, her young face furrowed in consternation, the small traces of ice melting beneath her fingernail, and looked toward the door, where she had expected to see her father more than an hour before. She was now late for school, but as this had become a common occurrence over the past few weeks, and as it was *school* after all, she wasn't very worried. She just would have liked for him to be there so she could ask him what had made the sound. But then, so often had she wished he were there, and so rarely did she see him, that she had begun to wonder if he existed at all anymore, or if, like the flurries of snow that whirled by the window, the sadness had simply swept him out of her life.

Indecision kept her in place for a few moments. She was cold. Her father usually had a fire lit by now, but, like cooking her breakfast and taking her to school, it had become another neglected duty in an ever-increasing list. She worried that he was sick, that maybe like the house, with its peeling wallpaper and cracked wainscoting, he was slowly coming apart in the wake of her mother's passing. It was a thought that filled her with dread. She couldn't lose him too. What would become of her without someone to look after her? She had no relatives that she knew of. Her only remaining grandfather had passed away the winter before. She would be well and truly alone, though in truth, even at such a young age, she already knew what abandonment felt like.

One day in the fall, her mother had gone down into the basement. This was nothing new. Her studio was down there. Sometimes she stayed there for days on end. This time, however, she was down there for weeks, until Father went down to retrieve her. The girl had rounded the curve of the stairs just in time to see him dragging her mother into the hall by her ankles. She wasn't moving.

One look at her face and the girl knew why.

She was blue, her eyes the color of rubies. Her tongue was black and poking from the side of her colorless lips as if she had died making a joke. There were odd marks on her neck, like snakes made of ash. The girl stood frozen upon the stair until her father looked up and roared at her to go to her room. His eyes were red too. She could tell he'd been crying. This scared her more than anything, more than the sight of her lifeless mother being hauled like a bag of coal out of the basement, so she had done as he'd demanded and retreated to her room.

Once, she had been able to depend on her dolls for solace, but that day she saw no comfort in their faces. She saw nothing at all in their idiot stares. Worse, the pallor of their skin and the lifelessness of their glass eyes only reminded her of her dead mother. She realized henceforth they would never be able to comfort her again, and as she gathered them up one by one and stowed them in the darkness beneath her bed, where they would stay until the house collapsed in on itself three winters hence, she felt the onset of an awful kind of maturity, the death of magic and of innocence. Her toys, her only friends, often her only company, were now nothing but empty shells, childish distractions from the agony that had been waiting all along to strip her contentment away.

She never saw her mother again, though she knew where she was buried, had watched from behind her bedroom curtain as her father dug a deep hole in the back forty and tumbled the body in as if it was nothing but the carcass of some animal they had found on the road. The girl could tell from his movements that he was angry. He shoveled dirt into the hole as if he was feeding it and feared if he dawdled, it might eat him instead.

Afterward, he made dinner and stared at the bowl of rabbit stew as if it was the only place left in the world to find answers, a cauldron of knowledge, and when she excused herself, he did not acknowledge her departure. He simply brought another spoonful of stew to his mouth and *slurped*.

He had dolls eyes too.

Since then, she had moved like a ghost through the house, running her fingertips along the cracked walls and gathering dust from the windowsills with her fingertips. She drew pictures in her room and grew angry when they didn't turn out right. Where once she had prided herself on the straightness of her lines and the accuracy of her depictions, now she saw only ugly, melted renditions of unfamiliar things. She tried to read books—her abridged and illustrated versions of *Treasure Island* and *Heidi* and *The Count of Monte Cristo*—but the words seemed to spasm across the page like addled ants. The crosshatched illustrations perturbed her. They seemed to thrum like the struck strings of a violin. When she tried humming to herself just to have a sound other than the quiet or the intermittent settling of the house, it sounded alien to her ears, so she seldom did it for long.

The object smacking against the glass had not frightened her, but it had brought her back to herself in a way she hadn't felt since seeing her mother's body rolling over at the behest of her father's boot and tumbling down into the earth and out of her life forever. Now, she made her way into the hallway, careful not to look at the basement door, and called out for her father.

There was no answer.

She called for him again, and only the house responded, with creaks and groans and the occasional sneaky shuffle of snow sliding off the eaves. Every window was clouded by the cold, muting the light. Already her birds were fading. It made her uncomfortable, made her feel trapped, in danger of being erased too, as if the house was slowly becoming the hole in which her mother lay. Perhaps this was how ghosts were made: her mother buried, her father gone, and the girl left wandering the house until she too faded into the walls. People might wonder what had become of this once happy family, but nobody would ever find them, and soon they would be forgotten.

Weakened by hunger, she tightened her woolen coat about her, and tugged her hat down just below her eyebrows. The plan, such as it was, was simple: find her father and get him to take her to school. Ordinarily, she resisted being sent to that terrible place, with its strict, sallow-faced teachers and shadow choked rooms, where the other children looked at her with unkind eyes, and the walls were speckled with mildew, but it was the only place left where she could be free of this place. Gladly would she endure the smell of chalk dust and disinfectant, and the taunts and jeers of people she had once hoped could be her friends, if it only meant escape, even for just a little while.

Stomach rumbling, she hurried to the front of the house, where she saw that her father's boots were not in their usual place by the door. Nor were the floorboards wet with melted snow, which meant he had gone outside but had yet to return.

She opened the door. The morning sun against the snow made a blazing white void of the doorway. Mittened hand shielding her eyes against the blinding glare, she cried out "Daddy?" and listened to her voice become a parody of itself as it shuddered across the fields and died in the trees at the far edge of their land. She stepped through the door and out into the cold, blinking to adjust her vision.

Slowly, the world came into focus.

Before her, a short stretch of snow-covered yard led to the barbed wire fence her father had erected around the fields. It has stood there since before she was born and a lack of maintenance over the past few years had left it looking like a sagging clothesline. The wire was rusted now, the wooden posts leaning this way and that like drunken revelers. There were snatches of sheep's hair snagged on the barbs, though the animals to which they might have belonged were long gone. It did not present much of an obstacle to the girl. She stepped gingerly over the flaccid wire, leaving it vibrating behind her, and into the field, her boots plunging into the bank of snow on the other side.

Around the field, ranks of chestnut and walnut trees stood like sketches of black lightning against the pale white sky, the frenzied reach of their mangled arms seeming to suggest a desperate desire to close the distance between them. Otherwise the day was featureless, the landscape monochrome but for two distinctive figures, dark against the white. With no small measure of relief, and even though they were some distance away, she recognized the one on the left as her father, purely because he was ambulatory. The one on the right was the scarecrow, a humanoid formation of old clothes and branches with a gourd for a face and desiccated boots for hands and feet. She had helped her father erect the scarecrow back when he loved her and the sun still rose on their lives, back when Mother would have watched them from the window above the sink with a small smile on her face. Back when the color was not restricted to her mother's paintings.

Before.

Shaking off the memory for fear the melancholy would drain her resolve and send her running back to the house and the fragile safety of her room, she trudged onward through the snow, following the clouds of her breath toward where her father was laboring over the scarecrow. Why he chose such a hostile day to attend to something that had ceased being useful a long time ago—the crows not only ignored the scarecrow, they often used its shoulders as a perch—was a mystery to her, but it hardly mattered. She was just relieved that he was there to be seen at all, because it was no longer a guarantee.

Cheeks red, teeth chattering, she navigated the snowdrifts with difficulty. It seemed to take half the day before she finally reached him.

After pausing to catch her breath, the words she had rehearsed along the way bubbling into her throat, she saw something so curious, so odd and unexpected, that it killed her desire to say anything at all.

Father was there, dressed in dungarees. He wasn't wearing his coat, only a checkered shirt with the sleeves rolled up, exposing the curly ginger hair on his forearms. He did not, however, appear to be cold. Perhaps his labors kept him warm. At his feet was a large pile of letters, old by the look of them, the once-white envelopes faded to a dark yellow. Each one bore his name in block letters, but the address was not familiar. He had his back to her, unaware of her presence, and as she watched, he retrieved handfuls of those letters and stuffed them violently into the gaping chest cavity of the scarecrow, which before today had been stuffed with old clothes. Now those clothes lay in a pile at its feet.

But this was not the strangest thing. Oh, how she wished that it were.

How she now wished she hadn't left the house at all, because the scarecrow's face was no longer the smooth featureless surface of an old gourd.

It was her mother's face.

Her father had nailed a black and white portrait to it—the one that had, up until today, been hanging in the upstairs hall—so that now the girl found herself being regarded by a more youthful and vibrant rendition of the woman who lay buried somewhere beneath their feet.

"Daddy?"

He had just reached down to scoop up more letters. Now he stopped, mid-stoop, and looked back over his shoulder at her. For the longest time he said nothing, just watched her with the one cold blue eye she could see. Then he straightened and turned around to face her, allowing her to see the bloody hole where his other eye should have been. The cheek beneath it was streaked with snow-flecked gore and blood, and now the girl had to back away in horror, one hand over her mouth, her body wracked with shivers she could no longer blame on the cold.

"Sweetheart," her father said, and when he opened his mouth, she could see that some of his teeth were missing too. "I'm so glad you're here."

Behind him, she registered what might be the oddest thing of all. Propped up in a heap of snow was something she had missed from a distance because it had blended in with the colorlessness of the day. Now that she could see it, she felt a curious mixture of emotions because although it didn't belong out here in the field, not now, not today, it was something she had desperately wanted for as long as she could recall.

"I got you a birthday present," her father said, his face spread in a smile she didn't care for at all.

It wasn't her birthday. Hadn't been for months, but she remembered the disappointment upon waking that day to find that, not only had she not gotten what she'd asked for, she'd gotten nothing at all, and the house was silent. No gifts, no celebrations, no cake, just her parents shut away in separate rooms and the girl left to pout all alone until she forced the dolls to join her in an impromptu and pitiful tea party.

"Do you like it?"

She had asked her parents for an easel and some paints. Watercolors would do if oils were too expensive, she'd told them. She wasn't fussy. Money was tight and really, she just wanted to make pictures on something other than another of her mother's raggedy old sketch pads. Her father had seemed ambivalent, her mother horrified, then angry, a reaction the girl didn't understand. She thought her mother would be proud that her daughter wanted to follow in her footsteps and become an artist.

Instead, her mother locked herself in the basement, which doubled as her studio, and tore the place apart.

But now here it was, the very thing she'd asked for, in the last place she expected to see it.

"Daddy…" She didn't know what to say. Part of her desperately wanted to appreciate the acquisition of the long-desired gift, but all of this felt so very wrong. What had happened to her father? Who or what had hurt him and why was he not hurrying to the hospital? And the letters…and the picture of her mother nailed to the scarecrow's face…it all felt like a nightmare. Only the biting cold told her that it wasn't.

"I'm sorry," her father said, and his face fell, his one remaining eye watering. "I forgot to get the paints. My head was hurting so bad. I was home before I remembered them."

Between the half-sunken wooden legs of the easel, she saw what might have been the handle of a shovel. She watched as her father walked to the easel, stepped behind it, and retrieved the object.

"But I have a way to fix that for you, honey."

It was not a shovel, after all, but his hunting rifle.

"What are you doing?" Her voice sounded brittle, as if it had become ice melting on her tongue.

He walked slowly toward her, the sadness still on his face though he was still smiling. Spots of blood marked his passage. He almost lost his footing as he approached where she stood paralyzed by fear.

"What she told me to do," he said and stopped between the girl and the easel.

"Daddy, please, I'm scared."

When he smiled, she saw that his lips were grey and trembling, his gums raw and bleeding.

"Don't be. I have something else for you too. Would you like it?"

She shook her head and backed another step away from him.

"There's nothing to be afraid of. All of this is the start of something wonderful. It's *freedom*."

Again, she shook her head. "Please, let's just go back to the house. We can light a fire and make some food, or…or…"

"Sweetheart, listen to me. I know I haven't been myself. I know I haven't been okay. But I'm going to make that up to you now, okay?"

A flock of ravens exploded from the trees to her right, but she paid them no mind. Couldn't have diverted her attention from her father's face even if she'd wanted them to. It had become her whole world.

"How?" she asked him, despite her terror. All she wanted was for everything to go back to the way it was before.

Still sad, still smiling, he reached into the pocket of his dungarees and produced a small stubby red pencil, no bigger than her pinky. He held it out, ice crystals sparkling in the edges of his hollow eye socket as the blood began to freeze.

"I want you to take this."

"Why?"

"I want you to take this and I want you to go over and write your name in the lower right-hand corner of that canvas."

"I don't want to." She was sobbing now. Her head hurt from the force of the tears and she tasted salt on her tongue. Her legs were shaking so bad she was not sure how much longer they'd keep her upright. "Please, let's just go home."

"Write your name like I asked you to and we can be done. But you must do it. Your mother said so."

"Why?"

"Because it's how you start over."

"I don't know what that means."

"You will, but you have to do what you're told. If you don't, nothing changes. And even worse, you'll be disrespecting your mother's wishes." Absently, he reached up a hand and scratched with a forefinger at the edges of the raw red hollow in his face. It bled anew. "And even though she's dead, she'll know, and that will be the worst thing of all."

The cold had crept inside her coat, inside her skin. She was powerless to keep from shaking. "W-why did sh-she die?" It was the question she had wanted to ask, a truth she needed to understand, ever since the day she'd watched him drag her mother out of the basement. She'd known, even if she hadn't fully comprehended how such a thing could happen, or why, that her mother wasn't well in the mind. In the weeks, perhaps months leading up to her death, she had changed, become a frightening shadow of herself. She had *faded*—yes, that was the word—as if someone or something had been slowly draining her of color. Now, her father looked the same.

"She died because she needed to," he said.

"Why did she need to?"

"Because she knew it was the right thing, the only thing to do if there was to be any hope of saving you."

The girl was confused and frightened and thus the tears came freely. She expected her father to take her in his arms, to hold her until the worst of the pain went away, to tell her, like he used to, that she was his special girl, that he would never let anything hurt her. But that's not what he did. Instead, he dropped to his haunches, wincing involuntarily at some unknown discomfort in his knee, and he looked squarely at her, one hand braced in the snow to steady himself, the other around the unbreeched stock of the rifle. He held the pencil out to her.

"Go write your name where I told you to."

Again, she wanted to ask why. None of this made any sense. She desperately wanted to defy him, to turn and run, maybe keep running until she reached the school. There perhaps she could find someone who would listen, and help. Maybe they would send an ambulance out to the farm and they could fix her father's eye and whatever else was wrong with him. Maybe the situation could still be salvaged before she lost everything.

But what if they took him away and he never came back? What then?

Again, she looked up at the scarecrow. The tears in her eyes made it appear to move and rendered her mother's smiling face a gray smudge beneath a windblown puddle.

"It was what she wanted for you."

As much as she loved her father, it was getting harder to meet what remained of his gaze, so she took the pencil, stepped around him, and walked the few short feet to where the easel stood waiting. Down in the lower right-hand corner of the easel, she wrote her name in cursive, the tip of her tongue protruding from the side of her mouth as a force of habit. At school she had been working on making her letters more like her mother's, but while there was certainly a touch of floridity to it, it still lacked the elegance of her mother's signature. Once done, she stepped back from the canvas. She was chilled to the bone now and couldn't help wondering how long she was going to be out here. There was no fire at home. If she pacified her father, would he come home and help her warm the house, perhaps make them something to eat? That the pantry was bare of food mattered little. It was his duty to provide.

But would he? And what was she to do if he didn't?

"Take the canvas down," he instructed.

She didn't ask why. It didn't matter anymore. She just had to do as she was told until she could figure out a better course of action. Fleeing was the dominant impulse, but she knew she wouldn't get far through the deep snow before he caught up to her.

She reached up and grabbed the edges of the large canvas and gingerly removed it from the easel. It was heavier than she'd expected and she almost went sprawling, but she redoubled her efforts, spreading her feet to compensate for the weight, and took a step backward.

But for her signature, the canvas was blank, the unblemished white making it seem as if she had signed her name on a piece of the winter sky.

"What should I do with it?" she asked.

"Kneel down and hold it in front of you as if it's a mirror."

"Why?"

"Because it soon will be."

She heard rustling behind her and, filled with the sudden and terrifying feeling that he was about to force his request upon her, she dropped down on her knees into the snow, the canvas propped up before her.

"Good girl."

"What do I do now?"

An eternity of cold confusion passed before he replied, long enough for her to start to worry that maybe he had just gone away and left her here alone.

"You become."

"Become what?"

She heard a sound that was both familiar and horrible: the ratcheting click of the hammer being drawn back on the hunting rifle. Instantly, she was paralyzed, her eyes widening, throat dry, the shakes intensifying. She felt her bladder let go and wet warmth spreading across her groin and down over her legs. The heat was merciful only for a moment before it quickly began to cool.

No matter her confusion and fear thus far, the only possibility she hadn't considered was that her father might want to hurt her, or worse.

"Daddy?" She didn't want to turn around, but desperately needed to, if only to assure herself that her father wasn't standing there pointing the rifle at her. Unable to bear it any longer, she risked a quick glance.

Her father was still kneeling in the snow and facing away from her just like she'd left him. She couldn't see the rifle.

"Look at the canvas, sweetheart," he said.

"What are you doing? Why are we out here?"

"Look at the canvas, honey."

"Daddy, please."

"Look at what's there to be seen."

Terrified to the core of her being, but equally afraid to disobey him, she could only do as he'd asked. Jolted by wave after wave of tears and shivering so bad her muscles ached, she looked at the canvas held in her hands, at the endless expanse of white blending in with the field and sky behind it and waited.

Enough time passed that she felt the wetness in her pants start to freeze.

Enough time for her to run out of tears and for darkness to begin to edge its way like spilled ink between the trees.

Enough time for her to reach a place where she now just wanted to sleep.

Then her father said, in little more than a whisper, "I love you, Beth," and she was instantly awake.

She looked up at the precise moment he pulled the trigger. The roar of thunder was so loud it might have come from inside her. She flinched, screaming as wet spray soaked her hair and carried on to drench the canvas before her.

All except the outline of her head and shoulders, now the only negative space in a dripping crimson picture.

She stared at the white portrait of herself amid the red until her muscles went numb, until sirens filled the air, until the light started to leave the sky and strangers beseeched her to rise.

Her father had told the truth. This was the start of something, at her mother's bequest. It was a gift. She could feel it, a small cold fire in the pit of her stomach, though she didn't yet know its full nature. But she knew she would never speak again, not in words anyone would understand, the same way the sheer power of the need to create had silenced her mother. She would have to paint her story for them and hope that made more sense.

Before they forced her to stand, she secreted the pencil in her pocket, her mind already filled with images she yearned to bring to life, each and every one of them red.

Biographies

Kealan Patrick Burke is the Bram Stoker Award-winning author of *The Turtle Boy, Kin,* and *Sour Candy*. Born and raised in a small harbor town in the south of Ireland, Kealan knew from a very early age that he was going to be a horror writer. The combination of an ancient locale, a horror-loving mother, and a family full of storytellers, made it inevitable that he would end up telling stories for a living. Since those formative years, he has written five novels, over a hundred short stories, six collections, and edited four acclaimed anthologies. He lives in Ohio with a Scooby Doo lookalike rescue named Red. Find him on the web at www.kealanpatrickburke.com

Kenneth W. Cain is the author of four novels, four short story collections, four novellas, and several children's books among his body of work. He is the editor for the anthologies *Tales From The Lake Volume 5, When the Clock Strikes 13,* and *Midnight in the Graveyard*. The winner of the 2017 Silver Hammer Award, Cain is an Active member of the Horror Writers Association as well as chair for the membership committee and the Pennsylvania chapter. Cain resides in Chester County, Pennsylvania with his wife and two children. www.kennethwcain.com

Somer Canon is a minivan revving suburban mother who avoids her neighbors for fear of being found out as a weirdo. When she's not peering out of her windows, she's consuming books, movies, and video games that sate her need for blood, gore, and things that disturb her mother.

Catherine Cavendish first started writing when someone thrust a pencil into her hand. Unfortunately, as she could neither read nor write properly at the time, none of her stories actually made much sense. However, as she grew up, they gradually began to take form and, at the tender age of nine or ten, she sold her dolls' house and various other toys to buy her first typewriter. She hasn't stopped bashing away at the keys ever since, although her keyboard of choice now belongs to her laptop.

The need to earn a living led to a varied career in sales, advertising and career guidance, but Cat is now the full-time author of a number of supernatural, ghostly, haunted house and Gothic horror novels and novellas, including *The Haunting of Henderson Close*, the Nemesis of the Gods trilogy (*Wrath of the Ancients, Waking the Ancients, Damned by the Ancients*), *The Devil's Serenade,* and others. She lives in Southport, in the U.K. with her longsuffering husband and black cat and can be found at www.catherinecavendish.com as well as the usual social media.

Alan M. Clark was born in Nashville, Tennessee in 1957, and grew up in a home full of old bones, Indian relics, and dusty medical books. He graduated in 1979 from the San Francisco Art Institute with a Bachelor of Fine Arts Degree and has been a freelance illustrator since 1984, a freelance writer since 1995. Awards for his work include the World Fantasy Award and four Chesley Awards. He has produced illustrations for textbooks, children's books, young adult fiction, and innumerable speculative fiction books. He is the author of 17 books, including 12 novels, 4 collections, and a full color book of his artwork. Mr. Clark's company, IFD Publishing, has released 45 titles of various editions, including traditional books, both paperback and hardcover, audio books, and eBooks by such authors as F. Paul Wilson, Elizabeth Engstrom, and Jeremy Robert Johnson. Currently, he and his wife Melody live in Eugene, Oregon. www.alanmclark.com

John Everson is a staunch advocate for the culinary joys of the jalapeno and an unabashed fan of 1970s European horror, giallo and poliziotteschi cinema. He is also the Bram Stoker Award-winning author of eleven novels, including his latest occult thriller, *The Devil's Equinox* and *The House By The Cemetery*, which takes place at a real haunted cemetery–Bachelor's Grove—in the south suburbs of Chicago. His first novel *Covenant*, was a winner of the Bram Stoker Award and his sixth, *NightWhere*, was a finalist for the award. Other novels include *Redemption*, the conclusion to the trilogy begun in *Covenant*, as well as *Sacrifice*, *Violet Eyes*, *The Pumpkin Man*, *The Family Tree*, *Siren*, and *The 13th*. Over the past 25 years, his short stories have appeared in more than 75 magazines and anthologies. He is the founder of the independent press Dark Arts Books and has written novelettes for *The Vampire Diaries* and Jonathan Maberry's *V-Wars* universe (Books 1 and 3), which will appear as a 10-episode series on NetFlix in 2019. He's also written stories for *The Green Hornet* and *Kolchak, The Night Stalker* anthologies. He has had several short fiction collections, including *Needles & Sins*, *Vigilantes of Love*, *Cage of Bones & Other Deadly Obsessions* and most recently, *Sacrificing Virgins*. For more on his obsession with jalapenos and 1970s European horror cinema, as well as information on his fiction, art and music, visit www.johneverson.com.

Shannon Felton lives in Buckeye, Arizona with her husband, Ben, and their four children. She has a debut novella coming out in late 2019 with Silver Shamrock Publishing. You can find her on twitter at @ShannonNova3

Kathryn Meyer Griffith has been a writer for over forty-eight years now and has had twenty-eight novels and twelve short stories published since 1984. She began her writing career as a mass market paperback horror author in 1984 with Leisure Books (Dorchester) and Zebra (Kensington Publishing), but has since moved on to write paranormal horror, romantic historical time-travel, suspense, romance, thrillers, and murder mysteries. Since 2012, she self-publishes exclusively in eBooks, paperbacks and audio books. Her horror novel, *The Last Vampire*, and her thriller, *Dinosaur Lake*, were both Epic eBook Awards Finalists in 2012 and 2014.

Jeremy Hepler is the Bram Stoker-nominated author of *Cricket Hunters*, *The Boulevard Monster*, and numerous short stories and nonfiction articles. He received the Texas Panhandle Professional Writer's Short Story Award in 2014, and his debut novel was a Bram Stoker Award finalist in the Superior Achievement in a First Novel category in 2017. He lives in central Texas with his wife and son, and is working on his next novel. For more information, you can follow him on Twitter, Facebook, Instagram, Goodreads, or Amazon.

Todd Keisling is the author of *Devil's Creek*, *The Final Reconciliation*, and *Ugly Little Things: Collected Horrors*, among other shorter works. He lives somewhere in the wilds of Pennsylvania with his family where he is at work on his next novel.

Born and bred in Tennessee, **Ronald Kelly** is an author of Southern-fried horror fiction with fifteen novels, eight short story collections, and a Grammy-nominated audio collection to his credit. Influenced by such writers as Stephen King, Robert McCammon, Joe R. Lansdale, and Manly Wade Wellman, Kelly sets his tales of rural darkness in the hills and hollows of his native state. His published works include *Undertaker's Moon*, *Fear*, *Blood Kin*, *Hell Hollow*, *The Dark'Un*, *Hindsight*, *Restless Shadows*, *After the Burn*, *Timber Gray*, *Mr. Glow-Bones & Other Halloween Tales*, *Dark Dixie*, *Midnight Grinding & Other Twilight Terrors*, *The Sick Stuff*, *More Sick Stuff*, and *The Buzzard Zone*. He lives in a backwoods hollow in Brush Creek, Tennessee with his wife and young'uns.

Allan Leverone is the *New York Times* and *USA Today* bestselling author of twenty-four novels and five novellas, as well as countless short stories. A former Derringer Award winner for excellence in short mystery fiction, Allan lives in Londonderry, New Hampshire with his wife of more than thirty-five years, three grown children and three beautiful grandchildren. Connect on Facebook, Twitter @AllanLeverone, or at AllanLeverone.com.

Chad Lutzke has written for Famous Monsters of Filmland, Rue Morgue, Cemetery Dance, and Scream magazine. He's had a few dozen short stories published, and some of his books include: *Of Foster Homes & Flies*, *Wallflower*, *Stirring the Sheets*, *Skullface Boy*, *The Same Deep Water as You*, and *The Pale White*. Lutzke's work has been praised by authors Jack Ketchum, Stephen Graham Jones, James Newman, Cemetery Dance, and his own mother. He can be found lurking the internet at www.chadlutzke.com

Elizabeth Massie is a two-time Bram Stoker Award-winning and Scribe Award-winning author of novels, short fiction, media-tie ins, and nonfiction. Her novels and collections include *Sineater, Hell Gate, Desper Hollow, Wire Mesh Mothers, Homeplace, Afraid, Naked on the Edge, Dark Shadows: Dreams of the Dark* (co-authored with Mark Rainey), *Versailles, The Tudors: King Takes Queen, The Tudors: Thy Will Be Done, Buffy the Vampire Slayer: Power of Persuasion,* and many more. She is also the creator of the *Ameri-Scares* series of spooky novels for middle grade readers which is currently in development for television by Warner Horizon (Warner Brothers) with Margot Robbie's company, LuckyChap, signed on to produce. She is a ninth generation Virginian who lives in the Shenandoah Valley with her illustrator husband, Cortney Skinner. Until her updated website launches, she can be reached through Facebook, Twitter, Crossroad Press, or through e-mail: emvirginia@yahoo.com

Robert McCammon is the New York Times bestselling author of twenty-four books. He is the winner of five Bram Stoker Awards and a World Fantasy Award. He is best known for *Swan Song* (1987), *The Wolf's Hour* (1989), and *Boy's Life* (1991). More recently, McCammon has published *The Listener*, which was nominated for a Locus Award, and *The Border*, and is writing the Matthew Corbett series, a nine-book series of historical thrillers that USA Network has called "the Early American James Bond." McCammon lives in Birmingham, Alabama.

Kenneth McKinley was born and raised in the small town of Bronson, Michigan. He grew up in the time of heavy metal mix tapes, VCRs, and library cards. Ever since that magical moment when he wandered into the adult horror section of the public library at the age of 11, he has always dreamed of being a writer. He is finally realizing his dream.

Kenneth graduated from Ohio State University and owns Silver Shamrock Publishing. He is a member of the Horror Writers Association and the Independent Book Publishers Association. He resides in Michigan with his wife, Kathy, and their four children. Kenneth is currently working on his next novel.

William Meikle is a Scottish writer, now living in Canada, with over thirty novels published in the genre press and more than 300 short story credits in thirteen countries. He has books available from a variety of publishers including Dark Regions Press and Severed Press, and his work has appeared in a large number of professional anthologies and magazines. He lives in Newfoundland with whales, bald eagles and icebergs for company. When he's not writing, he drinks beer, plays guitar, and dreams of fortune and glory.

Tim Meyer dwells in a dark cave near the Jersey Shore. He's an author, husband, father, podcast host, blogger, coffee connoisseur, beer enthusiast, and explorer of worlds. He writes horror, mysteries, science fiction, and thrillers, although he prefers to blur genres and let the stories fall where they may.

Thomas F. Monteleone has published more than 100 short stories, 5 collections, 8 anthologies and 30 novels including the bestseller, *New York Times* Notable Book of the Year, and Bram Stoker Award-winning *The Blood of the Lamb*. He's also written scripts for stage, screen, and TV. His fourth collection of short fiction, *Fearful Symmetries*, won the Bram Stoker Award. His omnibus collection of *Cemetery Dance* columns about writing, genre publishing, television, film and popular culture entitled *The Mothers And Fathers Italian Association* from Borderlands Press also won a Stoker. He remains co-editor of the award-winning anthology series of weird imaginative fiction, Borderlands. He is also the author of the bestselling *The Complete Idiot's Guide to Writing a Novel* (now in a 2nd edition). In 2017, The Horror Writers Association honored him with their Lifetime Achievement Award. Despite being dragged kicking and screaming into his seventies and losing a lot of his hair, he still thinks he is dashingly handsome—humor him.

Brian Moreland writes a blend of mystery, action-adventure, thriller, and horror. His books include *Shadows in the Mist, Dead of Winter, The Witching House, The Devil's Woods, The Seekers*, and *Darkness Rising*. Coming in 2020, he'll be releasing a new novel, *Tomb of*

Gods and a collection of horror stories called *Night Stalkers*. Follow on Twitter: @BrianMoreland

Lee Mountford was born and raised in the North East of England, in the small town of Ferryhill. Not much happens there anymore, but it has a surprisingly dark history... which probably helped cultivate his love of horror. He is a best-selling author with a huge passion for the dark, the scary, and the macabre. He still lives in the North East of England with his amazing wife, Michelle, and his two daughters, Ella and Sophie.

Kelli Owen is the author of more than a dozen books, including the novels *Teeth* and *Floaters*, and the Wilted Lily novella series. Her fiction spans the genres from thrillers to psychological horror, with an occasional bloodbath, and an even rarer happy ending. She was an editor and reviewer for over a decade, and has spoken at the CIA Headquarters in Langley, VA regarding both her writing and the field in general. Born and raised in Wisconsin, she now lives in Destination, Pennsylvania. Visit her website at kelliowen.com for more information. F/F

Jason Parent is an author of horror, thrillers, mysteries, science fiction and dark humor, though his many novels, novellas, and short stories tend to blur the boundaries between these genres. From his EPIC and eFestival Independent Book Award finalist first novel, *What Hides Within*, to his widely applauded police procedural/supernatural thriller, *Seeing Evil*, Jason's work has won him praise from both critics and fans of diverse genres alike. He currently resides in Rhode Island, surrounded by chewed furniture thanks to his corgi and mini Aussie pups. www.authorjasonparent.com

Glenn Rolfe is an author from the haunted woods of New England. He has studied Creative Writing at Southern New Hampshire University and continues his education in the world of horror by devouring the novels of Stephen King, Richard Laymon, Jack Ketchum, and many others. He and his wife, Meghan, have three children, Ruby, Ramona, and Axl. He is grateful to be loved despite his weirdness. He is a Splatterpunk Award nominee and the author of *The Window*, *Becoming*, *Blood and Rain*, *The Haunted Halls*, *Chasing Ghosts*, *Abram's Bridge*, *Things We Fear*, *Boom Town*, *Slush*. and *Land of Bones*. www.glennrolfescribbles.wordpress.com

Hunter Shea is the product of a misspent childhood watching scary movies, reading forbidden books and wishing Bigfoot would walk past his house. He doesn't just write about the paranormal—he actively seeks out the things that scare the hell out of people and experiences them for himself. Hunter's novels can even be found on display at the International Cryptozoology Museum. He's a bestselling author of over 25 books, all of them written with the express desire to quicken heartbeats and make spines tingle. Living with his wonderful family and two cats, he's happy to be close enough to New York City to gobble down Gray's Papaya hotdogs when the craving hits. You can find him and his works at www.huntershea.com

"A stand-out book for 2019."
—Sadie Hartmann, *Nightworms*

Most kids dream about a new bike, a pair of top-dollar sneakers endorsed by their favorite athlete, or that totally awesome videogame everyone's raving about. But thirteen-year-old Jake and his little brother Matthew want nothing more than to escape from their abusive father. As soon as possible, they plan to run away to California, where they will reunite with their mother and live happily ever after.

It won't be easy, though. After a scuffle with a local bully puts Jake's arch-nemesis in the hospital, Sheriff Theresa McLelland starts poking her nose into their feud. During a trip to the family cabin for the opening weekend of deer-hunting season, Jake and Matthew kick their plan into action, leaving Dad tied to a chair as they flee into the night. Meanwhile, the bully and his father have their own plans for revenge, and the events to follow will forever change the lives of everyone involved...

"An unpredictable, page-turning roller coaster."

—Chad Lutzke, author of *The Pale White*

Celia (Garcia) Lundy was fifteen in the fall of 1998 when Abby Powell, one of her five friends who called themselves the Cricket Hunters, disappeared without a trace. Cops scoured the central Texas town of Oak Mott searching for Abby. Interviewed everyone. Brought in the Texas Rangers to assist. Three key suspects emerged and were focused on, but no evidence was found. Eventually, the case went cold, and the passage of time buried the truth of Abby Powell's fate.

Fifteen years later, as the anniversary of Abby's disappearance approaches, Cel's life is upended when her husband Parker, also once a Cricket Hunter, goes missing. When bizarre clues surface that point to a link between Parker's and Abby's disappearances, Cel is forced to delve back into the past in order to navigate the present. With the help of her abuela, a self-proclaimed bruja, she embarks on a tumultuous journey fraught with confrontation and trickery, spells and spirits, theft and murder, in order to find out what happened to her husband, and why.

"Todd Keisling runs at the front of the pack."

—John Langan, Bram Stoker Award-winning author of *The Fisherman*

About fifteen miles west of Stauford, Kentucky lies Devil's Creek. According to local legend, there used to be a church out there, home to the Lord's Church of Holy Voices—a death cult where Jacob Masters preached the gospel of a nameless god.
And like most legends, there's truth buried among the roots and bones.

In 1983, the church burned to the ground following a mass suicide. Among the survivors were Jacob's six children and their grandparents, who banded together to defy their former minister. Dubbed the "Stauford Six," these children grew up amid scrutiny and ridicule, but their infamy has faded over the last thirty years. Now their ordeal is all but forgotten, and Jacob Masters is nothing more than a scary story told around campfires.

For Jack Tremly, one of the Six, memories of that fateful night have fueled a successful art career—and a lifetime of nightmares. When his grandmother Imogene dies, Jack returns to Stauford to settle her estate. What he finds waiting for him are secrets Imogene kept in his youth, secrets about his father and the church. Secrets that can no longer stay buried.

The roots of Jacob's buried god run deep, and within the heart of Devil's Creek, something is beginning to stir...